THE SECRET OF FATIMA

THE SECRET OF FATIMA

PETER J. TANOUS

ISBN: 978-1-5040-3511-8

Liberty Island Media Group
New York, NY
www.LibertyIslandMag.com

Distributed by Open Road Distribution
180 Maiden Lane
New York, NY 10038
www.openroadmedia.com

To

Theron Wade Raines
9/26/1925-11/05/2012
Founder, Raines & Raines, Literary Agents

and

Josephine Tanous

ACKNOWLEDGMENTS

I'm one on those people who actually reads authors' acknowledgments even though I don't know the author or his friends. Apparently you're like that too. The question is: why do we? Perhaps we are curious to know who helped the author and in what capacity. Or maybe we'll find a name or two we recognize. We might want to know who assisted with the complicated police scenarios or the intricate descriptions of a scary medical procedure. Is there a secret wink in there to a long lost relationship? I don't really know, nor can I explain why I spend the time reading these pages. Maybe you have a better answer.

So here goes.

I want you to know that the Secret of Fatima is a project I've been working on for over three decades. My wife, Ann, and I first went to Fatima in the 80s, and back again last year. How it has changed! It is a major pilgrim / tourist destination with a large, soaring chapel, dozens of hotels, and an esplanade that can hold over a hundred thousand visitors. I've been working on the book idea ever since that first visit. I started with the world's fascination over the third secret of Fatima, which has been locked in the Vatican archives since Sister Lucia, the survivor of the three children to whom Mary appeared, recorded it and sent it to Rome for safekeeping in the 1940s. It remained locked up until Pope John Paul II released it in 2000. Was that a major news story, you ask? You bet! It made the front page of the *New York Times*. But many believe that the real secret was never revealed. This novel addresses that question.

I could not have completed the work without the contribution of several talented editors who helped me at different stages. Heartfelt thanks to Erin Brown and Donna Peerce. More recently, I had the benefit or working with Blair Brown, a seasoned and talented editor who injected much life into the project. I'm grateful to have worked with her and richer as a writer for having met her. My editor at Liberty Island, Jay Merwin, offered additional plot input and he put the finishing touches on the manuscript to get it ready for publication. Thanks, Jay.

Many friends and colleagues agreed to read early versions of the manuscript and offer their comments and suggestions, for which I am understandably grateful. Everlasting thanks to, Katie Fleiss, Vienna McCartney, Alex Hoyt, Sarah West, Marysue Shore and special gratitude to Justine Moore, a fellow writer who contributed both sage advice and some sparkling dialogue for my female protagonist.

Others who offered specialized advice include Lucas Evans, Monsignor Seely Beggiani, and Will Tanous, who contributed thoughtful plot points which I gratefully used.

This book is dedicated to the man who was my writing mentor, advisor, and agent for over thirty years: Theron Raines. We lost him a few years ago and I miss him. Fortunately, his wife Joan Raines has picked up the baton and continued the work of the agency. I am grateful to her for all the efforts she made to market the book successfully.

The second dedicatee is Josephine Tanous my newest adorable granddaughter.

Given that I started this project several decades ago, I likely forgot to acknowledge some individuals who gave me important help and advice, and I will lose some sleep over it. If you're reading this and you fall in that category, please let me know so I can correct and make amends.

As always, thanks to family, including my trophy wife of 50+ years, Ann, my children and their spouses, Chris Tanous, Paul Bartilucci, Helene Bartilucci, Will Tanous, Julie Tanous, and four wonderful granddaughters, Olivia, Isabella, Lilly and Josephine.

And the final acknowledgment, dear reader, to you with thanks for joining me on this extraordinary adventure.

THE SECRET OF FATIMA

CHAPTER ONE

The Vatican

September 28, 1978

Folds of paper-thin skin draped over the man's eyes. His grim expression foretold the importance of the impending reading. His shoulders rounded forward, Monsignor Antonio Calvi emerged from an underground corridor deep within the Vatican, both hands clutching a jeweled velvet pouch at his chest. The pouch contained the wax seal of the previous pope, evidence the document within hadn't been tampered with since the seal had been affixed. As archivist and custodian of the Vatican's most sensitive documents, it was Calvi's sole duty to protect it.

Three Pontifical Swiss Guards waited for him outside the *Archivio Segreto Vaticano*. As Calvi approached, they joined him. The four crowded into a small elevator and rode to the top floor of the Apostolic Palace. Besides the elevator's grinding cables, the only sound was the thunderous pounding of Calvi's heart. He was sure everyone could hear it. But no one was saying a word.

The elevator stopped with a thud. One by one, the men stepped out. With his eyes focused forward, Calvi led the way to Pope John Paul I's private study in the papal library. The newly elected Holy Father had summoned Calvi, and the others, to his study where he'd break the seal on the jeweled velvet pouch and read the secret document inside. He alone was authorized to do so.

Cardinal Villot, secretary of state of the Vatican, greeted the men at the papal quarters. "Good morning, Monsignor Calvi. Join us, won't you?"

Nodding, Calvi joined Cardinals Silvano and Villot, along with several priests, standing around a large oval mahogany table in the papal library. Heavy red velvet drapes had been drawn at the windows, shutting out the glaring lights in St. Peter's Square.

The bedroom door opened. Smiling, John Paul I walked into the room. "Please be seated," said the pope, gracefully waving his hand over the table. The pontiff wore a white silk cassock with matching pellegrina and white fringed fascia. On his head was the white papal zucchetto. The pectoral cross hung loosely around his neck. With his salt-and-pepper hair, the pope was youthful looking; his slender face lit up.

Calvi could see why, just a month after his election, people were calling this one "the "Smiling Pope."

As Pope John Paul I seated himself at the head of the table, the others followed.

Slowly raising his eyes, Cardinal Villot nodded at Calvi.

Standing up, Calvi knelt to kiss the papal ring, and handed the jeweled pouch to the pontiff. The pope's hands, he was surprised to note, were shaking. *Probably from excitement and anticipation.* In respect to the pontiff's privacy, the monsignor turned and left the room, closing the door behind him.

Outside the study, Calvi and the three guards waited in silence. They stood erect, barely moving, lost in their thoughts. Calvi nervously paced the corridor, checking his watch repeatedly. When half an hour had passed, Cardinal Silvano flung open the door. His face fiery, lips pursed, he was noticeably unsettled, agitated.

"Calvi, come in!" Silvano bellowed, motioning frantically for him.

Confused, Calvi rushed inside, scanning the entire room. *Something wasn't right.* Then he saw. The pope was lying fully stretched out on the floor, his body half-obscured by Cardinal Villot, who was leaning over him. Calvi's heart jumped into his throat. The pontiff's eyes were shut, his face distorted in pain. He wasn't breathing. He was lifeless, drained of color.

"What happened?" whispered Calvi. He could barely form the words.

"We don't know," said Cardinal Villot, his mouth drawn into a thin line, his hands folded across his stomach. "It was sudden. Presumably a heart attack."

The manuscript lay facedown on the table, its pages strewn, splayed like a deck of cards, the jeweled pouch at one side. The Holy Father's reading specs were also there on the floor, shattered as if stomped on. Standing stupefied, Calvi gazed at the shards of glass. His heart was breaking like the glass before him. *This couldn't be happening!*

Then suddenly the burning reality of his mandate was overpowering. Calvi sprang to the table, hurriedly gathered up the manuscript's yellowed pages, refolding and inserting them back into the velvet pouch. He'd protect this secret document, no matter what, to the end. His job in this crisis was simple: to return the pouch, and its sacred contents, to the archives, unscathed.

Cardinal Villot requested holy oil to perform a last anointing. A monsignor handed him a vial.

"*Si capax, ego te absolvo a peccatistuis, in nomine Patris, et Filli, et Spiritus Sancti, Amen.*" Villot dipped his thumb into the vial, tracing the sign of the cross on the pope's forehead. "Through this anointing, may God forgive you whatever sins you have committed. By the faculty given me by the Apostolic See, I grant you a plenary indulgence and remission of all sins, in the name of the Father, and of the Son, and of the Holy Ghost. Amen."

Calvi was sobbing. *This couldn't be! A moment ago the Pope was healthy, smiling. How could His Holiness be no longer? Only a month into his papacy!*

And now, for the second time in a year, Cardinal Villot was the *Camerlengo*—the man who'd assume papal responsibilities until the time when the conclave elected a new pope.

Clutching the jeweled pouch, Calvi thought he might be sick.

A priest took a lit candle and, with the flame, softened a red stick of wax. When it melted, the priest motioned for the pouch. He dripped a liquid circle onto the strings to seal it, then gave it back to Calvi.

Bending down, Villot eased the papal ring from the finger of the deceased pope and soaked it in the pool of soft wax, creating the final seal of John Paul I. A young priest retrieved a silver hammer from its ceremonial case in the study. Then, in keeping with sacred tradition, Cardinal Villot took the silver hammer and smashed the seal on the papal ring, marking the end of the papacy of John Paul I.

Turning to the six men present, Cardinal Villot addressed them. "It is September 28, 1978. On this day, His Holiness John Paul I has died. No man present here in this room will discuss what's transpired here today. From this day forward, let it be known to all, our beloved pontiff passed in his sleep while reading '*Imitation of Christ.*'"

Calvi nodded, his eyes closed, his heart heavy with a foreboding. *These damnable pages! What were they about?* Calvi might never know. The document was accessible only to the pope. Faithfully, Calvi was following the rules to the letter. He knew one thing: Whatever was in that document had caused the death of the leader of the Catholic Church. *Who'd be next?* Calvi shuddered. His life's work was safeguarding this document. Whatever its purpose or mystery, it was his solemn and sole mission to protect it. Even if it meant giving up his life for it.

CHAPTER TWO

Washington D.C.

Present day

Basketball practice started at seven-thirty a.m. sharp on weekdays. Father Kevin Thrall always told the boys to be there on time. On this day, as usual, he was early. He yawned, shaking off the stressful uncertainty caused by an unexpected four a.m. phone call. Groping to get to his bedside lamp for the phone, he'd knocked over a glass of water; when finally he'd answered it, no one was on the line. There were many who might have called. None good.

Glancing over the basketball court, Father Thrall noticed another sizeable chunk of the concrete had come loose. *Hell, the damn parking lot was in better shape.* The basketball court stood adjacent to the parking lot by St. Anthony's main building, a Fifties structure which hadn't seen repairs since its construction during the Eisenhower Administration. Southeast Washington, D.C., especially the Anacostia neighborhood, was a ramshackle area taken over by the African-American community and a few immigrant families. Kevin was happy here in this job. Kevin, as Father Thrall, could make a difference.

The students were tough city kids who longed for the chance to get out in the world and do something. Be somebody. Escape this life. Most of them in Father Thrall's basketball squad had stuck it out, a tribute to their abiding respect for him and his program. And to their gratitude to him. They'd pegged him as a rebel, an iconoclast, and they admired him because they identified with him. It made it easier to deal with his military style of discipline.

At forty-two, Kevin Thrall was aware, and had come to terms, with his appearance. He knew he looked older than his years. It didn't surprise him, given the knots in his life. Already his chestnut hair was speckled with flecks of gray and his blue eyes were lined more than they should've been. He didn't mind. His six-foot, lean stature made him attractive to members of the opposite sex, which might've meant more to him if he'd been in another line of work. Still, it didn't hurt to have women looking, smiling coyly at him. Some didn't seem to care he was a priest.

This morning, Kevin had planned inter-squad drills, five-on-five, half-court. The boys, ranging in ages from thirteen to sixteen, fell in, played hard. With Father Thrall around, there could be no trash talk. That was the rule, unless the trash talk came from Father Thrall himself.

Kevin whistled at a particularly nasty foul; the play stopped.

"What the—? Sean, what was that, huh? A mugging?"

"I'm sorry, Father," Sean said. Six feet tall and lanky, as if he hadn't quite grown into his arms and legs, the fifteen-year-old bent to help a teammate up off the concrete.

"You okay, Lamar?"

"Yep, Coach. Fine."

Kevin whistled, and the scrimmage started anew, just as Lamar drilled a three-pointer from the corner of the court.

A minute later, Bob Mather, St. Anthony's headmaster, appeared suddenly on the edge of the court, signaling to Kevin. In his mid-fifties, Mather, partially bald, was on the heavy side. "Too many doughnuts," he'd always say, patting his belly.

As the headmaster paced, Kevin couldn't help but notice the tension pulling on his face. *What now?* The last thing Kevin needed was a confrontation with a self-important, pain-in-the-ass administrator who thought he was running a major university, not a third-rate high school.

"Excuse me, Father Thrall," Mather hollered. Kevin motioned for play to continue while hustling to the sideline.

Out of the earshot of the players, Mather began speaking, his finger waggling, “Listen, Kevin, I’ve got a problem with Sister Helen. Apparently, your team has snazzy new uniforms. Her girls’ hockey team has no uniforms at all.”

Kevin grimaced. “You know where they came from, Bob? Me. I bought ’em. I’m not interested in hearing Sister Helen’s complaints.”

“Yeah, well it looks real bad if some teams have ’em and others don’t.”

“Listen, these kids have lousy home lives. What they need is personal pride and conviction. The uniforms provide that.” Kevin turned to the court, yelping, “Barkley, post up! Post up!” His look lingered on the lanky sophomore. What kind of world did these kids have without team sports? Most were products of single moms, drug-infested homes, poor nutrition, and the absence of paternal or spiritual guidance. Kevin wanted to help. Sometimes it was a losing battle, but when it was going well, he felt whole and satisfied. It was a special feeling, sacred, sublime joyfulness.

Mather straightened to his full stubbiness, squaring his shoulders. His face was rosy, aglow. “My decision is no new uniforms, unless all the school teams get them,” he said with as much authority as his high-pitched voice could muster. To Kevin, he looked like a squirrel with nuts stuffed in his cheeks.

Kevin glared at him. “Please, you’re interrupting my practice.”

“This isn’t over.”

“For now it is.” Kevin turned away.

“Not so fast, Father. You’ve got a visitor in my office. An emissary. From the Vatican.”

“What?” said Father Thrall, whipping his head around.

“Yessirree. Showed me his ID.” Mather grinned smugly. “Maybe some disciplinary committee from Rome. I wouldn’t be surprised.”

Suddenly Kevin remembered the early morning call he’d missed.

“Sean, take over the drill!” Yanking the cord from his neck, Kevin tossed the whistle to the young man. His mind racing, he traipsed behind Mather into the school building.

At the far end of the school’s main corridor, Mather’s office showcased an assortment of vintage sports trophies, stacks and stacks of books, and an enormous World War II-era desk with ladder-back chairs.

The Vatican emissary stood stoically to the side, briefcase in hand. He appeared roughly the same age as Kevin, with olive skin and black eyes. His face was proud and dignified. On first impression, perhaps from his polished manner and speech, Kevin assumed this guy came from a well-heeled Italian family. He was dressed in formal priestly attire, a dark suit with the traditional white turned collar. However, he wasn't just a priest. The red buttons dotting his vest told his story: This guy was a monsignor. Standing in Mather's office, his formal appearance contrasted markedly with Kevin's, who sported a tattered gray tee, beat-up sneakers, and his couture-of-the-times, long, baggy basketball shorts.

"This is Father Kevin Thrall," said Mather.

"Good morning," the monsignor said with a nearly perfect American intonation. With a slightly limp wrist, he offered his hand. "I'm Monsignor Massimo Drotti from Rome. I'm sorry to intrude at such an early hour."

"No problem. Nice to meet you," said Kevin, shaking his hand.

"The pleasure is mine, Father Thrall," Drotti said. "I'm here from Rome to talk to you."

"Oh, was it you who called my cell at four this morning?"

"Indeed it was," Drotti replied with an unapologetic smile.

"Now, please," said Mather, interrupting the two men, pointing to the chairs in front of the desk. "Please. Have a seat." He walked to his desk, seating himself, and opened his appointment calendar.

Watching Mather, Kevin suppressed a smile. He recognized the headmaster's behavior. He was puffing up, trying to look important.

"Are you American?" Kevin asked Drotti.

"Well, yes and no. My father is American, my mother Italian. I was educated at Boston College, but since then I've spent my time in Rome. I understand you were in Rome for a while, as well."

"Yes, I studied at the Theologica," Kevin replied. He was twitching in his seat, eager for the monsignor to get to the point. Whatever it was bringing him all the way from Rome, it must be mighty important.

Drotti said, "Mr. Mather, I'm here to inform you that Father Thrall has been summoned to Rome and will be taking a leave from the school."

What? Kevin beamed laser eyes on Drotti, then looked back at Mather. *What the hell?*

Mather's eyes widened. He snapped, "Without the bishop's consent, he's not going anywhere."

Kevin felt his fate being played, back and forth, like a ping-pong ball.

Drotti smiled, nodding. "Of course. The papal nuncio here in Washington spoke with His Excellency this morning. It's all arranged. I thank you for your attention to protocol. Now, Mr. Mather, I must speak privately with Father Thrall."

"Hmph!" said Mather. "That's fine. Well, I have things to attend to." Flustered, Mather busily gathered up an eclectic assortment of gewgaws from his desk.

When Mather was gone, Monsignor Massimo Drotti removed a leather attaché from his briefcase and held it on his lap. "Kevin . . . may I call you Kevin?"

"Of course."

"I don't want to be overly dramatic. I'm not sure where to begin. I guess it'll be in the middle."

"I'm all ears, monsignor."

"Thank you. First, I know Massimo is a bit of a mouthful. Please call me 'Max'. If you agree to what I'm about to ask of you, we'll be spending some time together."

Kevin said nothing. Maybe his reserve would have an effect, would draw out this seriously bottled-up dude. An old CIA trick.

"The directives and information I'm about to share with you come directly from the church's highest source. If you assume that'd be His Holiness, you'd not be wrong. I say this not to get the drums rolling, but to emphasize both the urgency and the importance of our mission. In short, we're facing an immediate crisis which threatens the very core of our Catholic Church."

"That's unquestionably dramatic," Kevin exclaimed dryly.

"It's true, I'm afraid. You've been the subject of the most detailed and extensive investigation ever undertaken by the Church. I'm happy to report it was the right thing to do: you've been cleared. You're being reassigned to the Vatican. This'll mean dropping what you're doing here and coming to Rome immediately. Of course, you'll be held to our strict rules of confidentiality far more stringent than those in the military and the CIA."

"I was never a direct employee of the CIA," Kevin said.

Max looked down at his notes and continued, "Yes, I see that. You were officially employed by a paramilitary group called 'Grey Associates' assigned to the CIA under contract, correct?"

Kevin nodded. "Correct."

"Then—" began Max.

"Excuse me, Max. What if I were to turn down this assignment?" Kevin's head was reeling.

"Not an option, Kevin."

Kevin couldn't argue. Not now, anyway. "What else can you tell me?"

The monsignor stroked his chin. For a moment, he was contemplative as he looked out at the barren street. Pink buds and young leaves hinted of the coming of spring. On the horizon, clusters of smoky storm clouds were congregating.

"We believe there's a serious threat to the leadership of the Church. It's coming from within. I'm afraid that's all I'll disclose now."

"And how was I so lucky to get tapped for this special—ah, dangerous—assignment?"

"You came recommended by a highly-placed source—His Eminence, Cardinal John Porter," Drotti said.

"When I was studying in Rome, Porter was a bishop, and my mentor." Kevin nodded. He didn't add that Porter also happened to be his savior. After his snafu in the army had gone public, if it hadn't been for Porter, he might have been defrocked as a priest.

"Then you know he's now a cardinal. He runs the Instituto per le Opere Religiosi, the Vatican Bank. He's a powerful man and His Holiness has great confidence in him and his judgment. Besides his vote for you, our investigation into your military background also confirmed you're precisely the person we need."

Kevin cleared his throat. "You thoroughly checked my background?"

"If you're asking if we're aware of your army court martial, the answer is yes, of course." Drotti glanced at his notes. "According to the Code of Canon Law, Canon 1040, paragraph 4, a person who has committed voluntary homicide is considered 'irregular' regarding receiving Holy Orders." Drotti looked up and smiled. "The Holy See has granted you a dispensation."

A shrill bell rang out through the halls. Terrified, the monsignor jumped at the sound as if a gun had just gone off. Kevin thought to himself the bell's timing must be a sign from heaven. He was ready to get going.

Kevin rose. His body language spelled closure. "Well, if there's nothing more to discuss, I've got a class to teach, Max. Where do we go from here?"

"First, forget about the class, Kevin. Go home, start packing. Our plane leaves Dulles at seven p.m." Monsignor Drotti handed Kevin a single sheet of paper, confirmation of his reservation on United Flight 966 to Rome.

A chill was slithering down Kevin's spine. *What to do? What to do? Fight it or play along? Was God behind it? And what about the boys?*

"I'll need time. I've got to take care of obligations," Kevin said firmly.

"I'll see you at Dulles Airport. No later than six p.m." Drotti smiled faintly. "You wouldn't want to disappoint His Holiness."

It wasn't delivered as a question. Of course he wouldn't want to disappoint His Holiness. What should have been a question came off as more of an order. Before Kevin could say another word, Monsignor Max was leaving Mather's office.

Kevin stood still for a moment, clenching his jaw, watching the storm clouds converge higher in the sky. Sighing deeply, he left Mather's office. Tentatively, he headed to his classroom to bid farewell to his kids. He knew this wouldn't be easy for them. Or for him. But he also realized, for the moment, he hadn't a choice, especially if he wanted to keep his good standing in the Church. And with God.

After Kevin told the players, DeShaun, a bright junior on the team, stood up and walked to the front of the room to hug Kevin. "We're going to miss you, Padre. No one else here to kick our asses when we need it." He was speaking for the team.

Kevin smiled. "Hey, I'll keep score; if any of you mess up while I'm gone, when I'm back I'll kick your asses twice as hard."

"How long you gonna be gone?" asked another student.

"Don't know for sure," Kevin answered. "But I'll be back. You guys remember what I told you. Heads high, two hours of homework every night, and stand tall."

After a few more hugs and high fives, Kevin left, his heart heavy. *Dammit! I love these kids.*

Kevin didn't bother saying goodbye to Headmaster Mather. He wasn't in the mood to pretend he was happy about leaving. When it came to these kids, they were a different story.

Before packing, Kevin took out his checkbook and a spiral notebook, scribbled a note, ripped out the page, then wrote out a check and stuffed them both in an envelope addressed to Mather. The note was brief. "Here's for the uniforms."

And then through the fog in his brain, he thought of his final remaining conundrum. Katie. She was an entirely different story.

∞∞∞∞

CHAPTER THREE

Washington, D.C.

The next thing Kevin did was call Katie. They'd planned a while ago on having dinner in Georgetown that very night. He opened the conversation by apologizing for having to break their date.

"Rome?" Katie asked. "They're sending you to Rome?"

"That's right."

"And you don't know why? I mean—crazy thought—but, did you ask why?"

Hearing this, Kevin burst out laughing. Katie was completely serious. It all was happening so quickly he hadn't digested the weighty reality of it and the unintended implications. Nothing else to do but LOL—laugh out loud.

"What's so funny?" Now Katie was annoyed.

"Nothing, Katie. I wasn't laughing at you."

"Okay, you think I'm being bossy and aggressive, the kind of girl you—"

"No, Katie. I'm laughing about Katie being Katie."

By this time, Katie was miffed. He was pushing her buttons, not taking her seriously. Everything else in his life was deadly serious—except her.

"Sorry, Kevin," she said. "I'm an attorney, you know. That's what I do. It comes naturally. I know, I know—I sound like my Bosnian mother."

Oops. Kevin had ruffled her feathers. Katie was the product of a combative Croatian father and a willful, dominant Bosnian mother. The combination had produced the relentlessly inquisitive, chirpy Katie.

"I'll take you to the airport, okay?" Katie said.

"Sure, that'd be great."

As he hoisted his suitcase from the depths of the closet, Kevin reminded himself that theirs was, by any measure, an unusual friendship. She, a high-powered attorney; he, a Catholic priest. She, so much in and of this world; he, more often in the next. What a bizarre combination! People raised eyebrows and . . . well, probably with good reason.

Kevin often thought about how they'd met. Both had been undergraduate students at Georgetown University in Washington. Kevin had been newly initiated to the Jesuit way of life, the teachings of St. Ignatius Loyola, and the Jesuits' special way of defending their teachings. Reading the theologians, he'd felt, for the first time in his life, connected. Empowered.

Given his early indifference to the church and its teachings, Kevin's gradual connection later in college to the Jesuit mystique surprised him. Kevin's parents, devout Catholics, had dragged him to Mass on Sunday. They'd enrolled him in a Catholic high school. But at that time nothing theological was sticking. It wasn't so much that he disbelieved, as he deemed the stuff of religion just plain dull and impractical. That is, until he matriculated at Georgetown and discovered for himself the lot of scintillating philosophers and theologians.

Only a Jesuit institution of higher learning offers an assortment of esoteric courses, in epistemology, ontology, and logic. It's all about wild gossamer journeys into abstract spheres. There, in one of these lofty philosophy classes, Kevin first set eyes on Katie. A beauty by any discerning eye, her auburn hair flowed to her shoulders, framing a sculpted face. Kevin always thought that if Katie's face were plastered on the cover of a girly magazine, it'd sell a zillion copies. It was a face to sink a zillion hearts. Yet it wasn't her looks alone driving Kevin toward her.

On campus, in classes, Katie had become famous for her aggressive questions. At every chance imaginable in philosophy and religion classes, Katie would take upon herself to challenge time-honored Catholic teachings. Kevin often revisited an early incident. It was pure Katie.

The professor in the class, a middle-aged Irish Jesuit, already had covered the concept of the Holy Trinity. The Holy Trinity should be thought of as one: the Father, the Son, and the Holy Spirit, and they should be thought of as equal to one another.

Hearing this, Katie shot her hand up immediately. "So Father, if the Father, Son, and Holy Spirit are equal, we must assume they look the same, right? If I were to accost them, how would I tell them apart?"

Audible muffled hoots filled the room, but the earnest student asking the question wasn't amused. She was dead serious.

The professor laughed. "Ah, my dear Katie," the priest said in a lilting Irish brogue. "I often wonder if the Good Lord sent you to me as punishment for some long-forgotten transgressions in the old country . . . so be it." The priest made an exaggerated sign of the cross while the class again erupted in laughter.

Katie would have the final word. "I meant no disrespect, Father," Katie said, smiling. "Aren't the Jesuits known for having all the answers?"

"Indeed, Katie. It's a legend we've worked hard to propagate." Lowering his head in a moment of reflection, the priest continued. "With respect to the Trinity, they're equal but also separate and different. Were you to accost them, as you suggest, you'd relate differently to each. That's how you'd know them apart."

After class, having heard this amusing vignette, Kevin made a point of introducing himself and suggesting they go for a cup of coffee. They chatted for a while about school, Washington, friends. Wanting to know more about her, Kevin started asking questions about her childhood and her interests. At first elusive, it didn't take long before they were comfortable with each other. Soon she was opening up.

"My parents were born in what was then Yugoslavia," she said. "After Tito died, the country fell apart and broke down into sectarian conflicts. I was a kid. My older brother and I were frightened and my mom wanted us to get out of there."

"Did your family move to the U.S.?" Kevin asked.

Katie's expression saddened. "I wish they had," she said. After a moment she looked up. "Have you ever heard of a town called Vukovar, Kevin?"

Kevin thought for a moment and shook his head. "Don't think so."

"It's a town in Croatia. That criminal Milosevic invaded it in 1991. His army should have won the battle in a few hours. Instead, the townies wanted to fight. My dad was one of their leaders. Against all odds, they held the town for a long time against the much larger Serbian Army."

Kevin wanted to ask the gruesome details of what had happened, but hesitated. Katie read his mind.

"They were massacred, Kevin. All of them. Massacred. Then they were buried in mass graves. Oh, there's an impressive memorial in the town." She sounded more angry than sad.

"I'm sorry, Katie. I don't know what else to say."

"Well, all my life it's been an issue for me. At that time, in the town, my dad was a hero. But the price was too high; it cost me a father. Never have I forgiven him for that." She turned to face Kevin and smiled. "How the hell did you get me to talk about something I hate talking about? You are devious, Mr. Thrall."

"Not me, Katie. You want to talk about it. And it's good for you. Helps with the pain," Kevin said, smiling back. There was something about this hot-headed rabble-rouser diva that was getting to him.

They got to talking about their dreams for the future. Katie expressed interest in law school. Kevin said his post-graduation plans already were in place and spoken for: he was enrolled in ROTC. After college, military service.

* * * * * * * * * * * * *

And it seemed they both weren't far off from what transpired. As the years unfolded, Katie enrolled at Georgetown Law. Kevin, a freshly minted U.S. Army second lieutenant, went first to Ft. Benning, Georgia, for infantry training; then to Airborne and Ranger School, then a combat unit in Iraq. Kevin's army stint, however, ended badly. Understandably, after that, he wouldn't revisit it often.

Before graduating, Kevin and Katie had become more than friends. It started one evening when Kevin invited Katie to dinner at his place in upper Georgetown, offering to cook for her. Apologetically, he explained his apartment was small, a studio. Katie was charmed and undeterred, teasing that she'd go anywhere to have a smooth cowboy cook for her.

True, his efficiency apartment was barely big enough for one person, let alone two. But it was cozy. He was cooking his specialty, shrimp scampi with linguini. Well, not so much a specialty; it was the only dish he cooked with any confidence. Wanting everything to be just right, Kevin picked up a couple bottles of Chianti. As his pièce de résistance, he'd stopped by the Catania Bakery for a tiramisu, Katie's favorite. When they'd gone out for Italian, she'd always ordered it. To add to the deliciously smoky ambiance, he lit a couple of candles on his wobbly card table.

When she walked through the door, he'd known it'd be a special evening. She looked radiant. As she turned her head, her shoulder-length hair would tumble over her oval brown eyes and full lips. On that night, instead of her loose-fitting student garb, Katie had opted for a black knit dress accentuating her curves, showing off endlessly long legs.

"Oh, this is nice," Katie cooed. She'd not been to his apartment, though on a few occasions she'd invited herself. She flung her small black Kate Spade backpack on a chair.

"Would you care for the VIP tour?" Kevin joked, brandishing his hands in the air.

Kevin's stomach was in somersaults. He was jittery. This was just Katie. *No big deal.* They were the best of friends.

"If you'd like me to get lost while you're cooking, I brought homework," Katie said, pointing at the backpack.

"Uh, not what I had in mind," he said.

"Me neither." She beamed. "But I stirred things up in Catholic Theology class today."

"Really? Big surprise," Kevin said, smiling.

"No, this is serious. We were analyzing The Lord's Prayer. It's the one that Jesus himself wrote, right?"

Kevin wasn't sure where she was going with this one, but on this evening, wrestling around God-riddles wasn't what he'd hoped for.

"OK," Katie continued, looking up through the ceiling as if to the heaven beyond. "I have a real problem with the line: 'Lead us not into temptation.'"

"And that would be. . . ?"

"Why must we implore God *not* to lead us into temptation? Is He so mean-spirited that unless we call him on it, he'll say: 'Oh there's Kevin down there. Let's throw some temptation his way, see how he handles it?"

Kevin laughed. "You might have a point, Katie. An idiotic one, but a point."

"Don't patronize me, Kevin. Assuming Jesus wrote this, what the hell did he have in mind? The prayer says: 'Lead us not into temptation.' So writing it, was Jesus saying, 'Father, please stop hurdling these bolts of temptation before us mortals. We're pathetic and can't handle it.'"

"Katie, let's cover this another evening or maybe leave it to the theologians to worry about. I'm only an occasional cook, don't want to burn dinner."

Katie grimaced good-humoredly, then reached for the girly back-pack.

"I brought you something," she said, hiding her hands behind her back. Her arm swished around with a flourish. "Here!" she said coyly.

Kevin accepted the small box from her, wrapped and topped with a bow with a wide grosgrain sun-yellow ribbon.

"Open it."

Carefully Kevin unwrapped the package, peeking inside as he did. He smiled broadly. "A Mickey Mouse watch? Ha!" The watch had a gold frame, a black leather band, and Mickey's gloved hands pointing to the hours and minutes.

"Turn it over," Katie said, smiling.

Kevin did as she asked, wondering what'd possessed her. He turned it over. On the back there was a personalized inscription. "Don't Take Yourself Too Seriously. Love, Katie."

Kevin stared at it for a few moments, beaming. "Thanks, Katie. How kind of you."

And then he thought the irony of this gesture was that on this special evening, at least, it was Katie who was taking things too seriously.

"The real reason for this early birthday gift is that you're a serious guy, Kevin. And I want this silly watch to be a constant reminder to you that there are many ways to see things in life. Now get on with our dinner. I'm famished."

* * * * * * * * * * * * *

"This is absolutely divine," Katie said, heaping what she realized was an unladylike portion of the linguini onto her plate. "I'm impressed, Kevin. You can cook."

"There's tiramisu for dessert."

"What? You made that?"

"It's tempting to say, yes, of course I did, which would lead me to chastise you, my darling, for leading me into temptation!" Reaching for the garlic bread, Kevin hoped she wouldn't take umbrage. He was tempted to go on about the temptations in our daily lives, his sermon in the studio—but he stopped himself. He was pleased with himself for steering past disaster and catching himself. He'd already said enough. He'd softened the mood and calmed the beast. "No, bought it from a little bakery down the street."

"I'm sure I'll love it," she said, laughing.

Kevin opened the second Chianti. She accepted it gladly. Not wanting the night to end, Kevin said, "How about watching a movie with me?"

"Sure," she said. "What is it?"

"*A Man and a Woman.* It's a French film by Claude LeLouche. It's romantic with beautiful scenes of Normandy. Music by Francis Lai. I think you'll like it."

"Didn't it win a Palme d'Or at the Cannes Film Festival, way back when?" she asked.

"You know it?" Kevin was surprised. The film was released in 1966. Not many remember it.

"I'm a film buff," Katie said. "For a second, I thought you'd produce the likes of the more subtle *Casablanca*."

Kevin smiled. "Lucky I didn't. I could have. Then you've seen *A Man and a Woman*?"

"No, but I've always been meaning to," she said.

"Awesome," he said. Kevin refilled their wineglasses and started the DVD. Katie gently kicked off her heels, folding one leg beneath her, patting the seat beside her. Kevin sat down, kicking off his shoes as well.

Nursing the wine, watching the movie, they quipped back and forth, commenting on this scene and that, enjoying themselves. During a romantic moment, Katie's eyes filled with tears. Kevin put his arm around her. She didn't resist, and snuggled closer, her head nestled on his shoulder.

Finally emboldened, Kevin leaned over and kissed her, tentatively at first, then passionately. As his hand moved up her back, Katie sat up. Taking a deep breath, she laid a tender hand on Kevin's face.

"Well, Kevin, it seems we've hit a crossroads. It's no longer about temptation. Now it's about brushing temptation aside. Mortal Sin, anyone?"

He looked at her quizzically, loosening his grip, as if to say: I don't get it.

"I think you know." She stood up. "Let me make this easy for both of us. Yes, I care about you, and yes, I'm dead set on staying over tonight."

Kevin smiled. Katie turned to him and gracefully stepped out of her dress. It wasn't long before they moved, in a lingering embrace, from the sofa to his bed in the corner of the room. Soon thereafter this spot would become their regular soul sanctuary. After this sensual evening, there were more to follow, nights of making love to the steady beat of French drums. *Bolero, anyone?*

The next morning, before Katie escaped to her apartment to change for class, they toasted ceremoniously with orange juice to the end of their celibacy and the beginning of their newfangled, sentient friendship. Kevin loved her and knew, without a doubt, she loved him. Still, he wasn't quite ready to go the distance with her.

* * * * * * * * * * * * *

After a romantic period, Kevin and Katie went their separate ways. Kevin joined the army to fulfill his ROTC obligation. When possible, he and Katie saw each other. She continued with her studies and soon leveraged her way to become an attorney in Washington, D.C.

After leaving the army under questionable circumstances, Kevin consulted with the CIA in Washington. He and Katie were living in the same city and started to see each other, resuming the close relationship they had begun in college. After a few months of dating and commuting between their respective apartments, Katie casually suggested they live together. Kevin hesitated. Something powerful and mysterious was burning and growing inside him. A calling. A life path. He dreaded telling Katie about it. Telling her, saying it out loud, would finalize his resolution. He wasn't ready. She wouldn't get it. What woman would? And then without knowing exactly when it happened, one day a decision was made.

One afternoon Katie and Kevin met in a café on 36th Street in Georgetown, just blocks from campus. The sky was filled with dark rain clouds. Outside it looked dreary, sunless, solemn. Kevin was the first to arrive and was fidgeting with his cup of coffee. When she joined him, his eyes avoided hers. If he looked at her, he'd lose the nerve to speak his mind.

"Katie, there's something we should talk about," he said, folding his hands and looking at his coffee.

"OK," she said, unconcerned, stirring her cappuccino. "What's up, Kev?" Kevin knew his body language would give him away. He was nervous, wanted to get this over with.

"You know how much I love you," Kevin said.

"Of course," said Katie. *Good Lord! Maybe he was going to propose.* Her heart softened. She reached out, took one of his hands in hers. It felt cold. "Kevin, you know how much I love you, too. Right?"

He nodded.

"Something's come between us. I . . . I've made a decision—about my career—that will change . . . how we relate."

"Is the CIA relocating you?" she asked. *She would not let him leave without her! This was the perfect time to get married.*

"No, no . . . it's nothing like that," said Kevin. Withdrawing his hand, Katie noted that he wasn't wearing the Mickey Mouse watch.

"Is it . . . another woman?" chortled Katie.

"What?" Kevin looked at her, surprised. "No, not another woman, nothing like that."

"Then, what?" asked Katie. Her eyes were dark and defiant. "If you have to move somewhere, I'll come with you."

"No, Katie . . . .it's not that." *How could he possibly tell her?*

"Look, we love each other. Circumstances necessitated we spend time apart in the last few years. But it doesn't have to always be that way," said Katie. "We can make this work. I don't want us to be separated again—not now, Kevin. So no matter where you have to go—even if it's to the moon—I'm ditching my job and coming with you!"

Kevin squirmed in his seat. He had to tell her. "Katie, I . . . well . . . I've decided to move forward. To do it. To become a priest."

"Oh, my." Katie dropped her cappuccino, spilling it on the table.

"Look, this is tough," Kevin said, trying to look her in the eyes, "and I know you can't possibly understand what I'm feeling. This has been haunting me for over a year."

Katie's mouth popped open, her eyes big. "I'm speechless . . . I . . . don't know what to say."

"Remember the problems I had in the army?" Kevin said. "I won't explain them now. What matters is that at the end of the whole fiasco, I was close to God. I took much comfort in Him. That's how I got through it all, Katie. I talk to Him. He talks to me."

"What do you mean He talks to you? Do you hear voices? Are you crazy? Kevin, it's the schizophrenics who hear voices!" Katie wiped away a tear, conscious that she was shrieking, her voice elevated.

"Look, Katie, there's lots of biblical cases of exactly this—beyond our rational understanding. It starts with true faith in God." He took a breath, noticing the tears streaming down Katie's cheeks. "Believe me, Katie. Or have you lost your faith? Remember Joan of Arc? She heard voices and followed them." He reached out to take her hand. But she winced, rolling away from him.

"Joan of Arc?" Katie snapped. "Are you plagued with visions of burning at the stake, too? You sound delusional. Either that, or you're cracking up."

Kevin shrugged. "Okay, if you must, call me delusional. But Katie, He is calling me to the priesthood. It's my calling, Katie. The priesthood. Look, I fought it at first. Crazy idea. No way. But the more I fought it, the stronger it grew. I could hear Him telling me he wanted me in His service. And when I've looked at other options—you and me getting married—it wasn't right. It receded into darkness, faded out of the picture. Disappeared. There's nothing else for me."

Katie was inconsolable. "After all this time we've been together, you're telling me this now?"

Shaking his head, Kevin's eyes dropped to the table. "In this past year, it's only become more real for me. Honestly, I wish I could explain the power of this force. I hope you'll believe me, trust me when I tell you it's real."

"Kevin, there are other ways to serve God! Lots and lots of other ways. Are you just going to throw our love to the wind? I don't understand how you could possibly think that's what God wants?"

Again, Kevin reached for her hand, but again she pulled away. "No, of course not. But our relationship, the one we now enjoy, will dissolve. We'll still be friends. We love each other. Everyone needs love, Katie, even priests."

Holding her hands in the air, Katie was mocking him using finger quotation signs: "Just friends, right?"

"C'mon, Katie, don't take it that way."

"Don't take it like what? Spurned? Jilted? Thrown out for the priesthood? At least if there were another woman I'd have a fighting chance. What'd you expect? Good God, it'd be easier if you told me you preferred boys!"

"You don't mean that, Katie," Kevin said.

"I've just one question for you, Kev," said Katie, staring deep into his eyes. "Are you sure? Are you absolutely 100 percent sure this is what you want for the rest of your life?"

Kevin couldn't bear to look in her eyes. In them, he saw the pain and the hurt, and he knew he'd caused it. He looked away, nodding. "I'm sure, Katie. It's been torturing me."

She bolted up. "Then, I don't think there's anything else to say. Good luck with your Jesus. I hope he keeps you warm at night."

Before Kevin could say good-bye, Katie already had snatched up her purse and stormed from the café. Visibly shaken, Kevin's world was changing forever. He'd miss Katie. But this was something bigger than him. A power had possessed him. A decision, yes, but really not: there'd been no choice.

Packing his suitcase, in his mind's eye Kevin could see the hurt on Katie's face. But they wouldn't remain apart. One wish had come true for him: Over the years, they'd drifted back to each other, sometimes at first uncomfortably, but over time, their separation had become comfortable and familiar terrain. It'd even deepened their relationship. Well, maybe Katie wouldn't get married, maybe she'd go on loving him, on his terms. Maybe no one would ever come between them.

Often Kevin had tried to pinpoint when it was, exactly, that he'd made the fateful decision to serve God as a priest. Thinking about it, different scenes popped into his thoughts. He remembered studying about the concept of free will. God had created many different kinds of creatures on earth, but He gave free will only to one of them: man. Animals could be trained, but they couldn't make decisions; they acted only on instinct. An animal wasn't equipped to distinguish right from wrong. Animals were simple, followed their God-given instincts. Man, on the other hand, made choices. A great gift, but one that came with heavy responsibilities. In God's eyes, we are accountable for the choices we make.

Over time, Kevin knew he'd made some questionable choices. On active duty in the U.S. Army, he'd killed a man. He was following the orders of his army commanders, but had he the right to take a life? At the time, he'd thought he had, and that God was supporting him. But he was young. Following the army dictates seemed enough. Later, he realized there were other ways to see the issue. Others would question what he'd done.

While on active duty, if he saw evil in a man, he'd go after him—even kill—with impunity. He had little or no guilt regarding his actions; felt no remorse. He often wondered why. He wasn't sure. He was following orders.

And then he'd think, *Hey, Kevin, who are you, acting both as judge and jury?* Well, no, he wasn't the judge and jury. But some evils were self-evident. Case in point: the rapist of a young girl. In the army, he'd killed a man for raping a girl in Iraq. Later, he'd chastised himself. He'd come to terms with his God-given free will. He'd made a choice to kill the man. The peanut gallery talked about his having an anger management problem. Yeah, maybe.

One day, in church attending Mass at Holy Trinity in Georgetown, he was in a pew directly in front of a statue of the Blessed Virgin Mary. She wore her standard blue robe and was holding the infant Jesus in her arms. Gazing at the statue, he was transfixed. Staring back at him, she morphed into flesh and blood, and he heard her message. Never had he shared this mystical occurrence with anyone. Who would believe it?

∞∞∞

Kevin awakened from a state of reverie to focus on the matter at hand. Getting ready to go to Rome, he decided to wear jeans and a black sweater on the plane. He wanted to be comfortable and not draw attention to himself. He packed his priestly garb and a civilian suit. He retrieved his passport from his desk, ensured his iPad had reading material, and packed the leather breviary his parents had given him upon his ordination. He was ready.

Minutes later, Katie pulled up in her new red BMW convertible, a longtime temptation she'd weakened for, thanks to last year's bonus at her law firm. She signaled her presence with two quick beeps. Kevin grabbed his bags, looked around the apartment one last time for anything he might have forgotten, locked the door, and went downstairs.

Was this trip to Rome tied to his calling? Kevin had trained as a priest as thousands of other Jesuits had done. Yet he was unique. He was a priest who'd mastered the military skills of cold-blooded combat, expert marksmanship, espionage and deception, cool-headedness in the face of danger, and the ability to kill as necessary. Even with these unusual skills and training, at his core he was proud to serve God as priest, whether in a schoolyard, or in a fight for world order. It was complicated, this duality. As a priest, he practiced humility before God. As a soldier, well, the opposite. There were intrinsic conflicts. Now, as he rolled his suitcase behind him, he was reflecting on these irregularities, bouncing the suitcase down the stairs.

"You bought this beauty with a stick shift instead of an automatic?" Kevin said, after climbing in. Pressing on the pedal, Katie zoomed onto the Beltway surrounding Washington. Along the horizon, the sun was setting in vivid reds and yellows.

"I like to drive," Katie answered without taking her eyes off the road. Having just come from the office, she was wearing a tailored navy blue Armani suit. Her hair fell in curls on her shoulders. He liked it that way. Often, she wore it tied back off her face. Either way, his appreciation of her beauty intensified when he hadn't seen her in a while. Otherwise, he accepted her, loved her, thought of her as a part of himself.

* * * * * * * * * * * * * * * * *

"So how long, Kevin?" Katie asked.

"Not sure. I think I might be there for some time."

Katie shook her head. "What about your job, your apartment, your life, your friends?"

Kevin shrugged. "The job will wait. The church takes care of my apartment, as you know. And my thousands of friends will just have to get along without me." He looked over at her and smiled. "You know you're my one and only real friend."

Katie didn't let her composure slip. "Yeah, right." There was sarcasm in her voice. "And you don't know why they picked you?" She veered the car off the Beltway and onto the access road leading to Dulles Airport in Virginia.

"They didn't tell me much, except that they need a wolf dressed as a lamb. Obviously, it has to do with my background in the army and CIA."

"Do they know about. . . ?" Katie abruptly abandoned the question and went silent.

"The trial?" Kevin obliged. "Apparently so—and they still picked me."

"I've got to take some depositions in Brussels next month on an international trade case," she said. "Want me to come back via Rome?"

"You'd do that?"

"Sure," she said. "Why not? Hey, I'm not the one who joined the priesthood."

Kevin smiled at her. "Just as long as you don't expect me to put you up."

Katie smiled back. "What? Priests can't put up their friends? There's no rule against it that I know of."

"Yeah, it'd really look great to the Vatican if they knew Aphrodite was staying with me," Kevin said.

"A girl can always dream."

"A man can always dream."

Katie pulled onto the access ramp of the multilevel Dulles Terminal, stopping in front of United's check-in. As Kevin removed his bags from the trunk, she got out of the car and stood by him. A breeze was lifting her curls and she was wearing the same perfume she'd worn on that first night they made love so long ago. The scent . . . and the memory . . . was electrifying.

Kevin's attention was diverted by the figure of Monsignor Drotti standing on a curb nearby. Kevin thought about introducing Katie, then thought better of it. No need for stimulating curiosity.

"Thanks for the ride, Katie," Kevin said. "I'll be in touch." He hugged her and their eyes locked, exchanging more than words.

Watching her getting back into the Beemer and gracefully folding her legs inside, Kevin's feelings of virility resurfaced. The priesthood never could cloud these moments.

She waved and sped off, leaving Kevin standing tall, his forbidden fantasies and his belongings beside him on a curb.

Spotting him, Drotti wasted no time coming over. "I've checked in already," he said. He, too, was wearing non-clerical garb, slacks and a sports jacket.

"I got a ride to the airport from a friend," Kevin explained.

Drotti smiled. "Miss O'Connell?"

Kevin was more annoyed than surprised. "Sounds to me like your investigative work has crossed the line," he said.

"I told you we were thorough."

Kevin decided not to pursue it. Clearly, when it came to Drotti and the guys in Rome, nothing in his life was private.

Onboard, business class was an unexpected treat. Both men ordered Scotch. Chivas Regal. Kevin grabbed some magazines and nuzzled in, sitting all the way back. Drotti fussed with papers in his briefcase.

"Can you tell me more about this assignment?" Kevin asked.

"In due time, Kevin." Drotti finished his Scotch and ordered another.

Kevin drifted off to sleep. Soon he was afloat, airborne, flying not toward Rome, but toward an airy, puffy cloud where a beckoning, lovely Katie awaited him.

CHAPTER FOUR

Rome, Italy

Arriving at the Leonardo da Vinci Airport outside Rome, Kevin and Monsignor Drotti gathered their carry-ons from the overhead bins, joining the queue exiting the plane. Entering the sleek steel-and-chrome terminal, soaring glass panels offered magnificent vistas of a clear spring day. The airport was alive with businesspeople stampeding the gates, Starbucks and briefcases in hand. Clusters of tourists were headed to line up at customs along with Kevin and Drotti. These days, customs control was little more than a passport check. Then baggage claim to retrieve luggage. So far, on this trip, Drotti was tight-lipped.

Stepping outside for fresh air, Kevin took a deep breath. Not quite the great outdoors, but better than the recirculated air of a nine-hour flight. After hopping on the shuttle bus, they rolled their luggage to the parking lot where Drotti had left his car.

"Nice wheels," commented Kevin when they approached Drotti's gleaming black Alfa Romeo.

"Thanks," said Drotti. "Probably not something you've ever seen in the States."

"Oh I don't know," Kevin replied as he inspected the car. "It's a 1990 or 1991 Spider Veloce, four cylinder super-charged engine, with Panasport wheels. Good condition, too."

Drotti smiled. "I'm impressed. Would you care to drive it?"

"No thanks."

They climbed into the sports car, and Drotti drove out of the parking lot and onto the freeway.

Ten minutes into the drive, in the side view mirror, Kevin saw something he didn't like. He turned to Drotti. "I changed my mind. I'll drive."

Drotti raised his eyebrows, but said nothing. In a few moments, he pulled over at a rest stop where benches, a table, and wooden structure housing toilets were nestled in a park-like area.

Kevin opened the car door and got out. Drotti did the same.

"Do you know how to get to the Vatican from here?"

"Sure, I lived here for eighteen months, remember?" said Kevin. "But let me tell you why I want to drive. We're being tailed. Let's just say my James Bond background may be better suited to handling this."

Drotti frowned, looking around. "I don't see anyone."

"They're over there. In that souped-up Fiat," Kevin said, motioning towards a car parked in front of a bench.

"What are you going to do? Lose 'em?" Drotti asked, blinking his eyes as if trying to see more clearly.

"Maybe. I want to know why they're following us."

Drotti shook his head. "What do you plan to do?"

Kevin smiled. "You'll see. Let's find the men's room."

Coming from the restroom, Kevin glanced toward the black Fiat. One of the men was stocky, with fine tufts of hair, smoking a cigarette, leaning ever so nonchalantly on the back of the car. The other was inside the car at the wheel. Upon sighting Kevin, the man standing put out his cigarette and hopped in the vehicle.

Drotti tossed the keys to Kevin, and they were off and running. Truth be told, Kevin was just enough of a cowboy to relish the feel of Drotti's Alfa. He shifted effortlessly through the gears, savoring the high pitch of the engine as they picked up speed, watching the speedometer hit 140, 150, 160 kilometers an hour. The Fiat struggled to keep up.

Once in Rome off the freeway, they slowed, navigating their way toward the Vatican, down Via Aurelia, into a working-class neighborhood with small shops, the occasional outdoor café, and bicycle repair businesses and merchants. Young men and women on motorbikes were whizzing past them.

At a stoplight Kevin abruptly veered left on to a side street. Sure enough, the Fiat was following. The two priests continued along the cobbled road until it turned into a gravel and dirt footpath.

Pressing down on the accelerator of the Alfa Romeo, spewing dust and gravel under the tires, Kevin shifted into fourth gear, churning up a dark dust ball astern. The Fiat was still hugging the Alfa's bumper.

Now there was only one thing to do.

Kevin turned the steering wheel 45 degrees while simultaneously slamming on the brakes. First a skid, then the car spun around. Now it was facing the other way, headed straight toward the Fiat.

This tricky maneuver Kevin had mastered in the CIA. Not bad. A reversal of fortune.

Drotti, gasping, clutched the seat underneath him.

Approaching the Fiat, Kevin again slammed on the brakes, turning the Alfa across the entire road, skidding to a full stop.

The Fiat was still heading for them at high speed. Kevin knew the car, a Fiat Linea made in Turkey. A piece of junk, a low-end model at least eight years old. The driver could do one of two things: stop or crash. He had about five seconds to decide. The Fiat screeched to a halt.

"Stay in the car," Kevin said. Glancing over at Drotti, the monsignor's color drained from his face. He was ghost-like.

Opening the door to the Alfa Romeo, Kevin calmly stepped out, walking over to the stopped vehicle. The driver and his companion got out of the Fiat.

Now, let's see who's gonna make the first move, Kevin thought, clenching his jaw. He was acutely aware that he wasn't armed. They might be. Kevin assessed his situation. He expected that one man would approach and the other stay at a distance. Standard procedure. He knew he could take one of them, but could he neutralize the second one?

The tall, dark-skinned driver was dressed in workman's jeans. The smoker was shorter and rounder with a balding head, wearing jeans and a plaid flannel shirt. He was trailing behind.

The driver, wearing Ray-Ban aviator sunglasses and a fitted leather jacket, walked quickly toward Kevin. As he drew near, Mr. Sunglasses reached inside his jacket.

Kevin knew the guy wouldn't be reaching for a cigarette. His instincts took over. He lunged and tackled the thug at the waist, knocking him to the ground. They hit the surface hard, but luckily, Kevin was cushioned by the man's body. As the driver's Ray-Ban's spun off, he was trying to get at the pistol inside his coat. As the thug withdrew the pistol, Kevin grabbed his outstretched hand. In a split second, Kevin kneed him in the groin, then karate-chopped him on the neck. The man crunched up in pain.

Kevin picked up the pistol and stood up. A Glock ASP. *Very familiar, thank you.* Using its butt, he struck the guy on the head with the full force of the gun, knocking him out. Kevin looked around just in time to see Mr. Baldie rushing him. He, too, was holding a pistol, and this one was aimed at Kevin's head.

Kevin fired a shot into Mr. Baldie's shoulder. The man buckled to the ground, yelping in pain, his gun flying from his hand, out of reach. Kevin turned back to the driver, still lumped on the ground, grabbed his collar, yanked him up to a sitting position, and spoke through clenched teeth. "Do you want to live?" Kevin pushed the pistol into the side of the man's cheek.

The man was coming to, regaining consciousness. He gasped a barely audible 'yes.' Apparently, he understood some English.

"Start talking."

Monsignor Drotti was peeking out from behind the Alfa Romeo. Kevin motioned for him to come over. Drotti tentatively approached. The man who'd been shot in the shoulder was on the ground, moaning. Keeping his eye, and his gun, on the two of them, Kevin yelled over to Drotti, "Max, pick up that gun and hand it to me."

Looking terrified, Max went over and picked the pistol off the ground with his thumb and forefinger.

"Max, now I want to get this guy to talk. Get over here. My Italian isn't as good as yours."

"This man's bleeding, Kevin. We've got to do something."

"Max, ask him why he's following us, who he works for—the important details. Tell him if he doesn't, he's roadkill."

"I can't say that!" Drotti winced.

"Just do it, damn it." Kevin kept his gun pointed at both of them.

Nodding, Drotti came over and handed the gun he'd picked up to Kevin, who stuck it in his jeans. Still pale and shaking, Drotti translated as they talked, but Kevin understood most of it. After a lot of Italian jabber, Drotti said they'd been hired by a group called Columbo to follow them wherever they went, and report back who they talked to. For the job, they were paid 2,000 euros. The thug said he worked regularly for Colombo, but didn't know his identity or any of the bosses. They were originally contacted over the Internet, so they didn't even know the names of the guys hiring them or their intentions. For ordinary thugs like them, this was simply a source of income. Nothing personal.

"Okay, that's all we're going to get out of them," Kevin concluded. Nothing new here. He'd assumed they were just hired guns.

Reaching into his pocket, Drotti pulled out his cell.

"What are you doing?" Kevin asked.

"Calling an ambulance," Drotti responded.

"No. Put that phone down."

"Kevin, this one's bleeding to death. We can't just let . . ."

Kevin grabbed the phone. "We'll call for help, but not on your phone. They'll trace the number."

He reached inside the jacket of the man who lay bleeding on the ground.

Kevin searched Baldie's pocket, found a mobile phone, and threw it at Drotti. "Here. Use this one. Don't let them know who you are."

"They'll find out, won't they? Shouldn't we stay until the ambulance comes?"

"Just make the call, Max. Trust me. These guys won't say a word. If they do, next time I won't be so kind and gentle."

Drotti called the emergency number, gave the location, and requested an ambulance. Snatching the phone from him, Kevin removed the SIM card with the stored data.

From his pocket Kevin found a clean handkerchief and handed it to Baldie to stop the bleeding. He then searched the pockets of the driver who was still on the ground, squirming in pain. Kevin found his cell, yanked the SIM card out, and dropped the phone on the ground.

"C'mon, Max, let's get out of here."

They got into the Alfa Romeo and sped away, rubber to the road, toward the Vatican, Kevin at the wheel.

Drotti was still visibly shaken up. He whined, "Kevin, if this is the way it's going to be, I'm not your best partner material. I'm a priest. I've no experience or appetite for this."

"I'm a priest, too, and I'm not sure that you should be my partner, either. But given how this assignment is starting, I'll need someone who's not afraid to get his hands dirty."

After a while, Drotti asked, "Kevin, forgive me for asking, I'm terribly curious, how does a man like you become a priest?"

Kevin didn't answer. *Interesting question, monsignor. I'm a priest who roughs it up with the best of them. Excites me, that adrenaline. How do I reconcile this with my calling to serve as a priest of God? Does it matter? It's who I am, what I want. I'm divided, a split personality. I am two, Kevin the brave and fearless warrior, and Father Thrall, the humble servant of God. What's mind-boggling is that they're opposites. Kevin, meet Father Thrall. Father Thrall, meet Kevin.*

Finally, Kevin turned to Drotti. "When I find out, I'll let you know," he said. He pushed into fifth gear as an ambulance, sirens screaming, passed them.

CHAPTER FIVE

Vatican City

The dome of St. Peter's Basilica, the world's largest church, appeared in the distance above the sand colored buildings. Nearing the city limits of Rome, Drotti took the wheel as the car slowed in the heavy traffic on Via Aurelia.

St. Peter's, built over a span of more than one hundred years by the greatest Italian architects of the era, was the most recognizable place of worship in the world. Built of travertine stone, combining eclectic architectural styles and adornments, it seemed nothing short of a miracle that this edifice, more than 500 years old, sustained such splendor over the ages. In addition to housing its works of art, including Michelangelo's masterpiece, the Pieta, St. Peter's houses the tombs of 91 popes, including that of the first pope, St. Peter. Vatican City is the heart of Rome, surrounded by the city itself.

As they approached, a burst of sunlight from above was flooding St. Peter's Square, as if it were a part of heaven itself. As always, tourists were milling about, snapping photos in front of the stately columns and fountains. Kevin had seen many of the great churches of the world, yet none affected him as viscerally as this one. To him, it was the holiest of holy places. It made him proud to be a priest.

Kevin opened the car window to take in the air, the smell, the aura of this place he'd once called home while training for the priesthood. There was something about being here. Even with his eyes closed he knew exactly where he was, and he liked it. As a city, the entirety of Rome was sacred: just being here lifted his spirits.

From time to time, Kevin noticed Drotti looking at him quizzically. Kevin knew Drotti was still ruffled by the skirmish with the thugs. To a shielded soul like Drotti, the incident must have been upsetting. Every time Kevin looked at Drotti, he'd see that question on his face. *How does a man like you become a priest?*

Drotti drove to the side of the columns, through the gates to the Vatican, and stopped at an administrative building. The two men said little. When they stopped, Drotti got out. "I'll pick up the keys to your apartment; be right back," he said. "Stay out of trouble while I'm gone?"

"I didn't start the trouble," said Kevin defensively.

"I know," Drotti said. He was stiff and slow, with a wise, all-knowing look on his face, as if he knew more than he was telling.

Drotti went to the villa's gated reception area. Kevin watched him, thinking, *Why had he been brought here?*

When Drotti returned, he climbed back into the driver's seat and started up the engine.

"Everything OK?" asked Kevin.

"Sure. I got your key. No messages from the thugs." He looked at Kevin, smirking.

Kevin allowed a half smile, knowing their scuffle with the thugs was only the beginning. This wasn't a pleasure trip.

Drotti drove the Alfa Romeo up a hill lined with towering pines. Kevin rolled down his window, relishing the fragrance of the pines and the freshness of the morning air, a welcome contrast to the smog and hustle-bustle of the city. The Sistine Chapel's steepled roof was on his left, the Vatican Museum on his right.

Slowing in front of a four-story brick building, the Villa Domenica, a Romanesque villa with manicured gardens, Kevin recalled it was the one he was looking for. They stopped. Kevin wondered why he'd be staying in such splendor. This place was for VIPs, like diplomats, celebrities, or high-ranking church officials.

"Welcome to your home away from home," Drotti said dryly.

"I'm staying here?"

"I think you'll like it." Drotti nodded.

"You think it's secure?" asked Kevin.

"As secure as anywhere here," Drotti said. "Best we can do."

The men left the Alfa Romeo and Drotti led Kevin through the villa's reception area to his apartment on the first floor. Kevin whistled. "This is a welcome surprise."

"Pretty luxurious, isn't it?"

It was far more than Kevin had expected. A VIP setup with a living room and flat screen TV, separate bedrooms, outfitted in modern furniture, and a fully stocked refrigerator and bar with whiskey, beer, and vodka. *Mmm*, thought Kevin. *Drinking is one of the vices tolerated in the priesthood.* He was grateful for that.

"Try to get some rest. I will too," Drotti said, his face drawn. "I'll be by for you at five o'clock. We have a meeting."

"Who with?"

"Tell you later. Make yourself comfortable. Please, no shootings or gangsta-like shenanigans."

"Duly noted." Kevin beamed, grinning from ear to ear.

"If you need anything, you have my number. But my offer is good for emergencies only," said Drotti.

"Don't worry, I'll be fine."

When Drotti had left, Kevin unpacked quickly, finding ample room in a walk-in closet and dresser for storing his things. He plugged in his laptop, placing it on the desk, and was relieved to see a card offering Wi-Fi with a password. The apartment had all the office equipment a guest might need, including a copy machine and a fax.

Once everything was put away, Kevin laid his breviary, the liturgical book of the Latin rites of the Catholic Church, on the bedside table. He never traveled without this little book. Exhausted, he flopped onto the bed. He had a throbbing headache. The jet lag, plus the charade with the thugs, had done him in.

"*Colombo*," the thugs had said. *What did that mean?* Kevin had no idea. At least, by the end of it, Kevin had gotten his hands on a couple of pistols. He'd need to figure out how to get ammunition. That shouldn't be too difficult. Maybe he wouldn't need it, but his experience told him otherwise. Later on, he'd search the SIM cards.

Kevin's iPhone beeped. A text message from Katie:

"Going to Brussels next week. Afterwards shall I come to Rome for a couple of days?"

Kevin had no idea of his itinerary—he'd just gotten here. A visit from a woman might be problematic. But then it was Katie. The thought of her warmed him.

"Sure," he texted.

∞∞∞∞

CHAPTER SIX

Seville, Spain

Carlos Alameda's shabby one-room apartment was nestled among rows and rows of same-size houses in the poorest section of Seville. The paint on the buildings was peeling, exposing rotting wood beneath. The apartment was ascetic. Simple. A rickety metal cot covered with a thin blanket, a small wooden table and chair, and a light bulb hanging from the ceiling on a string. Once upon a time, the walls may have been washed in white, but now were gray.

Wet from a shower, Carlos Alameda stood in his underwear facing the window. This was his home. Carlos was interested in utility only, not comfort. This bare-bones décor was what he needed. Standing at the window, he noticed the sun hovering over the buildings in the distance, ushering in the dawn of the day.

Carlos's trim body and taut muscles glistened from his shower. If there'd ever been an ounce of fat on him, there was no trace of it on this body that had been muscled and toned years earlier under the expert training of the Franco Youth Brigade. Carlos often prayed to the founder of the brigade, his own grandfather who, during the Spanish Civil War, had fought alongside Generalissimo Franco as part of the ultranationalist movement in the thirties.

Falling to his knees, he prayed out loud in his native Spanish. At fifty-four, Alameda was the trusted and obedient servant of the Visitor, the leader of Opus Mundi. He'd been working for the Visitor for more than thirty-five years.

The morning's quiet was broken by the sonorous clang of bells from Seville's cathedral. The bells reminded Alameda of his start with Opus Mundi. It was after he'd completed his studies for the priesthood. He'd been given the mission of violence with Opus Mundi. Should he get ordained? It seemed pointless. He never had.

Back in 1980, the Visitor had taken notice of him and his talents. Alameda was special. He was recruited to train a contemporary, Mehmet Ali Agca. The young Turk being trained by Carlos was determined to do whatever he could to save his family from starvation and penury. They told Agca he could also retain his farm for his parents and siblings in Yozgat. But the deal was that he must do as they ordered, without question. Agca agreed, of course. But he didn't realize he was selling his soul.

At about the time he was thinking of being ordained, Alameda trained the young Turk to be an assassin. His mission: to assassinate Pope John Paul II.

Finishing his prayers, Alameda dressed in black trousers and shirt, as was his custom. Now it was time for another ritual. In a small bowl on the table were six shiny steel knives, each with a short handle and a six-inch blade. Once thrown, the knife would spin twice, then level out, blade first, on its trajectory to the target.

No one was better at throwing knives than Alameda. This morning, he grabbed the knives and placed his target on the wall with a piece of tape. It was a recent photo of His Holiness Quintus II.

Alameda backed up ten meters, spun around, and in a fluid, practiced motion of speed and balance, launched a dagger. The knife sailed through the air, striking the target in the forehead. Alameda performed the same motion twice more, striking the target precisely in each eye. He was a master.

Alameda smiled, remembering how he'd trained young Mehmet Agca for his day with the pope. But when the day had come, the attempt had failed. On May 13, 1981, he shot Pope John Paul II in St.

Peter's Square. The pope fell, but hadn't died. Instead, Agca was captured and imprisoned. The Opus Mundi had upheld their end of the bargain. While Agca was sentenced to life in prison, his family survived, though modestly.

The bells were now tolling again. Alameda checked his wristwatch. Time to get to work.

CHAPTER SEVEN

Kevin's Mission, Vatican City

Monsignor Max Drotti arrived at Kevin's executive suite promptly at five p.m. Drotti was clean-shaven, looking eager. Kevin, too, was refreshed. He'd grabbed a nap, showered, and downed a beer. Ready to go.

"Did you find everything here satisfactory?" asked Drotti.

"Perfect. Everything was great."

"No visitors or shootings?"

"Well, well," said Kevin. "The monsignor has a sense of humor!" Kevin slapped him on the back good-naturedly.

"Just looking out for you," said Drotti, dryly. "I hadn't realized you were one of those rambunctious American cowboys."

"Oh, you ain't seen nothin' yet," said Kevin. He smiled at the monsignor. *Maybe they'd be friends, after all.* "So, who're we meeting?"

"Your good friend, Cardinal John Porter," Drotti said. "If you're ready, let's go."

Kevin relished the idea of seeing his old friend Porter, but he knew the meeting wasn't because Porter was missing him.

Kevin grabbed his watch and key and locked the door, following Drotti outside. Together, they walked through the damp chill of the late spring afternoon around St. Peter's Basilica. Kevin loved the history of the place. It seemed uncanny that since the fourth century there'd been a church on this site. Since Caligula was the Emperor, a granite Egyptian obelisk had stood in Rome. And then there was the *power* of this place. An indisputable lingering and mysterious *energy* which couldn't be ignored.

A pope's responsibilities are staggering—leading a church of more than one billion souls. And with the Curia, overseeing 2,500 dioceses, more than 150 Cardinals, 5,000 bishops and 400,000 priests. Kevin himself was one of those 400,000 priests. Probably the only one who'd been in the CIA. Maybe not, but thinking about it made him feel special.

In addition, there were over a million clerical brothers and nuns, plus 500 citizens, all living in this inner circle, a one hundred-acre area called Vatican City. And of course, there were museums and administrative offices and colleges, tucked around and behind the Grand Central Piazza, stone buildings marked by bronze plaques.

Cardinal Porter's office was on the second floor of the *Governatorato*, the Palace of the Governatorate, a tall, boxy building in the heart of the formal Vatican Gardens. Though it wasn't as well-known as the Apostolic Palace, where the Constantinian Basilica of St. Peter's was constructed in the first half of the 4th century, this was where the serious business was orchestrated. The most important behind-the-scenes management of Vatican City happened here, and the city's 1,500 employees were hired and managed from these offices.

"Please, this way," said a uniformed attendant as he opened the door to Cardinal John Porter's office. As Drotti and Kevin walked into the room, Kevin let out a low whistle, but checked himself, remembering where he was. Things here were tighter, more reserved than where he came from.

Kevin and Drotti found themselves enveloped by the creation of a medieval ambience. Tall ceilings and walls of filigreed gold statues. Italian Renaissance furniture glistening with gold trim. Three period chairs faced the antique desk where His Eminence stood, smiling. Porter looked to be around sixty years old and stood six feet tall. He was slim with beautifully groomed silver hair, blue eyes, and a movie star sculpted face. If Hollywood ever needed a senior cleric for films, Porter would fit the bill.

Kevin was genuinely pleased to see his old friend again.

"It's great to see you, Kevin!" Cardinal Porter said, hugging him. He turned and shook Drotti's hand. "Nice to see you, as well. I wish the circumstances were different, of course. Come, let's sit at the conference table where we'll be more comfortable."

"So, how have you been?" asked Kevin once they were seated on forest green velvet-covered chairs around an oval oak table. Kevin thought the place was truly regal.

"I'm doing well. May have put on a few pounds." Cardinal Porter patted his stomach. "I have to tell you, I really miss our training sessions in the gym, Kev. Can't get any of my colleagues to work out with me."

"The extra pounds come with age," Kevin said. He smiled. "I'm starting to feel it, too."

"Maybe we can get in a game of racquetball while you're here?"

"I'd like that," Kevin said, "and my game is a lot better than it used to be."

"Really? You're telling me I'm not going to win this time around?"

Kevin shook his head. "Sorry to tell you, Eminence, you haven't got a chance."

"We'll settle that later." Cardinal Porter smiled. "But back to the present reality. Kevin, you're here because we need somebody with your special skills. For a major crisis."

"So I gather," said Kevin. "I'm surprised I was chosen. You're one of the few who really know me—and the truth about my background."

"We considered your background carefully, Kevin, and to tell you the truth, that's precisely why we need you." The cardinal smiled, settled in his chair, folded his hands, and took a deep breath. "I trust you, Kevin."

"Thank you, sir," said Kevin. "I appreciate that."

"I suppose you've been following the international news. There's a risk of war between Iran and Israel. The Israelis might strike at any time."

Kevin raised an eyebrow. The Vatican has been involved in many world events, but the possibility of the Church taking a role in a Middle East war was preposterous, borderline wacky. Kevin remained reticent, nodding for the cardinal to continue.

"No doubt you're wondering what it has to do with us. Simply put, this war could be nuclear, hence, apocalyptic. There are predictions in the Bible as well as in various Revelations about such an apocalypse opening a new era for Christianity. The official position of the Church is that when the time comes, God will tell us how to proceed."

Very interesting, Kevin thought. *An apocalypse? Are we being serious?* Glancing over at Drotti, he noted his eyes were wide open and his mouth slightly agog.

"I know what you're thinking, gentlemen," Porter said. "You're thinking this is strange. But hear me out." The cardinal walked over to the floor-to-ceiling cabinet of rare books. Up on his tiptoes, he reached, retrieved a leather Bible, blew off a thin film of dust, and flipped through the pages.

"Here it is," he said without looking up. "Matthew 24."

Porter began to read:

"*And as he sat upon the Mount of Olives, the disciples came unto him privately, saying, 'Tell us, when shall these things be? And what shall be the sign of thy coming, and of the end of the world?'*

"*And Jesus answered and said unto them, 'Take heed that no man deceive you. For many shall come in my name, saying,* I am Christ; *and shall deceive many. And ye shall hear of wars and rumors of wars: see that ye be not troubled: for all these things must come to pass, but the end is not yet. For nation shall rise against nation, and kingdom against kingdom: and there shall be famines, and pestilences, and earthquakes, in diverse places.'*"

Flipping the page, Cardinal Porter continued. "*And many false prophets shall rise, and shall deceive many.*"

Porter closed the book.

Drotti and Kevin looked at each other, puzzled.

Porter smiled. "You're not understanding?"

"Not really," Drotti said. "My personal recollection of Matthew 24 is the ending in which he talks about the weeping and gnashing of teeth, which I always found somewhat colorful."

"What does this have to do with us?" asked Kevin. "More specifically, what does it have to do with me?"

"The group, Opus Mundi, believes today's Catholic Church has strayed from its original teachings. They contend the Church is being led by a 'false prophet.' In this case, His Holiness, Quintus II. As the passage suggests, 'nations shall rise against nations,' resulting in a war. Simply put, a war will fulfill the prophecy, and then the false prophet will be replaced. See where this is heading?"

As the men looked at each other, a loaded silence followed. In the hallway, a clock chimed. Everything seemed surreal. Kevin felt as though time had stopped. Finally he spoke. "Are you saying they're going to kill the pope?"

Cardinal Porter shrugged. "That's possible. Wouldn't be the first time."

"How does the pope feel about all of this?" asked Drotti.

"The pontiff is aware of it," said Porter. "But he insists on 'business as usual,' on keeping his schedule. However, security has been heightened."

"Well, even if the Pope dies, Opus Mundi can't replace him," Drotti said. "Only the College of Cardinals can elect a new pope. Am I missing something here?"

"We don't have all the answers," the Cardinal said. "That's why Kevin is here and on the case. We believe Kevin has the resources and gumption to find the answers we're looking for."

"I'll do my best," said Kevin. *Good God, what did this mean? Would he have to eliminate the would-be assassin?* "How did you learn of this, Eminence?"

"Here at the Vatican, we have a special IT team monitoring the online flow of communications 24/7 for chatter related to crimes against the Vatican and the pope. They search for keywords and other data that might be relevant. The IT team is modeled after the National Security Agency in the States, but nowhere near their capability. In any event, in recent days our internal security has reported increased Opus Mundi chatter online, which could mean a major operation is brewing—especially after your attack this morning."

Resting his elbows on the table, the cardinal unfolded his hands, then folded them again. There were lines around his blue eyes, highlighting his worry and fatigue. "We intercepted one message possibly related to Opus Mundi's plans. It's in code. We don't entirely understand it. I'm going to share it with you in the strictest confidence." The cardinal looked over at Drotti, whose eyes were transfixed on the paper in Porter's hand.

"I understand," said Drotti.

Kevin nodded. Over the years, he'd heard rumors about Opus Mundi. Those in Opus Mundi were fanatics who held to some catastrophic worldview. They'd been around for over a hundred years. If the Masons had deep secrets and an aura of mystery surrounding them, well, they paled next to Opus Mundi. According to legends, and documents uncovered over the years, Opus Mundi believed that a false messenger of God would appear threatening the Church. The advent of this false messenger's reign would be preceded by a major calamity, like a world war . . . or an apocalypse. How was the Colombo group connected to Opus Mundi? He'd have to do some research to connect the dots.

Cardinal Porter handed the paper to Kevin and he read:

Transcription intercepted 5/22 NSA 43T/29QA
VISITOR 5/29 BEIRUT. TRIGGER SALE
SATIN PO$ 6/2
(Note: unsure of correct translation but nothing better found)

Kevin shrugged his shoulders. "I have no idea what this means." He handed the note to Drotti.

The cryptic message meant little to Kevin, but he'd figure it out. He took out a piece of paper and a pen from his pocket, and started jotting down a list.

Cardinal Porter said, "Visitor is the pseudonym—the code name—for the leader of Opus Mundi; that much we know. Beirut is a mystery unless Visitor or his designee is going there or expecting someone from there. The next words don't make sense. We tried variations of *satin* since the Church uses that fabric extensively; nothing came up."

"Sir, give me a little time with this. I'll work on it. Get some help if I need it." As he finished his list, Kevin stroked his chin.

Cardinal Porter nodded. "Certainly. Anything else you need?"

"I made a list." Kevin handed the cardinal his piece of paper.

"Ammunition, a secure cell phone, a Taser gun? Goodness, Kevin! I hope you don't need all these things. Sounds like you're going to war."

Kevin half-smiled, raising his eyebrows. "You never know."

"Did you forget a knife?" Drotti smirked.

"I brought my own," Kevin replied.

"I cannot overstate the gravity of this, Kevin," Cardinal Porter said. His voice was grave.

"Of course," said Kevin.

"Believe me," said Drotti. "Kevin will know what to do with this stuff. I've seen him in action."

"I know," said Cardinal Porter. "That's why he's here. And, gentlemen, in Vatican Security parlance, we believe this is a 'Code Red.'"

"A James Bond movie?"

"I'm being serious, Kevin. To us, it means that Opus Mundi has entered into the Action Phase of their mission to annihilate the Catholic Church." He looked pointedly at Kevin. "Kevin, they must be stopped. By any means necessary. I hope I've made myself clear."

By any means necessary? That's why they picked me.

"I understand." Kevin nodded his head. "Give me a couple of days to put all this together and get back to you with a plan."

"Don't take too long. That attempt on your life this morning won't be the last."

"I'll do my best," said Kevin. He swallowed hard. This was no game.

"And I'll help in any way I can," added Drotti.

"I knew I could count on the two of you," said the cardinal. "Now, come. I'll let you two get some rest tonight. You can get busy first thing in the morning. If you need anything, Kevin, call my direct line. Max has my number."

"Thank you for having confidence in me," said Kevin.

"Of course, old friend."

The cardinal rose from his chair and Kevin and Drotti followed quietly out of the room.

"Thank you for coming, Kevin, and you, too, Max." The men shook hands.

Cardinal Porter turned to Kevin and repeated, "I'm counting on you."

"Thank you, sir. I won't let you down."

∞∞∞∞∞

Once outside, they could see the sun setting in spheres of red and yellow, creating a golden orb in the spring air.

As they headed towards Kevin's apartment at the Villa Domenica, Kevin asked, "Max, what do you know about this Opus Mundi group?"

"You probably know as much as I do. They're crazy. Been around for a long time. They're a group of far-right conservative Catholics who think the Church is plagued by false prophets. Their solution is to insinuate themselves into the pulse of the church, to exorcise the ever false prophets."

"That's what I've always heard about them."

"The thing is, Kevin, they'll stop at nothing. Once they decide the pope is the false prophet, they'll eliminate him. They're our Hezbollah and just as dangerous."

"Where did they get these ideas about false prophets, anyway?" Kevin walked slowly along the ancient stone path, taking in the scent of fresh basil wafting through the air. Being a resident of the Vatican had its delicious advantages.

Drotti shrugged. "As you've just heard from Cardinal Porter, it's from the Bible. Some say it's in the prophecies, and the appearances of the Virgin Mary through the centuries."

"Strange that this group has lasted all these years underground."

"Indeed," Drotti added. "They are small, secretive, and invisible, though they're international. This isn't Opus Dei, who may be conservative, but are in line with Church doctrine. This group is more secretive than the Masons. Their secrets and rituals are more deadly."

The two men continued their brisk walk to the executive suite.

Suddenly, Drotti stopped to face Kevin. "We suspect this Opus Mundi was responsible for the 1981 assassination attempt on John Paul II."

"Really? That's one hell of an accusation."

Drotti nodded. "I know. Sounds crazy, doesn't it? But it gets more interesting. John Paul II was shot by a Turkish man, Mehmet Ali Agca on May 13, 1981, in St. Peter's Square. If you recall, the square was especially crowded that day; it happened only seconds before the pope was going to read the third secret of Fatima. The date chosen for the reading and the assassination was the anniversary of Mary's first appearance to the children at Fatima."

The children of Fatima. Kevin reached back in his memory. In 1917, the Virgin Mary appeared six times to three children in the small village of Fatima in Portugal. Drotti was right on the mark. The first of these appearances was indeed on May 13th.

"You're right. I remember it now," Kevin said. "In 1978, after only 33 days in office, John Paul I died. Then his successor, John Paul II, was shot in front of St. Peter's in 1981. So, what's the connection?"

Drotti didn't respond. He knew more, but wouldn't reveal it to Kevin just yet.

"And now you guys think a secret group within the church is trying to kill this current pope?"

Drotti nodded, his brows furrowed. "Opus Mundi believes the current Church leadership, meaning the pope, is leading us to hell—literally. They're out to kill the false messiahs." Drotti looked to the sky, pointing his finger. "And they're taking their fanaticism from their reading of the scriptures!"

"Will they try again—to kill the pope, I mean?" Kevin asked.

"Here's what I'm worried about," Drotti responded. "The current pope is rumored to be making an announcement in the next few days that'll mandate a major change in Catholic doctrine. It'll incense the conservatives."

"Do you know what he's going to say?" Kevin asked.

"I have an idea, yes, but I'm going to keep it to myself."

"Sure," said Kevin. "But if it could help us with our job in this, let me know."

"I will," said Drotti.

The men strolled quietly for a few minutes, until they came upon Villa Domenica.

Kevin took his key from his pocket. "Max, please don't plan anything for me Thursday or Friday. I'll have visitors in town."

"Your lady friend?" Drotti smiled.

"Just visitors, OK?" said Kevin, irritated. Drotti seemed to know everything about him.

"We don't have much time to figure this out, Kevin," said Drotti.

"Don't worry," said Kevin, "I'll be working all the time. I have resources. If you don't mind, I'll need a little privacy."

Drotti nodded. "Sure. You have my number. Oh, and the cardinal's."

"Thanks," said Kevin. "I appreciate it. And thanks for everything."

"No problem. I'll have everything on your list delivered tomorrow. Have a good night, Kevin." With that, Drotti turned, leaving Kevin alone for the evening.

Once inside the executive suite, Kevin noticed right away that his laptop was open and the screen on. Who'd been using it? He was sure he'd closed it before leaving. *What the hell?* He approached the desk and sat down. He looked at the screen. A message scrolled across the screen in large, black letters. The message: GO HOME.

A threat? Had someone from Colombo been here? Opus Mundi? Maybe they're playing hardball, Kevin thought. *No matter. It's one game I know how to play, too.*

Kevin opened the refrigerator and grabbed a Peroni. Plopping in the leather chair, his mind was scrambled by what Cardinal Porter had told him. And now, the laptop with a message.

Often Kevin prayed to God and Jesus and Mary. He decided to ask them all about his new assignment and the quandary of the church. *What's the mission at hand? To save the Church? To save the pope? Uncover a menacing secret society within the Church? Eliminate the would-be assassins? Or could it be something else, something even more portentous and earth-shattering?*

As Kevin gulped down a deliciously cold slug of beer, his mind drifted to Katie. *How about giving all this up and leading a normal life?* With his advanced education, he could get a job in finance or consulting. New York would be an interesting place to live. *And kids?* As a result of a bad case of chicken pox at a young age, Kevin knew Katie couldn't have kids.

What? Wake up! What are you thinking, knucklehead? He couldn't leave the Church. In his head, a chorus of angelic voices were blaring, powerful and demanding. The idea of breaking his vows was unthinkable. *Okay, everybody. Calm down. I'm not leaving the Church.*

Kevin sat up, alert. He hoped someday, somehow, to find the key to silencing this tug of war in his mind—his love for Katie versus his love for the Church. *Was this a given for priests? Did all priests have this screeching cacophony, this tortured conflict?*

Back on track to the assignment. He was here to investigate a possible overthrow of the Catholic Church by a radical group. They think a false prophet has gone soft regarding doctrine. *Sounds easy enough.* Kevin sighed.

Kevin remembered the intercepted message Cardinal Porter had given him. He stopped moving and retrieved it from his pocket.

VISITOR 5/29 BEIRUT. TRIGGER SALE
SATIN PO$ 6/2
(Note: unsure if correct translation but nothing better found)

An idea came to him. He grabbed his iPhone and called Toby Beck, a CIA friend, an expert in crypto. He and Toby went way back. In Iraq they were army officers together. From their time there, they shared some dark secrets.

Toby answered his phone. "This you, Kevin?"

"Yes. How are you, Toby?"

"Good, good. What's going on?"

After explaining he was in Rome on a Church mission, Kevin continued, "I need some decoding help, buddy. I have an intercepted message that needs your eye."

"I'm in that business, Kev," Toby said. "I can give you a secure number to relay it as a PDF. Can you do that?"

Kevin recalled he had a copy machine in his quarters. He jumped up to see if it could scan and send the document to Toby. It could. "Can do, Toby. I'll send it right away."

"I'll get back to you," Toby said and hung up.

His iPhone buzzed a half hour later. *It couldn't be from Toby, could it?*

"Kevin, it's Max. I just got an advance copy of the papal encyclical that's coming out tomorrow."

"How bad is it?" Kevin asked.

"Bad. The pope appears to be changing the rule on birth control. Contraception will be permitted for married couples."

"Is that a big deal? For decades American priests have been avoiding it in the confessional. The majority of practicing Catholics pay no attention to that rule."

"The short answer, my friend, is that it's a very big deal. Church leadership must have known this would enrage conservatives like Opus Mundi. I just hope they're prepared for how it'll affect them."

Kevin had nothing to say. A second call beeped in on Kevin's mobile. "I'll call you back, Max," Kevin said, and hung up. He answered the second call. It was Toby.

"My ass is on the line for this, pal, but frankly I don't give a shit. I've got some stuff for you," Toby said.

Kevin knew he'd need to return the favor someday, but it was worth it.

"You're a good man, Toby. I appreciate your help," said Kevin.

"Anyway," Toby continued, "Visitor is likely just that—a visitor or someone by that name. Satin Po$ 6/2 has nothing to do with cloth. When you go through the various combinations it appears that this isn't even in code. Your guys got lucky. Satin should be two words, Sat in. It likely means Satellite in Position 6/2, or June 2nd. That's early next month. The word 'trigger' is puzzling. One of our guys thinks it means to initiate, the other one thinks it's literal, means what it appears to mean—a trigger, like on a weapon."

"This isn't making much sense to me, Toby."

"Well, this might help. The Vatican owns three satellites which were launched privately. They're used primarily for communications and for Vatican TV broadcast transmissions. Anyway, our guys tracked a signal directing one of the satellites to a new orbit starting on June 1st. We don't know why they did that, of course, but the new trajectory is interesting." Toby paused. "This is a strange question, but does the Vatican have any, uh, initiatives in the Middle East?"

"Not that I know of," Kevin said, although Cardinal Porter's comments about a world conflict popped into his head.

"Well, maybe you should dig a little deeper. We tracked a top Israeli official on his way to Beirut today. Don't know what he's doing there. Nobody in Israel is volunteering any intel. That Vatican satellite I just told you about was directed to a new route over Iran, Syria, and Israel."

"Thanks, Toby. I'll work on putting this all together."

"Okay, buddy. But you'd better work fast."

∞∞∞∞

CHAPTER EIGHT

Seville, Spain

Although there was a specific, Opus Mundi-related reason that Carlos Alameda, also known as Columbo, resided in Seville, he wanted to be there. In all of Spain, Seville was Alameda's ideal choice for residence.

At the cultural and religious center of the city was Seville's Cathedral, ranked as either the largest in the world, according to the *Guinness World Records*, or the third largest, depending on how you measured it. It was the largest Gothic cathedral in the world, but its ranking in size was not of importance to Columbo. There was simply not a more expansive and majestic place of worship in the world.

It was no coincidence that Kevin felt equally partial to this Spanish city and its church. He looked forward to visiting the cathedral, and the sights and aura of the magnificent structure took his breath away. The original was a mosque, built in the twelfth century when the Moors controlled Spain. When Ferdinand II of Castile reconquered Seville in 1248, Christianity was reestablished and the Aljama Mosque was converted to a cathedral. Both men knew all this, but Alameda likely knew the history even better than Kevin did. Indeed, Alameda's knowledge was deep enough to qualify as a tour guide. But there were other reasons for his expertise.

In the fourteenth century, following two earthquakes, the church as it is known today came into being. The Giralda Tower dominating the skyline originally was built as the mosque's minaret. In the sixteenth century, the bell tower crowning the Giralda Tower was added, bringing in a much needed harmony to the Islamic and Renaissance elements of this magnificent structure. Every visit Alameda made to this cathedral was a fresh experience. Every visit he enjoyed watching first-time visitors entranced by its towering structure and beauty.

Alameda, dressed like a Franciscan monk in a long brown tunic and hood, kneeled before the Capilla Major, the highest and most breathtaking altarpiece in the Christian world. Measuring twenty meters high, it was protected by a bronze grill, itself a work of art. The altarpiece behind the main altar featured massive gold covered carvings of lifelike saints. It was all so unusual and majestic, it took his breath away. He wasn't the only one who experienced such sublime feelings in this holy place. Pope John Paul II had visited the cathedral in 1982 and as his eyes took in the altarpiece for the first time, he was said to have wept.

His prayers completed, Alameda looked about for the man he knew as Visitor. Soon enough, Visitor, similarly attired like a Franciscan monk, joined him and knelt before the altar. "God bless you," Alameda whispered in Spanish.

Visitor knelt, his eyes fixed straight on the altar. "The Vatican has summoned an investigator from America," he said. "He must be dealt with. He is not our usual ecclesiastic enemy."

"I know what happened to the agents who followed him from the airport," Alameda commented while shaking his head. "I believe I must go to Rome and personally assume command of the mission." For a moment, Alameda hesitated before asking the next question.

"Excellency, does the American know about the Secret?"

Visitor continued to stare ahead at the altar. "We do not know what his superiors have told him. Perhaps the Vatican leaders will want to observe him for some time before discussing the Secret."

Alameda nodded respectfully.

"There is much at stake," Visitor continued. "Operation Delorgio begins in one week." He gazed again at the altar. "You will be met by the customary personnel. Pray for guidance."

Visitor crossed himself and left.

Alameda prayed for a few moments, crossed himself, then got up to leave. On his way out of the cathedral, Alameda made his habitual stop at the tomb of Christopher Columbus. The explorer who'd discovered America had been a resident of Seville. His remains were first interred in Santo Domingo, then in Cuba. After Cuba broke from Spain in 1898, his remains were transferred to a mausoleum in the Seville cathedral in 1902. Alameda was aware that Christopher Columbus would play a role in the cataclysmic events Opus Mundi saw coming. In a gesture of allegiance, he'd adopted the code name "Columbo" as his alternate identity, a tribute to Columbus.

He gazed reverently at Columbus's coffin, held aloft by four massive bronze statues, kings in arms representing the four original kingdoms of Spain: Castile, Leon, Aragon, and Navarre. *We know what mysteries you hold,* Alameda said to him in his mind.

Visitor had just confided to Alameda that Operation Delorgio, named for the founder of Opus Mundi, would launch in two weeks. The excitement within him was explosive.

∞∞∞∞

CHAPTER NINE

Rome, Italy

Entering the lobby of the Hotel Hassler where Katie was staying, Kevin admired the gilded architecture and design. This hotel had earned its reputation as the finest in Rome. The antique furnishings, crowned by a dazzling crystal chandelier from a doge's palace in Venice, complemented a staff of attendants graciously greeting guests. As Kevin was dressed in his clerical suit and collar, they welcomed him with a small bow. Kevin thought how blessed it was that Katie was doing so well she could stay in such a hotel.

Lovely Katie was waiting in the lobby. The sight of her stirred feelings that Kevin continued to find hard to manage. She looked statuesque, with the most au courant accessories: Hermes scarf, kitten heels, Prada purse. And what a dazzling smile!

After a warm hug, he said, "A nice flight?"

"Yes," Katie said. "Although first class isn't what it used to be."

"Be grateful. Better than the alternative."

"Right." She smiled up at him coyly, flashing her eyes.

Taking her arm, they walked out side by side onto the Spanish Steps.

"I wasn't sure what to wear. You didn't tell me where we were going," she said, while Kevin admired her style. She was wearing an unadorned black dress with a fitted linen jacket. On her earlobes were big, playful bauble earrings.

"You look terrific," he said. "And you're wonderfully overdressed for where we're going tonight."

"Thanks. Are you going to tell me or surprise me?"

"Your choice."

"Then tell me," she said with a forced smile. "I've had my fill of surprises from you."

Ouch! Kevin let the comment pass. "We're dining in Trastevere, the oldest part of Rome," he said, mustering up as much enthusiasm as he could.

"Sounds adventurous." Again she smiled, just happy to be with him.

They hailed a cab and crossed a bridge into what seemed like a bygone era. Narrow, windy streets paved with cobblestones were barely wide enough for a single car. The area encompassed the Jewish quarter. Colorful awnings shaded small outdoor restaurants. As Kevin wasn't sure of the restaurant's address, they stopped, paid the driver, and started out on foot. Strong aromas of garlic and herbs wafted through the air.

"I love it!" said Katie. "Feels like we've been transported back in time."

"I thought you'd like it," Kevin said.

They wandered the streets until Kevin spotted strings of lights dangling from a restaurant's awning. It had a dozen outside tables and rows of low hanging multi-colored lanterns, gently swinging in the breeze. As they approached the entrance, they were greeted with music and song, a lively operatic aria from *La Traviata*. The singer's energetic gusto compensated for his lack of talent.

Da Meo Pattaca was a favorite historic tourist restaurant known for its old-fashioned ambiance, strolling gypsy musicians, its food with medieval portions of pasta, and tableside serenades by underemployed opera stars.

A rotund, grinning waiter, menus in hand, approached with vibrant gesticulations of welcome. Soon they were seated al fresco under a clear sky of stars. A lit candle on the table was flickering as though dancing in the breeze. Kevin noticed Katie wearing the gold-plated bracelet he'd given her years ago. It was without value—except to her. She still wore it. It tugged at his heart.

In turn, Katie noticed the watch on Kevin's wrist, the Mickey Mouse watch she'd given him. She pointed to it. "You're still wearing that?" she asked.

"Given to me by someone special," Kevin replied.

"Do you remember the message on the back of it?" Katie asked playfully.

"'Don't take yourself too seriously,'" Kevin said. "That admonition hasn't always been easy."

After they'd ordered from an oversized souvenir menu, Kevin asked, "How was Brussels?"

Katie fidgeted with her phone, answering while reading a text message. "Oh, not bad. I did three depositions, got asked out to dinner twice—declined—and walked around the Grand Place. I'm working for an interesting new client. Worldwide trading company and my firm is racking up the fees!" Finishing with her text message, she felt Kevin put his hand on her phone.

Katie looked up. "Sorry! That's it. I promise, no more."

"It's our time, okay? It's rare enough these days," Kevin said.

"So tell me about your Mission Impossible assignment."

"Not going well," Kevin responded. "Even though I'm sworn to secrecy, I decided I want to tell you what I'm doing here."

"Telling me sacred secrets, Kevin? Like old times."

Old times? She still had a way of getting to him. Kevin struggled every day with thinking about *old times* with Katie. Why couldn't he banish them completely, stop thinking about them? God could be cruel sometimes. *Lead us not into temptation.*

Kevin looked at Katie and resisted the temptation to reach for her hand. "For the first time the Church is allowing married Catholics to use birth control."

"Is that such a bad thing?" asked Katie. She wanted to reach out and touch him.

"Look, Catholics mostly ignore that rule anyway, but the conservative wing of the Church is not going to take this well."

Katie shrugged. "Why is that so important?"

"Our problem is that there's a lunatic branch of the Church that doesn't tolerate liberal changes like this, and it could put them over the top."

"So what'll they do? Post a nasty message on Facebook? Picket the Vatican?"

"It's more serious. This wacky group has threatened life of the pope."

"You're not serious? And if you're worried, then this is scary, Kevin. I'm worried about you. "

Kevin smiled. "Thanks. I can take care of myself."

"Are you sure you know what you're doing?"

"I'll be all right," said Kevin. "I just wanted to let you know what's going on."

A waiter hurried over with a plate balanced in each hand. Kevin's ossobuco and Katie's angel hair pasta had arrived.

"Absolutely delicious," said Kevin as he dove into the ossobuco, an Italian dish of braised veal shanks with a zesty gremolata of parsley, lemon, and garlic.

Hungry, they ate without talking and finished quickly. When the waiter approached again, they were thinking about dessert. But his smile was gone; he was frowning.

"Padre," the man blurted in Italian. "There is a man next door—he's my neighbor—and he is ill. Can you help?"

"Of course," said Kevin.

Kevin translated for Katie what he'd said and rose from the table.

"I'm going with you," she said. Katie threw her napkin on the table and leapt up.

They followed the waiter out of the restaurant, crossed the street, and started climbing the rickety stairs of a rundown two-story building to the second floor. The waiter led the way.

In an open doorway to an apartment, an elderly woman, wearing a knee-length flowery dress and a cloth headpiece, stood waiting. "Oh, please come," she begged. "The doctor will be here soon."

The bedroom was dimly lit. Several elderly people with sad faces surrounded a bed where a gaunt man lay under the covers.

His face was scrunched up, and his eyes were closed. Clearly he was in pain.

"He's dying," the woman whimpered.

Kevin asked for some water and prepared to administer Last Rites.

Pointing at Kevin's black suit and turned collar, one of the mourners mumbled something. The woman who'd let them in turned to Kevin and said, "Oh, Father, the man isn't Catholic. He's Jewish. This is his family. I am their friend."

Kevin nodded to the family members around the bed. "What's his name?" he asked.

"Jacob," an elderly woman replied. "I'm his wife."

In the semi-darkness Kevin moved to the head of the bed. He stood by the old man who was now opening his teary eyes. Raising his right hand, Kevin placed it over the man's head and began to chant:

"*Ma she bayrach avoteinu, Avraham, Yitzak, v'Yaakov, Moshe, Aharon, David, u 'Shlomo, hu yivarech v'rapayethaholeh Jacob. Ha kadosh baruch hu, yimaleh rachamim alav lehachalemo u 'larapoto u' hachazeko . . .*"

At the sound of Hebrew the man's eyes lit up. The family members sighed and bowed their heads.

Katie looked completely bewildered. One of the relatives, sensing she didn't understand what was going on, accosted her and spoke in English. "My dear, the priest is conferring the Jewish blessing on the sick. Let me try to translate . . . *May he who blessed our fathers, Abraham, Isaac, and Jacob, Moses, Aaron, David—and others—may he bless and heal the sick person, Jacob.* "

The woman added, "How wonderful that this man of God knows Jewish traditions! Bless him!"

Kevin continued the ritual he'd learned so well while studying Hebrew. He prayed God would hear him in the language of the Old Testament.

Jacob's eyes now gazed into Kevin's while continuing to chant. " *. . . ulhachayoto v'yishlachlom' hayra rifuah shlaymah minhashanayim leyrmach avarav ushesa gidav betoch sh'ar choley . . .*"

As Kevin finished the prayer, the man reached over and took his hand. Kevin kissed the old man's forehead.

Just then a middle-aged bearded man in a black suit arrived and immediately began tending to the patient. He examined the old man, exchanging a few words and preparing an injection. After the shot had been administered, the doctor rose and called for an ambulance.

When Katie and Kevin prepared to leave, the family members came forward offering their thanks. The doctor broke through, grabbing Kevin's arm. "You're indeed a man of God, Father," he said softly. "Please accept my gratitude."

Kevin and Katie walked down the stairs and followed the waiter back to the restaurant. There was still time for dessert. Katie grinned. "You're just full of surprises. You know Hebrew? You never told me."

Kevin returned her smile. "The seminary is six years. I learned as much as possible about other religions. I'm particularly fascinated by Judaism. After all, it was Christ's religion."

Back at the restaurant, the waiter appeared with a tray of tiramisu, chocolate mousse, and semifreddo. "With our compliments, Padre. Grazie."

Katie looked at Kevin again, this time seriously. "I was about to tell you something before we were called away," she said.

Kevin smiled, pointing. "I'm sure you noticed the tiramisu on the tray. I remember it's your favorite dessert, Katie. Go ahead. Have a piece. Tell me what's on your mind later."

"No, I don't feel like it. Honestly."

"Well, it must be something really important." Kevin motioned for the bill. "I'll walk you back to your hotel."

The bill settled, they strolled leisurely under the full moon, its silver light casting a warm glow over the cobblestone street.

"I've been trying to tell you this for a while," Katie said, "and, as a bit of a preface to what I'm going to say . . . I still love you. I want you to know that."

Her words were like a stiletto cutting its way to Kevin's heart. He wanted to tell her that he loved her, too. But he couldn't.

Kevin took her hand, squeezed it, then let it go.

Katie didn't expect him to respond. She continued, "I've been seeing someone in Washington."

His jaw dropped. Now the stiletto felt real. After he took a deep breath, he opened his mouth to speak. Nothing came out.

"He works for an investment company," Katie went on. They walked slowly and she avoided his eyes. "We've been going out for a couple of months. I met him at church. I thought you'd like that."

"Well, if he's Catholic, at least that's something," Kevin said, trying to lighten the mood.

"As a matter of fact, he's Jewish. He comes to our church because he's interested in Catholicism, as well as other religions, too. He's kind of like you."

Kevin shook his head. "You're full of surprises, Katie."

Katie smiled awkwardly. "I'll bet his Hebrew isn't as good as yours, though."

"Why haven't you mentioned this until now?"

"There's been a major development, Kevin." She paused for a moment. "Well, he's asked me to marry him."

Kevin didn't want to ask the next question.

"And you said?"

"Kevin, you know I would've married you, don't you? I've told Jimmy about you. That's his name, Jimmy Stein. He knows about us. Under different circumstances, he may not have been the man of choice, but I do love him. Kevin, I want a family," she said with a faint sob.

They stopped walking. She turned to Kevin. "I said yes."

Kevin was struggling for control of his emotions. "I don't know what to say," he whispered. "I know I let you down. A family, Katie? I thought you can't have children."

"That's true, Kevin. We'll adopt. I've been speaking to Father O'Hara at Holy Trinity. He was close to my mom. He told me about a number of orphans in Bosnia and Herzegovina, part of the former Yugoslavia, where my mother's family came from. These are children who need parents."

"Oh my God!" Kevin said. He looked at her. *Could she see his utter despair, the sadness in him?*

Katie could see it, felt sorry for him and close to him. But it would be different between them now.

"Katie, does it make sense for me to consider renouncing my vows?"

"Stop it, Kevin. Please. Every time this comes up, you become tentative and insecure. Every major decision in life has consequences. You sacrificed us, Kevin, and now, following you, I am, in turn, sacrificing you, and us."

Kevin looked at her again, his eyes pleading, but his look wouldn't betray the heartbreak inside him. Instead, he said, "Have you set a date? I need to find a tux that fits."

"Not yet. But with Father O'Hara's help we're already working on the adoption."

"I guess your mom must be proud you chose a child from her homeland," Kevin said.

Katie smiled in acknowledgment. "We've found the baby's mother. A lovely seventeen-year-old Bosnian farm girl. Wouldn't consider aborting, but she has no means to care for the infant. I've signed all the papers."

Kevin closed his eyes and took a deep breath. "I'm sorry, but this is a lot for me to take in." Without thinking, he grabbed her hand and held onto it tightly.

She pulled her hand away. "Sure, Kev, it's soooo hard on you," she said, her voice dripping with caustic sarcasm. "You really don't get it. You have no idea how painful it's been for me sitting back waiting for you. To be with you, to love you, but not be able to really love you. My life has been passing by while I hang around like an idle schoolgirl, waiting for you to pay your penance, or whatever the hell it is that you're doing in the priesthood, and come back to me. But that's not going to happen. And I have finally gotten that through my thick, legal-laden skull. Maybe someday you'll come to your senses and want that life with me. By then it'll be too late, Kevin. My decision to marry Jimmy, to start a family, is irreversible. Final. I've stopped waiting for you."

"Katie—"

"I want to be a wife and a mother, Kevin. Strange, huh? I want a husband and a baby so badly I wake at night thinking I hear him crying for me. And that baby needs me more than you do. More than you ever did." As she turned toward her hotel, Katie was shaken. "I have to go."

"Okay," Kevin said, keeping pace with her. He desperately wanted to comfort her. Deep down, he'd known this day would come, but knowing hadn't made him any more prepared for it. He hadn't realized she could break his heart. He'd thought he was tougher than that, that his heart was unbreakable.

It was going to be a sleepless night.

"I'll come see you tomorrow. We can talk."

"You know what, Kev?" The anguish on Katie's face was exacerbating Kevin's own. "Don't."

With enough self-loathing to last a lifetime, Kevin watched Katie walk, by herself, along the cobblestone street and disappear into the vapors of the night.

"I love you, Katie." His voice was a whisper.

Turning towards the Vatican, Kevin bent down to tie his shoe. He wanted to be sure the man who'd trailed them earlier wasn't now following Katie. With a sigh of relief, Kevin walked on.

∞∞∞∞

CHAPTER TEN

Rome, Italy

After years of working in cloak-and-dagger services, Kevin had acquired a sixth sense of when danger lurked. It was not easy to describe; it was a sort of acquired skill.

As Kevin entered his apartment, that sixth sense was percolating. There was somebody in the room. Kevin killed the lights and crouched low, heading toward the cabinet where he stored the pistols. Quietly, he reached inside the cabinet, grabbed one of them, and peered through the semi-darkness. No one in the living room. He tiptoed to the bedroom door, and heard a rustle inside. Kicking the door open, he pointed the gun in front of him. "If you move, you die!"

A slight but powerful body smashed into him. The glint of a knife caught Kevin's eyes as he grabbed the intruder by the throat. The guy thrashed his arms wildly through the air, stabbing Kevin where he could. Kevin smashed his gun into the man's mouth and watched him crumple to the floor, knife in hand.

His adrenaline pumping, Kevin wanted to end this once and for all with a single shot to the guy's head. Instead, pointing the gun straight at the man, he turned on the light.

Curled in a ball on the floor, the perpetrator was covering his eyes. In Italian, Kevin ordered him to get up, slowly, and put his hands over his head.

The man did as he was instructed.

Kevin's fury gave way to surprise and shock. His assailant wasn't the professional pit bull he'd thought. Rather, he was a skinny youth in jeans and a blue short sleeved shirt. A kid.

"How old are you?" Kevin blurted out in Italian.

"Eighteen," the youth answered in English. "My Italian is not so good."

Kevin couldn't identify his accent right away. *Middle East, perhaps?*

Blood was trailing down from an open gash on the boy's head and nose.

Keeping his gun pointed at the kid's head, Kevin said, "Start talking and you'd better tell me everything, young man."

"I . . . I did not mean to harm you."

"Well, you could have gotten yourself killed," said Kevin. "Hold on a sec, and don't move." Kevin retrieved his first aid kit from the closet, opened it and took out some bandages and iodine.

He laid the gun down and applied iodine to the boy's head. Then he taped bandages on the gash to stop the bleeding. As he inhaled big gulps of air, the teenager's entire body shook.

"Thank you," the young man said, bracing for what might come next.

"What's your name and where are you from?" asked Kevin.

"My name is Ali Recip. I . . . I . . . am from Turkey. I'm sorry . . . "

"What are you doing here, Ali?" Kevin asked.

Ali had fear and confusion in his eyes. Something didn't fit. The kid didn't seem like a teenage punk who'd do things like this.

"I was hired to break into your apartment, sir." He slowly reached into his pocket and removed a thumb drive, which he held up for Kevin to see. "I was supposed to find your computer and download info to this drive."

"Why?" asked Kevin.

"Because I was a good student at computer school."

"Who hired you?" Kevin asked, trying to put the pieces together.

"I . . . please sir, I cannot say. My family . . ." The boy's lower lip was trembling.

"Take your time." Kevin was giving him a few moments to compose himself.

"I am being forced to do things I do not want to do," Ali said. "But my family is poor and they are paying me good money. My father has no work. My sisters . . ." His voice trailed off.

"Who do you work for?" Kevin asked more forcefully.

"Sir, if I say, they will kill me . . ."

"Tell me."

Trembling, Ali said, "His name is Carlos. I do not know his last name. He knows my uncle, from the time he was in jail."

"Why was your uncle in jail?"

"He shot a pope. Mehmet Ali Agca."

"Agca's your uncle?" Kevin made no attempt to conceal his surprise.

"Yes."

"But why break into my apartment? What could I possibly have on my computer that would be of use to this guy?" As he was talking, he went to get a glass of orange juice from the kitchen and gave it to Ali, who gulped it down.

"I heard them talking about you. They said you committed a crime in the U.S. Army and then it was covered up."

"And this so-called crime would be on my computer?"

"Yes, they thought so."

"What else did they say?"

"They plan to use this information against you."

"Listen to me, Ali. Think hard. What else do you know?"

The boy sat silently for a minute, deep in thought. "They talked about an operation. Something to do with Iran. Please . . . that is all."

Looking at the kid, Kevin felt compassion for him. "Go back to where you came from. Tell them I came home before you could accomplish the job. You can tell them you fell on the way out and that's how you got cut. Got it?"

"Yes sir," he replied.

"I want you to memorize my phone number." Kevin recited it to him and made Ali repeat it back to him. "Call me with any information you get, understand?"

Ali nodded.

"Now, give me your phone."

Ali pulled a cell phone from his shirt pocket and handed it over. Kevin flipped it open, removed the SIM card, and handed the phone back to the young man. Then he reached into his pocket and pulled out 200 euros. He handed the money to the boy, who hesitated, but then took the bills, putting them in his pocket.

"Take the money and don't get into any more trouble. Next time it may not turn out so well." Kevin led him to the door.

Ali stared at Kevin with big, questioning eyes. "I . . . thank you, sir." He reached up and put his arms around Kevin, then broke away.

Kevin opened the door to his apartment and followed Ali down the corridor to the main entrance. He watched as the teenager scampered away, turning every few yards to look back at Kevin, until he disappeared down the path leading to St. Peter's Square.

When Ali was out of sight, Kevin retrieved the SIM card he'd taken from the airport thugs and put it on the desk alongside the one from the boy. He placed the first card into his Italian cell phone and scrolled through the numbers. Only four calls on the thug's card, three to the same number. Kevin recognized the country code as Spain and transcribed the numbers onto his laptop. Then he inserted the boy's SIM card into the phone and found over a dozen numbers. Comparing the numbers on Ali's phone to the ones he'd transcribed from the thug's phone, *bingo!* A match. From Spain. Kevin determined it was time to impose again on his personal CIA mole and friend, Toby Beck. Listening in on cell phone lines may have been outside the wherewithal of the Vatican, but it certainly wasn't of the CIA and NSA.

Kevin dialed. Toby picked up right away.

"Hey, buddy. How's it going?" Kevin could be as facile and nonchalant as any of these CIA guys.

"Good. How's it going for you?"

"Need your help again," Kevin said. "I've got some phone numbers in Spain from two sets of bad guys. Can we get NSA to monitor for some of the usual suspect keywords?"

Kevin heard a slow whistle at the other end of the line.

"You're escalating this about three notches, Kev."

"I know. Sorry. Can you do it?"

A deep sigh. "What the fuck, send 'em over," Toby said.

∞∞∞∞

CHAPTER ELEVEN

Rome, Italy

The next morning, Kevin went for an early morning run. As busy as he was in Rome, he was keeping his physical routine. In Washington, it was easier: working out with the kids on the basketball court. At the Vatican, it was proving a challenge.

Returning home for breakfast, his phone rang. When he picked up, he nearly stopped breathing. It was Katie.

"Kevin, I'm back in D.C. I wanted to apologize for the way we left each other."

"I understand, Katie. What's that old cliché from the movies? Love means never having to say you're sorry?"

"From that movie we saw together, *Love Story*," Katie said flatly.

Kevin smiled. "Oh, yeah. Well, then, no apology needed, not this time, or ever, OK?"

"I don't want to lose you as a friend." Her voice was charged.

"You won't, Katie. Like the sun at the break of dawn, I keep coming back, don't I?"

Flustered, Katie mumbled something. "I just need you to stay my friend."

"You won't lose me. I'm praying for you, and all the best with your marriage. You deserve it."

"I'm glad we cleared the air on this, Kevin, and I need your advice on something else."

"Sure."

"I think I told you about this major new client of mine. The one I went to Brussels for.

His name is Greg Maggio. I had dinner with him last night—"

Dinner? Kevin thought. *Do you often have tête-à-tête dinners with your male clients?*

"—and he asked me about some large money transfers, like how could I help him quietly transfer a large sum of money without getting the authorities suspicious."

"So?"

"There are rules, and this comes close to the edge. He's my biggest client and if he's legit I don't want him to just go *poof!* Some other law firm will grab him."

"How can I help?"

"I know you still have connections within the intelligence community. If I give you the name of his company, can you get someone to discreetly check it out?"

Kevin hesitated. "Katie, my best source is Toby Beck, but I've been leaning on him a lot lately."

After a brief moment of silence, Katie said, "I understand. Forget I asked."

"No, leave it with me. I'll work something out. What's the company name?"

"Consolidated Investors United. A pure bullshit name he dreamt up for an LLC we registered for him. Thanks, Kevin."

Seeing another call coming in, Kevin interrupted her. Area code 703. Northern Virginia. "I'm sorry, Katie. I've got to take this call."

"OK. Talk soon."

Without small talk, Toby got to the point right away. "I got to tell you, buddy, I don't know exactly what you're doing over there, but you might be in over your head."

"How's that?"

Toby continued, "We intercepted a couple of calls. The numbers you gave me are registered to a cleric named 'Carlos Alameda', goes by the name 'Columbo.' NSA approved my request to listen in. Man, this stuff gets messy. I'm looking at the transcripts now."

"Send them to me?" Kevin asked.

"I can't. My sweet ass is in enough trouble as it is. I don't want to push the boundaries here." Toby went silent for a spell. Kevin wondered if the connection had been lost. Then Toby went on. "Are you alone in your unit?"

"Yes, of course. Why?"

"Go to your laptop and dial in this URL." Kevin did as his friend asked and powered up the Dell. As Toby read off the address, Kevin typed it in.

When he'd finished typing, a blue screen appeared. A series of numbers dotted the screen at a rapid pace, then abruptly stopped. A white box formed.

"Type this code in the box," Toby continued. "Once you do that, I'll be able to control your screen." Toby read off the code.

"What?" Kevin responded, typing it in as he spoke.

What was on the screen faded, replaced by an overhead image of an outdoor café in filtered sunlight, tables with patrons sipping drinks, palm trees, white jacketed waiters, and a nearby pool with frolicking bathers. Kevin gazed at the image, puzzled. "Am I supposed to know what this is?"

"Since you already gave us some useful intelligence, and you might be able to tell us more, I got permission to share it with you. It's the pool area of the St. Georges Hotel in Beirut. It's a satellite shot."

Kevin continued to study the screen, not connecting the dots in his head. What is this? Then the screen's image zoomed in on two men at one of the café tables.

Toby went on. "The hunky fellow on the left with a cigarette in his mouth is Dov Leibotski, Israel's deputy intelligence director. We can't ID the other guy; his face is blocked by a fedora, probably on purpose. Take a closer look."

The image zoomed in to reveal a grainy picture of a dark-skinned face, partially obscured by the brim of his hat. "Who's that?" Toby asked.

Kevin kept looking and shook his head. "Sorry, Toby. No idea."

"Well, Israel won't tell us anything, which spells trouble. We think it's Carlos Alameda. We traced one of the phone numbers you sent me to him. He was talking to someone with a heavily encrypted phone number. We couldn't figure it out. We know he called the Vatican, but we don't know who in the Vatican."

"How do you know he called somebody? I don't see a phone," Kevin said.

"The phone's in his pocket."

"You can track a phone in his pocket?"

"Don't ask. Keep your eyes on the screen."

A Google Maps app with an image of a blue earth now appeared and zoomed in rapidly on another city: Teheran, Iran. A close-up of a street became visible, then changed to sand colored buildings in what seemed the outskirt of Teheran, busy streets and minarets dotting the landscape. As the picture zoomed in, an image of a man wearing a coat and hat, entering a tall building, formed. "That's the same guy from Beirut," Toby said. "We have this guy who talks to the Vatican, then meets with an Israeli Intelligence official, then he trots over to Tehran to chat with one of leaders of the Supreme Security Council of Iran. That building is where the Council's office is located."

"Toby, I met with Cardinal Porter in the Vatican. There's a fringe group wanting to start a nuclear war. To fulfill some Biblical prophecy," Kevin said.

"And they're well underway. They might succeed. Let me give you some background," Toby continued. "It's no secret that Israel has nuclear weapons. The French built their nuclear facility at Dimona back in the sixties. Today the threat is Iran. Remember that message your guys intercepted that had the word 'trigger' in it?"

"Sure. You figured out that it also said something like 'satellites in position.'"

"Right," Toby said. "Putting this all together, the 'trigger' must be a reference to a nuclear trigger, a special device that sets off a nuclear explosion. There are only a few countries with these triggers, including the U.S. and Israel. Iran needs them to activate nuclear warheads."

"Geez. Scary stuff," Kevin said.

"It gets better. One scenario is that the Iranians have lassoed a source for getting these triggers."

"Well, so far as I know, the Vatican doesn't have nuclear triggers. What source, Toby?"

"My best guess: Pakistan. Pakistan has got enough nukes to obliterate half the world. Pakistan could always use some cold, hard cash. Look at your screen again."

Kevin watched as a map of Iran appeared.

"The three blinking lights are the suspected nuclear sites, Kevin." An arrow swirled around the screen and stopped. "This is Natanz, a small village; another one is over here; and the third is the Fordo facility, near the Holy City of Qum." As Toby identified the locales, the blinking arrow darted like a firefly around the screen. "We think the reason the Israelis are mum is they're planning a preemptive attack on a nuclear assembly facility in Iran. Only one of these facilities houses the triggers, but the Israelis don't know which one."

"Where does the Vatican fit in all this?"

"That coded message that your cardinal buddy gave you had the first clue. It mentioned a trigger and a date. Our guys think this Alameda character knows where the triggers are going. He's trying to sell that information to the Israelis."

"So why did he visit Tehran? That doesn't make sense."

Toby sighed. "Yeah, we haven't figured that out either. Working on it. Right now, the big worry is that the Israelis would bomb the shit out of the trigger site so the Iranians can't build a nuclear bomb. That's why the Israelis aren't talking to us. If Israel were to attack Iran, we wouldn't have known about it in advance, which gives us Washington's favorite state of affairs: plausible deniability."

"Great! I should have stayed home. The parish priest life is starting to look just fine."

"Well, it seems that you've been called on to do a lot more than an average parish priest."

"What's your take, Toby?"

"Have you considered that your higher-ups may be playing you?"

Kevin thought about that for a few seconds. The more he thought about it, the angrier he got. "Why would they do that?"

"I don't know. But I suspect they're not telling you everything."

If that's even remotely true, Kevin thought, *I'm outta here.* His next thought was even more chilling. *What if I'm being framed, set up as a scapegoat for something?*

"I'll look into it," Kevin finally said.

"I'm sure you will, pal, but I've got another problem. Given what we uncovered here, I can't sit on it. I have no choice but to send this stuff to Defense and the White House, especially since June 3rd, the date on the encrypted note you sent me, is only a couple of days away. Since the lead came from you, your name will be smeared all over this."

Kevin shook his head. *Damn!* "Do what you have to, Toby."

Kevin hung up, hoping the pause and quiet would calm him. It didn't. Cardinal Porter had mentioned the Israel-Iran war which Opus Mundi might use to justify fulfilling a prophecy and taking over the Vatican. *But could the Vatican, or Opus Mundi, for that matter, be involved in this, in starting the war?* If so, had they told him everything? And what was his role in it?

Toby's questions about his role in this rang loud and clear. *Was he being played? How could the whole thing possibly have eluded him?* His temper was now ready to burst, and he knew how dangerous that could be. There was only one way to get some answers: Cardinal Porter.

While he was still fuming, his blood pressure rising, Kevin's mind quickly turned to Katie's dilemma. He couldn't ask Toby for anything else right now, so he decided to do some research himself. He googled Greg Maggio. Precious little came up. He was a member of the Sons of Italy organization and had been involved in various import/export businesses that mostly traded with Italy. A couple of awards, a wife, then a divorce. Nothing else. Consolidated Investors United produced precisely nothing.

Kevin closed his laptop and went back to stewing about why he was here in Rome.

∞∞∞∞

CHAPTER TWELVE

Rome, Italy

Kevin always had to have the last word.

"I quit," he said as he walked into Cardinal Porter's office. Without being invited, he'd barged in and flung himself in the chair facing Porter's desk. He took note of the ornate, gaudy trappings, a gold and white Vatican flag, a Louis XVI desk, an assortment of gaudy baubles and gewgaws, high ceilings, and a communications array on the desk that'd make a general proud. Kevin thought he was perfect in his new role. It was good to be a prince of the Church.

"What's going on, Kevin?" Porter asked, sitting down at the desk. The cardinal was dressed in a simple black cassock, a ribbon of red buttons signaling his lofty post in the hierarchy. His gray hair was combed immaculately, and was a cloud obscuring his blue eyes.

"I don't have all the details, and I don't know what the hell I'm doing here. I want out. I can't do an assignment like this half-assed, and that's how it's turning out." Kevin felt his anger festering at a dangerously high level. He was fighting to keep it in check.

"Calm down. Please." Porter inhaled deeply. "What specifically is bothering you?"

"I'll tell you, cardinal. I think I was brought here as some kind of scapegoat or distraction . . . I don't know. I'm afraid I've been played like a puppet. I need the truth!"

"And what truth would that be?"

"For one, who are the bad guys? So far, I've been told that a gaggle of clerics in Spain are waiting for a war—which they'll use as a cover to take over the Church. Well, there's more to it than that, and you know it. Now, thanks to Father Kevin Thrall, the White House is involved and my friends in high places think I'm being played. So I need you to come clean. The entire story. Or I'm out of here."

Pursing his lips Porter started tapping his fingers on the desk. Finally, he spoke slowly and deliberately. "You are not being played. You were being tested, son. What you have uncovered in such a short time was your first test. Yes, we knew about the threat from Seville. But we don't know who's giving the orders in the Curia. We would have told Washington in due course, but there is no assurance that anyone, at this point, can stop the Israelis."

"Where does the Church fit in all this?"

"As I told you the last time we met, Opus Mundi wants Israel to attack Iran to start a nuclear holocaust. In their twisted psycho-drama reasoning, this will trigger the apocalypse when Jesus, or someone posing as Jesus, will return to earth. They believe God is upset at the Church for becoming so liberal. To them, the Church has strayed from where it began and God will punish the liberal leaders unless corrective action is taken—by them. Their solution and strategy is to replace the leadership, by force if necessary, to steer us back on the righteous path—as they see it."

Kevin stared in disbelief. "Let me get this straight, Opus Mundi is prepared to start a nuclear war over liberalism in the Church?"

"The Church is a constituency of over a billion people. The vast majority will need to be convinced their new leadership is the right one. They'll prove it by pointing at the false prophets and the corruption in the Catholic Church. The war is a necessary, integral part of the prophecy—remember Matthew 24."

"'For nation will rise against nation, and kingdom against kingdom,'" Kevin recited from memory. For a few seconds he closed his eyes before speaking again. "Are we talking about a direct attack on the pope?"

"We don't know. But this is the group who masterminded the 1981 assassination attempt of John Paul II. You can take it from there." Again, Porter started drumming his fingers on the desktop. Clearly he was agitated.

"Why was I was being tested? Why was I kept in the dark?"

"We hadn't planned on telling you so soon." Porter leaned back and took a deep breath. "Kevin, there's a deeper and more sinister mystery lurking. It's highly secret, and it's the reason we wanted you here. We needed to test your skills in action first, before exposing you to the big one. You passed with flying colors."

Gee, isn't that great. It all felt ridiculously juvenile—this being tested. Kevin still couldn't grasp the real reason he'd been brought to Rome. If his only friends in the Church, including the man he respected more than anyone, were playing games with him, who could he trust? Kevin's confidence in the Church was slipping into a dark abyss.

"Anything else to tell me, Eminence?" Kevin asked.

Cardinal Porter looked at his watch. "We've got a lot to tell you. In thirty minutes, meet me at the gate of the Apostolic Palace."

Briefly, Kevin stewed over this. "I'll be there, Eminence. And after I hear what you have to say, I'll make up my mind about two things: whether I'm sticking it out with you and your melodramatic puppet show, and whether I'll be staying in the priesthood."

∞∞∞∞

CHAPTER THIRTEEN

Pope Quintus II

Following the contentious meeting, Kevin walked back to his apartment to freshen up before the appointment at the Apostolic Palace. Although the clear air lifted his mood, his calm was abruptly eclipsed by the buzz of his cell. He hoped it was Katie.

It was Toby.

"I think we solved the Teheran mystery."

"Meaning you know why Alameda went to Tehran?" Kevin asked.

"Precisely. We got some good intel that Alameda brokered the sale of the triggers between Pakistan and Iran. The Tehran trip was to complete the sale. After that, the Iranians arranged for delivery by truck from the Pakistani embassy in Teheran to the nuclear site. Problem was, the package had a secret tracking device, a thin array of electronics built into the brown wrapping paper, to tell Alameda exactly where it went. But when the package location data was uploaded, the signal, the tracker, fizzled into burnt cardboard."

"So now what? We don't know where it is?" Kevin asked, keeping an eye on the time.

"No. We assume Alameda sold this information to the Israelis so they'd know which site to bomb. I'm telling you this to give you a sense of how dangerous this is. If you can find out anything—anything at all—about these wackos or their plans, pass it on."

"OK, OK. I will, Toby. Promise."

With no time to spare, Kevin turned around and went straight to meet Cardinal Porter. In short order, he arrived at the black iron gates marking the entrance to the largest building in the Vatican, the Apostolic Palace. He waited for security to let him in.

Moments later, Kevin saw Cardinal Porter approach. He was dressed formally in a scarlet red cassock, a red mozzeta cape, and the traditional red biretta cap. He was the picture of a prince of the Church.

The cardinal nodded to Kevin, who nodded back.

The colorful Swiss guards on duty made their way over to Kevin, where officiously they scrutinized his credentials. They didn't ask to see Cardinal Porter's credentials. With a snappy salute, the guards affirmed both could pass into the dark hallway leading to the offices of the most powerful men in the Catholic Church.

Kevin was curious about the next meeting. *Who would be there? Would he finally get the first honest briefing on his mission since this whole mess started?*

As shoes pounded the wooden floors, the clatter echoed through the cavernous halls. A welcoming party consisting of two monsignors and two Swiss guards approached Cardinal John Porter, walking on either side of him. Kevin followed the group up three flights of stairs to a large regal room. At first, it seemed to be a library. Period desks and chairs, gold candelabra, and tall cherry bookcases were clues to his whereabouts. The coffered ceilings were, Kevin guessed, easily twenty feet tall. A magnificent vista of St. Peter's was visible through the window. Kevin was impressed by the whole aura of opulence. This would be a high-level meeting.

As the library door opened, a dark-suited official with a chain around his neck and a silver walking stick entered. He banged the stick on the floor, commanding the immediate attention of everyone in the room.

"*Il Santissimo Padre!*" the man announced in a high-pitched voice.

Behind him stood the recognizable figure of Pope Quintus II, his white zucchetto resting elegantly on his head, descending to layers of white silk robes. As always, a large pectoral cross hung from his neck.

As the pope entered, everyone in the room bowed simultaneously. The pope waved the traditional backhanded greeting.

Cardinal Porter approached the pontiff with reverence, kissing his ring. "Your Holiness," Porter began, "may I present Father Kevin Thrall."

Instinctively, Kevin bowed his head.

The pope addressed him in nearly flawless English. "I am happy to meet you. Come, sit over here." His Holiness directed Kevin to a table and chairs. With a simple hand gesture, he dismissed some of his official entourage, leaving Cardinal Porter, Kevin, Cardinal Claudio Marini, and Cardinal Gianni Serrano alone with him in the papal library.

Marini was well known, a cardinal who'd spent most of his career behind Vatican walls in a variety of top-level posts. His face was unusual, with contours which, on first glance, made it seem like he'd been pummeled at birth.

Cardinal Serrano had been bishop of Venice and now was in charge of special missions, a job calling for experienced administrative and managerial skills. At sixty-eight, he was young by senior church standards. He stood tall and had a stately demeanor and a regal Italian expression.

"Welcome back to Rome, Father," Marini said in serviceable English.

Cardinal Serrano nodded, his hands crossed on his lap.

Kevin thanked them in Italian. To Kevin, this was all surreal. He was sitting in the presence of the spiritual leader of a billion Catholics. It defied reality. Kevin noticed the pope's skin was darker in the light of day than it had appeared in pictures, perhaps reflecting his Tuscan origins. At only sixty-three, his relative youth explained his exuberance and high energy. Kevin recalled how impressed he'd been when he first read how Pope Quintus II had revolutionized the Vatican by bringing in a top management consulting firm, KPMG Consulting. They'd swarmed over the place, looking for ways to improve its efficiency.

The consultants' conclusion was that the venerable institution had a long way to go to undo eight centuries of deeply-rooted, essentially ineradicable habits and systems.

"I have heard much good about you from Cardinal Porter, Father," the pontiff said. "How have you found your assignment so far?"

"I'm honored to be in your presence, Your Holiness." Feeling unsure of himself, Kevin decided to not say more, and listen for what was coming.

The pope looked over at Cardinal Serrano and nodded for him to continue.

"Father Thrall, do you know about the secret of Fatima?" Serrano asked.

Is this what they brought me here to ask? Kevin thought a moment and decided he'd best play along. *Let's see if I pass their little test.* "The Virgin Mary appeared to three children in a village in Portugal in 1917 and told them secrets. When the villagers disbelieved them, Mary performed a miracle called the 'Miracle of the Sun.' Seventy thousand people were present and observed the sun spinning on its axis, plunging to earth. That is, until it stopped."

"Very good," Cardinal Serrano said, brushing his palms together in mock applause. Apparently, here was a cleric well versed in ecclesiastic sarcasm. "Now, how much information have you learned about the secret—the last secret?"

"Well, for many years, the secret was known only to Lucia, the surviving child, who wrote it down sometime during the Second World War, I believe, and sent it to the Vatican to be read only by the pope," Kevin said. "It was rumored to contain apocalyptic information that, if released, would terrify the world."

"Very good, indeed," said Cardinal Marini.

"I happen to be a student of Fatima," Kevin said. "Given that it was witnessed by thousands and widely reported in the press at the time, I find it the most credible of miracles."

"I agree," Marini said. "So you're probably aware that His Holiness, John Paul II, revealed the secret publicly in the year 2000."

Kevin still hadn't a clue why he was discussing the secret of Fatima with the leaders of the Catholic Church. "Of course. I recall that the secret predicted that a future 'bishop in white' would be shot or assassinated. In 1981, that's what happened to John Paul II. He was shot in St. Peter's Square."

"Correct," Marini said.

His Holiness joined the conversation. "Father Thrall, you might not be aware that the date on which John Paul II was shot, May 13, 1981, was the anniversary of the first apparition at Fatima."

For Kevin, it took a moment for that information sink in. "Actually, I was aware of that, Your Holiness," Kevin said, recalling his conversation with Max Drotti on the same subject. "It is indeed a remarkable coincidence."

"Perhaps not a coincidence," Cardinal Serrano added. "We believe there is a connection between the secret and Opus Mundi's attempt to take over the Church. If His Holiness's life is at risk, we must find out what it is in the secret that has them so worried. Some believe there's nothing to this, but others . . ." Marini raised his eyebrows and looked in the direction of the pontiff. Marini seemed to correct himself and continued, "Others believe that we must explore this possible connection."

Kevin was confused. "The secret was made public, so we have as much access to its contents as Opus Mundi, correct?" The men nodded. "So, what is it that they seem to know that no one else does? This doesn't make sense."

Cardinal Porter spoke up, "We have an Opus Mundi defector who told us that the key to their operations was the secret of Fatima. But all we know is that the secret accurately predicted that a bishop in white would be shot. Then there's the remarkable coincidence that the assassination attempt on John Paul II occurred on the anniversary of the first apparition at Fatima. Beyond that, we're stuck, Kevin. We need fresh eyes on this mystery." Porter looked at the pope and then back at Kevin. "You were chosen for this assignment because of the combination of your skills and your devotion to the priesthood."

Kevin nodded, keeping his eyes on the floor while he gathered his thoughts. *If you only knew, Blessed Father, how my priestly obligations are challenged every day.*

The pope's secretary, a young man dressed in a black suit and tie, entered and whispered in the pontiff's ear.

As he stood up, Pope Quintus II nodded and announced softly, "This meeting will end now. Thank you, my friends."

As the pontiff left the room, the men all rose. Cardinal Porter walked out with Kevin and they chatted quietly.

"The meeting was short, I know," Cardinal Porter said, "and there's something else you need to know about John Paul I."

Kevin stopped in his tracks and looked at His Eminence. "I remember. Quite a shock. He was the one who died in 1978 after being in office just a month. What about him, Eminence?"

"I must share with you one of the most sacred secrets. You need to know it. The pope's death occurred on the thirty third day of his reign, while he was reading the secret of Fatima."

Kevin was speechless. This conversation was getting just too bizarre. "He died reading the secret?"

"Yes," Cardinal Porter said. "And it is a mystery. We've all read the secret. It was made public in 2000. There's nothing in the secret that would—or should—cause a heart attack."

"Maybe it was unrelated to his reading. Could it have been a coincidence? Maybe it was his natural time to die."

Cardinal Porter shook his head. "We don't think so. He had no previous heart problems. Remember, Opus Mundi believes there's an apocalyptic message in the secret." The cardinal stopped and rubbed his eyes. "The problem, Kevin, is that we really don't know exactly what John Paul I saw and we don't know what Opus Mundi sees or what mayhem they're concocting. That's why we sent for you."

Kevin nodded but said nothing.

"Look," Porter continued, "I took a risk sending for you, given your colored background." Porter paused for a moment, looking for the right words. "You're a good priest, Kevin. Your calling was genuine, your faith is strong. I want you to hear this from me because I trust you completely."

"Thank you, Eminence." Kevin breathed deeply. "I appreciate your confidence and I'll do everything I can not to disappoint you. I'm overwhelmed by all this new information: papal assassinations, wars between nations, and now a mystery surrounding the secret of Fatima . . ."

Well, this was certainly getting more interesting, Kevin thought silently. One pope died reading the secret of Fatima just a month after being elected. Another pope, John Paul II, was shot, but survived. When the secret of Fatima was revealed publicly to the world, it predicted 'a bishop in white'—the pope surely fit that description—would be assassinated. But nothing in the secret, revealed publicly, pointed to a cataclysmic event that would have given an earlier pope a heart attack and excite a fringe group to commit atrocities against Church leaders. *So, what was hiding in the secret that no one but Opus Mundi could see?*

The awkward silence passed. Finally, Kevin said, "I'll do everything I can, Eminence."

Porter seemed relieved. "May I answer other questions you may have?"

"Did Monsignor Drotti know about the test I was given?" Kevin asked.

"Yes, he did."

"Okay, I'll stay on the job, Eminence. But Drotti must go. I can't work with him. I want him off."

"As you wish."

"And I'll need him replaced with someone I can trust," Kevin said.

As the men exited the Apostolic Palace, Cardinal Porter stroked his chin. "That will take some time, Kevin."

"Then, in the interim, I'll work alone."

∞∞∞

CHAPTER FOURTEEN

Rome, Italy

Back at his apartment, Kevin collapsed on the bed, mentally wiped. For any Catholic, a meeting with the pope would be emotionally draining. In his case, given the weight resting on his shoulders, it was both exhilarating and enervating.

Kevin clicked on the flat screen TV. CNN was showing an ominous screen title in a box just below the picture: *Middle East Turmoil.* The news stories were ablaze with reports that Israel had bombed a nuclear arming site near the holy city of Qum in Iran. In its third "Special Report" of the morning, CNN was saying that the U.S. President was expected to make an announcement from the Oval Office imminently.

Then CNN was airing live scenes of ambulances with sirens screeching and dense black smoke hovering over minarets in Iran. Minutes later, the White House appeared on the screen with the president facing the cameras from the Oval Office. His address was brief and to the point. The United States had nothing to do with the attack. That said, the United States was committed to the defense of Israel. An attack on Israel would result in an immediate and appropriate response from the United States.

"All parties involved are encouraged to remain calm and resolve their differences through negotiations to be hosted by the United States." The President paused. "And I urge outside parties to refrain from involvement in this situation. If left to ourselves, we will peacefully resolve this."

When the President had completed his statement, NBC announced that Hezbollah, the Shiite party funded by Iran, had launched a missile attack on Israel from the South of Lebanon. In retaliation, the Israeli Army was moving to invade Lebanon.

The world paused in anticipation of the Iranian reaction to Israel's strike. Did Iran have nuclear missiles?

Kevin sat up in bed, clenching his jaw. He was transfixed by the images on the screen. His nap had been short and was over now. No way could he go back to sleep. The world was teetering on the brink of a nuclear holocaust.

He went into the living room, turned on the television there, and got himself a Peroni out of the fridge. He kept the TV volume on low and as the stories were now getting repetitive, decided to do something while he watched.

Kevin retrieved his two pistols from safekeeping and started cleaning them. He reassembled the smaller Glock, then put the weapons away.

His mental inventory of recent days was hitting overload. Like shuffling through files, he organized his thoughts: a review. First, he was brought to Rome, initially, as some kind of test, because of his one-of-a-kind military skills, traits, and experience. Now he'd learned that the real mission was for him to solve "The Big One," which had something to do with the famed secret of Fatima. The only problem was that Opus Mundi was cognizant of things in the secret that nobody else could figure out. So, the first task would be: Read the actual text of the secret as written in Lucia's hand. *But would this be possible?*

Second, according to the news, a nuclear war was about to start. That had been part of his initial assignment, the "test," so to speak. Kevin had gotten wind of the plot to bomb Iran and the Israelis did just that. Now the world held its breath waiting for the Iranian response. *Would it be nuclear? Where would they hit?* It seemed inconceivable that a shadow organization like Opus Mundi could have had a role in starting this war, but the evidence was pointing in that direction. And despite the devastating consequences of a nuclear war in the Middle East, why was the Vatican more concerned about the secret of Fatima?

Kevin picked up his phone and pressed the numbers for Cardinal Porter's office. His request was simple and direct. He needed access to the primary source, the original text of the secret of Fatima. The cardinal's chief of staff put him on hold, then came back on the line, explaining that Kevin would be given the access code to an encrypted website where he could read the secret in both its original form and in the translation. *Well, they've come a long way,* Kevin thought. *To think that he now could access a secret document held in the Vatican archives, via electronic technology!*

Minutes later, the link appeared on Kevin's laptop. He typed the access code. The original, handwritten text of the secret popped up on the screen, followed by the English translation. Kevin first studied the original, then the translation.

J. M. J.

A terceira parte do segredo
revelado a 13 de Julho de 1917
na Cova da Iria - Fátima.

Escrevo em acto de obediên-
cia a Vós Deus meu, que mo
mandais por meio de sua
Ex.cia Rev.ma o Senhor Bispo
de Leiria e da Vossa e mi-
nha Santíssima Mãe.
Depois das duas partes
que já expus, vimos ao lado
esquerdo de Nossa Senhora

TRANSLATION

The third part of the secret revealed at the Cova da Iria-Fatima, on 13 July 1917.

I write in obedience to you, my God, who commands me to do so through his Excellency, the Bishop of Leira, and through your Most Holy Mother and mine.

After the two parts which I have already explained, at the left of Our Lady and a little above, we saw an Angel with a flaming sword in his left hand; flashing, it gave out flames that looked as though they would set the world on fire; but they died out in contact with the splendour that Our Lady radiated towards him from her right hand: pointing to the earth with his right hand, the Angel cried out in a loud voice: "Penance, Penance, Penance!"

And we saw in an immense light that is God: "Something similar to how people appear in a mirror when they pass in front of it," a Bishop dressed in White; "We had the impression that it was the Holy Father. "

Other Bishops, Priests, men and women, and religious groups going up a steep mountain, at the top of which there was a big Cross of rough-hewn trunks as of a cork-tree with the bark; before reaching there the Holy Father passed through a big city half in ruins; half trembling with halting step, afflicted with pain and sorrow, he prayed for the souls of the corpses he met on his way; having reached the top of the mountain, on his knees at the foot of the big Cross, he was killed by a group of soldiers who fired bullets and arrows at him, and in the same way there died one after another, the other Bishops, Priests, men and women Religious, and various lay people of different ranks and positions.

Kevin zeroed in on the famous passage about the "bishop in white" being "killed by a group of soldiers." The Church had interpreted this passage as forecasting an assassination attempt on John Paul II in St. Peter's Square on May 13, 1981, the sixty-fourth anniversary to the day of the first apparition at Fatima.

Eerie, Kevin thought. *Coincidence? Maybe. Maybe not.*

As Kevin read and reread the secret, he could find absolutely nothing that might be suggestive of a threat or prophecy. After a couple of frustrating hours, Kevin stretched out on the sofa and did what was becoming a habit—he called Toby Beck at CIA.

"Let's see," Toby said playfully answering the phone, "So, kid. Another shoelace needing help?"

"How'd you guess?"

Toby chuckled.

"Toby, I'm going to send you a link to a document. Since you're Catholic, you'll know what this is about. It's the secret of Fatima as transcribed by Sister Lucia in 1944. Now here's what you don't know. There's a rebel group within the church who thinks the message contains an apocalyptic foreboding of some catastrophe. A doom and gloom message from the grim reaper. The problem is that no one else looking at it sees that or can figure out what they're talking about."

"I'll resist asking if you've been drinking. Maybe you spent too much time reading *The Da Vinci Code*. You know, Tom Hanks was great in that role and the scene—"

"Toby, please."

"Sorry, pal. Okay, we'll have a look."

"Thanks," Kevin said, relieved. "And dare I say it's urgent?"

"Isn't it always? I'll get back to you ASAP."

Kevin sent Toby the link and passcodes and asked him to find something, anything, in the secret that might prompt someone to see an apocalyptic prediction, no matter how far-fetched.

As he ended his conversation with Toby, Kevin heard a knock on the door. He rose from the couch, asking who was there.

"A message from Cardinal Porter," the man said.

Kevin opened the door. He felt the jolt of thousands of electrical volts zapping his body. A gun was jammed into his stomach.

∞∞∞∞

CHAPTER FIFTEEN

Fallujah, Iraq

September 2006

Another hazy, infernally hot day in the desert meant another series of patrols. Today, Captain Kevin Thrall knew his mission would be the toughest one of his tour. He was to lead his men on a cleanup mission to a nearby Iraqi village, where reports of a massacre had reached the base. *Just another day at the office*, Kevin thought.

Upon arrival, Kevin's patrol validated the earlier report. The Iraqi village had been viciously plundered by forces sympathetic to al Qaeda. The ravaged village now consisted of a dozen small houses, a street with two small stores, and smoldering fires. No one had been spared.

Kevin ordered his platoon to break into a destitute house. The men smashed the wooden door and entered to acrid smells of sweat and rotting garbage. Kevin led the way, his rifle pointing straight ahead, his goggles partially clouded with sand. It was dark and hazy inside with only a small window above a sink filled with dirty dishes.

Cautiously, Kevin traipsed through the house, motioning for his men to follow. Hearing moans on the other side of a cardboard wall, he moved in the direction of the sounds. He and his men came upon a group of bearded, shabbily-dressed men torturing women.

When the American soldiers had entered the small clay house, most of the torturers had fled. But one of them remained, still raping a young girl who looked no older than twelve, maybe thirteen. Her attacker was holding her by force against the wall. She was staring up at the ceiling, her brown eyes glazed over, while the bearded bastard finished with her. Kevin went ballistic. He grabbed the rapist by the hair and smashed the butt of his rifle into his throat. The man fell. Kevin stomped his boot on his chest.

As she slumped forward, Kevin caught the young girl. He would never forget the fear and hopelessness in her eyes. When one of his men came in, Kevin said, "Here, please get her out of here."

Her lips mouthed, "Shukran." He knew it was Arabic for "thank you." His teammate picked her up and carried her out.

Kevin turned to the assailant, who was lying flat on his back. As he started to get up, a knife in his hand, Kevin kicked the hand, and the knife spun out. He grabbed the man by the neck and raised him up against the wall.

"Who the hell are you?" Kevin shouted.

"Ahmed," the bearded man replied. Blood trickled from his lip. "Look, I want revenge, justice."

"Really? You call this justice?"

"I know my rights," he said.

Staring into the man's eyes, he punched him in the face. "Your rights, asshole? You just better hope the girl lives."

Kevin's team searched the house for other combatants and survivors. Finding none, they went outside to secure a perimeter around the house. Kevin followed, dragging the rapist, now his prisoner.

Two other soldiers also dragged corpses outside—a man, a woman, and a boy—the young girl's family. Kevin gagged at the sight of the bodies. The rape victim was lying outside on a makeshift cot.

Another American soldier, Kevin's friend and roommate, Toby Beck, sensed what was happening and approached Kevin. "Take it easy, Kevin," he said.

"Look at that poor girl, Toby," Kevin hissed as he kept his hands wrapped around the rapist's neck. "I'm not done here."

The girl was eyeing both men, tears streaming down her face as she looked at the bodies around her. She was sobbing inconsolably.

Toby reached for Kevin to restrain him. Ahmed, the perpetrator, sensing his chance, shoved Kevin and broke loose. Kevin pushed Toby aside and raced after Ahmed, grabbed him, and slammed him back against the wall.

"This is war. I know my rights," Ahmed said.

"You have no rights!" Kevin shouted.

Kevin grabbed the knife he'd taken from the rapist and pointed it at Ahmed. "Look at her!" Kevin shouted.

The man smirked. "This is war."

"Yes, I get it. It certainly is."

Kevin lifted the knife, placing it before the man's eyes, while holding him securely against the wall with his other hand. "This is what you deserve."

The man smiled. "I know the rules, Captain. I've surrendered. You can't touch me."

"Try this rule," Kevin said. He stabbed Ahmed in the leg. Ahmed buckled over and screamed.

"Help me!" Ahmed cried. "This man is insane!"

"Insane? Oh, how right you are." Kevin plunged the knife again, this time into the man's abdomen. "You feel that, you sicko?"

The rapist's eyes widened. For the first time, Kevin saw terror in his eyes. But Kevin was too enraged to care.

"You know what's coming, don't you?"

"No!" he cried, just as Kevin thrust the knife into his abdomen again. Blood was everywhere.

"That will hurt for a long time," Kevin said, teeth clenching, "and in the end, you will die." With that, Kevin retracted the knife and kicked him to the ground in a pool of blood.

The young girl witnessed the killing. If she felt any revulsion or horror, it didn't show. "Shukran," she said again to Kevin. And for the first time, he saw defiant hope in her brown eyes. He knew he'd never regret what he'd done.

Two soldiers from Kevin's patrol ran over. "Leave him," Kevin ordered. "Take care of the girl."

At the court martial, most of the soldiers in Kevin's detail claimed he'd acted in self-defense, while others reported that Kevin had murdered the man.

Secretly the military judges were relieved to acquit Kevin of the charges. But when the court martial was over, the presiding judge requested to confer privately with Captain Kevin Thrall. His message was simple and direct. "Son, you've got anger management issues."

"I know," Kevin said humbly.

"Get help," said the judge.

The press statement that followed the court marital reported that the slain man was a local militia member, and Captain Kevin Thrall had acted in self-defense.

∞∞∞∞

Rome, Italy

Present Day

The nightmare was back. Kevin's eyes shot open to complete darkness. What'd happened? His memory was returning slowly. He was now remembering. An ambush outside his apartment in the Vatican. A stun gun zapping him.

Kevin tried shaking off the grogginess. His head was foggy. He could see he was in a room without windows, poorly lit by a suspended lightbulb dangling on a coarse string. The foul stench of urine permeated the air.

The room also had a couple of wooden chairs and a small, rickety card table. Kevin's arms and legs were tightly bound by ropes to the legs and the back of a chair. His mouth felt rough like sandpaper and parched. He ached for water.

Minutes later, a door opened and blinding bright light flooded into the dark space. A tall, spectral silhouette loomed on the threshold of the doorway. It moved closer. The hair was dark. It was dressed in a suit with no tie, its eyebrows furrowed and forming creases in the forehead. Its mouth was thin-lipped, giving its weathered complexion a somber expression.

The man, it was a man, set about untying one of Kevin's arms. When he'd freed the arm, he handed him a bottle of water. Clutching it, Kevin started gulping. When he'd finished, the man retied the hand to the chair.

"What do you want?" Kevin asked.

"*Shhhhh*," the man whispered in English with a thick Italian accent. Smiling, he put his forefinger to his lips. "We ask the questions, not you." Whereupon he turned and left the room, slamming the door behind him.

Kevin assessed his situation. He couldn't tell how long he'd been out, but his numbness, along with his parched mouth and scratchy throat, suggested he'd been unconscious for several hours. One at a time, he moved his limbs. Everything was working. He was unarmed, of course, but if the guy came into the room again he could probably take him. *How many more of them were there? And what did they want from him?*

Of the knots binding him to the chair, he figured with time and fidgeting, he could slip out of them. Wriggling his hands through the knots, his wrists were raw and bloody. After what felt like an hour, he was making progress with one hand and figured it'd be free in a short while. The rest would be easy. He prayed to God for help.

The door opened again and banged shut. Three men stormed in. *Another pair of thugs*, Kevin thought. *Where do they get these guys?* Two of them appeared to be in their mid-forties, in slacks and tee shirts. The third looked monk-like in a long brown robe, the head veiled in a hood. Kevin guessed he was the leader. He spoke first. "Father Thrall, we hope you'll choose the easy path."

A sly, crooked smile crossed the monk's dark face. He appeared older than the others. A shiver shot up Kevin's spine. One didn't want to cross this man.

"What'd you want to know?" Kevin asked. Out of the line of vision of the intruders he was continuing to twist slowly and gently. His one hand was now almost free.

The monk's head was bent forward, the hood shading his face.

"Tell us about your Vatican activities, Father. We'd like to know what it is you're looking for."

"Oh, not much. Spiritual renewal."

As Kevin spoke, his hand wriggled free, but he wasn't ready to make his move.

The monk nodded ponderously. "I suppose we'll have to do this the hard way, Father," he said, "much to my regret."

The monk eyed one of his henchmen, who promptly scuttled over to Kevin and punched him hard in the face. A trickle of blood, warm and salty, flowed from Kevin's mouth. *Ouch! Dammit!*

Kevin now freed his other hand. He grabbed the man by his shirt, slamming his head against the wall. His legs were still roped to the chair legs, so he just dragged it along.

With his hands clasped in front of him, the monk stood calmly at a short distance as the second henchman sprang to his cohort's rescue. Reaching into his pocket, the monk withdrew a small knife, a sliver of light glinting off it from the light of the hanging bulb.

Again Kevin hurled the thug's face against the wall, twisting and slamming his chair against the body. Just as he was readying to throw the knife, Kevin saw the monk out of the corner of his eye. With perfect timing, Kevin pulled the man away from the wall, positioning the thug in front of him as a shield. The knife whizzed through the air with deadly aim toward Kevin. Instead, it struck the thug Kevin was holding in front of him in the back. As moans filled the air, blood gushed from his wound.

Kevin held him upright, by his throat.

How many knives did the brother have, anyway?

Now henchman number two tried grabbing Kevin.

The hooded man stood calmly, another knife at the ready, while the second seized Kevin, who was still roped to the chair.

"Sit still," the second thug shouted, locking his arm around Kevin's neck and shoving his chair to the floor. He smelled of cheap cologne. His breath was hot and putrid on Kevin's neck.

Kevin let go of the wounded man, who crumpled to the floor in a pool of blood.

The monk put the knife back into his pocket and smiled again, a sly, crooked smile. The other henchman retied Kevin's arms to the chair. This time, the knot was tight; Kevin's hand went numb. At that moment, Kevin knew he'd been defeated.

Henchman number two then examined his cohort lying on the floor. Rising slowly, he looked at the monk.

"He's dead," he said.

"You're armed, correct?" the monk asked.

The man nodded.

"Then finish it." The hooded man went to the door, opened it, and slammed it behind him.

Kevin braced himself. His time had come. He prayed the man would do it, execute him mercifully. "Dear Lord, lift me to your eternal embrace. I am your faithful servant."

And then there was nothing.

Kevin opened his eyes, peering from slits into the darkness. Henchman number two was untying him from the chair, working methodically.

Kevin looked to see if he could make anything out about the man. As near as he could tell, his eyes seemed blank, devoid of emotion. As he finished untying the knots, Kevin noticed he was middle-aged, although fit and agile. He put his finger to his lips and whispered, "*Shhh.*"

When Kevin was free, he stood up from the chair and faced the man. Now he was pointing a handgun at him.

"Leave through that door," the man said, waving the pistol at a door on the far end of the room. "There is a bicycle for you."

Kevin scrutinized the man, not getting what was happening. *Was he a friend or foe? Was this a trap?* For a couple of minutes, Kevin stared blankly. In a barely audible whisper, he asked simply, "Why?"

"Do you remember the young Ali Recip who was in your home?"

Kevin nodded.

"I am his father. He is my son. Please go."

Then he pointed in the direction of the other door.

∞∞∞∞

CHAPTER SIXTEEN

Rome, Italy

The room was still. Kevin hadn't moved in hours. The only sound was the insistent hiss from the air conditioning grill until a cell phone buzzed. It woke Kevin from a long, dreamy nap. Opening his eyes, he took a few seconds to realize he was lying on the sofa at his Vatican apartment in the Villa Domenica. He remembered that not long ago he'd had a narrow escape. He'd bicycled to escape his captors to the Porta Maggiore on the east side of Rome, abandoned the bicycle, and then checked his pockets for money. His cash was still there. After a taxi ride to the Vatican gate, he'd staggered to the apartment.

Kevin had made a mental note to call Vatican authorities, and request that a security system with video surveillance be installed. The thugs knew where he lived and had gotten to him easily. Come to think of it, he'd have Cardinal Porter's office get on the case, thereby ensuring it'd get done pronto. But his first priority was to shower and get some sleep. A helluva night.

Now he was alert enough to worry about the buzzing phone. Kevin's pulse quickened, wondering if it was Katie. It wasn't. Area code was 703. Virginia. Toby Beck.

"Hey, Toby."

"Not so good news for ya, buddy," Toby said. "I've had no less than six crypto guys go over your secret of Fatima. We found nothing. Not a threat, not a message, not anything."

Kevin shook his head. "Toby, I know there's something there. How could this be?"

"Maybe Opus Mundi is just plain cockamamie. There's nothing here, buddy."

"OK, thanks, Toby. We'll deal with it. Talk to you later."

Kevin still wasn't convinced. He got up, went to the bathroom, and downed three Advil. A part of him was dejected, feeling like he'd hit a dead end. Yet there was hope. He must be missing something. He wished he had an Opus Mundi operative on hand. He'd beat the answer out of him.

Kevin pressed the TV remote, clicking on CNN. The United States had positioned two aircraft carriers in the Persian Gulf awaiting the Iranian response to the Israeli attack. Oil had jumped to over $180 a barrel and citizens and politicians were screaming for relief at the pump. The stock market had plummeted. Now, somber talking heads were speculating about a nuclear holocaust.

A loud rapping at the door dashed his thoughts.

With the searing memory of the last time he'd opened this door, Kevin moved cautiously, picking up one of the pistols from his bedside table, and moving toward the door.

"Who is it?"

"Kevin, it's Max."

Kevin opened the door a crack. There stood Monsignor Drotti, dressed in his clerical garb. He was looking disgruntled.

Drotti spoke quickly, gesturing nervously with his hands. "Look, I know you don't want to see me, but I need to talk to you."

Kevin nodded, gesturing toward the living room. He walked over and laid the pistol down on the table.

"I know you're upset with me, Kevin. But I couldn't tell you everything. I had my orders, too."

"Yeah, sure," Kevin said, as they sat down in the only two armchairs in the apartment.

"The test of your abilities was important, Kevin, because the next assignment—the one you're on now—is really, really serious."

"More serious than a nuclear war?" Kevin asked.

"Yes," Drotti said. "At the moment, I don't know much more. I came to see you because I knew you were upset with me. Please accept my apology. I'll understand if you'd prefer not to work with me."

"It's about trust, Max, it's—"

Buzzzzzzzz. Kevin glanced at his ringing cell, perplexed. He didn't recognize the number.

"Excuse me, Max," he said.

"Father Thrall?" the tentative voice asked in a thick accent. "This is Ali Recip. I remembered your number."

Kevin smiled. "Ali, small world. Yesterday your father saved my life."

"Well, my father is dead, sir. That must have been just before they killed him."

Kevin's jaw dropped and his stomach was churning. *That must have been because of me.*

"I'm so sorry, Ali. Oh my God!" Kevin cried out. He was horrified. He was responsible for the man's death.

"Thank you, sir. I'm calling you because he wanted me to tell you something in the event of . . . in case he was no longer here."

"Sure . . . please continue." Kevin looked over at Max, who was frowning with worry.

"My father said to tell you Operation Delorgio will happen today at noon."

"Operation Delorgio? What does that mean, Ali?" Kevin asked.

"I do not know, sir. . . . I . . . I . . . must go now." The phone went dead.

Kevin looked at Max, shaking his head.

"What is it?" Max asked.

Kevin explained what had happened to him yesterday and what Ali had just told him.

"I . . . I . . . feel so guilty. It's my fault the kid's father was killed. Now, he's given me a secret message about Operation Delorgio. What does it mean?"

"Operation Delorgio is a code name for an Opus Mundi event, but we don't know exactly what it might be," said Max.

"Ali said 'noon today.'"

Max looked as though he'd been struck by lightning. "My God!"

"What?"

"Today is Sunday. The pontiff will be giving his blessing from the window above St. Peter's Square. At noon exactly. He addresses the crowds every Sunday!"

Kevin checked his watch. "Oh my God! That's a half hour from now. Call Vatican security!"

Monsignor Drotti shrugged. "Certainly. But to do what? Protect the pope from half a million Catholics in the Square? No way His Holiness will skip his Sunday blessing."

Kevin went into the bedroom and withdrew the other pistol. "If they're going to take a shot at him, it won't be from the Square up at the window," he said. "The pope speaks from his window on the top floor of the Apostolic Palace. They'll need an expert marksman with a powerful rifle. That wouldn't happen if the assassin is on the ground, in the crowd."

Max looked at the pistols Kevin was cradling. "What are you saying?"

"The assassin has to have a better vantage point." Kevin was pointing at a large framed photo of St. Peter's on the bedroom wall. The color aerial shot showed St. Peter's with the semi-circle of Bernini columns framing the square, in front of the Basilica. To the right of the colonnade stood the Apostolic Palace.

"There," Kevin said, pointing at the photo. He pointed to the top of the semi-circle of columns, fingering a spot closest to the window of the Apostolic Palace. This is where the pope addresses the crowd. "It's the best vantage point for an assassin."

Drotti studied the picture. "They'd have great difficulty accessing that building," he said, pointing to the same spot. "The Vatican police know the top of the colonnade would be an assassin's best vantage point."

Tapping his finger on the photograph, Kevin reflected for a moment. "They're right. That spot would be the easiest shot for a good marksman."

"And that's why you can't get up there," Drotti added.

Kevin looked again at the picture of the Square and the columns. "Wait," he said, pointing at the other side of the semi-circle of columns. He tapped on the image at the top of the semi-circle, this time at the roof of the colonnade farthest from the Apostolic Palace, on the other side of the esplanade.

"What?" Drotti asked.

Kevin was still tapping. "I figure about eight hundred yards. An expert sniper with the right equipment could make a shot from here. It wouldn't be easy, but it's feasible. How secure is that side of the colonnade?"

Drotti shrugged. "It's indisputably a controlled access, but not as closely watched as the other side."

"Could someone sneak up there at night?"

"Well, I guess so . . ."

Kevin pocketed the guns. "Let's get going, Max."

Drotti swallowed hard. "Kevin, we're just speculating . . . we don't know anything will happen!"

"Would you rather sit here watching television?"

Max shook his head and stood up.

"C'mon," said Kevin.

Both men raced from the apartment, Kevin dressed in the jeans and polo shirt he'd put on after returning from his kidnapping, Drotti in his black clerical garb. In calculation of a measured run to the center of the Square, they estimated about six minutes. But they couldn't factor into their calculation the variable of the crowds. How much would the crowds slow them down?

Exiting the Vatican gate to the left of St. Peter's, throngs of people were gathered, awaiting the pontiff's blessing. The sun shone brightly, illuminating the Square, creating a kaleidoscopic blur of colors and shapes against the crowd. Thousands upon thousands of pilgrims and tourists were milling about, some singing, others clicking photos with cell phones and cameras. The constant hum of anticipation was ominous. It hung over the Square.

"This way," Drotti directed. The two fought their way through the dense crowd, peering upward occasionally at the window where the pope was due to appear.

"Scusi, scusi," the men shouted as they muscled their way through the throngs. Drotti led the way, aiming for the guard station at the foot of the far columns. A wood shack, just big enough for one guard, protected the entrance to a stairway that led to the roof of the colonnade. The roof connected the Bernini columns at the top, completing the semi-circle of the colonnade. Amidst bursts of laughter, chatter, and songs, the din of the crowd grew louder. A gentle breeze elevated everyone's mood.

The pope's window was open, the microphone in place, and the red papal banner, which had just been unfurled beneath the open window, was slapping against the side of the building. The crowd roared, knowing this red banner signaled that the pontiff would soon appear.

Kevin and Drotti clawed their way to the sealed and guarded stairway under the colonnade. Drotti addressed the guard who was checking his credentials.

Drotti explained as calmly as he could what was happening. Kevin saw the guard's eyes widen in alarm. Kevin breathed heavily, impatient with small talk. His mind was roaming back to Iraq, which was the last time he felt this kind of pressure in his chest. Adrenaline was pumping throughout his body. *What was this elation he was feeling? Was it fervor over the prospect of meeting death? Or, was it because he was rabidly determined to win this battle?*

Impatient, Kevin brushed the guard aside and rushed to the top of the stairs. Drotti followed. The guard hollered into the intercom, summoning help. Kevin checked his watch: three minutes to twelve.

On top of the colonnade was a slanted roof, forcing the men to go along the bottom edge by the railing. From this vantage point, the crowd below had morphed into a cluster of milling insects.

Locating the papal quarters where the pontiff would appear, Kevin stopped to orient himself. The window was open, the banner beneath it. Mentally, Kevin measured the distance from the papal window to the columns, calculating he was roughly 800 yards from the optimum spot from this side of the colonnade to shoot.

Over on the other side, Kevin now saw security guards on top of the columns, fully armed, ready to ensure the pope's safety. Kevin recalled the many hours he'd spent in Iraq talking shop with some of the expert sharpshooters in his battalion about similar situations. He had no idea then that some of that banter would one day become so important. Perhaps God had prepared him for this moment. But no time to think about God now.

He motioned for Max to crouch down and follow him along the railing. They had to go slowly; every few feet, statues of saints stood in their way.

Kevin pointed to the far extension of the columns. "Over there is a shooter's best vantage point." He reached into his pocket and handed one of the pistols to Max. "You want to be my partner? Take this." Before giving it to him, Kevin cocked the pistol and chambered a round. "It's like a Kodak Instamatic: Just point and shoot."

Max took the pistol, making sure to keep his finger away from the trigger. He was nervous, having never held a gun in his hand before.

Crouching all the way down, the men made their way around the curve of the colonnade. The tin roof crunched, making metallic clatter with every step, but the din of the crowd drowned it out.

Suddenly, as trumpets blared, the all-white figure of Pope Quintus II appeared in the window, hands extended. His figure was visible only from the waist up. The roar of the crowd was deafening.

Kevin motioned for Drotti to stop. They got down on their hands and knees and crawled around the roof of the colonnade, searching for the shooter.

Nothing.

Crawling a bit farther for a better view, Kevin motioned for Drotti to follow. They crawled ten yards ahead and looked up.

Nothing.

They repeated the maneuver. Their crawling became more rapid and proficient. They looked up again.

Nothing.

Had he overreacted? Had he miscalculated? Nervously, Kevin focused on what he'd concluded was the optimal spot to take a shot, the closest point to the window from the far side of the columns. Straightening up, his head was poking again above the steep roof of the colonnade.

Then the target came into full sight.

Further ahead on the roof, the figure was sleek and elongated, clothed in a muddy jumpsuit camouflaged to match the brown color of the plaster, with a ski mask of the same color to cover his face. He was hard to spot just a few yards away, more difficult from above. This guy was a pro. Beside the sharpshooter lay a long cloth case where his rifle was stored.

His Holiness began with a papal blessing. The crowd quieted.

Deliberately, the assassin unzipped the case by his side and took out a sleek rifle with a telescope. The rifle rested on a small tripod attached to the barrel. He crouched into position.

His finger to his lips, Kevin signaled Max to follow him up the slanted roof. The shooter's attention was entirely on the Apostolic Palace. He checked the rifle sights, clicked a knob, and then positioned himself, looking into the telescope sight.

The time had come. More than 700 yards away, the pope's voice was loud and clear echoing over loudspeakers in the Square below, invoking the words of Jesus.

Kevin now had two options and he had to pick one fast. He could try a shot at the assassin from here, but with only a pistol, he might miss. Even if he hit the target, the man might still get a shot off with his rifle. The other option was to get closer for a better shot, and in the process create a distraction to keep the shooter from firing at the papal window. Only this option meant Kevin was substituting himself as the target. Or at least, the shooter's first one.

Kevin's decision came swiftly and his movements turned automatic. Conjuring skills learned years ago, he jumped on the roof, careening down the other side toward the shooter. In a split second, the shooter saw Kevin, sprang up and whipped his rifle around, pointing the barrel straight at Kevin.

Like a cheetah, Kevin dove to the ground and slid down the roof toward the assassin. Behind him, Max's clumsy footsteps were lacking subtlety, inviting disaster. "Down, Max!" Kevin shouted while aiming his pistol at the assassin. In this game, whoever fires first, fires last.

The assassin got off the first shot. But in this one, things were playing out differently. His aim was off. He missed. The bullet whizzed over Kevin's head, close enough to make his hair stand on end.

Kevin pointed his gun and squeezed the trigger. *Nothing.* The pistol jammed. He banged it on the tiles, as the sharpshooter positioned for another round.

Another shot rang out, but this time it wasn't from the assassin. It was from Drotti. *Thank God for Drotti!*

Drotti jumped down next to Kevin on the tiles, shaking, gun in hand, ready to take another shot.

"Give it to me, Max," Kevin said.

"Gladly," said Drotti.

The assassin was wounded, but still standing. He readied his rifle again, aiming it at Kevin and Max, but was now moving too slowly. Kevin rose. Holding his pistol straight in front of him, he shot the assassin in the chest.

Kevin remained standing, anticipating the man's collapse, but he didn't. Instead, the shooter grimaced. Kevin realized he must be wearing a Kevlar bulletproof vest. A wicked smile plastered across his face, the guy was aiming the rifle at Kevin, but his smile was fading. Mustering his wartime *sang froid*, Kevin held the pistol steady with both hands and shot first, emptying his cartridge into the assassin's skull. The assassin's eyes grew wide, then closed as he collapsed into a heap on the roof, blood oozing out of both sides of his head. A dozen security men with guns rushed to the scene, pounding the tin roof toward Kevin and Drotti.

"Monsignor, what happened here?" asked a security guard.

By the way he took control, Drotti assumed the guard was the leader of the security team. Drotti signaled to the leader, "All under control!" Drotti explained that they'd gotten a heads up on a possible assassination attempt against his Holiness. He motioned toward Kevin, explaining that he was a special U.S. Emissary to the Vatican.

The security guard looked at Kevin, nodded, and matter-of-factly asked where the clerics had happened upon the guns.

Puffing up his chest further, Drotti said, "Inspector sir, this matter must remain top secret. Am I making myself quite clear?"

The man nodded, saying, "As you wish, monsignor. I'll handle this thing appropriately. We'll remove the body discreetly."

"Good," Drotti said. "Further instructions will follow from the Vatican."

After additional cautious words from Drotti, the security men headed toward the assassin's body.

"Thanks, partner," Kevin said.

"No problem," said Drotti.

Drotti had some balls, after all, thought Kevin. *Sometimes he comes across like a donkey, but under pressure, he looked like a Triple Crown race horse.*

∞∞∞∞

CHAPTER SEVENTEEN

Rome, Italy

Exhausted, Kevin and Drotti pushed through the crowds, heading back to Kevin's apartment. As they collapsed in armchairs, Drotti was wailing, "I'm having a heart attack."

"How do you know?" asked Kevin.

"Throbbing in my chest."

"I can fix that, Max," said Kevin. He got up, went to the kitchen and poured two glasses of Scotch. He handed one to Drotti. "This is what the doctor ordered."

Drotti took the glass, downed a swig. "I never imagined I'd do such a thing."

"What? Drink Scotch?"

"No, shoot a man."

"Well, you only wounded him. I was the one who killed him. I did what I had to do and my conscience will deal. I've been there before."

"Want to talk about it?" Drotti asked.

"I don't want you as my confessor, if that's what you mean."

"No, no, that's not what I meant. I meant talking helps . . ."

"My faith is deep, Max. It's the one thing I'm certain about. But there's this other side to me that's harder to quantify. I believe in justice and—"

"Was it justice, Kevin," interrupted Drotti, "or revenge?"

The comment stung. Kevin didn't like to admit some things about himself.

"To be honest, I've been told I have an anger problem, Max. And maybe it's true. When I was stationed in Iraq, I killed a man. I was put on trial for it."

Drotti nodded, looking away.

"I deserved to be tried," Kevin continued, avoiding eye contact. "Not only did I kill him, but also I made sure that he suffered while dying . . . and . . ."

Drotti's mouth was wide open.

"Look, Max, this is hard to talk about," said Kevin, noticing the stunned expression on Drotti's face. Waiting for Drotti to respond, Kevin took a big gulp of Scotch.

"I know it's important to let it out," Drotti finally said. "Did you confess this sin, Kevin?"

"Sure . . . yes." Kevin nodded. "Cardinal Porter, who was then a bishop, absolved me. But, you know what? If I had to do it over again, it wouldn't be different. I'd do it all over. That man deserved what he got."

"I've never met a man who killed another man . . . on purpose," Drotti said. "Are you are suggesting you have no remorse?"

"You don't know the whole story," said Kevin.

"But Kevin, you're a priest. You took solemn vows. It's a mortal sin."

"So is missing Mass on Sunday. Back off," said Kevin. "You don't understand."

"You're frightening me with this kind of talk."

Kevin shot up from his chair, shouting, "The man I killed had raped a young girl, Max! Judge that, will ya? What would you have done? Grant him absolution and tell him to say three Our Father's and three Hail Mary's?" Kevin's face was beet red. He looked away from Drotti. "Max, every night I see her face. I've never seen such fear and hopelessness." Kevin's eyes were moist. "And after it was all over, she found the strength to look at me and thank me."

"I'm sorry," said Drotti. "I didn't know any of this. I can see this must have been an impossibly difficult situation for you."

"Yeah, it was hell. A kind of hell you had to be there to understand."

"I can't begin to imagine," said Drotti.

"I wonder what you'd have done, monsignor?"

"I don't know," Drotti said slowly. "I honestly can't say." Drotti paused for a second. "But you aren't God."

"I'll deal with God," said Kevin.

"Look, I didn't mean to make you angry, Kevin," Drotti said. "Clearly, this is not easy for you."

"No, it's not," said Kevin. "And since I wasn't an ordained priest then, the situation was different. Still, I stand by my actions."

"Why don't we just leave this subject, discuss it another time?" asked Drotti.

"Sure," said Kevin. "Sorry I got so angry"

Drotti stood up. "Look, Kev, I need to go. I'm saying Mass tonight at 5:00."

"OK"

"Why don't we have dinner later after you've had some time to rest?" asked Drotti. "I know a great little trattoria not far away."

"Sure."

After Drotti gave him directions, Kevin sat in his apartment alone, nursing a Scotch. He wasn't sure why he still got so upset about his time in Iraq. Perhaps one never gets over something like that. Not even with absolution and the gift of priesthood.

∞∞∞∞

CHAPTER EIGHTEEN

Rome, Italy

At eight p.m., Kevin waited at the bar of San Angelo, not far from St. Peter's. This was the kind of place which tourists all hoped to stumble upon. It was an old-fashioned trattoria with only a few tables, and lots of wall-mounted photographs showing its steadfast celebrity clientele. There were lively young Italians three deep at the bar, noisily chatting it up, drinking.

Waiting for Drotti, Kevin ordered a Scotch at the bar. When he joined Kevin, Drotti was a half hour late and was huffing and puffing. "Sorry I'm late."

"It's OK, Max," Kevin said. "I just fended off a beehive of great looking women."

Max caught his breath. "Just before I left, I received a call from Cardinal Gianni Serrano. You met him in the pontiff's office, remember? He told me he was taking charge of the 'incident' that happened today, as he called it, and news of it mustn't leak out. He said it'd be handled internally."

"Fine with me," Kevin said, gulping the last slug of his Scotch. "C'mon, let's sit down. I'm hungry."

Kevin was beginning to like Drotti. He'd relaxed and was more accessible and understanding. He knew his way around the Vatican and had insight into the circle that counted. But there were rules Kevin wanted to discuss.

The two men got up and secured a quieter corner table so they could hear themselves talk over the noise.

A waiter approached them and asked, "*Un po di antipastino per cominciare*?"

The waiter ran through a litany of antipasti appetizers to start. Kevin's stock answer was no, because a first course would spoil his appetite. But tonight he was ravenous. "*Che cos'è*? *Affettati*?" he asked.

"No, no," said the waiter. "*Un po di questo, un po di quello, tutto caldo*. It's a little of this, a little of that, and all of it is warm."

"OK," said Kevin. "Sound good to you, Max?"

Max nodded good-naturedly, happy Kevin was no longer dispirited from their earlier conversation.

As the little plates started arriving, there were two small crostini—made of *pane di lariano* and topped with whipped ricotta, drizzled with freshly pressed extra virgin olive oil. Then a wooden trencher full of steaming *sugo*-topped polenta with a sprinkling of fragrant parmesan. After a stressful day, it was just what they needed.

After Kevin and Drotti made small talk, Kevin got serious, clearing his throat. "Max, I'd like to designate you as my good friend. My best listening friend, if that's all right with you."

"Of course." Max nodded while munching on a piece of bread.

"And as my friend, I'll talk to you about things that I wouldn't discuss with anyone else, you understand?"

"Of course."

"First, complete honesty. No backhanded deals or divided loyalties. OK?"

"Agreed."

"Good. Then let's start with the real reason I'm here."

"I don't understand. What do you mean?" asked Drotti.

"Don't play games, Max. If we're going to be friends, you can't be evasive with me."

Drotti put down his fork, and looked Kevin straight in the eye. "It's true that we didn't tell you everything at the beginning, but now you know the real reason. I understand His Holiness himself told you about the secret of Fatima. We believe there's something in the message that we're not getting—that we don't fully understand—which may ultimately destroy the Church."

Kevin shook his head almost imperceptibly. "Look, I believe in the Church and its mission. But this hokey fairytale of secrets told to children by the Virgin Mary appearing all over the place for them, is far-fetched."

"Well, I do believe in miracles," Drotti said. "Don't you?"

Kevin hesitated. "Not sure."

"My beliefs come from deep faith and from hard evidence. Kevin, remember, at Lourdes, Bernadette came back with the phrase, 'the Immaculate Conception'. A fourteen-year-old peasant girl wouldn't have known such a phrase."

Kevin nodded. "I know. I know. I'm not saying I don't believe in miracles—I do. But not all of them. Fatima is about as real as it gets for me. There were 70,000 witnesses to the miracle of the sun. It's the so-called 'secrets' Mary supposedly voiced that I take issue with. These were a bunch of kids. They might have misunderstood."

"Wait a minute," Max said. "Before we talk about the secrets, I want you to look at something." He grabbed his leather briefcase from a side chair and pulled out his iPad. "Here, my dear Doubting Thomas, take a look at this!" Max pressed a button on the tablet; it sprang to life. "Let's see what you think of this. Do you recall the Virgin Mary's appearance at Zeitoun in Egypt in 1968?"

Kevin searched his memory. "I don't remember."

"In April 1968, the Virgin Mary appeared for weeks over a Coptic Church in Zeitoun, a suburb of Cairo. But unlike appearances in the nineteenth century when there were no photographs, in 1968 we had television! And there are shots of her appearance. Plus, it was broadcast live. On Egyptian television."

"Are you sure about this?" Kevin asked.

"Look it up. There were numerous articles and photos in the press at the time. Here." Max placed the iPad on the table. "Here is a photo taken of one of the appearances."

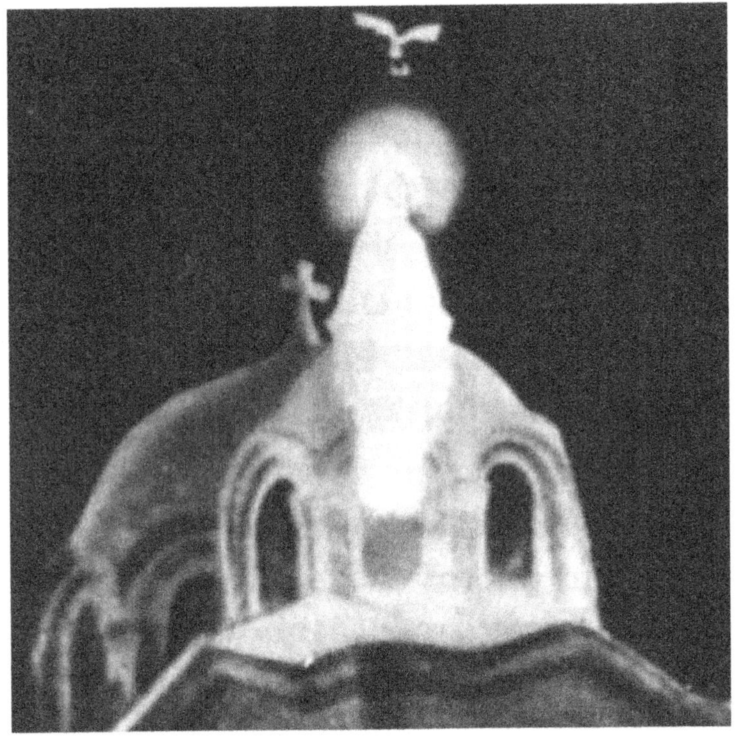

Kevin stared at the picture. "How do you know it's not photoshopped?"

Drotti smiled. "We're not fools, my friend. The picture was examined and reexamined by experts, and remember, hundreds of people witnessed this. It's real."

"Impressive, Max," he said. "But right now, I've got a problem with another miracle, the one I was summoned here for. I've got some good friends at the CIA and they told me the *secret* contained no discernible secret message. So what was it Opus Mundi saw that no one else could figure out?"

Drotti took his napkin, dabbed his mouth, then lifted his wineglass. "Maybe you and I should look at the original."

Kevin picked up his wineglass, too, and took a sip. They'd chosen Prosecco, a much-loved sparkling wine from the Veneto area of Italy.

"Yes. Good point. I think we need to see the original," said Kevin.

Max said, "Only the pope can touch the secret of Fatima. Perhaps an exception can be made, no?"

"And I know just the person to do it." Kevin smiled while raising his glass in a toast.

The waiter approached with their entrees of lasagna al forno. With layers of noodles, meat, ricotta cheese, and a tomato sauce, it smelled delicious.

"What is it about this secret, anyway?" asked Kevin as he dove into the lasagna. "The pope reveals it to the world in 2000, and it's still causing problems."

"It's still a big deal, Kevin. Right after the pope made the secret public, on May 14, 2000, the *New York Times* ran a front page story about the revelation of the secret of Fatima. Mind you, on the front page!"

Drotti refilled both their wineglasses.

Kevin asked, "Can you get us permission to see the original by tomorrow?"

"*Vediamo*," Max responded. Another clink of glasses. "We'll see."

But Kevin took a deep breath, confident his new best friend was the best man on the job.

∞∞∞∞

CHAPTER NINETEEN

Rome, Italy

Kevin woke up groggy. Too much Prosecco, and the Scotch chasers didn't help, either. He finished his second cup of coffee when the phone buzzed. Katie. Her call couldn't have come at a better time. Just hearing her voice brightened his mood.

"How are you, Kevin?" Katie asked. Her voice sounded like honey melting on a hot biscuit.

"Fine . . . sort of," he said.

"Oh? Did something happen?"

"It's too much to go into right now."

"God, Kevin, I hope you're taking care of yourself."

"Mmm, yes and no. I could use some help in that department."

Katie laughed faintly, but ignored his innuendo.

"I have a favor to ask," she said.

"What? Your boyfriend needs Hebrew lessons?"

"Funny. Listen, I got a letter from the agency in Bosnia. My new baby boy is expected to be born in three weeks. I need to go there to pick him up."

"Congratulations, Katie. You'll make a wonderful mother."

"Kevin, I want to ask if you'll join me at the orphanage and baptize my son."

An awkward silence followed.

"Kevin?"

"I'm here, Katie." Kevin didn't relish the thought of being with her when she picked up her new son. *Would she bring her fiancé?* His heart ached at the thought of seeing her under these circumstances. Frankly, he dreaded it.

"Of course I'll do it," he said, casting off the warning bells.

"That's great. And Jimmy will be coming, too, so you'll get to meet him!"

"Wonderful."

"Thanks again, Kevin. This is so important to me. We'll meet in Sarajevo. I'll email you the details."

"Great, Katie. Can't wait."

"Another question if you don't mind," Katie said, her tone serious. "Did you and your friends check up on Greg Maggio's company that I asked you about?"

Kevin hesitated a split second. He had not wanted to burden Toby with this, so he had just googled the man's name and the company name and found nothing of interest. "Yes," Kevin replied. "Nothing particularly suspicious at this point."

"Thanks, Kev. That's a relief. Look forward to seeing you in Sarajevo!"

Hanging up, he wondered how he'd get out of this. One thing he was sure of: He didn't want to meet "Jimmy" and watch his beloved Katie go off with him and a new baby to "happy ever after."

Kevin remained sprawled on the couch, the phone clutched in his hand. He knew there was no way out of this. If he declined to baptize Katie's baby, she would be hurt and disappointed. It would create an obstacle to their continued relationship, one she wouldn't forget.

Thank you, Lord, for yet another challenge.

∞∞∞

CHAPTER TWENTY

Rome, Italy

The following morning, when Kevin opened the door to his apartment, Monsignor Max Drotti greeted him warmly.

"Mornin'," said Kevin.

"Mornin' to you, my friend. It's all done!" Drotti exclaimed. "Permission granted. I redeemed a special favor for this. Shall we go?"

Kevin smiled. "Great. I knew I could count on you, Max. I'll get my jacket."

Drotti and Kevin went to the office of Monsignor Antonio Calvi, archivist of the Vatican since 1974. The archives were located in a subterranean network of offices and storage facilities beneath the Vatican museum complex. Calvi, eighty-four years old, was waiting for them at the door, grinning, looking every bit his age.

Sister Mary Catherine Powell, his assistant, an American nun from Massachusetts, sat by his side.

"*Bienvenuto!*" the old man greeted them enthusiastically. Introductions were made all around. Sister Mary Catherine seemed particularly pleased to meet them. Kevin noticed she was tall and pretty with auburn hair like Katie's. Probably around thirty years old. To Kevin, her perky demeanor and flashing blue eyes made her seem more of a high school cheerleader than a nun.

Calvi spoke good, but not fluent, English. "May I escort you in a piccolo tour before we sit?" he asked.

Without waiting for a reply, Calvi led them past towering shelves of old books and manuscripts, through the room containing records of every bishop and cardinal's appointments for the past six hundred years. The ambiance made Kevin imagine the set of a witchcraft gothic horror movie where cobwebs were hanging from the ceiling of a dungeon filled with books.

Calvi led them down the corridor of indulgences—the official granting of exemptions from suffering for those who'd earned the right to spend less time in Purgatory. Apparently, there weren't too many students or scholars with access to this trove of exclusive information.

As they moved along, Calvi gave explanations of the various documents. Another turn brought them to the *Miscellanea.* Kevin's heart skipped a beat when his eyes landed on the file containing the letters of Joan of Arc, used against her in 1431 at her trial. He'd always been fascinated with the whole story of Joan of Arc.

Arriving at Calvi's office, Kevin thought to himself that it was exactly what he'd imagined: Worn wooden furniture, a carved Italian table resting below a brass chandelier hanging from the cathedral ceiling. *Dracula would love this place,* Kevin thought as they took seats around the table. He couldn't help but think nostalgically of the times he and Katie had watched horror movies. Knowing he'd miss those trysts, he winced.

"I've been told about your mission, Father Thrall," Calvi began. "I'm quite surprised. No one, besides the sitting pope of course, has ever touched the secret. But I know I must follow orders." Calvi threw his head back and struck a pose, looking upward, as if to say his order had come from the highest authority.

With that, Calvi rose and removed a painting of St. Mark from the wall, to reveal behind it an embedded safe. He squinted dialing the combination numbers. "I can assure you," he said, "since I knew you would be coming, this is only a temporary placement. The secret is normally stored in the most secure part of the archives."

From the safe, Calvi removed a jeweled velvet pouch sealed with crimson wax on which a mark had been embedded. As he broke the seal, his face was gnarled with pain. Slowly, his eyes focused as he gingerly removed four sheets of yellowing paper, handwritten and dated 1944. He placed them on a table directly in front of Kevin. "Here," he said. "Please don't take long. It's fragile."

Kevin picked up the pages one by one and examined each one. He couldn't fully understand the written Portuguese script, although the writing was clear and the letters well formed. *Was there a clue in something other than the text?* Kevin perused the secret while the others in the room with him held their breath. The haunting quiet continued for several minutes. No one dared interrupt while Kevin absorbed the document's contents.

Finally, after about twenty minutes, Kevin laid the pages on the table and signaled to Monsignor Calvi that he'd finished. Calvi breathed a sigh of relief and went about reinserting the pages into the pouch.

"If I may, monsignor, I'd like to ask a few questions," Kevin said.

Monsignor Calvi looked at Monsignor Drotti for a signal and Drotti nodded ever so slightly. "Yes, Father," Calvi said. "*Prego*."

Kevin took his notebook out of his jacket. "Would you confirm for me the last time the secret was removed from the safe?"

Calvi's voice dropped an octave. He sounded grave. "It was May 13, 1981, the day John Paul II asked to read the secret."

Sister Mary Catherine piped in, "Monsignor Calvi personally took it to the papal library. That was the day His Holiness was shot by Mehmet Ali Agca in the Square. His Holiness was whisked straight to the hospital. He didn't return to read the secret." Her head dropped in sadness.

"His Holiness Quintus II hasn't read it?" Kevin asked.

"He has, Father, but he read it here in the archives. It wasn't removed."

Kevin nodded. "Did anyone else have access to the secret that day in May 1981?"

Calvi shrugged. "The secret was in its pouch on the table in the library. When the pope was shot, everyone ran to the window to observe the . . . uh . . . activity in the Square. There was much shock, much commotion, as you can imagine."

"So it's possible that it was compromised," Kevin commented.

Sister Mary Catherine said, "Over the years, we've asked that same question. The truth is, we just don't know."

"Who was in the library at the time?" Kevin asked.

Calvi thought for a moment. "Cardinal Umberto Silvano, Cardinal Claudio Marini, who is with the secretariat of state, Cardinal Serrano, and Cardinal Bartilucci, who was the predecessor of Cardinal Porter. And there were several junior clerics and attendants. Of course, I was present."

Kevin scribbled some notes, put his notebook away. "Monsignor Calvi, what do we know about the circumstances under which Lucia wrote the secret in 1944?"

Calvi frowned. "We know that what you've just seen she wrote in the presence of the bishop of Leira and a young man, a cousin of Lucia, who assisted the bishop." Calvi hesitated for a moment before continuing. "In fact, before she died, I met Lucia, along with her cousin who helped her when she wrote the document in 1944. Her cousin went on to become a priest, you know."

Kevin signaled to Max that it was time to leave.

"Thank you for your time," said Kevin. "And thank you for allowing me to read the original document."

"You are most welcome. I hope it's helped," said Calvi.

∞∞∞∞

Max Drotti accompanied Kevin back to his quarters, retracing their walk past St. Peter's and up the hill to Villa Domenica. The sun was setting in faint orange hues along the gardens and the west side of St. Peter's Basilica.

"You look troubled, Max," Kevin said as they were approaching his apartment.

"I thought you ended that meeting rather abruptly," Drotti said.

"Yes, but for a reason. I've got an idea, Max. I need you to do some research. I did a quick calculation in the meeting. The cousin who was there when Lucia wrote the secret had to have been a teenager in 1944. We were told that he later became a priest. If he's still alive he'd be in his eighties. Would you find out his name and see if he's still with us? I'd like to meet him."

∞∞∞∞

CHAPTER TWENTY-ONE

Fatima, Portugal

It took Max only a couple of hours to get the answers he was looking for about Lucia's teenage cousin. Yes, the teenager who'd helped Lucia in 1944 was alive. His name was Father Alberto Salazar. He was a retired priest who lived close to Fatima, near Lisbon, Portugal.

Drotti arranged for the pope's secretariat to phone Father Salazar and inform him that two priests from the Vatican wanted to talk with him. When the pope's chief of staff called Max back, he cautioned that Father Salazar was very perplexed by the request, but felt it was his duty to oblige. The meeting was set for two days from now. Drotti made the plane reservations for him and Kevin to go to Lisbon.

The day before their departure, Kevin phoned Max to brief him on strategies.

"We've got to assume the Opus Mundi crowd is watching us," Kevin said. "We obstructed their plot to assassinate the pope, so we need to take special precautions. They've already come after me once; I'm sure I'll still be a target."

"I'm worried that I'm in over my head, Kevin. You have far more experience with this sort of frolic."

"Max, don't worry. There's method to my madness. We'll stick together. You'll be fine. Here's what we'll do. First, we won't travel to the airport together. We'll split up. Max, I want you to take a cab tomorrow morning to the main railroad station—"

"Stazione Termini," Max said.

"Right. You'll likely be followed. Take a commuter train. At the second stop, jump out just before the doors close. Chances are they won't get a chance to follow you. Take the first train back to Termini and then grab a cab straight to the airport. I'll meet you there. Then we'll board our flight to Lisbon separately."

"This sounds like espionage intrigue. What about you?" Max asked. "How are you going to get there?"

"Don't worry about it. I'm used to this stuff."

The following morning, both men arrived at Leonardo da Vinci Airport. They didn't acknowledge each other's presence. When he spotted Max, Kevin breathed a sigh of relief. He suppressed a smile at Max's dress: flashy sport jacket, tie, and leather briefcase. They boarded their flight, but sat in different rows.

Once they landed in Lisbon, Kevin and Max rented a car and drove the two hours to Fatima. To get to the small community in the hills north of the capital of Portugal, they wound around twisting narrow roads, a harrowing car ride, indeed.

Finally, once in Fatima, Kevin and Max parked in a public parking lot, and wandered the streets of the town, strolling the undulating cobbled paths, flanked by an endless number of small hotels, colorful souvenir shops, and quaint *pensiones*.

"Let's find a place to stay the night," said Kevin.

"This looks good," said Drotti as they came upon a hotel with distressed green shutters. It had a sign with two stars, and an inviting lobby was furnished with simple, functional sofas and a reception desk. The clerk offered them a room for two, with a half bath, for sixty euros a night, including breakfast and dinner. The room had two small beds and a crucifix on the wall. It suited them fine. After settling in around five p.m., they had the rest of the evening to do as they wished.

Dinner at the hotel was served promptly at eight p.m. They were told not to be late. Their meeting with Father Alberto Salazar was scheduled for nine a.m. the following morning, and they wanted to get to bed early. A translator would be provided by the Vatican.

Kevin and Max made their way to the Shrine of Our Lady of Fatima.

One problem for Kevin with this special assignment was that his priestly routine was being compromised. Kevin hadn't said Mass in over a week, and now he'd arranged with the rector of the Sanctuary of Fatima to say Mass in one of the most special places of worship in Christendom. Being from the Vatican had its privileges. In Washington, rarely would Kevin go more than three or four days without saying Mass. Since his arrival in Rome, his routine had fallen apart. He yearned to get it back.

Approaching the basilica, both men were awed by the huge expanse of the esplanade, an area that could hold several hundred thousand souls during the Season of the Miracles, when pilgrims gathered to commemorate holy apparitions. This wide area that culminated in the imposing Basilica was originally the *Cova da Iria*, an ordinary patch of hilly land where villagers had once herded sheep and led simple, pastoral lives. No longer. A rotunda, almost as big as the one in front of St. Peter's, encircled the neoclassical church with a single gleaming spire. The approach to the church was surrounded by a colonnade, creating a plaza where the attendants could stand and participate in services of prayer and meditation. Some made their way to the basilica on their knees, praying the rosary as they inched forward.

The men entered the basilica on their way to the rectory and knelt before the main altar. They marveled at the striking painting above the altar depicting our Lady of Fatima along with the three children. In particular, Kevin noticed the mural with the portraits of several popes. Missing was John Paul II, who credited the secret of Fatima with saving his life when Mehmet Ali Agca shot him in St. Peter's Square in 1981, on the anniversary of the first apparition at Fatima.

After a few moments, Kevin and Max rose and proceeded to the rectory and a reception area for visiting clergy. A Franciscan brother checked the men's credentials. Upon recognizing Kevin's name, he straightened smartly.

"Arrangements have been made, Father," he said. "You will be saying Mass at the Chapel of Apparitions." He handed a stack of vestments to Kevin and turned to Drotti. "And you, monsignor, may say Mass at altar number four in the basilica. These are dedicated to the Mysteries of the Rosary." The two priests might have concelebrated Mass at the same altar, as permitted by Vatican II, but Kevin preferred to say Mass alone.

Both men took their vestments and went to an adjoining room to change. Max didn't say anything, but gave a look to Kevin that implied, "*How did you arrange that?*"

Dressed for the service, Drotti went to his assigned altar in the basilica while Kevin went back outside, down the stairs to the covered, open air chapel to his right. His heart raced as he approached the white marble pedestal on which stood the statue of Virgin Mary, perhaps the most beautiful one he had ever seen. She held a gold rosary in her hands, which were joined together in prayer. On her head rested a large gold crown to which precious jewels were added as adornment.

In 1917, this was the exact spot where the Virgin had appeared to the young shepherds. To Kevin, this felt sacred.

Looking at the Blessed Mother, Kevin felt the pull of a special allegiance with her. *I know you,* he thought. *And you know me. I don't know why I'm here, but I accept your command with all my heart.*

Bowing, Kevin turned to the altar where he was scheduled to say Mass. The altar was a simple slab of white marble on which stood a gold chalice and two candles. A number of pilgrims and nuns sat attentively in a semicircle around the altar, awaiting the start of Kevin's Mass. Kevin arranged the items on the altar, still unnerved by the thought of standing on the spot where the Virgin Mary had appeared to three peasant children.

To serve God, to honor Mary who speaks to my soul, sending me messages I cannot know the meaning of? Is this what my life is about? he wondered.

* * * * * * * * * * *

After Mass, Kevin and Max reunited and walked through the narrow streets of the village to their hotel. As night fell and the time of the candlelight procession approached, the crowds swelled. To participate in the procession from the basilica to the site of the apparitions, many pilgrims carried candles.

Kevin was taking it all in. "There's truly something special here," he said. "More than at other miracle sites."

"The spirituality is penetrating. I feel it in my bones," Max said.

I feel it, too, Kevin thought. *It's a feeling which envelops me relentlessly and never lets up.*

Dinner at the hotel was a lively affair with a number of pilgrims, clerics, and others. Everyone was seated side by side at long communal tables in the hotel's modest restaurant. At the end of the dinner, Kevin raised his glass in a toast.

"No matter what happens tomorrow, here's to our being together. I'm glad we came. Thanks, Max."

Max seemed overcome by Kevin's words, his lower lip quivering. He looked away at the diners in the restaurant, but said nothing.

After a brief walk outside for some fresh air, they retired to their room, read for a while, and called it a night.

∞∞∞∞

The meeting with Father Salazar, who in 1944 had helped the teenage Lucia, transcribe the secret, would take place in the rectory of St. Anthony of Padua, a small church on the outskirts of town. The two-story building had an office downstairs, and a small apartment above where Father Salazar lived.

Apart from a table and a few chairs, there was little else in the room. A large poster of Our Lady and a wooden crucifix adorned the far wall.

The young nun greeting them had a familiar face. Kevin recognized her right away.

"Hello, Fathers." She smiled. "It's good to see you again. I'm Sister Mary Catherine. We met in Monsignor Calvi's office."

"And you will translate?" Max asked.

She smiled. "I'm from Fall River, Massachusetts. We speak more Portuguese there than English!" Indeed, at one time, Fall River was the largest Portuguese American community in the United States.

"Call me MC if you like." Her voice was distinctive, high-pitched, like a schoolgirl's.

As they were conversing, Father Salazar was wheeled into the room. His head lowered, his hair was tousled. He wasn't smiling. As he peered up, his eyes were sad. And he looked older than his eighty-six years. With a nod, he invited the guests to sit at the oak table in the center of the room. Kevin sensed some hostility to their visit. He concluded that the old priest didn't want to answer any questions at all, but given the source of the request, he was obliged to obey.

Max spoke first. He started by saying that their mission was authorized by His Holiness himself. This didn't seem to move Father Salazar. His dour expression remained unchanged. Max went on to say that they had a few questions for him, and they'd be obliged if he'd do his best to answer them.

Kevin spoke next. "Thank you for receiving us, Father," he began. "I understand that, as a young man, you assisted Sister Lucia dos Santos in 1944 with the transcribing of the secret of Fatima."

Father Salazar nodded, speaking quietly. "But why are you asking me these questions?" MC was scribbling away, translating for those present.

"I can't give you answers, Father," Kevin replied. "I can only say the security of the Church is at stake."

With a puzzled look, Salazar turned to Sister Mary Catherine. She whispered something to him. He nodded.

"Yes, I was with Sister Lucia," he replied. "She was ill, worried she might die. She spoke to the bishop who advised her to transcribe the last secret and send it to Rome. The next day she had a vision from Mary, who told her to do as the bishop had requested. That's when I helped her."

Kevin didn't respond immediately. His next question was important. Leaning over, he whispered to Max. Then he went on. "I must ask you certain questions, Father. I hope they'll not offend you, but I must ask them. First, have you yourself personally read the secret?"

MC scribbled, reread her notes, and translated in a fluster.

Salazar was appalled at the question. "Of course not!"

Kevin continued without pausing, "How many have you told about assisting Lucia with the letter?"

Father Salazar frowned and continued in a weak voice. MC stopped writing and translated directly. "I spoke with Pope Quintus II, Monsignor Calvi, and His Holiness Paul VI."

"And would you remember how many pages in total Lucia had written at the time?"

Another quizzical look from the old priest.

"*Seis*," he responded.

"Six?" Kevin repeated.

Max and Kevin locked eyes, eyebrows raised.

"*Seis*," the elderly priest confirmed.

After a few more questions, Kevin and Max thanked Father Salazar, apologizing for having taken so much of his time. Sister Mary Catherine showed them out.

∞∞∞∞

As they checked out of the hotel and booked a late afternoon return flight to Rome, the men were deep in thought, feeling reflective. They said little as they drove south to Lisbon.

Finally Drotti said, "It's about the pages, isn't it?"

Kevin kept his eyes on the road, nodding. "Right. I think so, anyway. I held the secret in my hands. There were only four pages. So whatever it is that's spooked Opus Mundi is on the two pages that are missing. The two missing pages of the secret must have disappeared sometime between May 13, 1981, when Agca tried to kill John Paul II, and last year, when Quintus II read it. The four pages I read contained nothing alarming. We've got to find those two missing pages."

Max tapped the dashboard. "So from this we can deduce with certainty it must have been the last two pages that caused John Paul I's fatal heart attack."

Kevin nodded.

Max shook his head. "I just can't imagine what could be on those pages that would incite Opus Mundi to kill the pope."

"Something scarier than we can even imagine."

CHAPTER TWENTY-TWO

Rome, Italy

His arms propping up his head, Kevin was sitting at the desk deep in thought, his eyes fixated on the laptop screen. Katie's email reminded him that he'd made a commitment he really didn't want to keep. He was knee-deep in the mystery of the secret and finding the two missing pages was his priority. But where to begin? In her email, Katie had said she was thrilled Kevin would be coming to Sarajevo, to baptize the baby and to meet Jimmy. She was planning to arrive on Tuesday and hoped Kevin could join her for dinner. Jimmy was travelling from New York and wouldn't arrive until later that night. Dinner alone with Katie? Kevin thought. Not a tough decision. In fact, a no-brainer.

When Max phoned, Kevin had settled on the sofa with his laptop to check flights.

"I'm going to be away for a few days next week, Max," Kevin said.

"Shall I guess why?"

"No. You'll likely guess right, which'll just piss me off."

"Can I help?" Drotti laughed.

"No, thanks. I'm going to Sarajevo to baptize Katie's adopted child," Kevin said.

"Sarajevo? I'm coming over, Kevin. I have things to tell you."

Kevin barely had put the phone down when Max arrived, out of breath, holding a folder under his arm. He wiped sweat from his brow and plunked down in the armchair facing the sofa.

"If I said your behavior was strange, it'd be a gross understatement," Kevin said. With a Peroni in one hand, he offered one to Max, who accepted it without saying a word.

Max pulled a map out of the papers he was holding. "Medjugorje is about 160 kilometers from Sarajevo. Our Lady wants you to go there."

"Please tell me you're not plagued by apparitions, too, Max."

"No, no. Be serious. You're familiar with Our Lady's appearance at Medjugorje. These are the most trusted recent apparitions by the Virgin Mary. She appears regularly to six visionaries and has told them a total of ten secrets."

Kevin nodded. Maybe Max was on to something.

Max pulled another page from his stack. "Listen to this. It's a transcript of Our Lady's message to the visionaries on August 25, 1991. Here, I'll read you the salient parts:

"*Dear children, today, I also invite you to prayer, now as never before when my plan has begun to be realized. Satan is strong and wants to sweep away plans of peace and joy and make you think that my Son is not strong in His decisions . . . I invite you to renunciation for nine days so that with your help, everything I wanted to realize through the secrets I began in Fatima may be fulfilled.* "

"She referenced Fatima?"

"Yes!" Max almost shouted. "You've got to go to Medjugorje, Kevin. Our Lady must have planned this."

"Let's not get ahead of ourselves. And if I go, what would I be doing there?"

"Obviously, trying to see one or more of the visionaries. Maybe they'll help us with what we're missing in the secret of Fatima."

"And how do I do that?"

Max was prepared for the question. He scribbled something quickly on a piece of paper and handed it to Kevin. "Here's a name and contact info for a friend there. Ivan Koncik. He's not a cleric, but he's well connected, knows everybody in town. He's a friend I studied with. I'll let him know you're coming."

Standing up, Kevin traversed the room. Pacing back and forth, he wasn't sure what to do, but Max's plan certainly wasn't without merit.

"Any questions?" asked Max.

Kevin sat down again. "Tell me what you know about the Medjugorje secrets."

Max consulted his notes. "The apparitions started in 1981. The Virgin Mary appeared to six children, now called 'the visionaries.' Ever since, she's been appearing to three of them. By the way, if they were children in 1981, they're now in their fifties."

"And there were secrets?" Kevin asked.

"Correct. Ten of them. This becomes confusing." Max consulted his notes again. "Three of the visionaries have received all ten secrets; three haven't. When all six visionaries have received all the secrets, Our Lady will stop appearing to them. One of the visionaries chosen by Mary, a lady by the name of Mirjana, will receive the most important message when Our Lady makes her final appearance. We don't know when, except we know Our Lady's last important message will come during Mirjana's lifetime."

"Any clues as to what it is about?"

Max shrugged. "There's speculation, of course. But other revelations suggest a need for prayer to prepare for a major event." Max handed the folder of information to Kevin. "Here's some reading material for your trip."

"While I'm gone, see if you can make progress on the missing pages."

"I'll do my best."

"Thanks, Max," said Kevin.

"I'll try, but if they've been missing a long time, this may be water under the bridge. Impossible." Max said.

Kevin smiled. "Max, the impossible is what we're good at."

∞∞∞∞

CHAPTER TWENTY-THREE

Sarajevo, Bosnia

The flight from Rome to Sarajevo was short. Kevin was studying a guidebook on Sarajevo he'd picked up at the Rome airport.

Kevin hadn't been to Sarajevo, but he'd studied it in college. Sarajevo was the capital and largest city of Bosnia and Herzegovina. In 1914, it'd been the site of the assassination of Archduke Franz Ferdinand of Austria, which had triggered World War I. More recently, during the Bosnia war for independence, following the breakup of Yugoslavia, the city had become infamous for the Serbs' siege of Sarajevo. For four years, from 1992 to 1996, the city was under attack. It was the longest siege in modern history.

On the taxi ride from the Sarajevo airport into town, Kevin was struck along the way by the number of dreary, homogenous Communist-era apartment buildings, detracting from the breathtakingly beautiful mountain vistas and idyllic countryside.

Once in town, the charm of the old city revealed itself and Kevin was eager to take a tour. He checked into the Bristol Hotel, where he and Katie had agreed to stay. The desk clerk said Katie had already arrived.

Kevin went to his room and unpacked. He'd brought his vestments to perform the baptism, including an alb, the long, white garment worn by priests, a stole, a cincture, a braided white cord worn around the waist, and a chasuble, the long, colorful cape. Unpacking, Kevin had to smile, remembering one of his students seeing him in his vestments and saying he looked like Batman.

Before leaving for an exploratory walk, Kevin dialed Katie's room. No answer. He left a message and went out. Dressed in his travel clothes, dark jeans and a blazer, he hadn't shaved; he knew he looked scruffy, but didn't care.

Old town Sarajevo was much as he'd imagined it, a fairytale labyrinth of uneven streets and quaint buildings, some dating back to the sixteenth century. An open-air market was bustling with bargaining patrons filling their bags with fragrant flowers and fresh vegetables. In close proximity, highlighting the new and the old, were churches, mosques, and synagogues, contrasting ancient and modern architecture. Packed cafés and charming restaurants were doing a brisk business of well-dressed young people chatting away.

Kevin went into St. Anthony's, the Catholic Church completed in 1912. His gaze was drawn to the stained glass windows radiating a mosaic of rich purples, reds, and yellows. Then he went to the statue of the Virgin Mary and knelt before her.

Kevin looked up at the Virgin Mary, into her eyes. He began to pray, and then was distracted by a childhood memory of an old church custom. Entering a Catholic Church for the first time, a newcomer would get three wishes. Smiling, he decided to reenact the custom in this new church.

But he then realized he wasn't sure what to wish for. *Something about Katie? What could he possibly ask? About his future as a priest?* He wanted no part of that, preferring to give God the leverage on that one. *So what else was there to wish for? Not much, really. That he learn quickly about what was in the two missing pages of the secret.*

Kevin said a few prayers and left.

Back at the hotel, he dialed Katie's room and this time she picked up and the familiarity of her voice cheered him.

"I'm so happy you're here, Kevin. I can't tell you how much!"

"Wouldn't miss it for the world," he said.

"I spoke to the orphanage. We're meeting there tomorrow morning. They've asked if the mother could join us. They said she wanted to meet us."

"What did you say?"

"I wasn't sure at first. But then I said it was fine. I wanted to assure her the baby will be in good hands with me. And having you there as my support will boost me."

"Sounds good to me. Is Jimmy here?"

"He doesn't get in 'til later. Let's have dinner together."

He was counting on this. He didn't let on that this was reason enough for the entire trip.

∞∞∞

At the front desk, the concierge of the hotel directed Kevin and Katie to a local restaurant, Nanina Kuhinja, whose stone walls and arches had the feel of an old Parisian wine cellar. The two were seated and offered scrolled menus with elaborate calligraphy. As lovely as they were, the copy was completely illegible. With the help of the waiter, they ordered a dish, one with lamb, and a cornucopia of colorful vegetables.

As they were eating, Katie asked, "What's going on with your 007 super-secret assignment?"

"Yep, that's me. James Bond." Kevin smiled, his expression turning serious. "This is my life, Katie. Here is something no one knows. When somebody tried to assassinate the pope not long ago, my friend and I stopped it."

Katie almost choked. "My God!" she said. "You're not joking?"

"Nope. Deadly serious."

"How'd you stop it?" She put her fork down and looked intently at him, wanting to reach out and touch his hand.

"Let's just say I got to the assassin before he got the pope."

"You . . . you mean you killed him?"

"Well, yes . . . something I had to do."

"My God, Kevin. But . . . but . . . are you now in danger?"

"I'll be fine, Katie. Let's not talk about it now; let's celebrate your new baby."

"Kev, is anyone following you?"

"You've been watching too many detective movies!" said Kevin, trying to lighten the mood. Knowing this was one of the last times he'd be with Katie alone, he didn't want to spoil it.

"I . . . I just don't want anything to happen to you, Kev. It sounds like you might be in too deep."

"I can handle myself."

"I know that . . . but . . ."

"But nothing, OK?" He touched her hand with his, then withdrew it. "Dessert?"

Reaching over, Katie took Kevin's arm in hers. She turned his wrist and smiled. "The Mickey Mouse watch?" she said.

Kevin smiled. "I kind of got used to it," he said.

Katie pointed to the pin on her blouse.

"Oh yes, I noticed it," Kevin said. "I guess there're parts of you and me that'll always be there."

Katie refilled her wineglass. "Often I've thought the moment you really fell in love with me was when I gave you this watch. I can still the expression on your face—"

"Wrong," Kevin interrupted, smiling. He realized the wine was loosening their tongues, maybe too much.

"Hmmm." Katie was thinking. "Then maybe it was when I told you about Vukovar, and my dad dying a hero?"

"Wrong, again," Kevin said, playing along.

"Then, when?" Katie asked, lowering her voice, frustrated.

Kevin hesitated a moment. "It was before you gave me the watch. It was that day when we were in Teehan's having a beer after class and you challenged a classmate for thanking God for saving his life. Remember?"

"Not sure . . ." she said.

"Some guy had been in a bus crash on the way to Georgetown. He was one of three survivors. Twenty people died. He thanked God for sparing him. You had a fit."

Katie nodded. "Damn right," she said. "God had nothing to do with it. I said, 'Listen, asshole, if you think God spared you, then why'd he let the other twenty go? What makes you so special?' God doesn't choose either the survivors or the ill-fated. How dumb!"

"I agree, Katie. I admired your spirited resolve that day. You weren't afraid to speak your mind, and you did confront that guy."

"Okay, do you really want to know when I fell in love with you?"

Kevin sensed the conversation was heading in a dangerous direction.

"Let's leave it, Katie."

"Okay." She looked away.

After dinner, they strolled through the cobblestone streets. Kevin again resisted taking her hand.

"I really hope you'll like Jimmy," Katie said. "I want you two to be friends."

What a great idea, Kevin thought. Inside, he groaned. Katie had just brought up the one subject he'd hoped wouldn't come up tonight. It was ruining the wonderful feeling, the utter denial, the joy of hope. He was enjoying just being with her . . . alone. Now he was left with the cold truth: This would probably be the last time he'd be with her.

They kept sauntering quietly through the dark streets, now illuminated by tall lampposts.

"You're quiet, Kevin," Katie said.

"I've got a lot on my plate these days." But in fact, he was consumed by feelings he knew he shouldn't be having. As they walked, Katie put her arm through his. It felt good and natural.

As they approached the hotel, Kevin reciprocated, taking her arm in his, and turned toward her. With half a smile, she pecked his cheek. He caught the faint scent of lavender.

"Meet me downstairs at 9:30 tomorrow morning?" she said.

Sure. Good-night, Katie. Sleep well. Can't wait to meet your guy. Kevin smiled as the elevator door closed shut. He didn't feel like going up to his room. As he exited the hotel, his cell rang.

"Are you in Sarajevo?" Max asked.

"Yes, just finished dinner with Katie."

"Your voice sounds terrible. What's wrong?"

"Nothing and everything. Let's not get into it. What's new there?"

"A lot. I suggest you go to your room and turn on the news. Pope Quintus II is dead."

"My God! What happened?" The image of the robust pope flashed before his eyes. Inconceivable the man had died.

"A heart attack."

"Good God!"

"Kevin, when're you coming back?"

"Katie is picking up the baby tomorrow morning. We'll have a baptism ceremony, then I'll rent a car to go to Medjugorje to see your friend. Depending on how long I stay there, I should be back in Rome Wednesday or at the latest, Thursday."

"Come back Wednesday. Cardinal Porter will see you at three p.m."

As Max hung up, Kevin stood staring at his phone. This couldn't be—*the pope. Dead?*

∞∞∞∞

CHAPTER TWENTY-FOUR

Sarajevo, Bosnia

Kevin hardly slept that night, tossing and turning. His mind went from thoughts of Katie to news from CNN and the constant news coverage of the tragic death of the pope. His first thought was that Opus Mundi had been behind it, but official reports all spoke of a heart attack. Given the tremendous pressure the pope had been under, which Kevin knew more than almost anyone, a heart attack was within the realm of possibilities. Now he was regretting his promise to Katie to baptize her child. His mission was getting more complicated and dangerous. There was little room to veer from his mission for any personal distractions whatsoever.

He was counting the minutes of agitated sleeplessness (unicorns, sheep, cows, goats, the steps of the cathedral, the steps to heaven) until the sun was rising and it was time to get up. He would get through this somehow, but his mind kept drifting back to Katie. Being with Katie was one thing, but he dreaded the thought of meeting the man who'd replaced him.

Slowly putting on his cassock, the alb and cincture, and the green chasuble, he looked in the mirror. "FATHER Kevin Thrall, Father Kevin, Father Kevin Thrall."

If only he could convince himself. Besides his personal neuroses, he had a mission to accomplish in Rome which was getting complicated. The death of a pope brought everything in the Vatican to a standstill. But Kevin couldn't stand still.

Meeting in the lobby, "Good morning, Father," Katie said. She was beaming. Next to her, Jimmy was grinning, like the cat who'd swallowed a canary.

"Kevin, I'd like you to meet Jimmy Stein." She turned to the new Mr. Katie and Kevin took a quick take, extending his hand.

He wore a gray business suit, white shirt, and a bowtie with white pin dots. Jimmy was tall and slim. The bowtie, ridiculously goofy.

"Pleased to meet you," Kevin said.

"Likewise, Father," Jimmy said. "I've heard a lot about you."

"Call me Kevin, please, Jimmy."

"Sure." Jimmy seemed monstrously full of himself.

"I've got a car and driver outside waiting to take us to the orphanage," Katie said. "It's twenty minutes outside of town."

"Well, let's go," Kevin said. "I'm eager to meet your new baby."

They left the hotel and climbed into the black sedan. Kevin sat in the front seat with the driver. Katie and Jimmy sat in the back. As they pulled away, the driver put on some classical music. They sat together in silence looking out the window at the lush and verdant landscape of rivers, farmlands, and hills.

"A beautiful day for a baptism," Katie commented. No one responded.

Entering the driveway to the orphanage, a young Sister ran out to open an iron gate. The driver stopped in a shaded parking area. His passengers got out and walked the gravel path to the wooden double door where an elderly nun, no doubt Mother Superior, was awaiting them. The main building was a huge stone structure with small framed windows. Nearby, a steepled roof topped the orphanage's chapel.

"Welcome, Father, and welcome Mr. Stein, Miss O'Connell," the Mother Superior said warmly. "I am Mother Rosa in charge of this orphanage." She had a Slavic accent and wore a dated nun's habit with a white headpiece covering her gray hair. Through it, her face was rosy and reassuring.

Without waiting for handshakes, Mother Rosa said, "Come inside."

They entered a long vestibule and followed the nun into a parlor furnished in well preserved, turn of the century, rustic furniture. Small tables were covered with hand-embroidered white lace doilies.

"Please have a seat." Mother Rosa gestured toward some worn chairs and a sofa. "Knowing you must be impatient to see your son, we'll complete the paperwork formalities after the ceremony. Before I introduce you to him, may I know the name you have chosen?"

"William Kevin O'Connell," Katie said.

Kevin's heart skipped a beat. He looked pointedly at Katie, aghast.

"William was my father's name and the Kevin in the name is for Father Thrall here, a longtime family friend," Katie said.

"Well then, let us proceed." Mother Rosa approached a side door to the parlor and opened it. A young woman entered, cradling a tiny infant swaddled in white. A middle-aged man in a suit, with a stethoscope hanging from his neck, followed behind her.

"Father Thrall, Mr. Stein, Miss O'Connell, may I introduce you to William Kevin and his natural mother, Gileesa?" Mother Rosa turned to the man with the stethoscope. "And this is Doctor Florian Janiusz. Under our laws, the doctor must give a health report on the newborn to the adopting mother."

Dr. Janiusz nodded and smiled.

Gileesa, the child's mother, smiled at them. She wore a floor-length sky-blue peasant skirt. Her head was covered with a white scarf. Without a word, she handed the infant to Katie. Kevin watched Katie closely. If eyes could convey love, he saw it in hers. The infant's eyes were open and alert, his little hands closed in two tiny fists.

Kevin leaned over and smiled.

"Hello, William Kevin," Katie said as a tear ran down her cheek.

Dr. Janiusz approached Katie and patted the baby's head. "I have performed the examination. He is healthy," he said. His voice was stern and deep, his accent pronounced, although he had a good command of English. "Breathing, blood pressure, hearing, and sight all normal," he added. The doctor unwrapped the baby, pointed to his legs. "He has a case of *talipes equinovarus*, which in English means congenital clubfoot. His right leg turns in. When he's older, this can be corrected."

Katie's face went pale.

"That isn't serious, Katie," Kevin said.

"I . . . I . . . understand," she said slowly. "And he's otherwise healthy, doctor?"

Dr. Janiusz smiled for the first time. "Yes, he's is a healthy infant boy."

Katie covered the child and held him tighter. Kevin touched the baby's forehead and the child's mouth contorted into what seemed like a smile.

Gileesa stood by saying nothing, her expression blank. Kevin noticed that she had light brown hair and a beautiful oval face with refined features. Her wide almond-brown eyes were her most pronounced and unusual feature.

"Does she speak English?" Kevin asked.

"No," Mother Rosa replied. "She is a farm girl. Only eighteen."

Kevin offered his hand and she kissed it out of respect. Kevin blessed her and she bowed her head. When the blessing was over she said, "*Shukran*."

"What did you say?" Kevin asked, startled.

The young girl looked surprised.

"What did she just say to me?" Kevin asked, upset. *Had she just thanked him in Arabic?*

Mother Rosa spoke to the girl in Bosnian, and she answered.

"She said *hvala*," Mother Rosa answered. "It means thank you in Bosnian. Was there anything wrong?"

"No, no. I'm sorry. I must have misheard her. My apologies."

Yet Kevin was sure he hadn't. He'd heard the word *shukran*, which was "thank you" in Arabic. The last person to say the word to him was the young girl who had just been raped. *Of course, it couldn't be the same girl*, Kevin realized, *for she would be much older now*. Perhaps he'd imagined it.

Entering the chapel, they approached the baptismal font. Another priest, Father Ducek, introduced himself as the priest of the orphanage. "May I assist you, Father?" he asked.

"Of course," Kevin replied.

Katie undressed William Kevin and put on his baptismal clothes, a white lace gown she'd purchased in Washington. When she'd finished, Kevin proceeded with the baptism ceremony.

Jimmy stood next to Katie, whose eyes were riveted on the little boy. Kevin was amazed at her instant fluency with the cooing mumbo jumbo of baby talk. *Something natural to new mothers,* he thought.

When the moment came to lower the infant into the baptismal font, little William Kevin cried briefly, then stopped as Kevin lifted him up and handed him back to Katie. Father Ducek said a prayer in Latin and looked on. Kevin wished he could share her happiness, but knew it wasn't appropriate. He didn't want his unresolved romantic feelings to muddy the joy of a baptism and a new adherent to Christ.

When it was time to leave, Katie embraced Gileesa and told her she would stay in touch. When her son departed, Gileesa showed little emotion. Everyone knew how painful the separation must have been for her. But she was strong and brave. Probably she consoled herself with the hope for a better life for her baby.

But Kevin noticed her eyes betraying the pain she was feeling. When she bid good-bye to him, once again she fell to her knees and kissed his hand. He looked into her eyes for the last time. Her eyes lingered in his, and he saw her pain.

In the car on the ride back to Sarajevo, Katie was cooing to her little boy.

Jimmy, seated by Katie and the baby, said to Kevin, who was in the front seat, "I just want you to know, I love Katie very much, and I'll take good care of her."

Kevin nodded. "Thank you. I know you will," he said. He had no more to say.

At the hotel, they parted. For Kevin, this awkward moment couldn't have ended soon enough. He hugged Katie. They said their good-byes.

"Thanks again, Kevin. I won't ever forget."

"I won't, either," he said.

"And thanks from me, too," Jimmy said. "This meant a lot to Katie, so it meant a lot to me, too."

Kevin rode the elevator up by himself, up to his room to change. He didn't want to indulge his troubled heart. The little boy had made a lasting impression on him, knowing indifferent times in a different life, this little creature might have been his, and he might have been a husband, dad, lover, to Katie. This was a love that wouldn't let go.

But in life, irrevocable choices have to be made, and he'd made this one, for better or worse. Now was the time to prepare for the next challenge, a test of wills and strength against an unseen foe, and a secret which might change the course of the Church. Adrenaline was rushing. It was the thrill, the rush of the chase. It was about winning and losing. Combat time.

We've been expecting you, Mr. Bond.

∞∞∞∞

CHAPTER TWENTY-FIVE

Medjugorje, Herzegovina Region

Kevin had promised Max he'd go to Medjugorje. With the pope dead, he also wanted to get back to Rome as soon as possible. But Medjugorje was nearby and there'd been reports of Virgin apparitions there for decades. Maybe he'd find a key to the mystery of the secret of Fatima. Kevin decided to do it, to make it a fast trip and head back to Rome.

The car Kevin rented for the trip to Medjugorje was a lemon—rickety, with a stick shift. Kevin ground through the gears.

On Max's suggestion, Kevin stopped in the village of Mostar to find a place for the night. Pulling into the Motel Sehrer, in the center of the old town, Medjugorje still was another twenty-five kilometers away.

The motel room was modest, with a bed, a desk, and a chair, also featuring a panoramic view of the parking lot. Propped on the single, creaky bed, Kevin phoned Ivan Koncik, Max's friend who was meeting him in Medjugorje.

"Yes, yes, Father," Koncik answered cheerfully. "Massimo informed me of your visit and I'll help in any way." Koncik spoke good English, with a thick Slavic accent.

"Many thanks, Mr. Koncik. However, my trip has been cut short, so I only have this afternoon and tomorrow morning. May I see you today?"

"Yes, of course. Please accept my deepest sympathy on the loss of His Holiness. What a tragedy."

"Thank you."

Kevin bought a panino sandwich with crusty country bread, salame, mortadella, tomatoes, and lettuce from the motel restaurant and, while driving to Medjugorje, ate in the car. Medjugorje is located in the Herzegovina region of western Bosnia and Herzegovina, close to the border of Croatia. By this time, Kevin had read the material carefully from Max. But it was puzzling, almost a riddle. The Virgin Mary had given the six visionaries ten secrets. Some of the secrets were personal to the visionaries; others were universal, and would impact the entire world. One secret foretold a sign over a mountain near Medjugorje, now dubbed "Apparition Mountain."

Mirjana was the visionary whom Our Lady assigned to divulge the secrets. No specific date was given, but Our Lady had said the secrets would be known during Mirjana's lifetime. As hearsay would have it, Mirjana also had received from Our Lady a tangible physical parchment with the ten secrets written on it, along with the precise dates each event would occur.

Kevin's interest was in one particular secret—the one linked to the secret of Fatima. In this case, it'd give him the missing pieces of the Fatima secret. *But how likely was it that the visionary would reveal the secrets to him?*

Koncik had suggested they meet at the Church of St. James, nestled in the heart of Medjugorje. Once Kevin entered the village, he had no trouble finding St. James, which he'd seen in the guidebook. It was built in a neo-Gothic 1960s modern style, with soaring twin towers identical in every detail, including the clocks on each tower.

Kevin parked his car and made his way on foot to the church. Kevin dressed in a clerical black suit to simplify the identification for Ivan Koncik. Max had given Kevin a good idea of Koncik's style.

Milling in the crowd, and fitting Max's description, was a middle-aged man with long hair and a beard, a rumpled jacket, and a general appearance that might be characterized as unkempt. Kevin knew it was his man, and wasted no time accosting him and shaking hands.

"So nice to meet you, Father," Koncik said.

Kevin smiled back. "Call me Kevin, please."

"Indeed, Kevin. And, of course, I am Ivan. Welcome to our holy village. Let me show you around."

Entering the church, Kevin genuflected and made the sign of the cross. The interior of the church was dark and vast, with rows of wooden pews.

Ivan gave a brief history of St. James and then said, "Come, I'll drive us to Podbrdo Mountain. It's too far to walk."

"Apparition Mountain," said Kevin. "Correct?"

"Correct," said Ivan. "That's its nickname."

Once there, they hiked up the steep, rock-strewn path leading to the location where Our Lady appeared. Tens of millions had climbed this very path—pilgrims from all over the world.

Reaching the top, they paused, looking down on the village. St. James dominated the landscape, nestled amongst stone cottages and winding streets.

"In 1981, this is where it all began," Ivan said, looking out across the horizon. "Apparition Hill." He gestured toward the town. "In this village, we are all believers."

"It feels holy and sacred," said Kevin.

"It is. Come, I'll take you to the exact spot of the first apparition." As they started down the path, Ivan motioned for Kevin to follow.

Not far away, they happened upon a plain wooden cross partially buried in a mound of rocks. "This is it," Ivan said. "This is where Our Lady first appeared to Mirija, not to be confused with Mirjana, who's also one of the six."

Seeing the cross, Kevin knelt down and said a prayer.

"Down below," Ivan said, pointing to a footpath leading down the other side of the hill, "I'll show you the other cross."

Kevin nodded.

Continuing down the footpath at the bottom of the hill, they found another wooden cross, this one painted blue. Near the base of the cross stood a wooden statue of Our Lady.

"This is where another man, also named Ivan, also a visionary, comes regularly, and the Virgin Mary appears to him."

Kevin looked back up to the top of Apparition Hill. "Is it that, up there, where the 'permanent vision' the visionaries spoke about will take place?"

"Yes," Ivan responded. "We don't know what it'll be, but it'll be like nothing we've ever seen. And it will be permanent."

"Ivan, do you believe the revelation about the 'permanent vision'?"

"Of course. But when I've seen it I'll believe even more." Ivan smiled wryly.

"I understand," said Kevin.

"Come, let's head back to the car. That's all I have to show you," Ivan said.

"Sure, but could we go sit somewhere when we get to Medjugorje? A café or something? We need to talk."

"Yes, of course."

The two men climbed into the Fiat and drove back to the hamlet. Once they parked on the side of the street, Ivan selected an outdoor café in the middle of Medjugorje. Priests, brothers, and nuns were crowding its main square.

Kevin ordered a coffee, Ivan, a cold beer.

"May I ask what you do?" Kevin asked.

"Years ago I was a mechanic," Ivan said. "But when the Virgin Mary appearances began, I devoted my life to the Church. I know the visionaries. They trust me."

"That's good," said Kevin, stirring a sugar cube into his coffee.

Ivan's bushy brows furrowed, and his eyes narrowed. "I don't abuse my relationship with them. My money is earned as a tour guide." Ivan leaned in, winked at Kevin, and continued. "Let me share something with you, my friend. Miracles are good for business."

"I imagine so," said Kevin. He didn't relish the idea of miracles being traded like business commodities, but at the same time, he didn't think Ivan's soothsaying could be far from the truth.

Leaning back, Kevin took in the full view of Apparition Hill. A throng of pilgrims were strolling around the town square.

"You wanted to talk?" Ivan sipped his beer, folded his hands on the table, and leaned forward.

"Ivan, I need your help," Kevin said. "There's a monstrous threat to the Catholic Church. You and I both love the Church and are committed to it."

"What's this threat?" asked Ivan, his eyes growing bigger.

"I can only tell you that it has to do with the secret of Fatima. I'm here because many trusted observers have claimed that the Fatima and the Medjugorje revelations are related. Does that ring a bell with you?"

Ivan nodded. "Indeed, it does. And I've heard it from the highest authority, if you understand what I'm saying." He paused, leaned forward, and whispered, "One of the ten secrets is about Fatima, of that I'm certain."

"Which one, Ivan? And how is it related?"

"I cannot say."

"Well, perhaps you could arrange for me to meet one of the visionaries?"

Ivan shook his head. "As a rule, they don't talk to outsiders, but perhaps I could convey a message?"

Kevin thought for minute. "Look, I need to know about the secrets they've heard. I've got to find out if and how their secrets are connected to the secret of Fatima. It'll be easier for me to figure it out if Mirjana, or one of the others, is willing to talk directly to me. If it'd help, I'll get a high Vatican official to endorse this."

"I understand, Kevin. I do. But the visionaries have their own rules." He pointed to the sky. "I will see what I can do. Could we meet here again tomorrow?"

Kevin had played his hand, gone as far as he could. "Yes. Thanks very much, Ivan. Can we meet in the morning? I'm returning to Rome tomorrow afternoon."

"Certainly. Ten o'clock. I'll wait for you here."

∞∞∞∞

When Ivan left, Kevin lingered in Medjugorje. He hadn't made plans for the evening and he was drawn to this place, curious about it. Since 1981 it'd attracted more than twenty million visitors. The Virgin Mary had appeared to three children, who were now grown adults, and she was continuing to appear to some of them daily! The Vatican hadn't officially sanctioned these apparitions as miracles, but on the other hand, they hadn't discredited them, either. To Kevin, it was fascinating.

Like most towns where a religious occurrence had taken on fantastic proportions, the economy was thriving. Lourdes, Fatima, and now Medjugorje, all had a bustling industry of inns, restaurants, and tourist shops.

Kevin walked down the street and went in one of the shops. Rosaries were a big seller, as were statues of the Virgin Mary and a solar-powered miniature of the children waving. Exploitive commercialism was everywhere. Kevin wondered how much of this was a hoax, engineered by the greed of these villagers.

Kevin walked back up Apparition Hill. He was drawn to this mystical place. But when he got there, his thoughts turned to Katie. It would be hard for him to get past her marriage and her having started a life with another man. Even if he left the priesthood, it was too late: The only woman he'd ever loved had committed to someone else.

Kevin wasn't sure about Jimmy. He seemed decent enough, but in Sarajevo, Jimmy had gone out of his way to say as little as possible to him. Perhaps Jimmy was still wary of Kevin's past with Katie. But surely he knew Kevin wasn't still a threat. Something bothered Kevin about him, though. He wasn't sure what.

Kevin dined alone in Mostar at an outdoor café. He was looking forward to getting back to Rome. When he finished his meal and got back to his room, he turned on the TV and clicked on CNN. The death of Pope Quintus II was still the main story. After a while, the coverage became unbearably repetitive. Kevin turned it off and went to bed.

In the morning, Kevin rose, prayed, and dressed in civilian clothes. His three-day beard had turned into a scruffy four-day beard, and his jacket was musty and wrinkled. He didn't care. He had more serious things to worry about. He checked out of the hotel, then drove to

Medjugorje and parked near the café. Ivan was there already, seated at an outdoor table and nursing a breakfast beer.

The café was half-filled with tourists and clerics. The sky was bright and the aroma of coffee filled the air.

"Good morning, Kevin." Ivan rose and shook his hand.

"Good morning, Ivan." Kevin sat down, gestured for a waiter, and ordered a croissant and a double espresso. "Any news for me?"

Ivan squirmed in his chair. Finally, he leaned over and spoke in hushed tones. "Last night I met with one of the visionaries. I can't say which one."

Kevin realized that whatever it was that Ivan was going to say, it wasn't going to be easy for him.

"Perhaps this is my imagination, but the visionary seemed to know you," Ivan said.

"Oh? How is that?" Kevin asked.

"The visionary nodded repeatedly when I spoke of you and your visit and your interest in Fatima."

"Go on."

"The visionary said to give you a message. I . . . I wrote it down." Ivan fumbled in his jacket pocket for a piece of paper. "Forgive me, but I wrote it in Croatian. I will translate."

"Yes, please," Kevin said.

"The visionary said, 'Dear Father, please understand that Our Lady prays for you. Your true mission begins now. Please be careful. Much rests on your success.' That is the message from the visionary." Ivan crumpled the paper in his fists and looked up.

"Ivan, are you sure that's all there is? It tells me nothing."

"I'm sorry, Father. I wrote faithfully what was said." Ivan hesitated for a second, then continued. "The visionary added something she said was for you personally, Kevin."

"Oh?"

"She said, Mary has heard you. You will soon find answers to questions about your life."

With his sophisticated counterintelligence training, Kevin was above emotional entrapment. Rarely in these situations could he be provoked into reacting. But this time, it was hard not to, to maintain his reserve. He shivered. The message was both personal and jarring. After a moment of awkward silence, he said, "I'm very grateful for this message, Ivan. As you indicated, it'll all become clear in time."

"I hope this has helped," said Ivan.

"Yes, yes, it has."

Kevin settled the bill and the two men walked to his car.

"Thank you again, Ivan," he said. "You have been a true friend."

Ivan bowed and then put his hand on his heart, adding with a broad smile, "God bless you, Father. And should you know of others coming for a pilgrimage to Medjugorje, please remember me."

Just before Kevin started the car, his phone buzzed. A text from Katie. *Made it home OK. Got a nanny for little William K. Off to Cayman Islands with Greg next week to set up a new offshore company. Oof!*

Something troubled Kevin, and it wasn't just that Katie was off to the Caribbean with her client and occasional dinner companion. It didn't ring right, but he wasn't sure why. Jealousy? Uncertainty? He couldn't rationalize the concern but his instinct had always been his friend. To add to his discomfort, he had only given Katie a perfunctory report on the company she had asked him about, not wanting to bother Toby with it. He searched through his Google history and came up with the names. He called Toby and gave him the names of Greg Maggio and Consolidated Investors United. Toby agreed to do the work and didn't even make a wisecrack about it. Everyone needs a friend like Toby.

∞∞∞∞

CHAPTER TWENTY-SIX

The Vatican, Rome, Italy

On the flight back to Rome, Kevin slept the whole way. He was only jarred awake when the plane's landing gear jolted the passengers as its wheels hit the runway. Yawning, he switched his phone on, just as a text buzzed in from Max: "I'm here at the airport."

"Thanks," Kevin texted back. "Just landed."

When Kevin got off the plane and had made his way through customs to exit, he saw Max waiting for him.

"Hey, thanks for picking me up," said Kevin.

"No problem," said Max. "Good flight?" He was dressed in a cassock and mozzetta, uniform for those with the title of monsignor.

"I slept the entire way."

"Was the trip successful?"

"Yes, somewhat," said Kevin. "I'll explain more later."

"I'm parked over here," Max said, motioning to the Alfa Romeo in the parking lot.

The two men walked quietly to Max's car and got in. As Max drove back into the city, following the signposts to the Vatican, they spoke little.

Max commented on how Rome had changed. The pending election of a new pope had given the city an aura so electrifying, you could feel it humming through the streets and cafés.

As Kevin rode in the car, Max reminded him about the last time the two of them had made this trip from the airport.

"No one's trailing us this time," said Kevin. "I've been looking out."

"That's good," said Max. "I don't really enjoy a cat and mouse chase—especially when it involves guns."

"I know," said Kevin. "Oh, they're too preoccupied with the conclave to bother with us."

"Right," said Max. "Nine days from now, the Assembly of Cardinals who've been summoned will meet to elect the new pope. It usually starts fifteen days after the pope's death."

"When will he be buried?"

"He's lying in state at St. Peter's, but must be buried within six days of his death. That's Friday."

"That's right, I remember," said Kevin. "Cardinal Porter wanted to see me?"

"We're going there now. I've been invited along."

"OK, but first let me go change into a suit for our meeting," Kevin said as Max pulled into a parking space in one of the Vatican garages.

"Sure."

In fifteen minutes Kevin was ready to go to Cardinal Porter's office. Both Max and Kevin had to go through the routine protocols for admittance. It went quickly. Soon they found themselves standing before Cardinal Porter.

Cardinal Marini and Cardinal Serrano were seated at a conference table. When Cardinal Serrano saw them, he raised his hand in acknowledgment, but did not smile or speak. Marini fussed with his paperwork, but didn't look up. His face, like Cardinal Porter's, was puffy, with swollen eyes.

"Sit down, gentlemen," Porter said, motioning to the table where Cardinal Marini sat.

Kevin noticed Cardinal Porter wasn't offering coffee or refreshments. This wasn't a social visit.

Porter went to the door and peeked outside. No one should hear what he was about to say. Satisfied they were alone, he closed the door and went back to the table where the men were sitting. "As you may know, one of Cardinal Marini's portfolios is Vatican security. Cardinal Serrano supervises the papal guards. What I am about to tell you, as you will see for yourselves, is of the highest confidentiality."

Both Kevin and Max nodded.

"Allow me to get right to the point." Porter's breathing was heavy. "His Holiness did not die of a heart attack. He was poisoned. It happened during his meeting with staff members."

What? Kevin froze. Max's mouth fell open. Neither moved a muscle.

"How?" Kevin asked quietly.

"There was evidence of poison in his cup of tea."

"Who served the tea?" Kevin asked. Max shook his head in disbelief.

"At the moment, we don't have all the details," said Serrano. "But we will get to the bottom of this. Please remember, for now, until we know more, it's imperative we keep this quiet. This news is too shocking to release to the public."

"Of course." Kevin and Max nodded in unison. They were aware that the rumor mill—inside and outside the Vatican—posited Serrano and Marini as rival candidates for the next pope. Every word they said publicly, as well as internally, would be scrutinized.

Porter looked directly at Kevin. "Father Thrall, you are charged with heading the investigation of the pope's death. Monsignor Drotti will assist you."

Kevin rose. "Thank you, Your Eminence. We'll do our best."

"How can I help?" asked Porter.

"The first thing I'll need is a list of the staff members who were with the pope. The next thing is the toxicology report."

"Of course. We've anticipated this request. I already have them for you." Porter handed Kevin a folder. "Cardinal Marini is keeping Vatican security out of this for the time being. We simply don't know who to trust."

Kevin nodded. He was beginning to think no one could be trusted. Except Max.

"When this happened, what was the purpose of the meeting?" Max asked.

"It was routine," said Cardinal Porter. "An international assemblage of clerics from different orders. About fifteen people in all."

"I'll do everything I can to get to the bottom of this," Kevin said, his mouth parched. When he came to Rome, Kevin had no idea how serious or critical to the Church his trip and participation would become. *If this were a baseball game,* he thought, *they'd just switched to serious hardball.*

"Thank you, gentlemen," said Cardinal Porter. "Now if you'll excuse me, I must prepare for the conclave. The cardinals will soon be arriving from all parts of the world."

∞∞∞∞

CHAPTER TWENTY-SEVEN

Rome, Italy

The next morning for breakfast, Kevin ate a couple of chocolate croissants with French roast coffee. The previous evening he'd spent a long time going over the list of people who were at the last meeting with Pope Quintus II. He had some new theories. Disconcerting ones, at that. As he sipped his coffee, his cell phone rang to *Stairway to Heaven.*

"Hi, Father, it's MC." The voice was female, young and alive.

"Who?"

"Oh sorry, it's Sister Mary Catherine. Remember, in Portugal I translated for you?"

"Sure," he said. *The cheerleader nun.* "What can I do for you?"

"Father, I just got a call from Father Salazar, the priest we visited in Fatima. He said he had some additional details he wanted to share with you. Mind if I come over?"

"Um . . . sure . . . that's fine. Give me a couple of minutes."

Sister Mary Catherine chuckled. "I'll be there in a half hour."

Kevin put another pot of coffee on to brew and scurried about the room, smoothing the comforter on the bed and tidying up. He wasn't used to having female company, even a nun.

MC arrived right on time. Kevin watched her approach his door on the security monitor, which was installed after the kidnapping incident. She was wearing a navy blue blouse, and a short, black skirt that swayed as she walked. Her outfit was complemented by black knee socks. No head covering. With her short, tousled brown hair, she looked more like a schoolgirl than a nun. In fact, the only sign pointing to her religious affiliation was a gold cross around her neck.

"Hi!" she exclaimed as Kevin opened the door.

"Hey, Sister. C'mon in. Want some coffee?"

"I'd love some! Can I help?"

"Nah, already made it."

Kevin's cell phone buzzed. It was Max. Before answering, he pointed the nun toward the kitchen. "Coffee's in there, Sister. Cups in the cupboard. I've got to take this call, OK?"

"Sure," she said, smiling again. Was this nun really batting her eyes at him? *Youth,* he decided. *Just her youth. Undoubtedly she was used to men's attentions—even as a nun.*

"I'll be back in a minute." Kevin went into the bedroom, closing the door behind him.

Holding the cell phone to his ear, Kevin listened to Max blather on about nothing in particular. He interrupted him. "Um . . . Max, if this isn't urgent, I'll call you back."

"Sure, it can wait," Max said. "You busy?"

"I have company," said Kevin. "I'll explain later. But stay close, okay?"

Before joining Sister Mary Catherine in the living room, Kevin grabbed the Glock from the drawer and put it in the back of his pants at the waist.

"So, what's the message from Portugal?" he asked.

"Mmmm, the coffee's soooo good," she said, holding the cup to her lips.

"I know. My special blend. Glad you like it."

"Love it, Kev. It's delish. I poured one for you," MC said in a singsong twitter, pointing to the mug on the table.

Kevin hesitated a moment, seemingly distracted. "Hey, I don't like it too hot. Why don't you have a sip of it for me?" he said.

"Oh, I've got my own. Not too hot."

"No, I insist," Kevin persisted.

MC looked rattled. "What do you mean, Kevin?" she inquired with a pout.

With that, Kevin grabbed the pistol from his back pocket and pointed it at Sister Mary Catherine. She reacted slowly, staring at the gun, incredulous.

"What's this, Kevin? You're frightening me," she said, her voice trembling.

"You see, Sister, I have a list of those who were in the room when Quintus died. He was poisoned. Tea, wasn't it? Coffee would work as well. You were there. Your name was on the list. So, shall we say, I decided, if anyone who'd been in that room visited me, I'd use extreme caution."

"A man can't be too careful, I suppose," said MC, struggling to regain her composure.

"Move into the bedroom," Kevin said, continuing to point the gun at her. Just in case she had friends close by, he wanted her out of view of the living room picture window.

"Of course, that sounds like fun," said MC, stepping into the bedroom and stopping by the bed. She was taking this whole thing lightly, as if it were some kind of joke.

Kevin closed the door behind them. "I saw you pouring something in my coffee. It's your turn to talk," he said.

Mary Catherine set her coffee cup down on the nightstand, looked around the room, then back at Kevin. "You know, you're an attractive man, Kevin," she said. "The poison in your coffee wasn't personal. We can be on the same side. We don't have to be enemies here." She removed her sweater and started unbuttoning her blouse.

"What're you doing?"

"Oh, it's mighty hot in here." MC fanned herself, then removed the blouse and started unbuttoning her skirt. Carefully she stepped out of it, never taking her eyes off Kevin.

"Look! I don't know what you think you're doing, but—"

"Oh, Kevin . . . gorgeous Kevin . . . don't be a fuddy-duddy."

She stood before him in nothing but her French bra and matching barely-there thong.

Holy hell! Why didn't this ever happen before I became a priest? Kevin wanted to smile, but quickly repressed it.

"Enough!" Kevin ordered, the gun shaking in his hand.

"Don't judge me, Kevin. You know you want to play. You're good looking, you have needs, and mmm . . ." MC said, "let's see, you remember who first saw the resurrected Jesus, right? Of course you do! It was Mary Magdalene. And she was a Really. Bad. Girl, Kevin."

She started moving closer to Kevin.

"Please don't go any further, MC. This is hard enough." Clearly his resolve was weakening, but the gun was still on her.

"Oh, I know it's hard! Are you going to shoot me, Kevin?" she asked playfully. "Will it hurt?" MC reached back and unfastened her bra. She removed it, revealing full, round breasts. She slid off her thong. "What's crossing your mind right now, Kevin?" MC moved playfully closer to him.

"Back in high school, I had fantasies about moments like this," Kevin said.

"Well, well . . ." MC smiled and opened her arms wide, revealing the full shape of her naked body. "Come and get it."

Good God! Kevin was helpless. He couldn't physically prevent her from undressing and still keep control of the pistol. *Then again, did he really want to stop her?* He couldn't help but admire her body, her full breasts. Everything was desirable about this young woman. *Oh God, his body wanted her! It was on fire, screaming for her.* His blood pressure was rising, his breath quickening.

"I want you, Kevin," she whispered, moving closer. "Come here . . . please."

Maybe just this time . . .

"Aroused, Kevin?" Moving closer to him, she reached over to stroke him. The gun in his hand slipped, nearly dropping. "Let me help you with that."

With a young naked woman in front of him, offering her body, Kevin had only seconds to decide. *Hell, he was a man, after all. But God sends tests to measure faith. And He asks: Who are you? A common man or a man of God?*

Just before throwing her on the bed and taking her, reality came screeching.

As if lightning was striking, he moved back abruptly and yelled, "Good God, woman! You assassinated a pope! And now you tried to kill me. And you're wanting to fuck me?"

"Well . . . no . . . yes . . . I mean . . . I didn't kill him, Kevin. I could never have done that. I didn't even know it was going to happen. Someone else poisoned him. But yes, I was there."

"But killing me is okay because I'm a low-ranking priest?"

"I didn't want to kill you, but like you, I'm a soldier. I follow orders. But I don't want to kill you. You can join me. We don't ever have to mention it again. We can make love, forget all about the poison."

"Have you lost your mind?" Kevin shook his head. "Has Opus Mundi totally brainwashed you? Now, put your goddamn clothes back on. You disgust me."

"Oh, Kev . . . c'mon. You know you want me."

"No, I don't. You're delusional. Now, get your clothes on. I mean it." He pointed his gun at her.

Sighing, MC put on her clothes. She said, "I believe in Opus Mundi and its leaders. You just don't know enough about us. We're on the angels' side of the Church. The devil has infiltrated the Vatican. Our mission is to stop him."

"You're out of your mind," Kevin said. He kept the pistol pointed at her while he made a call.

"Who are you calling?" she asked, buttoning up her blouse.

"Security. They'll take you away; you'll likely spend the rest of your life behind bars."

"I'm leaving now," she said, as she fastened the last button on her blouse.

Kevin held his arm out and motioned her to stop. "You're not going anywhere. I'll shoot if I have to."

"Oh, I believe you, Kevin," she said as she headed to the living room. She turned her head back and added, "I know your violent history."

Kevin yelled, "Stop right there."

She turned around and smiled at him again.

"Tell me about Opus Mundi," Kevin asked. "Who runs it? What's in the secret of Fatima? What's in it that Opus Mundi's so frightened of?"

"Oh, Kevin. Silly boy. Join me—join Opus Mundi!"

"Look, tell me. I'll get your sentence lightened. Otherwise, you're gonna have a lot of time in prison to think about it."

The distant sound of sirens whistled in the background. MC approached the table and reached for the cup of coffee she'd poured for Kevin.

"Your coffee was really good," she said. "Time for a refill."

"Don't!" he shouted. He lurched forward to grab the cup from her hand, but he was too late. In two quick gulps, she swallowed the coffee.

"It's really better this way, Kevin," she whispered.

Sister Mary Catherine's face was contorting and foam was bubbling from her mouth. She collapsed in a chair, her body jerking in spasms.

Dropping the pistol, Kevin grabbed her by the shoulders. "Don't die on me! Do you hear me? Don't you dare die on me!"

Just then the Vatican Secret Service banged on the door. Kevin let go of MC and ran across the room to open it.

Three uniformed men rushed in. Kevin pointed to the floor. "She poisoned herself. She may still be alive. Hurry! Get her to the hospital immediately."

One of the Secret Service men ran over to Sister Mary Catherine in the chair and examined her. She was still convulsing, but less violently than before. He put his face next to hers to listen for breathing. Then, he put his hand on her neck, looking for a pulse. "Not dead, but she will be soon."

The other Secret Service men rushed in with a stretcher. They placed MC on it, covered her, and whisked her out to the waiting vehicle.

Kevin watched the ambulance speed away, its lights flashing, sirens blaring. He couldn't believe what had just happened. He held his trembling hands out in front of him and shuddered. *God, please, help me!*

Slowly, calm overcame him. Kevin called Max. "Get over here, Max."

"Kevin, is everything all right?"

"Please, Max. Just get over here." Then he went into the bedroom, lay down on the bed, and sighed deeply. *Lord, is this really what you meant for me? I'll embrace whatever it is you want me to do, but please, please let me know what it is.*

∞∞∞∞

CHAPTER TWENTY-EIGHT

Rome, Italy

Max listened in disbelief as Kevin recounted the episode he'd just had with Sister Mary Catherine. Kevin sat in his easy chair, clinging to a wool blanket draping his body.

"Good God! She poisoned the pope?"

Kevin was still shaken. "She said she didn't, that it wasn't her doing, and I believe her. Another Opus Mundi operative was there. He did it. But apparently she didn't have qualms about snuffing me, though. After I let her know I was on to her, she tried poisoning herself with the dose that was meant to kill me."

"Oh, Kevin, I'm so sorry. Lucky you studied that list last night," said Max.

"I know. If I hadn't recognized her name, I'd now be in the morgue. Max, get in touch with the hospital."

"You want to talk to her?"

"Yes, let's see how she's doing. I need to talk to her. She's an important link to Opus Mundi. She's our best hope to get wind of their plans with the secret of Fatima."

Max nodded. "I'll get right on it. It's a mess out there, though. The cardinals are coming in from all over the world and the conclave begins in the morning. When they gather in the Sistine Chapel, they'll be crawling all over the place with their extended entourage."

"I know," said Kevin. "It's a complete mess. We have our work cut out for us."

The papal conclaves were held in secret in the Sistine Chapel. Kevin was familiar enough with the chapel to know there were a series of small rooms accessed by a secret door to the left of the altar. While the conclave proceeded, they were there for the cardinals to relax during breaks.

Max made a couple of calls, name-dropping his VIP status, and managed to summon the doctor in charge of treating Sister Mary Catherine.

Hanging up, Max turned to Kevin, "She'll live. They pumped her stomach before damage occurred. I told them she was to have no visitors unless I approved. This was from the highest authority. So far, you're the only one approved to see her."

"When can I visit?"

"The doctor says she should rest today, but she should be up to talking to you tomorrow."

"Thanks, Max. It should be an interesting conversation."

Kevin heard his phone buzzing across the room on the dining room table where he'd left it. He got there just in time to pick up Toby's call.

"That guy and that company you asked me about?" Toby started. "Well, it gets interesting. This guy Maggio used to be known by another name, and he's got an international rap sheet with Interpol. I'm trying to get more info, but there seems to be a Vatican connection here. All well-hidden."

Kevin sighed. What had Katie gotten herself into?

Toby rattled on. "Meantime, buddy, I sure as hell wouldn't let my girlfriend travel with him! I'll call you when I get more."

As soon as Toby rang off, Kevin dialed Katie. No answer. He left a terse message. *Do not go anywhere with Maggio before speaking with me.*

∞∞∞∞

CHAPTER TWENTY-NINE

Vatican Hospital, Rome, Italy

A brisk walk on a hazy day brought Kevin to the Vatican Hospital shortly before nine a.m. The facility was small, containing fewer than forty beds, and was staffed by a dozen doctors and nurses. At the entrance, Kevin was stopped by an armed Vatican security officer. After the incident with Sister Mary Catherine, Max had ordered a security detail to stand guard. Seeing them there, Kevin was relieved.

The guard checked Kevin's credentials and ticked his name off a list.

Inside, Kevin was directed to the second floor. A nurse station in an all-white corridor checked him in a second time while orderlies and nurses scurried about. Funny how hospitals look the same all around the world.

A doctor appeared to accompany Kevin to MC's room. "I am Doctor Sergio. Please, Father Thrall, come this way," said the doctor. He was obviously Italian by his thick accent.

The hospital tended to the health needs of Vatican employees, for whom the services were free, handling minor emergencies.

Dr. Sergio said, "Fortunately, one of the doctors attending to Sister Mary Catherine has experience in poison toxicology. Her recovery is proceeding nicely."

"Thank you, Dr. Sergio," said Kevin. "I won't be long today."

When the doctor left, Kevin approached MC's bed. She lay quietly, attached to a heart machine and a drip. The room was a single, the walls white, adorned by a large crucifix over the bed. An electronic heart monitor stood at the side of the room, its green lines zigzagging across the screen. The machine emitted a steady beep; Kevin assumed it meant her pulse was normal.

MC's face was pale but her eyes were open.

"Hello, Kevin," she said softly.

"How are you feeling, MC?"

"Horrendous, thank you. You should've let me die."

Kevin smiled. "I'm happy you made it. Feel like talking?"

"About what? As if I didn't know."

"MC, you've done some bad things, and I hope you've had time to reflect on them. It's not too late to make things right. You're not a bad person. I think you've just been running with the wrong pack. Besides, I need your help."

"Kevin, you don't know them. They're monstrous."

For the first time, Kevin detected fear in her eyes. "I won't let them do anything to you, Mary Catherine."

MC frowned and put her hand to her heart. "I'm sorry. I made an oath."

"Look, MC. The authorities will get you to talk, one way or another. Do you understand what I'm telling you?"

She nodded, turning away to face the window. "Opus Mundi does what's right for the Church. I believe in them, Kevin. I . . . I don't agree with their methods, perhaps. I'm so. . . . confused. I suppose that's why I drank your coffee, I wanted to end it all . . ." She began to sob. Kevin stepped closer. He didn't know how to comfort her. *What could he say?* She looked so young. So vulnerable.

The head nurse knocked gently on MC's door, and entered the room.

"Excuse me, Father. It's time for a medical evaluation."

Kevin got up. "Sure, I'll wait outside."

Smiling faintly, MC held on to Kevin's hand before releasing it. "Don't go," she whispered.

"I'll just be outside the door," he assured her.

In the waiting room, Kevin picked up a newspaper from a table and took a seat. Down the corridor, from a distance, he watched the doctor enter MC's room.

Something about him bothered Kevin. He thought about it, went to the nurse's stand, and asked the duty nurse the doctor's name. She handed him a card.

Kevin took out his iPhone and Googled the name of the doctor. Nothing.

"Do you know this doctor, Signorina?" he asked the nurse.

"No, Father. I've never seen him before."

A familiar chill ran down Kevin's spine. He panicked. He might be wrong, but he sure as hell couldn't risk it. He bolted down the corridor to MC's room.

"Wait, Father. Please!" the nurse cried out, watching him fly down the hall.

Without knocking, Kevin barged into the room.

"Father, I am conducting an examination. Please leave us," the doctor said in an authoritative, superior tone. He certainly looked the part as he stood at MC's bedside. Her arm was exposed, the gown's sleeve rolled up. In his hand, the doctor held a syringe with a long needle.

"May I ask which of the Sister's doctors consulted you?" Kevin asked.

"Excuse me, Father. Not your concern. Now, leave this room before I call security."

"What's in your drip?" Kevin demanded. His voice was loud, challenging. He was getting angry.

"Get out! Security!" The doctor grabbed MC's arm and held the needle in place to inject it into her vein.

MC's face went pale. She screamed. "No!" She pulled her arm from the man. The doctor grabbed it back.

Kevin lunged at the doctor, who turned and pushed him aside with great force. Just as Kevin threw a left hook on his chin, the doctor was reaching into his pocket. Kevin slammed him back into the wall. The doctor stumbled, trying to hit Kevin back. Kevin punched him in the stomach. The doctor threw a punch, but Kevin rammed an uppercut to the man's head. The doctor's head jolted backward. A serrated knife slipped from his pocket to the floor.

Kevin grabbed the doctor by his white coat. The throwing knife looked familiar. Kevin's mind raced back to day he was drugged and kidnapped. A vision of the room where he was held captive came in a flash. This was the same kind of knife that had been thrown at him. Kevin had barely missed it. Kevin recalled hurling the henchman directly in the path of the knife. In the end, instead of Kevin, the henchman had been killed.

Kevin swung and punched the doctor in the nose. Blood spurted everywhere. The doctor scurried to the doorway. A small group of nurses and doctors piled into the room. Frantically pushing them aside to escape, MC's attacker fled from the room.

MC sat up in bed, her eyes wide with fear.

Kevin held up his hands and addressed the crowd. "You know who I am. It's under control," he said. He pointed at one of the doctors. "You, please call the Vatican police."

After a few minutes of murmuring among the hospital staff, the head doctor told them to get back to work. Kevin asked to be left alone with Sister Mary Catherine.

Closing the door to the room, Kevin sat on the bed beside her. "Those wonderful folks at Opus Mundi just tried to kill you, MC," he said. "I think it's time to rethink your loyalties."

MC nodded, tears streaming down her cheeks.

"It's time to talk to me," Kevin added.

MC reached for his arm and held it. "Will you give me absolution?"

Kevin thought for a moment. As long as she didn't confess to murder, he could absolve her. He wanted to. And that she'd tried to seduce him. . . . well, he'd just forget about that. "Yes, I will."

MC exhaled deeply and blessed herself, visibly relieved. "Then tell me what you want to know."

"Let's start with why you joined Opus Mundi," Kevin said. He was making an effort to keep his tone judicious, nonjudgmental.

Waving her hands as she spoke, MC began. "I was young and impressionable," she said. "You have to understand my upbringing. We were strict, old-fashioned Catholics and the Church's teachings made an impression on me. The new liberalization of the Church infuriated me, and I railed against it. Opus Mundi got wind of me. They sought me out."

"And you just signed up?"

MC shook her head. "It's more complicated than that. They send new potential recruits to a secret facility near Naples for testing. They want to make sure your convictions are real. Oh, I passed with flying colors." MC looked like she was about to start crying again.

"Take it easy, MC. We've got time."

"They tried to kill me just now!" she sobbed.

Kevin put an arm around her, and she snuggled closer. After a moment, he withdrew and moved to the foot of the bed. "When did you begin to have doubts?" he asked.

"At some point, it started to get weird," she said. "They did things I found strange."

"Like what?"

MC thought for a moment. "Well, it had something to do with Israel bombing Iran. I don't know how they did it, exactly, but they engineered it."

"Do you know why?"

"They don't let me in on all the high-level stuff, Kevin, but I think they were starting a major war in the Middle East. It would have served as their platform to take over the Church leadership. Once the pope was killed, they'd work to get their inside man in the job. The new pope would arrange some kind of peace in the Holy Land, and Opus Mundi would be in charge to pursue their secret agenda. I know they're afraid of something, but I'm not sure what it is."

"Who's in charge of Opus Mundi?"

"I don't know. We meet with him, but he's always covered, heavily clothed, his face totally masked."

"But he must be a cardinal if Opus Mundi expects him to be running the Church?"

MC shook her head. "I really don't know," she said. "I was told that anyone can be elected pope, not just cardinals."

"Listen carefully, MC, this is important. Have you heard anyone talk about the secret of Fatima?"

"Oh, yes. To them it's a big deal. I've heard talk that there is a prediction—a prophecy—in it that they don't want anyone to know about. It's a threat to them."

"Do you know what it is?"

"No. They don't let me in on it. I'm not important enough."

"Well, then, do you know where the secret is located?"

MC shook her head. "Kevin, I'm tired . . ."

Kevin touched her hand. "You've been through a lot."

"Can I tell you something?" she continued. "I always felt that I had a special role in the Church. That I was called to it for a reason, even if I don't know what the reason is."

Kevin nodded. "I understand."

"But what I feel around you is something similar."

"What do you mean?"

"I feel you have that same calling. Right in here." She pointed to her heart. "It's a special mission we're both destined to accomplish. But we don't know what it is. Maybe that's why I tried . . . to . . . a . . . you know . . ."

"Seduce me?"

"Yeah . . . that."

"Let's forget about that, OK?"

She nodded with an abashed smile.

Her comment about his mission was the very question he frequently asked himself. He knew he shouldn't make too much of it. But the question remained: *Who was this young woman? How did she fit in his life?*

"May I confess to you now, Father Thrall?"

"Of course." Kevin began his blessing. "In the name of the Father, the Son, and the Holy Spirit . . ."

∞∞∞∞

CHAPTER THIRTY

The Conclave

In a time-honored ritual, the princes of the Church and their entourages began arriving by air and train, joining the throngs of tourists and pilgrims flocking to Rome for the papal election. The cardinals who made their way to Rome for the conclave, all 112 of them, stayed in *Domus Sanctae Marthae*, the Vatican guesthouse designed and built precisely for this occasion.

At St. Marta's, the princes of the Church would be billeted in simple accommodations, with a bed in a small room, a kneeler for prayer, and a small bathroom. The cardinals were forbidden to talk to anyone outside the conclave, and especially not to the press. They dined together in their refectory on good Italian food and vintage Italian wine.

While a student in Rome years earlier, Kevin had studied the papal election rules. Following the death of the incumbent, under the rules for electing a new pope, the cardinals were summoned to the Vatican for the conclave to elect the deceased pope's successor.

According to the protocol, the candidate must receive a two-thirds majority to be elected. Most conclaves reached a decision in a matter of days, but just in case, a rule change made by John Paul II in 1996, *Universi Dominici Gregis*, stipulated that should the conclave remain deadlocked for over twelve days, the cardinals can change the rules, to elect by a simple majority. Thus far, Kevin was aware that the new rule had never been invoked. In theory, any baptized male was eligible to become pope, although in the unlikely event a layman were chosen, he'd have to be ordained as a priest, then as a bishop before assuming the mantle of Bishop of Rome, the official title of the pope.

No doubt, the most familiar part of the papal election process was the announcement of the results of the cardinals' ballots. If they didn't reach a two-thirds consensus on a candidate after a vote, straw was to be burned in a stove, producing black smoke wafting through pipes over the Sistine Chapel, indicating no new pope. This was a Catholic Church tradition known to all.

When consensus was reached, a chemical was added to the fire to make the smoke white, signaling to the world that a new pope had been chosen.

Kevin peered out his window at the procession of church elders in full regalia. The cardinals wore black cassocks with scarlet red sashes around their waists. They were capped by the skullcaps only cardinals could wear.

Today was the opening day of the conclave. This morning, the cardinals would gather for a solemn Mass of the Holy Spirit at the magnificent Pauline Chapel, whose walls were adorned by two of Michelangelo's masterpieces, *The Conversion of Saul* and *The Crucifixion of St. Peter*. After Mass, they'd form a procession, proceeding to the Sistine Chapel for their deliberations.

Kevin opened his apartment door for Max Drotti. Max carried two brown bags and rushed inside to put them on the table. The beer and sodas would go into the fridge.

"I got lots of stuff for our little party," he said. He was emptying the bags. "We've got three different kinds of cheese, potato chips, Chianti, beer, some sausages. Let's see . . . what else?"

Despite their elevated clerical status and a few important Vatican connections, the two had decided to observe the proceedings the way a billion other people would, by watching it on TV.

"Thanks, Max. We've got our own little feast here."

Max smiled, pleased with himself.

Kevin brought some plates and glasses from the kitchenette and the two men settled on the sofa and started eating.

The screen image showed the procession leaving the Pauline Chapel and heading into the *Sala Regia*, the great audience hall directly connected to the Sistine Chapel. The cardinals were dressed in their formal attire—a long, front-buttoned scarlet red cassock, and over it, a rochet, a white-laced robe. Topping it all, they wore a long bright red cape and the biretta, a scarlet headpiece.

Arriving at the *Sala Regia*, the *Camerlengo*, the chamberlain who served as acting pope, lectured the assembled cardinals as to how the new pope had already been chosen by God; and how their job was to pray and receive the grace to learn who, among them, He'd chosen.

Max glanced at the large bandage on Kevin's right hand. "Let me guess: You fell off a ladder?"

"You know better," Kevin replied with a smile.

"Yes, I heard about the melee at the hospital. And how's Sister Mary Catherine?" he asked.

"She'll be fine. And there's a small army guarding her now. I doubt they'll try again."

"Maybe one of the beers I brought will help the pain," Max said as he made his way to the refrigerator. "Want one?"

Kevin shook his head. "Too early for me."

The phone buzzed. The return call from Katie. Kevin was relieved.

"Your message sounded strange, Kevin," Katie said. "Sorry I didn't get back to you right away. I replaced my old phone."

"Look, Katie. This guy Maggio has a past. We're looking into it, but I'd stay away in the meantime."

"Kevin, you're talking about my largest and most profitable client!"

And frequent dinner companion, Kevin thought, but decided wisely to keep his mouth shut.

"Trust me on this, Katie. Make some excuse if you need to but do not under any circumstances travel with him. I'm still looking into it. Now, promise me. OK?"

Exasperated, Katie agreed. Kevin promised he'd get back to her soon. He rang off and turned his attention back to the action on the screen.

The television scene skipped to a shot of the doors of the Sistine Chapel. The last of the cardinals entered, and each took his place behind two long facing tables covered with gold cloth. The marshal at the door then shouted ceremoniously, "*Extra Omnes!*" which meant "Everyone out!"

When it was verified that no one but scarlet-robed cardinals were in the chapel, the doors were clanged shut and locked by three clerics.

"Now the fun begins," Max said.

"What happens next?"

"Well, there's not supposed to be any lobbying or politicking for the job, but inevitably it occurs. Cliques are formed, speeches made. Then they vote. As you've no doubt heard, the three favorites are Cardinal Marini of Genoa, the deputy secretary of state, Cardinal Serrano of Venice, and Cardinal Silvano, who's old even by papal standards."

"I remember meeting Marini and Serrano in the pope's office."

"Yes, both are powerful," Max said. "What're you thinking, Kevin?"

"I was just thinking about MC, Sister Mary Catherine. You know, Max, she's a fascinating young lady."

"Yes . . . so? Where are you going with this?" Max asked, his brow furrowed.

"Relax," Kevin said. "I mean she reminds me of a gorgeous college prom queen in search of world peace. But she got off on the wrong track."

"Yeah, with an insidious group that wants to take over the Church. She doesn't get much sympathy from me."

"I'm concerned about some of the things she told me."

"And you trust her?"

"I do. I heard her confession and gave her absolution. Afterward, she implied Opus Mundi killed the pope because they want to take over the Church."

"That's not hard to believe. I wonder if they've endorsed a candidate in the College of Cardinals?"

"That's what I was getting at."

Kevin and Max went into the kitchen and made some sandwiches on fresh baguettes. They listened to various experts prattling on the TV about the likely successors to the departed Pope Quintus II. Suddenly, the picture flipped to the roof of the Sistine Chapel and the small chimney, where the papal smoke would discharge. The cameras turned to a crowded St. Peter's Square, where voices rose in a clamor of anticipation. Then the scene switched back to the roof and the chimney.

Finally, smoke puffed out of the chimney into the cloudless sky.

Black smoke.

The conclave hadn't agreed on a candidate for pope.

The crowd exhaled and the sounds and murmurs of heavy disappointment swept over the Square. The pundits did their usual analysis, nothing more enlightening than that a new pope hadn't been elected.

Max and Kevin ate their sandwiches quietly, watching television. The coverage switched to "Breaking News" from the Middle East. CNN's Anderson Cooper was on-screen, in front of a colorful map in the background. Cooper announced that Iran had retaliated against Israel by launching a barrage of missiles at Tel Aviv. The experts' best guess: these were non-nuclear weapons.

Simultaneously, Hezbollah launched several hundred missiles across the southern border of Lebanon at Israel. Anderson Cooper opined that a new, and far more dangerous, Middle East war was imminent.

Kevin thought about how this conflict could become nuclear in an instant and turn into a Biblical apocalypse. *Was that what Opus Mundi wanted?*

Kevin put the sandwich down. "MC reminded me that a Middle East war was one of Opus Mundi's important agenda items."

"Did she say why?"

"No. She's too junior to know much."

A new image flashed on the TV screen. The smokestack on top of the Sistine Chapel was again in full display. The cameras panned the crowd in the Square. All eyes were looking up.

Finally, a stream of smoke.

Once again, black.

∞∞∞∞

CHAPTER THIRTY-ONE

Rome, Italy

With little difficulty, Kevin managed to resume his routine of saying Mass each morning. As he was easing back into his spiritual habits, it was giving him comfort and strength. He was spending the better part of his days talking to Max in person, and on the phone to Toby, his CIA buddy. He also checked in on Sister Mary Catherine, keeping his eye on CNN for the latest Middle East developments.

Over the following week, international political developments overshadowed the deliberations in the Vatican. Kevin monitored them closely. The Middle East conflict continued to escalate and rage. Missiles were flying between Lebanon and Israel, and occasionally between Iran and Israel. On their northern border, Israel invaded Lebanon.

The Hezbollah forces were waiting for them. Scurrying from house to house, the ragtag army set up mortars and anti-tank bazookas, fired shots, and disappeared. The Israelis countered with a barrage of fire, leveling buildings, homes, and anything that stood in the way. If Hezbollah wanted to play that way, the Israelis would stop at nothing to level their homes and kill their families. War was ugly. It was an ugly war.

The American president implored all parties to restrain their hostilities and to begin talking. It was no use. Casualties mounted—mostly in Lebanon—and the entire Middle East was in an uproar. *What country would enter the war next?* The entire world was watching and waiting.

Kevin, of course, was keeping a keen vigil on news at the Vatican. Two long weeks had passed since the conclave to elect a new pope had first convened. The eager crowds had seen nothing but black smoke.

At noon on the fifteenth day, the cardinal acting as *Camerlengo* announced a change: the 1996 rule instituted by John Paul II would now be invoked. The new pope would be elected by a simple majority of the conclave's votes, rather than the traditional two-thirds majority. When this news was announced, once again the crowd filled St. Peter's Square, knowing, with this voting rule change, that the announcement of a new pope certainly would come soon.

Kevin was spending time reviewing info he'd acquired about Opus Mundi and the secret of Fatima. In his eyes, it seemed certain Opus Mundi had in its possession the missing secret. They alone knew the message of the last two pages. *What could they have found in those pages that'd invoke such desperate and extreme acts, including the assassination of a pope? What could there be in this document written by a young girl in 1917?* The message had to be both frightening and credible. Scary indeed.

Returning to his daily Mass schedule was giving Kevin serenity and a renewed sense of duty to his Church. It felt good to meditate. He was feeling closer to God.

After Mass, Kevin knelt before the statue of the Virgin Mary and prayed for long spells. He developed a special relationship with Mary. His conversations with her were comforting. She spoke to him—not in words, of course—but in the way she directed his feelings, or chastised him for his wrongdoings. Whatever her message, Kevin heard it clearly. She was there for him, as he was for her.

It'd now been nearly three weeks since the conclave had first convened, and around St. Peter's there was massive discontent and frustration.

That morning after Mass in St. Peter's Chapel, Kevin strolled along the stone path, inhaling the scent of pine of early summer. The Vatican gardens were a peaceful refuge, a sanctuary removed from the deafening traffic. But the quiet was interrupted by a ring from his cell, a tune from the Grateful Dead.

"Hello, Toby."

"Hi, buddy. I owe you some thanks." Toby's tone was sarcastic.

"Really?"

"So, it happens I'm in Rome, staying at a fine hotel down the street, thank you very much—arrived this morning—it's all on Uncle Sam's dime. Thanks, buddy." Kevin detected something was wrong.

"Okay, where's the punch line?"

"Tell you when I see you."

"When is that?"

"How about right now?"

Kevin was as eager to hear what Toby had to say.

"Fine. Need directions?"

"Not really. Turn to your right."

Kevin turned quickly to see his friend walking along the garden's pebble path about one hundred yards away, phone to his ear, waving at him. Same old Toby. Same old CIA.

As he approached, Toby was grinning. He looked all of his forty-four years. The lines around his eyes had deepened.

Toby ran his fingers through his uncombed sandy hair. He was wearing a battle-worn brown sports jacket and casual slacks.

"Can't believe you're here," said Kevin, slapping him on the back. "Good to see you, Toby."

"Well, I'm surprised, too, if you want to know the truth."

"My apartment is just around the corner," Kevin said. "C'mon."

"It's nice here," Toby said.

"And convenient," added Kevin.

Kevin unlocked the door. They stepped into the apartment.

"Not bad," Toby commented, looking around. "If this fulfills your Church vow of poverty, I can't wait to see chastity."

Kevin smiled. "When your expense account runs out, you can stay here, too," Kevin said as they settled in the living room.

"Thanks." Toby made himself comfortable reaching into his jacket pocket for some papers. "To begin, old buddy, let me tell you that the White House is one of the reasons I'm here—and I should add that's how I got to fly business class, thank you."

"The White House?"

"You're the first one who tipped them off to the Israeli attack on Iran. Now it's heating up again. They want to know what's next—or at least, what your sources are telling you is next."

"I don't have any sources, Toby." Kevin thought for a moment, then added, "Well, actually I have one, I guess." Kevin trusted Toby and explained what had happened since they'd last spoken. The conversation that followed was mostly about Sister Mary Catherine and her role with Opus Mundi. Kevin omitted the part about the striptease.

"Can I talk to her?" Toby asked.

"No. She'll only talk to me."

"When do you see her next?"

"This afternoon. She's low-level, Toby. I doubt she knows much."

Toby grimaced. "Still, we'll take anything at this point. The Israelis are trigger-happy and we don't think we can control them. Unless some deal is worked out soon, we might be in a very hot war."

"She's been through a lot, Toby, so don't get your hopes up. How long are you staying?"

"It's up to me. If I'm finding out good intel, then I'll stay a bit."

"Great. You might be here for the announcement of a new pope. The rules changed, so we expect a proclamation any time now. It's quite an event."

"The announcement of a new pope here in Rome? That's history. You have pull to get us good seats?"

"Like on the fifty-yard line? Not a stadium event, Toby."

"Whatever you can do," said Toby. "Sounds like it might be interesting."

"You want something to drink or eat?" asked Kevin.

"Sure."

"OK, I'll be right back." Kevin went into the kitchen and quickly returned with two Peroni beer bottles and a plate of cheese and crackers.

"Thanks, Kev," said Toby, removing his jacket and throwing it over the back of the couch. "This jetlag has me all messed up. I'm starving."

Both men grabbed some cheese and crackers and chugged some beer.

Kevin clicked the flat screen on. The breaking news coverage switched back and forth between the crowd in St. Peter's Square and the White House, where negotiations so far were averting a major war in the Middle East.

Toby finished his beer and flipped through the papers he'd taken from his jacket pocket. "One more thing, Kevin," he said. "Do you know a Jimmy Stein?"

Why would Toby ask about Jimmy Stein?

"Yeah, I know him. Well, sort of . . . I guess. Why are you asking?"

"He's attracted the agency's attention. We opened a monitor filing on you after your intel on the Israeli attack proved so accurate. It just means we keep an eye on anything and anyone you're involved in who might be interesting. This guy Stein has been doing research about you. He also filed a Freedom of Information request about your court-martial."

"Son of a bitch!" Kevin blurted.

"Who is he?"

"Katie's new boyfriend. Why the hell would he be doing this?"

Toby shrugged. "Hold on. There's more." Kevin stared at the papers on his lap. "There's something else Stein and your friend Katie have in common: That guy Maggio's company United something is a client of both Stein's investment firm and Katie's law firm."

"I don't believe this! What do you make of it, Toby?"

"Beats me. His checking into you might mean he's working for someone who wants some dirt on you."

"Opus Mundi?"

Toby shrugged. "Or maybe he's just a typically jealous dude who's wanting to know more about the guy who's had Katie's affection all these years."

"I'm a priest, remember?"

"Yeah? I knew you before you did the priest thing."

Kevin was struggling to keep a lid on his fury. His head was racing with questions. *Was this guy Stein using Katie to get at him for some reason? And should he tell her, or would she dismiss it coming from him as sour grapes? And what about this Maggio guy's company?* Whatever he told Katie, first he had to find out more about Jimmy Stein.

"Did you check Stein out, Toby?"

"Yeah. We found nothing unusual. But that doesn't mean much. He could be working for somebody we don't know."

"Tax returns, employment? You guys have access to pretty much everything."

"The FBI has that stuff and, yes, we checked. Like I told you—nothing."

Kevin got up and put on his jacket. "I'm going to see Sister Mary Catherine. If you want, wait for me here."

"Thanks. Hey, bud, remember the favor I asked you? It's important, Kev."

Kevin nodded as he opened the door. "I know. I'll ask her to talk to you, but she's fragile. And very upset. Don't get your hopes up."

"I know," said Toby. "But try, will ya?"

"Sure, buddy."

As soon as Kevin stepped out of his apartment he rang Katie at her office. They had a brief but tense conversation. Yes, she knew that Jimmy was acquainted with Maggio and his company, Consolidated Investors United. In fact, it was Jimmy who referred Katie when Maggio asked for a lawyer recommendation. He explained their personal relationship but Maggio didn't seem to mind. No, she had no idea why Jimmy might have been checking up on Kevin.

The conversation ended inconclusively, which meant badly. Kevin tried to put it out of his mind as he headed to the hospital.

∞∞∞∞

CHAPTER THIRTY-TWO

Rome, Italy

When Kevin entered the room, Sister Mary Catherine was standing at the foot of the bed in nothing but her sheer hospital gown. With a big smile, she held out her arms to greet him. "Hi, Kevin! Look at the progress I've made."

Kevin dodged the hug. He knew trouble when he saw it.

"Nice to see you, MC. You look good—all refreshed, ready to go."

"Thanks. Gosh, I wish I could get out of here. Can I just leave? Dinner, maybe?"

"No. Let's sit and talk."

MC puckered her lips and crawled back into bed. She definitely was not like any nun Kevin had ever encountered.

Kevin sat down beside her on the bed, making sure there was plenty of space between them. "Have you thought about our earlier conversations? Anything you can add that'd help us with Opus Mundi?"

"I've been thinking, Kevin. Stuff comes and goes."

"I need some information about the connection with Israel."

MC put her hand to her head. "All I know is they wanted to start a war. I don't know why."

Kevin knew that much. She wasn't much help. "You'll be discharged soon, MC, and I'm trying to keep you out of jail because you're cooperating. I won't press charges against you, so it might work. But we can't forget that Opus Mundi already has made an attempt on your life. They might try again."

"I don't want to die, Kevin," she said, fixating on the door as if someone might burst in at any moment.

"I've arranged security. You'll be safe."

"I don't think I want to be a nun anymore. I'm realizing I'm not nun material."

"Ya think?" Kevin asked. *A new meaning for the word "understatement,"* he thought.

"I know you're making fun of me, Kevin. But I want to lead a good life and I got off to a bad start. I need your help, okay? As a mentor. Someone I can trust."

Apparently, she was determined to keep him in her life. And even though she'd tried to do him in, he remained intrigued. "I'll help in any way I can, MC. Or I should say, in any appropriate way I can."

MC smiled like a Cheshire cat. "Don't worry, Kevin. I know you're a priest through and through. And the word appropriate isn't lost on me." *Tally one for feminine smarts.*

"OK then." Kevin got up from the chair. "You've got my cell number. Call whenever you want."

"Thanks."

As Kevin got up from the bed, he leaned over to kiss her forehead, but then thought better of it. He proceeded to the door.

"Kevin, wait!" MC blurted, her arm waving. "There's something I forgot to tell you. It might have to do with the secret. You know, the secret of Fatima."

Was this a ploy?

Kevin stopped and turned back to her. "What?"

MC frowned, rubbing her forehead with all the theatrical *sturm und drang* of a diva in the exit scene. "Once, when we were in a meeting, I overheard Visitor talking to a man. I think it was the one who attacked me. They didn't know I could hear them. The man told Visitor about a precious document in Seville. They talked about visiting the cathedral."

"You overheard this?"

"They were speaking in Italian; I understood it."

Kevin remembered the cell phone SIM cards he'd retrieved from the thugs who'd attacked Max and him on the way in from the airport. Several revealed calls to Spain, as did the SIM card taken from Ali, the teenager who'd snuck into his apartment.

"Think hard, MC. This could be important." *But without the histrionics, please.*

"Oh my, I just can't recall any little 'ole thing right now." She sounded as if she was rehearsing in a Tennessee Williams' play. She exhaled. "Maybe later." She sighed. "Kevin, was this useful?" She looked at him, her eyes wide.

"Don't know yet, MC. Get some rest."

But Kevin did know. Now he had a solid clue as to the location of the missing pages of the secret of Fatima.

∞∞∞∞

CHAPTER THIRTY-THREE

Sistine Chapel, Rome, Italy

As Kevin walked to his apartment, he heard footsteps at a distance behind him. Turning around, he saw Max running at full throttle toward him.

"Hey, what's the hurry, Max?"

"The announcement is coming today . . . this afternoon," he said, catching up.

"How do you know?"

"A source in the kitchen. They've been told there'll be no more meals."

"C'mon over to my place. I have a visitor from the U.S. We can watch together. And that's not all. I just got a hot tip on the secret."

"Do tell," Max said, panting for breath, struggling to keep up with Kevin.

The enormous number of people within the confines of the Vatican could be seen scurrying and scampering everywhere and nowhere, underscoring Max's notion that something big was about to happen. All eyes were fixed on the chimney above the Sistine Chapel.

"MC overheard something about Seville and the cathedral there. Visitor was involved and he and another man talked about an important document."

"Hey, weren't some of the calls you traced from Spain?"

"Correct. And I gave those numbers to Toby Beck, my CIA friend who you're about to meet. I'll check to see if the numbers were from Seville."

Inside the apartment, Kevin made introductions. Max and Toby shook hands.

"Nice to meet you, Father," Toby said. "I've heard a lot about you."

"Just call me Max, Toby. I take it you work in Washington?"

"For the government." Toby smiled. "That can be anywhere, but yeah, mostly in Washington."

Max nodded, sensing not to pry any further. It was pretty evident Kevin's friend didn't work for the Department of Commerce.

"Toby and I go way back. He's been a big help to me," Kevin said.

"Yes, I know," Max said.

Kevin opened a drawer in his desk and removed a piece of notepaper with the phone numbers. He opened his laptop and typed a search query for the origin of the numbers. After a couple of seconds, he mumbled, "Yep, they're Seville."

Kevin rejoined the others, explaining to Toby and Max what he'd learned. "There's no proof that they were talking about the secret of Fatima," he said. "But I think it's a valid lead."

"So do I," Toby added. "Bring me up to date."

"Some of what I'm going to tell you is hard fact, Toby, but some requires faith, which works for Max and me, but might be less persuasive for you."

"Amen," Toby said. He blessed himself irreverently and smiled.

"We know that Opus Mundi was involved in getting a war started between Israel and Iran; it's fulfilling some biblical prophecy, at least as they see it. We know what they were talking about because Toby was able to monitor the numbers I got off the SIM cards. But the conversations have gone dead."

"Standard procedure," Toby chimed in. "They use burner phones and numbers. Every few days they switch them out so we can't track them."

Kevin continued. "On Max here's suggestion, I ventured to Medjugorje, where appearances by Our Lady, similar to those in Fatima, have been occurring. One of Max's contacts gave me a message from a visionary who speaks to Mary. And, believe it or not, she seemed to know of me."

Toby nodded.

"Toby, look, I know I might lose you with this, but hear me out. The visionary, the one who seemed to know me, sent a message to me, through Max's friend."

"A message?" Toby asked.

"She said, 'Dear Father, please understand Our Lady prays for you. Your true mission is beginning now. Please be careful. Much rests on your success.'"

Kevin purposely omitted the part about finding answers to questions about his life.

"Spooky," Toby commented.

"This is the part about faith," Max added clumsily. "To us, it appears to be a clear message from God. We take it seriously."

"Okay, today's not the day for radical conversions. I'll leave the God stuff to you guys," Toby said. "Let me stick to the facts. You've also got some guy in Washington snooping into Kevin's background."

Not wanting to go there, Kevin deftly switched the subject. "Cardinal Porter told us Pope Quintus II didn't die of a heart attack. That part was a Vatican cover-up. The pope was poisoned."

"Poisoned?" said Toby, taking a huge gulp of beer. "They killed the pope? I assume you suspect Opus Mundi."

"We know they're responsible," Kevin said. "And they've got a candidate for pope that they're pushing. We don't know who it is."

"For the Catholic Church, this all sounds very cloak and dagger," said Toby, who'd been raised Catholic. "But, hey, I'm learning there're crazies in every organization—even in the Catholic Church!"

"Well, if they succeed, we'll know it soon," Max said. "But since this has been the longest, most protracted conclave in modern history, all bets are off as to who'll be elected."

"The end of the trail is upon us," Kevin said. "The missing pages to the secret of Fatima. So far, we know they're connected to the death of Pope John Paul I. In 1978, he died while reading it, thirty-three days into his reign. Then, in 1981, a failed assassination attempt on John

Paul II, and a few weeks ago, the successful assassination of Quintus II. We've got to find those pages."

"That seems critical," said Toby.

"Well," Max said, "at least we have a clue to their location: Seville, Spain. Kevin and I will have to track them down. Once the conclave is over, I'll get Porter's office to authorize our trip."

The three men turned their attention to the TV, turning up the volume. The CNN commentators now were speculating that a decision was expected any minute. In the corner of the shot, the screen carried a live photo insert of the chimney.

Even Toby was feeling the excitement.

"Beer anyone?" Max asked. "It's almost showtime!" Max always had the final *bon mot.*

∞∞∞∞∞

CHAPTER THIRTY-FOUR

The Sistine Chapel, St. Peter's Square

While the world nervously awaited the big news from the Vatican, commentators were filling the interim by providing history and procedural details on the election of a pope. Kevin and Max tuned it out, but Toby, who didn't know much about these historical nuggets, was glued. To him, it was scintillating.

In 1492, to elect a successor to St. Peter, the first pope, the conclave was held for the first time in the Sistine Chapel. Since 1878, the conclave has followed the same general process and decorum. Only this time, the rule instituted in 1996, allowing the pope to be elected by a simple majority, had been invoked. The College of Cardinals apparently was deadlocked. By invoking the new rule, the criteria of "who" among the cardinals was (or was not) *papabile*, of sound papal character and eligibility, was tossed aside.

As the world waited, within the rooms reserved for the cardinals adjacent to the Sistine Chapel, the scrutineers were compiling the vote results, tallying the paper ballots and putting them in stacks. Next, the revisers retotaled the results, ensuring against error.

In the afternoon session, after the counting and recounting, a single candidate emerged with a simple majority of the votes. A new pope had been chosen!

For the final step, the secretary of the college and the scrutineers assembled the ballots: the burning of the ballots in the stove—a tower of pipes and scaffolding that looked out of place in the Sistine Chapel, where arguably the most treasured art in the world was housed.

The men proceeded to the oven and added straw to the mixture of ballots, to get the needed combustion. The final element, a chemical mixture, was spilled on the pile to provide the correct color as the smoke billowed from the chimney.

The color was white.

In the Sistine Chapel, the cardinals remained seated in their ceremonial chairs, awaiting the next step. Above them, Michelangelo's *Creation* towered over the assembly. A palpable silence echoed, like church bells ringing, within the chapel.

The importance of this moment was lost on no one. The dean of the college, elderly Cardinal Gianni Avellino, walked over to the new pope and addressed him in Latin, "*Acceptasne electionem de tecanonice factam in Summum Pontificem?*"

In English, "Do you accept your canonical election as Supreme Pontiff?"

"*Accepto,*" the pope-elect replied, his head bowed.

"*Quo nomine visvocari?*" the dean cardinal asked. In English, it meant, "By what name do you choose to be known?"

"*Linus secundus.*"

The new pope was Linus II.

The dean bowed slightly, taking two steps back. Both the pope-elect and the dean knew what was to follow.

Without further words, the dean of cardinals led Pope Linus II out of the Sistine Chapel, through the doorway to the left of the altar, through the chambers where the cardinals had assembled prior to the voting, and into the Room of Tears, a room where bygone popes were known to have wept upon becoming the new Vicar of Christ.

Leaving the darkened chapel, the remaining members of the conclave watched their new holy leader proceed from the room.

Once inside the Room of Tears, the pope-elect was left alone behind closed doors. The room had red walls, a kneeler, and a cabinet holding vestments for him—in three sizes. Being a relatively tall man, he chose the large sizes. After a moment of prayer on the kneeler, he rose and dressed. He put on the gold embroidered white silk cassock, the lace rochet, and the mozzetta, a short white silk cape. The new pope removed his scarlet red zucchetto and placed the papal white zucchetto on his head. Finally, he reached for the heavy, braided, pectoral gold crucifix, which he placed around his neck. He kissed the cross and hesitated slightly. The new pontiff returned to the Sistine Chapel to the applause and acclaim of the assembled cardinals. As he joined them, the cardinals rose and lined up in order of seniority to greet him. Aided by Vatican attendants carrying lists of their seniority, the cardinals found their positions in the queue. In turn, each one kissed the pope's hand, and pledged devotion to the church and to his leadership.

After the last cardinal in line had paid his homage, the cardinal dean gently took the pontiff by the arm for the ceremonial walk to the central balcony overlooking the square of St. Peter's Basilica. The time had come for Pope Linus II's presentation to the millions of Catholics crowding the Square and all of the streets leading into it . . . and to the world.

∞∞∞∞

Kevin, Max, and Toby watched the show on TV. The white smoke poured through the chimney atop the Sistine Chapel. With that, the thunderous clanging of the church bells rang out and even reverberated through the apartment.

Waiting in excited anticipation, Kevin and his colleagues sat quietly, their eyes fixed on St. Peter's and the papal balcony. The curtains parted and the cardinal dean emerged beneath a blazing sun, flanked by two priests. One priest held a leather folder from which the cardinal would read. The other adjusted the microphone.

In five languages the cardinal greeted the assembled brothers and sisters. Then he started reading, his voice echoing through the loudspeakers around the Square. "*Annuntio vobis gaudium magnum* . . ."

For Toby's benefit, Kevin translated. "I announce to you with great joy . . ."

"*Habemus Papam!*"

"I know that one," Toby said pompously. "We use that expression at the agency when we get a new chief."

The din of the crowd was reverberating through the TV's speakers. The world awaited the identity of the new pope.

The cardinal dean continued, "*Eminentissimum ac reverendissimum Dominum . . .*"

"The most eminent and most reverend . . ." Kevin continued. "I'm betting Serrano. Any other bets?"

"I think it'll be Marini," Max said. "For years he's been politicking, lining up support."

Toby finished his Peroni. "Sorry," he said. "I don't have any candidates."

Back on the screen, the curtains on the balcony parted again just as the cardinal dean proclaimed, "*Dominum Ioannes . . .*"

"Oh my God!" Max jumped up, knocking over a bowl of pretzels.

"*Sanctae Romanae Ecclesiae Cardinalem Porter.*"

"I can't believe it!" Kevin's jaw dropped.

"*Qui sibi nomen imposuit Linus Secundus.*"

"Guys, help me out," Toby said. "What's happening?"

Kevin said, "The Catholic Church has elected the first American pope ever. Cardinal John Porter. And he happens to be a mentor and a friend of mine."

"Holy shit!" Toby said. He quickly added, "Oops! Sorry."

"Holy shit is right!" Max said. "This is incredible."

"Interesting name he chose," Kevin said. "Linus the Second."

"Wasn't Linus a *Peanuts* cartoon character?" Toby asked in all seriousness.

"Linus was the second pope, the one right after St. Peter. Pretty gutsy name to pick."

Now the imposing figure of Pope Linus II appeared on the balcony, resplendent in the draped white cassock and the scarlet stole glowing in elaborate gold filigree.

The new pope raised his arms slowly and smiled, and the crowds let out all they'd pent up, screaming and screaming more. As tradition dictates, the pope imparted his first papal blessing, *Urbi et Orbi*, on the crowd below, addressing them in Italian and blessing them with the Sign of the Cross.

"I'm in total shock," Max said.

Turning away, Kevin suddenly looked sullen.

"Aren't you pleased?" Max asked. "He loves you, Kevin! Whistle a happy tune. You'll be a bishop in no time!"

"I think we're forgetting something," Kevin said. Toby's attention was now fully engaged. "Max, remember what we learned about Opus Mundi's ambitions?"

"Oh God, Kevin! You can't be serious! You know Porter better than anyone. He's a straight shooter."

"What?" Toby asked. "Am I missing something?"

Max inhaled deeply. "You're part of the team, right?" He looked over at Kevin for affirmation. Kevin nodded. Toby was in.

"We learned that Opus Mundi had a candidate for pope. They've been working on it for years."

Toby got up and asked everyone to stop talking. "Look, we may represent different sides here. Both of you need to remember that I'm representing the U.S. government. I'm here because Kevin tipped us off to the Iran attack. Our priority is to stop a nuclear war! Get it?"

"Sure," said Kevin. "We get it."

"Point is," said Toby, "and pardon my Latin, but this is fucking serious."

"You're right," said Kevin. "It's definitely fucking serious."

"Here's my take," said Toby. "The Opus Mundi dudes are behind the Israeli-Iran war. I need to follow that trail. I know you two are on the scent of some voodoo secret that, when decoded, has a scary message, the Cracker Jack surprise, right? I don't really give a rat's ass about that part, but I need intel on the group that's starting a war."

Kevin said, "We get it, Toby. But this is a two-way street. We'll keep you fully informed of anything having to do with the Mundi group. And you help us with our Cracker Jack prize. Deal?" Kevin continued. "I'll get you in with Sister Mary Catherine. She's in the hospital. I'm one of the few with access to her. I'll need her permission first, but I can do that."

Toby nodded. "And what do you want from me?"

"We got a lead: the missing pages of the secret are in Seville. Maybe connected to the cathedral there."

"It's important to follow that lead," said Max.

"We need you for the next step," said Kevin.

"Sure, OK," Toby agreed. "How?"

"You were able to track the calls on the SIM card numbers in Spain I sent you. How close can you come to the specific place where the calls were made?" Kevin asked.

Toby stroked his chin, contemplatively. "I'm trying to sort out if what I'm going to tell you is classified or not. So just assume it is, okay? I can trust you guys, right? You're bigwigs in the Church and all."

Max and Kevin both nodded.

"We can identify the cell tower the calls came from. That should get you pretty close."

"Could you be more specific?" Max asked.

"Cell phone signals are transmitted from towers on buildings or poles. You've seen a ton of them. I can locate the towers where the calls went. It'll put you in an area of maybe a block or two from where the calls originated."

"A block or two?" Max asked.

Kevin looked at him. "I'll settle for that, Max," he said. "Gives us a manageable area to search."

"Really? Like who and for what?" Max raised his eyebrows.

"I've got an idea, Max. Tell you later." Kevin looked at Toby. "Do we have a deal?"

Toby extended his hand. "When do I get to meet the good Sister?"

CHAPTER THIRTY-FIVE

Rome, Italy

Kevin was keenly aware of the pressure of the moment: The time to proceed was now. The three pulled it together faster than a speeding bullet. Max would make arrangements for the trip to Seville, Toby would call Langley right away to fine-tune the cell locations from Spain, and Kevin would take Toby to the infirmary to talk to the nun.

The men left the apartment, heading out on their respective missions. The air was crisp and the whispers and murmurs about the election of a new pope could be heard far and wide, from St. Peter's Square all the way to the far reaches of the Vatican's hilly paths.

Kevin and Toby entered the hospital without a problem. The guard recognized Father Thrall and waved him—and the man with him—in.

Once inside, Kevin picked up on the agitation in MC's room. The air was thick. Police officials jabbered loudly with doctors and nurses, while staffers huddled together sheepishly.

Kevin tapped a nurse who looked familiar. "What's going on here?"

"Oh, Father, you don't know? Your patient, Sister Mary Catherine, is gone."

"Gone? How's that possible?"

"She walked out. Found her habit and just walked out. As a rule, nuns aren't stopped coming in and out of here."

"Good God!" Then Kevin realized that he must have MC's cell number stored in his phone. She'd called several times. Scrolling through his contact list, he found her and pressed CALL.

Voicemail. "Hello, this is Sister Mary Catherine. Please leave a message at the sound of the beep."

He left a terse, cryptic message. "MC, it's Kevin. I don't know what you think you're doing, but you'd better stop. Call me back. Now! It's important. Call me!"

Toby looked disheartened. "Now what?"

"I honestly don't know." Kevin was unsure of his take on MC's actions. *What was she thinking, doing something this stupid?*

"Why'd she walk out on you?" asked Toby.

"I don't know," he said. "Women are always women, even if they're nuns."

"Meaning?"

"Meaning they're inscrutable, unpredictable, and flighty, that's what." Kevin was exasperated. He'd hoped he could trust MC. Either she was ditzy enough not to get that her life was endangered, or she was playing him.

The men left the hospital and walked to the little-used north end of the Vatican, away from the crowds in the square. They sat down in an unpretentious country café with red-checked paper tablecloths, and ordered sandwiches and beer.

In just moments, the server came with large, frothy mugs of cold beer and *Poplette e Panini* sandwiches. Kevin hadn't realized how hungry he was and wasted no time starting in.

"Stress getting to you, ole buddy?" Toby said, guzzling the beer.

Kevin looked up at him. "I'm up to here," he said, motioning to his forehead. "We've got a new American pope whom I've long admired. If it turns out he's part of Opus Mundi, I'll be crazy. Plus, I've a solid lead on the missing pages to the secret of Fatima, and I've got a missing nun who may or may not be playing me, whose runaway life is endangered."

"Mmm, I see," said Toby, chomping on his sandwich.

"And, thanks to you," added Kevin, "I got news that Katie, about whom I care deeply, may be unknowingly involved in this big mess."

"You talkin' about the Stein guy?" Toby asked.

"Yeah. What's worse, Katie loves him." It hurt to say, but it was the raw naked truth. "And now this shit about their joint client, Maggio."

"Remember what they used to teach us at the farm?"

"Prioritize."

"Correct," Toby said. "Can't solve all your problems at once. So prioritize. What's the most important? Girlfriend? Secret papers? Missing nun? The pope?"

"You're a big help," Kevin said. But Toby was right. "The pope's out. We won't get to see Porter for some time, given the roster of his new responsibilities. But I'm sure I can get an audience in due course. I don't know what to do about Katie and this guy—at least not yet. And Sister MC has fled. There's nothing to be done. She'll call me."

They ordered another round of beers.

Kevin had an idea. "Toby, you ever been to Spain?"

Toby smiled. "I know what you're thinking, but I'm not sure I can justify it."

"I can help. You're concerned about a war in the Middle East. The guys stoking it are guided by what's on the missing pages of the secret of Fatima Secret. That's what I'm after. MC gave me the Seville clue. And with your info, it's narrowed down to a few blocks."

"What would I do in Spain?"

"This is a rough crowd. As ruthless as any thugs or gangs in the U.S. Monsignor Drotti doesn't have our training, so if it gets rough, he's no help. Might even be a hindrance. There's no double-edged sword with him. He's a priest and only a priest. I need a partner. I need you."

Toby mulled this over, came to a quick decision. "Alrighteee, then," he said. "Get me the info. I'll book the flight with my Visa, courtesy of the government."

"Thanks, Toby. You're a fabulous guy." Kevin said. He patted his friend on the arm.

Kevin's phone buzzed. A text from Katie.

Kevin, I talked to Jimmy. He knows of nothing bad about Greg Maggio. He's been a good client of his for a while and that's why he recom-

mended me. He's hurt that you're suspicious of him. Also, I can't keep putting off my trip to the Caymans with Maggio. He needs to set up his offshore company and he needs me to do it for him. We plan to leave next Tuesday . . .

"Just what I need," Kevin mumbled.

This time his phone rang. The number told him it was MC. *Thank God.*

"Hi, MC. I'm glad to hear from you."

"I'm sorry, Kevin. I had to leave. I'm really frightened. They're going to kill me, I know—"

"It's OK, MC. Calm down. Let's talk it through. I'm here. I'm on your side," he said, lowering his voice to maximize the paternalistic affect.

"I believe you, Kevin, but I don't know if anyone can help me now."

"Where are you?"

"Here in Rome. I'm in a hotel. I used my passport. They don't know my real name. I'm safe for now."

"I'll come get you. Where are you?"

She didn't answer.

"MC, listen. The only way I can help is—"

"There's somebody at the door!" While lowering her voice to a whisper, she began sobbing.

"Don't answer the door! Where are you?"

"Hotel Saturnia. It's—"

"I know where it is. Listen to me. Do not open the door. Keep the bolt locked. I'll be right over. What's the room number?"

"403. Please hurry. I'm scared."

He could hear the loud knocking on her door.

"Listen carefully, MC. Talk to them through the door. They'll say they're from room service or try some other reason to be there. Pretend to go along. Tell them you just got out of the shower and need a moment to throw some clothes on."

"Should I call the front desk?" she asked in a shaky little-girl voice.

"Is there a phone in the bathroom?"

"No."

"Then don't phone. They might overhear you. Just stall for time. We'll be right over."

Throwing a handful of euros on the table, Kevin jumped up.

"What's going on?" asked Toby.

"It's MC," said Kevin. "She's in a nearby hotel. Someone was banging on the door, trying to get in."

"Shit!"

"C'mon," said Kevin. "Let's go."

They went outside and found a cab right away. Kevin gave the driver the address, saying *pronto*, and waving a fifty-euro note in his face. The cabbie nodded. He understood. He was hightailing it.

While the Fiat careened through the busy Roman traffic, Kevin told Toby exactly what'd happened. In less than six minutes, the taxi pulled up in front of the hotel.

The Hotel Saturnia was a three-star hotel, with a fancy awning out front, and a 1950s lobby. This place wasn't retro fifties, it was original fifties.

Kevin and Toby raced to the elevator, pushing in front of an American couple with numerous pieces of mismatched luggage.

On the fourth floor, they looked right and left. Not far down the hallway were two thugs in dark jeans and turtlenecks prying open MC's door. Kevin recognized one of them from when he'd been captured. It was the tall guy with long, dark hair and a craggy face.

"What are the chances these clowns are armed?" Toby whispered.

Seeing them approaching, the "clowns" froze dead in their tracks.

"Low probability," Kevin replied. "If they're caught with weapons in Italy, they get life."

One thug whipped a long blade out of a holster tucked into the back of his trouser belt, and pointed it at Kevin and Toby.

"Oh, boy," Toby said, "do you remember the kid at the Farm who taught us how to disarm a guy with a knife?"

Kevin nodded. "I do. Matt something. Very talented guy."

"I did pretty well in that class," Toby said, smugly, obviously pleased with himself.

"I remember that," Kevin said, raising his voice. "As a matter of fact, so did I."

The thugs looked at one another, trying to figure out what Kevin and Toby were talking about and, more importantly, what they were intending to do. So far, the long-bladed knife hadn't made a big impression.

"Well, Toby, time to practice our training." Toby sighed and started a slow strut toward the men at the door. "Hi, fellas, I don't suppose you speak much English but—"

"Stop!" craggy face shouted.

Toby kept walking. Kevin followed at a pace behind, keeping his eye on the second guy who wasn't talking. The first thug raised his arm, pointing the knife straight at Toby.

In a swift, fluid motion, Toby kicked the man's arm and the knife flew from his hand and onto the ground. Toby lunged toward the thug and punched him in the jaw, then jabbed him with a powerful blow to the stomach.

Kevin picked up the fallen knife and turned toward the second thug, who was throwing a punch. Kevin blocked it with his free hand and whacked him on the side of his head with the knife's handle. He screamed, crumbling in agony to the floor.

Kevin handed the knife to Toby, who was standing over the two men lying on the floor.

So far, their scuffling and commotion hadn't attracted notice, but that wouldn't be the case for long.

Kevin pounded on the door. "MC. It's Kevin. Open up."

"Kevin?"

"Yes, all clear. Open up."

She opened the door. Kevin stepped inside. She moved to hug him. He blocked her, bracing her arms firmly away from him. Seeing her, Kevin thought, what a loss to mankind that this stylish cupcake wasn't grounded in the secular camp.

MC was dressed in fitted taupe capris with a fifties-style side zipper, and a red striped blouse with a turned-up collar. Her hair was unkempt, falling over her shoulders. If nothing else, she had a sense of style.

"Kev, let's get these goons inside the room," Toby ordered. He held the knife in front of them, motioning for them to enter MC's hotel room.

"Let us go, Father," craggy face said to Kevin. "If you don't, you'll regret it."

"I regret it already."

Both men limped into the room.

Kevin rifled through the men's pockets. Nothing but a few euros. "No ID. These guys are pros."

Toby tore the cords off the lamp and the telephone and used them to bind the men's hands behind them and to a bedpost. Toby was exceptionally proficient at knots.

The thugs looked at each other and whispered something.

"Talk to me," Toby said with authority. "Who sent you?"

The men shrugged.

Toby looked at Kevin. "These knots aren't my best. They'll get out of these in a few minutes," he said, "but by then we'll be gone."

"Aren't you going to call the police?" MC asked.

"Not worth it," Kevin replied. "We've got to get you out of here. Get your stuff."

MC gathered clothes, toiletries, and an iPad and started stuffing them into her backpack.

The room had an old-fashioned metal room key which came in handy. Toby and MC left the room, and Kevin followed them out, key in hand. "They'll have to scream their way out," Kevin commented as he double-locked the door.

Outside, they hailed a taxi, and all three crammed into the backseat. Kevin told the cab to take them to da Vinci Airport. Then he smiled, looking at MC. "Sister Mary Catherine, may I introduce an old friend of mine, Toby Beck. He has a few questions for you."

∞∞∞∞

CHAPTER THIRTY-SIX

Rome, Italy

On the drive to the airport, the taxi weaved through Rome traffic at high speed. Motorbikes whizzed by, exacerbating the cacophony of street life in the Eternal City. Kevin stared aimlessly out the window, enjoying the relief of a few moments of mindlessness. The tree-lined streets of shops and flats were interspersed with occasional fields of lonely columns from another age.

The silence didn't last long.

Turning to face her, Toby started grilling MC about her Opus Mundi colleagues. "Is there anything you can tell us that might offer insight into their identity or their plans?"

"Well, I remember what some of them looked like and who attended the meetings—if that will help."

Kevin's phone buzzed.

"Kevin, it's Max. Where've you been?"

"It's been a little hectic, Max." Kevin filled him in on their rescue of Sister Mary Catherine. "We're now on our way to the airport, but there's been a change in plans. We're going to Spain, and we're taking the good Sister with us."

"They can go, but you can't," Max said.

"Of course I'm going, Max. And you need to meet us there, just as we'd planned."

"Well, listen to this, Kev. His Holiness has asked to see you. Alone. By yourself."

"What? Are you joking? He's been pope for less than twenty-four hours."

"It's a direct order. I'm not joking. The meeting is scheduled for five p.m. in the papal quarters."

"Are you going?"

"I'm not invited. Just you."

Kevin couldn't wrap his mind around this. He would comply, of course, but what did Porter—*His Holiness*—want to see him about? *And would he learn more about his mentor's undercover agenda? Was Porter, the new pope, aligned with the Catholic Church—or, God forbid—with Opus Mundi?* Kevin checked his watch. He had time to continue the cab ride to the airport with MC and Toby, then turn around and get back to the Vatican.

"Talk to you later," Kevin told Max. "I should be able to make the appointment on time."

"What was that about?" asked Toby.

"The new pope wants to see me this afternoon," Kevin said. "Can you believe that?"

"Geez. That's strange," MC said. "What about Seville?"

"Look, you two need to get to Seville. Check out the cathedral and the neighborhood where the cell phone towers are located. I'll join you as soon as I can."

"OK," Toby said. "We can do that."

MC stared blankly out the window. Kevin wondered what she was thinking about, but he didn't have the wherewithal to pry at the moment.

At da Vinci Airport, Kevin went to the Alitalia counter and bought MC's ticket to Seville. Next, Toby bought his own. Kevin stayed with them until Toby and MC cleared security and customs and were safely entering the boarding gate.

Since they hadn't planned on leaving so soon, Toby had no baggage. Kevin said he'd follow as soon as he could with their clothes and other necessities, one of them being two pistols which would be concealed in a check-in bag, in a lead envelope. That way, they would be protected from the X-ray scan.

"Good luck, you guys. I'll see you soon," said Kevin.

"Be careful," Toby said.

MC hugged him, telling him to hurry to Seville.

Since travelling by train was faster than a taxi through busy traffic, Kevin took one to Rome. Onboard, he had a good half hour to focus on his meeting with the new leader of the Catholic Church.

Years earlier, in the seminary, before he'd taken his final vows, Kevin had a personal crisis, grappling with the choices he'd made. He'd given up Katie, whom he loved deeply, and bet his future on a mystical calling to a life whose rewards wouldn't all come in this life. *And why?* The answer was that the voices in his head, what he dubbed the calling, were mysteriously insistent. Some would say it was a purely clinical psychological defect: obsessive behavior. Others saw it from a mystical perspective, as if an unrelenting pressure at his back, like a strong wind, was pushing him into the world of God. Escaping from this simply wasn't an option.

Only when Kevin relented to the calling had he found relief. He knew this was what God wanted. Who was he to balk? Serving God was his one mission. The Mother Mary would be his guide.

Now he was about to confront the leader of a billion Catholics, uncertain as to whether this pope was a follower of the Catholic Church, or an imposter for a Satanic cause. Kevin prayed for the wisdom to know the truth.

At the train station, Kevin grabbed a cab and rode to the Vatican, and his apartment. Once inside, he changed into his finest black suit and turned white collar. At the appointed time, he arrived at the gate to the Apostolic Palace. The Swiss guard snapped to attention while a clerk verified his identity. A male secretary dressed in a blue suit greeted him at the bottom of the stairs and led him up the wide marble staircase to the second floor. He was escorted into an antechamber and instructed to sit and wait.

At first, Kevin was too anxious to sit. He scanned the whole room, admiring the frescoes on the wall and the marble fireplace. Eighteenth-century oil paintings of religious themes adorned the high walls. The painted ceiling depicted clouds and angels floating in the sky. It was evident that the upper tiers of the Vatican hierarchy lived in lavish style.

Nervous for a few moments, he paced the floor, then sat in a Louis XVI chair.

Suddenly, a hidden door on one side of the room opened, and a young man, dressed in a blue suit, came toward him. He spoke in nearly perfect English, "His Holiness is ready for you, Father."

Kevin followed the attendant into the library attached to the pope's personal quarters, where the pope gave his Sunday blessing to those in St. Peter's Square. Kevin glanced around. There were shelves of leather tomes in bookcases, comfortably worn down chairs, and plumped sofas. Oil paintings of austere looking prelates, accented with picture lights, lined the walls. Kevin imagined they were the popes of centuries past.

Kevin stood quietly, waiting.

A few moments later, a chamberlain walked in and announced, "His Holiness, Linus the Second."

The tall figure of John Porter, dressed in papal white with the gold cross and chain around his neck, entered the room, smiling broadly.

Somehow, to Kevin, the reality of Porter as pope, and the setting, caused the whole scene to seem surreal, reminding him of Hollywood, red carpets, and the Academy Awards. "*The award for best portrayal of a pope goes to . . .*"

"Thanks for coming, Kevin," the pontiff said.

"Your Holiness," Kevin said while going through the motions of Church protocol and falling to one knee. He took the pontiff's extended hand and kissed the ring. It all still seemed unreal, like a dream. *Porter, the pope. Porter, his mentor and friend, the pope?*

"Let's sit over here." The pope gestured to a plumped sofa flanked by an equally plumped chair. Kevin followed him and sat down.

His Holiness waved his hand at the young man in the blue suit, who bowed, backing out of the room.

"I know you're surprised," the pope began, sounding like himself, "and you're not the only one."

"I don't know if congratulations is the appropriate thing to say, Holiness," Kevin said.

Porter smiled. "It'll do just fine. Would you like a coffee?"

"No, thank you."

"Then let's get down to business. Your mission. I need a progress report. Now that I've been elected, it's assumed an even greater importance."

The moment of truth. Kevin had wondered what he'd do if it came to this. And he was ready, for better or worse.

"Holiness, I've got a problem. We've made some progress in learning about Opus Mundi, but one of the things we learned has to do with their plans for leadership."

His Holiness looked at Kevin. With surprise.

Kevin spoke deliberately. "We understand Opus Mundi had planned to insinuate their leader into office as the newly elected pope."

Porter's face froze. Kevin held his breath. This powerful man could summon his security police and put Kevin in the dungeons forever. The Vatican was its own sovereign state. The pope was its universal, omnipotent leader.

Suddenly, Porter—Pope Linus the Second—began laughing. He continued for a moment, wiping his eyes, laughing even louder.

Kevin was spooked, witnessing the new pope laughing hysterically. *Was he missing something?*

The pope's laughing turned into a smile, and he stopped. Finally, Kevin smiled.

"That's the best laugh I've had all day! You thought I might be the puppet pope?" The pope pointed to his chest, wiping the tears from his eyes.

"I'm sorry, Holiness. It wasn't about doubting you. It was about observing the wiles of Opus Mundi. I had no choice."

"Well, let me help you out. You're partially right. There was a candidate who nearly got the votes—I'm not going to expose him because I'm not one hundred percent certain—but I believe he was the candidate you're concerned about, Kevin." Porter leaned across the table and stared directly at Kevin. "But it's not me."

"Sorry I even had to ask." Kevin still wasn't one hundred percent convinced.

"I know you'll want proof. We need to get this out of the way and get on with our mission. The Church is still in danger."

"I'm very aware of that, Holiness."

"Let's think through this logically. I'm the one who recommended hiring you. I know you better than anyone; you're the best for the job, Kevin. If I were the culprit, would I have done that, picked the best man for the job?"

"Thank you, Eminence . . . er . . . a . . . Your Holiness." *Good*, Kevin thought. But it still wasn't enough to ease his mind.

"Opus Mundi put the world on edge by starting the Israeli-Iran War. Now we're on the verge of a nuclear holocaust. We can't let that happen."

Kevin nodded. "I agree."

"So I have a plan, and I'm telling you first. I intend to call for a peace conference here at the Vatican. I will invite the Iranian, Israeli, and American leadership to attend. With God's help, we can work this out, cease the hostilities, the war, and whatever else could happen."

"Will they attend?" Kevin asked.

Porter smiled. "I'm not naïve, son. I sent feelers out this morning through diplomatic channels and have already received promising responses from Iran and the U.S. Haven't heard from Israel yet, but if the U.S. applies pressure, I expect they'll come. The Iranians won't meet directly with the Israelis—that's one of their conditions—but that we can work around."

Kevin felt an immediate sense of relief. This was major news, and if true, enough confirmation of whose side Porter was on. "That's wonderful news, Holiness."

"I've ordered Vatican security doubled and we're getting help from the United States Secret Service. I haven't forgotten my predecessor's fate." Porter took a deep breath. "But this isn't why I called you here."

The pope rose and walked to the window overlooking St. Peter's Square. He stared out at the crowds below as they milled around the Bernini fountains. "I want to talk about the secret of Fatima and Opus Mundi's interest in it."

Kevin thought that Porter had made a pretty convincing case of why he wasn't involved with OM; still, he'd reserve judgment. "Holiness, I've made some progress," Kevin said. He went on to say there were two missing pages to the secret and that there was something in those two missing pages that Opus Mundi feared most of all.

"What's more," Kevin said, "I have a hunch where the pages are."

The pontiff nodded and folded his hands. For a moment, he closed his eyes. "Strange. I've heard rumors over the years about those missing pages. This is the first confirmation of those rumors. You sure about this, Kevin?"

Kevin nodded. "I had the CIA go over the original secret, revealed in 2000. It's astonishing that it predicted the assassination attempt on Pope John Paul II, but mysteriously, what's got us tearing our hair out, is that there's nothing either coded or stated outright in those pages that's an apocalyptic prediction."

"Yet, you believe Opus Mundi sees something there."

"Not there, Holiness," said Kevin. "The answer came when I spoke to the priest who helped Sister Lucia transcribe the secret back in 1944. He told me there were six pages to the secret, and the one released in 2000 had only four pages. Hence the real secret must be on the missing two pages."

"If, by the grace of God, you find the pages, please keep in mind that I alone am authorized to read them," Porter said.

"Understood, Holiness."

"I asked for you to meet me today because I wanted an updated progress report." The pontiff smiled. "Well, I got one. Now, it's late and I have much to do. Kevin, I wish you Godspeed, and I will pray for your continued success."

Kevin rose and knelt before the Holy Father. Porter blessed him, making the Sign of the Cross above Kevin's head, a traditional gesture. Yet this was a time when things were unfolding that weren't traditional.

∞∞∞∞

CHAPTER THIRTY-SEVEN

Rome, Italy

Kevin lay stretched out on his bed, staring idly up at the ceiling, his heart racing. Sweat beaded his forehead. Anxiety was getting the best of him. He'd coped with multiple stressful events in his life. *But how had it all come to this?* He came to Italy for a small assignment, and now here he was in the middle of a world war, espionage entanglements, satanic plots, and the looming mystery of the secret of Fatima.

Never had Kevin doubted his calling as a priest, but often he'd wondered why he'd been called. Given his military background, he knew he wasn't a typical candidate by any measure. Now, perhaps, his mission was coming into focus. Kevin was becoming increasingly certain his calling and the fabled secret of Fatima somehow were divinely intertwined.

When his phone buzzed, Kevin found a text from Toby and MC. They were in Seville, at the elegant Alfonso XIII Hotel. Years ago, Kevin had been there. The hotel was nothing short of a palace. Commissioned by King Alfonso XIII for special guests of the Iber-American Exposition in Seville, it was built in the late twenties. It dazzled the senses with its majestic arches, colorful ceramics, brickwork, and ornamental towers.

Entering the hotel, Toby informed the desk clerk that he'd reserved a suite with two bedrooms. He and Kevin would share one room, MC would have the other, and Max could sleep on the couch and enjoy the wide screen TV in the palatial living room. *So much for travelling on a budget,* Kevin thought, smiling. *Thank you, Uncle Sam.*

When someone rapped on the door, Kevin rose from the bed, checked the security monitor, and opened it. There was good ol' Max, dressed for civilian travel: casual sport jacket, shirt, and slacks.

"Ready to go?" asked Max. He carried a small carry-on bag in one hand and rolled a large suitcase behind him with the other.

"Almost. We've got some more packing to do," Kevin said, referring to the pistols he'd stow in the one bag that'd be checked in at the airport.

"This one is Toby's," Max announced, motioning to the wheelie. "I got it from his room at his hotel after he called the manager."

"Mmm, good." Kevin was wary of smuggling the pistols through airport security, but knew it should go off without a hitch.

"How did it go with His Holiness?" Max asked as he stepped into the apartment.

"OK. Actually, good. The bottom line is I think I was wrong. In fact, if I ever suspected he was part of Opus Mundi, I was wrong. He wants us to find the missing pages of the secret and give them to him."

"Why are you so sure he's not working for the other side?" Max asked.

"Intuition. It was just something I felt. Besides, he's about to announce a new initiative that underscores his stance. I can't give you details, but we'll hear about it very soon."

Max smiled. "Sometimes, my dear friend, you seem to forget how well connected I am in the Vatican. His Holiness Pope Linus the Second is going to announce his decision to host a peace conference to settle the Middle East crisis. The announcement will come this afternoon."

"How'd you know? Your downstairs eyes in the Vatican kitchen?"

Max shook his head. "I have higher sources than the kitchen help, my friend."

"I understand Israel isn't yet on board," Kevin added.

Max smirked. “They came through an hour ago.”

Kevin shook his head. “Our new leader is a powerful negotiator, after all.”

“Something like that,” Max said.

“C’mon, Max.” Kevin looked at his watch. “Let’s get some lunch. I’m starved. We don’t have a lot of time. We need to leave for the airport in an hour.”

∞∞∞∞

CHAPTER THIRTY-EIGHT

Seville, Spain

News of the papal peace initiative flooded the media worldwide. Fox News broke the story first with a tip from an unnamed Vatican official. Kevin smiled and wondered if Max had been the source of the tip. The Vatican hadn't wanted news of the initiative released for another couple of days, until all the participants had prepared their own announcements.

Word spread quickly that parties in Iran, Israel, and the United States had agreed to take part in the papal peace initiative. Russia, France, and the Arab League would also attend and participate as needed. The initiative would personally be hosted by His Holiness in the Apostolic Palace in the Vatican.

Just another media circus at the Vatican, Kevin thought. After the irregularities of the recent papal election, he was glad he wouldn't be there for it.

On CNBC, the financial analysts reported that after the announcement, stock markets in Europe, the United States, and Asia rose nearly three percent during the day. Gold and oil fell as the prospect of peace reduced worldwide fear that a nuclear calamity was imminent. Now the chances of an oil blockade in the Persian Gulf seemed slim and the fear associated with a rise in the price of gold had abated. Leaders of the three countries participating in the peace initiative thanked the pontiff for convening the conference. Each leader claimed emphatically that his constituency wanted only a peaceful resolution to the conflict.

Nice start to your papacy, Your Holiness, Kevin thought.

During all this goodwill, Max and Kevin boarded the plane to Seville. Kevin had ensured his anti-tailing measures were in place, and now was relieved to know he wasn't being followed.

But something was bothering Kevin. He felt certain Opus Mundi had moved on to the action phase of their plan. He only wished he knew what that was.

To Kevin, Seville was the most beautiful, elegant, manicured city in Spain. The city sat on the banks of the Guadalquivir River, which flowed through the town. The town's history, some say, dated back to its founding by Hercules. Seville was one of Kevin's favorite cities in the world. He enjoyed its charm and cultural diversity. He was an avid student of the city's rich history.

From the early eighth century to the twelfth century, Seville was occupied by the Moors and under their rule the city entered its age of splendor. The cultural influences of the Moors, typified by the renowned Alcazar, still survived and were a stellar example of the Mudejar architecture and designs of Aragon and Castile.

But of all the visual wonders of Seville, it was the magnificent fifteenth century cathedral that Kevin loved most. The largest Gothic cathedral in the world, the interior of this holy place mirrored the majesty and power of God. The cathedral was built on the foundation of a Moorish mosque, which accounted for its unorthodox design. The nave of the cathedral soared skyward to a height of over 130 feet, higher even than the magnificent cathedral of Chartres.

And now, Kevin was excited to visit it again.

When talking about the secret document, MC had overheard the OM people mention the cathedral. The connection intrigued Kevin.

The flight to Seville was short. Soon, Kevin and Max found themselves in a cab riding from the Seville airport to Toby's hotel.

"Well, well," said Max as Toby opened the door, welcoming them. "This is beautiful." Max and Kevin stepped into a spacious suite where a Venetian crystal chandelier hung in the center of the living room.

"Glad you like it! Good flight?" asked Toby.

"Better than the taxi ride," Kevin said.

Toby said, "Hey, Max, go ahead and put your bag in the closet. You can use the bathroom in the hallway. I think you'll find the sofa comfortable for sleeping."

Max looked at the sprawling leather sofa and sat down to test it out. "Yes, it feels just right," he said.

Kevin and Max dropped their bags in Toby's bedroom, then came back out to the living area.

"Where's MC?" Kevin asked.

Toby grinned sheepishly. "In the spa . . . the girl likes luxury."

"All women like spas," said Max dryly. "Even nuns."

"Well, no matter. We don't need her for the operational planning. We need to get to work," said Kevin. "What've you got for us, Toby?"

Toby unzipped his leather portfolio and removed a large folded map of the city. He pointed to a red circle he'd made. "Here's the location of the cell tower where the calls were made. It's a neighborhood known as El Arenal, not far from here. I reconnoitered a bit and these are the four blocks we want." Toby traced lines with a pencil near the towers. "It's a mixed-use neighborhood, a few shops, a couple of cafés. I counted only four or five residential buildings. Of those, only three are multi-family. I suspect that's what we're after. These guys aren't likely to be living in a big villa."

"Too conspicuous," said Max.

Kevin and Max scrutinized the map.

"Let's find a vantage point," Kevin said.

"Right," Toby replied. "And we'd usually use a car. But we need all four of us. Kevin, you and I do the heavy lifting, you know, the contact stuff. Max can do surveillance, so nobody comes in after us."

"What's MC doing?" Max asked.

"She'll be identifying her former colleagues. We're looking to pinpoint who to go after," Kevin said.

"So with MC, we're back to four people," Toby continued. "And we can't have four people sitting endlessly in a parked car."

"We'll need a van," Kevin said.

"Right. But we'll have to modify the van so we can all see out. And if we cut up a rental car, Hertz will be real unhappy."

"At that point, do we really care?" Kevin asked.

"We don't want to leave tracks. The U.S. embassy has a consulate in Seville. I'll introduce myself to the consul, see if he can help."

"And maybe we can find a van with windows on the sides," said Kevin.

The double door to the suite opened and in walked a gussied up Sister Mary Catherine, in a short white skirt and dark blue pullover sweater. Her hair was feathered and spiked around her face. Kevin took a deep breath. *Oh boy,* he thought. *Here we go.*

"Hi, Kevin! Hi, Max!"

She waved and smiled at them. *Focus,* he said to himself. *There's a job to do.*

Toby put the map back in the briefcase. "Folks, let's plan on an early dinner. Here in Spain, that means before ten p.m. I hope that by tomorrow night we can be operational."

∞∞∞∞

CHAPTER THIRTY-NINE

Seville, Spain

Kevin and Toby awoke early to the clip-clopping of horses on the cobbled stone streets. Seville had a battalion of horse-drawn carriages to circle the cathedral and the old Jewish Quarter. Not far away, the palaces had magnificent wrought iron gates, allowing for easy viewing of the stylish private patios. Also, there were small shops and artisan outlets, as well as art galleries.

When Kevin got out of bed, he could hear Toby on the phone in the bathroom. Minutes later, Toby came out, his face ashen.

"What's up?" Kevin asked.

"That was the NSA about that guy Maggio who Katie's doing business with. Well, he's definitely connected to Opus Mundi. I'd be real careful."

Kevin's heart almost stopped. "What day is today?"

"Tuesday," Toby replied.

"My God! Katie's going to Grand Cayman with Maggio today!" Kevin grabbed his phone off the nightstand and pushed buttons.

"We're six hours ahead of D.C.," Toby said. "It's two a.m. there."

"She's not answering," Kevin counted off the rings, hoping for a reply.

Voicemail. *The owner of this phone has not yet set up voicemail. Please try again later.*

"Does she have a landline?" Toby asked.

"No," Kevin replied. He dialed again. Same result. "I'll keep trying during the day. Let's find the others and grab some breakfast."

Max was sitting in the living room, his blankets neatly folded and placed on a side table. He was showered, dressed, and ready for the day.

"Where's MC?" Kevin asked.

Max pointed to the bathroom. "Been in there over half an hour."

"Is there anything sharp in there?"

Max held his hands up. "My razor is in the hall bathroom," he said. "Are you still worried about her emotional state?"

"She tried to kill herself once," Kevin said.

"Well, if she's going to do it in there, she'll have to brush her teeth to death," Toby added.

A minute later MC emerged in a thick, white terrycloth robe and wet hair. "Just give me a couple, okay?" she purred and gurgled.

After MC dressed, they all partook in a buffet breakfast in the palatial dining room. While sipping coffee, Toby detailed the day's plans. "Spoke to the consul here. He's ex-CIA; we got along just fine. Years ago, we had the same asshole boss, so we bonded quickly. He's got a van for us. Can't be traced, and we can do what we want with it."

"Excellent," Kevin said. "We'll need some drills to make holes, some video gear, communications equipment, and weapons."

"Okay," Toby said. "Let's go shopping. My government credit card is looking for some action. We'll rendezvous back in the suite at seven p.m."

"Sounds good," said MC. "You boys have fun. Meanwhile, I'll enjoy this beautiful suite."

"Don't open the door. For anyone," said Kevin.

"I won't," MC said. "You don't have to worry about me."

Right. Toby, Max, and Kevin left and found shops to buy the stuff they needed. They then proceeded to the garage where the van was waiting. It was a beat-up, rusty old Dodge, maybe a dozen years old, with more than one hundred thousand miles on it. The van was white, nondescript, and without markings. Perfect!

In the back of the van, Kevin drilled a hole large enough for the lens of a small video camera, which was attached to a flat screen monitor. The van was equipped with two long side banquettes, running the length of the van, for them to sit. A digital hard drive would record the video.

After the equipment was hooked up and working, they did a test drive out of the garage. Behold! The camera worked perfectly. Then Toby returned the van to the garage, where it'd stay until after dark.

Kevin tried Katie's number for the fourth time. No answer. He took Toby aside.

"We can't let her get on a plane to another country, Toby. What do we do?"

"I know. I've been thinking. There can't be that many flights to Grand Cayman from D.C. Let's check them out and I'll have somebody intercept her at the airport."

Kevin was relieved. He grabbed Toby's arm. "Thanks, again, pal. And have the intercept make up some excuse why she can't go. We don't want Maggio to know we're on to him."

"Got that covered," Toby said with a smile. "The old dying aunt."

The three men went back to the hotel suite at seven p.m. They ordered room service for an early supper. They agreed it'd be best to forgo booze, given their plans for the evening.

When the food came, they ate, and shortly after eight p.m., Kevin, Toby, Max, and MC walked out of the hotel to the garage where the van was parked. They looked like everyday citizens, wearing jeans and T-shirts. MC and Kevin both wore baseball caps. They walked in silence, lost in thought. The importance, the magnitude, of what they were doing wasn't lost on any one of them.

After they climbed into the vehicle, Toby went over the plan one last time.

"I picked a spot on Via Turello right over here," he said, pointing at the map. "It's the best vantage point to observe two of the three residential buildings in the designated area. The third is around the corner. Anyone going to or from there will be crossing the street here. So we've got the space covered."

"We stay in the van, right?" Max said.

"Correct. Our parking spot is near a café. Kevin and I will get out and go inside and drink some coffee while you and MC watch the monitor. If you want a closer look, the camera has a zoom feature."

"Okay," Max said. "We'll be looking for anyone familiar to MC."

"Time to go, folks," Kevin said. He jumped into the front seat next to Toby. MC and Max got into the back of the van, where no one could see them. Toby fired up the engine and headed out of the garage.

∞∞∞∞

CHAPTER FORTY

Seville, Spain

At night, Seville is transformed into a dazzling festival of lights and winding cobblestone streets, jasmine flowers, orange trees, and serpentine alleys. The horse-drawn carriages, retired for the evening, were replaced by an idyllic quiet and gentle breeze.

Toby drove slowly, passing the Parque de Maria Luisa, a bustling public park by day, empty and lifeless by nightfall. He eased out onto a narrow street illuminated by lampposts.

"The first building is there on the right," Toby said. "We'll park here next to the café, at a safe distance from the lamppost." The street was semi-deserted, and many parking spots were open.

Toby reminded Max and MC that their field of vision, as detectives, included the two residential buildings on the right, and also they should keep an eye peeled for pedestrian traffic and any activities to, or from, the third building. Its entrance was around the corner, out of sight.

Once parked, Toby and Kevin got out and went into the café. They chose the table with the best view of the three-story building across the street. Lights were on in all but one of the apartments.

Kevin ordered a bowl of *samorejo*, a thick purée consisting of tomato and bread, a specialty of Andalusia in Southern Spain. Toby asked for a Caprese panini with smoked mozzarella and sparkling water. There were sandwiches in the van for MC and Max.

After three hours, the only activity whatsoever was an elderly couple exiting the first building and a young woman entering. After that, all they saw from the two buildings were lights shutting off as residents retired.

"Let's call it an evening." Kevin sighed.

"Yeah, looks like no action tonight," said Toby.

The men settled their bill and returned to the van. Kevin was vaguely disappointed, but he also knew it wasn't realistic to expect success the first time out.

Back at the hotel, Kevin got a call from Katie. She was furious.

"Kevin, how could you do that! You embarrassed me in front of my biggest client, pulled me off a plane because my favorite aunt was dying? All my aunts are dead!"

Kevin started to explain, but realized Katie was too angry to listen, so he made a decision.

"Hold on, Katie," he said, covering the phone with his hand. He turned to Toby. "Please speak to her. Tell her everything."

Kevin went back to Katie on the phone and told her he wanted her to talk to Toby, his friend who was a senior CIA operative. She agreed reluctantly.

Toby recounted what had transpired methodically and without emotion. He told her that her client, Greg Maggio, was an Opus Mundi operative, an executive with the very organization that was trying to take over the Church at any cost, including killing Kevin if they had to. Toby told her that in his judgment, they wanted her out of the country. He didn't know exactly why, perhaps to use her as a hostage in their fight with Kevin, and there was a good chance she might be in danger.

After that sobering account, he passed the phone back to Kevin.

Now Katie was in tears.

"Oh Kevin, what have I gotten into? I'm sorry I doubted you. Toby says these people are dangerous. What should I do now?"

"It's okay, Katie. Don't worry. Keep the business relationship going with Maggio. Don't let him know you're on to him. Just don't go anywhere with him. Remind him that your infant son has some physical problems that require your attention."

"Okay. I'll do that."

"Oh, and keep sending him those humongous bills!" Kevin added.

Katie let out a feeble chuckle. "You bet I will!"

The following day, the stakeout routine was repeated. Kevin and Toby, now regulars at the café, were greeted by a burly, amiable waiter and given the same table.

Three hours later, it was the same scenario as the previous day. Kevin and Toby ate sandwiches and soups, then paid their bill and left.

Back at the hotel, the foursome gathered for a glass of wine in the suite. No one was pleased. Everyone was doubting the plan.

Max spoke first. "I don't know if I can take much more of this. I didn't sleep well on the sofa, my neck is stiff, and tonight won't be any better."

MC said, "Look, this plan isn't working."

Kevin paced the floor. "Are you kidding? We can't expect action right away," he said. "These things take time and patience."

"What if these guys don't even live here? Or maybe they're preoccupied plotting another murder in Rome," Max said, frustrated at the day's end, the absence of immediate gratification.

"That's possible," Toby said. He looked at Kevin. "What do you want to do, Kev?"

Kevin too, was frustrated, but thought better of it. Patience was necessary. Patience might just get them what they needed. "Let's give it another shot. Let's start earlier tomorrow. If we don't get results in the next couple of days, we'll go back to Rome, try something else."

Everyone agreed.

∞∞∞∞

The next day they spent some time sightseeing. MC and Toby went to the Museo de Bellas Artes, one of the finest museums in Spain, located in a converted seventeenth century convent. Max went to a local church to say Mass. Kevin visited the cathedral again and marveled at the architecture, the soaring vaults, and the stained glass windows. Kneeling on a wooden kneeler in a pew, he prayed to the Lord, asked for guidance. Then he said a prayer to Mary, pouring out his heart and soul. “Blessed Mother Mary, what do you want from me? I feel your presence, but I don’t know what you want. Help me, Mary, please,” he whispered. Silently, he knelt for a while, repeating his words to Mary, then rose, made the Sign of the Cross, and left.

Just before five p.m., Kevin met the others at the hotel, and the four walked to the van. Unshaven, Max in his baggy slacks and sweater looked derelict. With her tousled do, holey jeans, and leopard sneakers, MC looked like a feral cat in the wild.

They took their places in the vehicle, and Toby headed out to their lookout point. On the other side of the street, he pulled up to the curb, a different spot than last night. Better not to be noticed parking where they’d been the previous evening.

As on the other two nights, Kevin and Toby got out of the van and went to the café. Max and MC settled in for another endless sitting session.

Shortly after six p.m., two young men, dressed in slacks, dark colored shirts, and cap, walked toward building number two. “Hey MC, check this out!” Max said under his breath.

MC hurried over to the monitor and said, “Zoom in!”

Max pushed the zoom button and the screen filled. Reaching the door to the building, the men’s blurry faces could be seen. “That one, I know,” MC said, pointing to one of the men on the screen.

“Okay, I’ll text Kevin,” Max said.

∞∞∞∞

While ladling his soup, Kevin’s phone buzzed. “A text from Max,” he said.

“What’s it say?” said Toby.

“MC recognized one of the guys who went into the building.”

“Let’s go,” said Toby.

Dropping some cash on the table, they hurried out of the café.

Once outside, Kevin and Toby climbed in the van’s front seat and turned around to face MC and Max in the back.

“Who’s the man you recognized?” asked Kevin.

MC said, "His name is Roberto. He's a young priest, very gung-ho in the Opus Mundi organization."

"Please explain gung-ho," Toby said.

"He's a former Italian paratrooper, who became a priest. He's devoted to Opus Mundi. And, I mean very. Like he'd give his life for the cause."

"He may get that opportunity," Kevin said.

"What about the other one?" Toby asked.

MC shook her head. "Didn't know him."

Kevin looked out the van window. "A light on the third floor just went on. The apartment on the right."

Toby said, "That's the spot all right."

Toby and Kevin watched the third floor lit window from the front seat, while MC and Max monitored the video screen.

"What's next?" asked Max.

"Let's wait a few, then go in," Toby said.

Kevin nodded. He reached into his jacket pocket and removed the Glock. He made sure an extra cartridge was in his pocket.

Toby checked his weapon and returned it to the holster.

"What are you going to do?" Max asked.

"We'll start with small talk," Kevin said, his jaw clenched.

"Please don't hurt them," MC said, reaching over the front seat and touching Kevin's shoulder.

"That's up to them," Kevin responded, turning to look at MC and Max. "Both of you, stay put in the van, and be on the lookout. This shouldn't take long. If we need you, I'll call you, Max."

"I just hate violence," Max intoned, in a slightly elevated trill.

"I do, too," Kevin said.

Toby grabbed a small satchel holding two flashlights, a roll of cords, and two Tasers. Opening the van's doors, he and Max jumped out. They strutted nonchalantly to the apartment building's large double doors and went inside. There was an unlit open courtyard with a three-tier fountain, barely visible. Exterior stairways flanked both sides of the building.

The two men chose the stairway to the right, and crept up two flights. The landing gave way to two doors, each with a nameplate. The one on the right was the apartment facing the street. Kevin and Toby whispered to each other, then, facing the door, knocked gently.

No response.

After a few moments, they knocked again, this time louder and more insistently. Someone was inside. They heard movement and muffled voices. Toby looked up at the ceiling to see if there were security cameras. Looking back at the door, he noticed a pinhole peephole. in the center Peeking inside, there was the distinct reflection of a tiny lens. *Shit, whoever was inside could see them!*

Nodding to one another Kevin and Toby drew their weapons. Kevin rattled the door handle. Locked. Stepping back, he fired a shot into the lock. Toby leaned back and kicked the door open. In case someone inside fired back, he and Kevin jerked back to flank the doorway.

The light in the apartment went out. Now there no was light anywhere. Kevin and Toby could hear voices inside whispering in Italian. They sounded angry.

Toby peeked around the door, and with one arm extended, turned on the beam of his flashlight. Bullets whizzed by his head. He ducked.

Without hesitating, Kevin and Toby rushed into the apartment, firing their pistols, and hit one target. A man fell back against a table, screaming obscenities in Italian.

Toby flicked the flashlight around the room, spotlighting the victim lying on the floor, his arm bleeding.

"Drop your weapons. Now!" Kevin commanded in Italian.

Toby circled the flashlight all around the space and found another man, hiding behind the couch. "Last chance, shit-heads!" Toby shouted in English.

"Don't shoot." The man stood up from behind the couch. He slid his weapon across the room.

Toby grabbed the gun and put it in his belt.

Kevin turned on a lamp on the end table by the couch. He spotted a pistol by the wounded man lying on the floor. With the agility and finesse of a seasoned soccer player, Kevin kicked it away from the victim, then picked it up.

Toby kept his gun pointed at the other man, who held his hands on his head.

"Anybody else in here?" Kevin asked.

The men didn't respond.

"Are you deaf?" Toby asked. "My partner asked you a question. You lie, you die."

Both men shook their heads.

Aside from the small kitchenette and living area, there was an open door leading to a bedroom and bathroom. Creeping inside, Kevin found no sign of life in either. "All clear," he yelled to Toby.

Kevin went into the bathroom and retrieved some iodine and bandages, then came back into the living area.

"This one's bleeding pretty bad," Toby said, motioning to the guy who'd been shot.

"Let me see your arm," Kevin said. The man was about thirty. His thin, dark eyebrows connected in the middle of his face above a large, peaked nose. His bushy hair was dark as night and as greasy as car gears.

"What's your name?" Kevin asked.

No reply.

"I'm not messing around," Kevin said. He backhanded the man across the face. "You're going to cooperate with us . . . or else. Now, what's your name?"

The man's eyes widened with surprise and fear. "My name's Gianni . . . Who . . . Who are you?"

Kevin smirked. "You know who I am."

Kevin ripped the sleeve from the man's shirt. "You're lucky, Gianni. The bullet went straight through." Pouring iodine on the wound, he applied a bandage. Gianni winced.

"You'll be playing bocce in no time."

"We're Italian TV salesmen," Gianni said.

Toby laughed. "Couldn't you pick something more glamorous?"

The other man, the one not wounded, put his hands down. He was stocky, a carrot top with a ruddy complexion. "Let's not be kidding, Father Thrall. Yes, we know you. What do you want?"

"Well, well, well, you must be the infamous Roberto," Kevin said, getting up from the floor, holding his pistol steady.

Roberto nodded. "I'd say it's a pleasure to meet you, but I can't quite find the words."

"Have a seat, Roberto, we need to talk."

Toby and Kevin grabbed a couple of dining chairs and shoved the two men into them. Then Toby retrieved the rope from his satchel and tied both men's arms behind their backs, strapping them securely into the chairs. After he'd tied them up, Toby and Kevin pulled up chairs for themselves and sat down for a tête-à-tête.

"I know Roberto is a priest. How about you, Gianni?" Kevin asked as he pointed his gun at them.

"Gianni isn't a priest," Roberto said. "He's a civilian. Works for our cause."

"Opus Mundi, I presume," said Kevin.

Roberto nodded.

"Guys, we can do this the easy way or the hard way. Your call. We want specific information. I can promise you're going to give it to us," Kevin said, "so why don't you just save us all some time, tell us what we need to know."

"We cannot and will not betray our faith," Roberto said solemnly.

Toby clapped his hands. "I'm so impressed you're a man of staunch, unwavering faith," he mocked. "We were in Iraq together." He motioned to Kevin. "That's right, and we ran a special unit that interrogated al Qaeda suspects. Once we'd start in on someone, we didn't stop until we got what we wanted. In fact, we took great pleasure in our interrogations."

Gianni was trying to mask the terror he was feeling, while Father Roberto stared blankly into the room. "Our faith will sustain us," he said.

Kevin's anger was peaking. He grabbed Father Roberto by his collar and jerked him up, chair and all. "Just one question, Roberto. Answer it, you live," Kevin said through clenched teeth.

Roberto was visibly shaken. "What do you want?"

Releasing his grip, Kevin stepped back. Roberto's chair fell back to the floor.

Toby kept his eyes on the two men. "Tell us where to find the two missing pages of the secret of Fatima."

"I don't know what you're talking about," Roberto said, looking down at the floor.

"I'm calling for reinforcements," said Kevin.

Nodding, Toby kept his gun on the men while Kevin pulled his cell from his pocket and called Max.

"Bring MC and c'mon up," Kevin said.

"Are you sure you want to do that?" asked Toby.

"Yeah," Kevin replied. "I'll uncover what these guys know one way or the other."

Minutes later, a knock on the door. MC and Max entered the room. "What's going on?" asked Max, looking at the two men tied to the wooden chairs.

"Oh, my!" said MC, gasping.

Roberto stared at her, trying to make the connection. "Sister?" he asked incredulously.

MC nodded, shifting her eyes.

Kevin said, "Max, you don't know these guys, right?"

Max shook his head. "No."

"MC, you know them, right? What do you know?"

MC hesitated self-consciously, shuffling her feet back and forth. "I know Father Roberto. Not the other one."

"You will die in hell!" Roberto screamed.

Kevin said, "MC, does he have the info I want?"

MC was unhinged, terrified—of Opus Mundi, of Kevin, of being in this situation, of the whole scene. After a few seconds, she closed her eyes, and nodded affirmatively. There was no way out. She began sobbing.

Kevin approached Roberto and stuck his gun in his face. "Last chance. Tell me where you hid the secret of Fatima."

Roberto spit in Kevin's face.

Kevin didn't react. Wiping his face, he turned to Toby. "Strip him to his shorts. Max, run the water in the tub."

"No!" Max shouted.

"Hell! Max, take MC and get out of here. Wait in the car. Now!" Toby ordered.

"I've read about waterboarding, Kevin," Max continued in a whining and accusatory tone. "You're a priest! How could you?"

"Get the hell out!" Kevin said. "Now!" He opened the door and shoved them both toward it. Max took MC's hand, and they scampered out. Kevin closed the door and locked it behind them.

"I'll run the water in the tub," Kevin said while Toby stripped off Roberto's clothes. "Let's see how brave this soldier of God really is."

∞∞∞∞

CHAPTER FORTY-ONE

Seville, Spain

Kevin knew well just how insidious waterboarding was. All the Congressional investigations, liberal protests, and religious admonitions aside, it was torture, pure and simple. And it usually got the needed results. It'd been used by the CIA, authorized by the Department of Justice.

Waterboarding is about placing a prisoner on a board, his hands and body tied down until he's immobile. The face is covered with a cloth, then water is washed over it. Gradually it soaks through, blocking the airflow through the nose and the mouth. When he can't breathe, it feels to him like he's drowning. Panicked, he twists and flails about, struggling to suck in air. Sometimes, in trying to breathe, hysterically gasping for air and escape, victims break arms or legs.

Toby filled the tub in the bathroom with hot water. Trained and experienced practitioners like Toby knew how to do waterboarding, making sure there'd be no escape. Each session of the process lasts for only thirty seconds. Then the cloth is removed and the prisoner is permitted a few gulps of air before it's placed again over his mouth. Few victims last more than a few minutes. The sensation of drowning and loss of air creates such panic, urgency, and desperation that prisoners will do anything to stop it.

With his hands and feet tied, Roberto was forced by Kevin into the bathroom. Roberto had no idea what was in store for him, that is, until he saw the ironing board.

"What . . . what are you doing?" Roberto screamed.

Ignoring him, Toby propped up the ironing board and measured it against Roberto's back.

"Looks like a good fit," Toby said. He tied the ironing board to Roberto's back.

Roberto began weeping.

With the board attached, both men lifted Roberto, placing him on the board in the tub. Kevin lowered a cloth over his face.

Toby said, "Remember that tough al Qaeda guy we worked over? That son of a bitch also said he'd never ever betray Allah before he gave us the info."

"Oh I remember," Kevin replied. "That bastard drowned right away, but not before blurting out a few gems."

"Nobody's perfect." Toby shrugged his shoulders. "OK. Let's get started with this guy."

Father Roberto pleaded, "Please, don't do this!" Then, he prayed, "God, help me, please!" Then he screamed, "God will punish you for this!"

Toby said, "Me, I don't believe in God." Adjusting the showerhead so the water would hit Roberto's face at the right angle, he turned on the faucet.

When the water began accumulating in his throat, Roberto gurgled, flailing wildly on the ironing board, screaming. His debut initiation to waterboarding torture lasted less than thirty seconds.

"Stop!" Roberto pleaded, imploringly.

"Ready to talk?" Toby asked.

Roberto nodded.

Kevin turned off the faucet while Toby untied Roberto, who gagged, squirmed, and twisted in the tub like a fish flapping out of water.

Let the interrogation begin.

"Spill it," Kevin said. "Or go back under."

"What you're looking for is in the Cathedral of Seville," Roberto said. "The tomb of Christopher Columbus."

Bingo! The moment of truth was upon them. Toby and Kevin exchanged mutually gratified looks that said, *Well, that didn't take too long.*

Roberto cried, "What now?"

Toby spoke. "Here's the way it's gonna go. We're going to leave you and your buddy Gianni tied up here in the apartment. We'll be back in a couple of days. If you've lied, well, I don't even want to tell you what'll be next."

Kevin added, "If you've told the truth, we'll give you some food and water. Then we'll tie you up again, until we're ready to call the police to come get you. Understand?"

Roberto nodded.

"Oh, and don't worry about visiting friends. There's a note tacked on the door explaining how you've left Seville, that no one's home right now."

Before gagging them, Kevin offered water to the men. Gianni drank, but Roberto declined.

"C'mon, let's go," said Toby. "I doubt Roberto will be thirsty anytime soon."

∞∞∞∞

CHAPTER FORTY-TWO

Seville, Spain

News of the pope's peace conference was trending nonstop from the Vatican all over the Internet. Within hours, the Associated Press and news reporters from around the world were dispatched to Rome. The following day, His Holiness, Linus II, would hold a press conference at two p.m. The talk of the town was about the pontiff being joined by world leaders.

Stock and bond market analysts held their breath.

Watching the news unfolding on the TV in his suite at the Alfonso XIII Hotel in Seville, Kevin was hoping these developments would herald the success of the new pope's ingenious diplomatic coup d'état.

"Toby, c'mon in here and watch this," Kevin said.

For three days, His Holiness had hosted a conference of foreign ministers from Iran, Israel, and the United States. Observers from the European Union and other nations were also on hand. The occasion marked the first time in history that diplomats from Iran and Israel had ever spoken, much less assembled together around a peace conference table.

News correspondents reminded viewers that the event recalled the famed Vietnam Peace Conference hosted by Henry Kissinger and Le

Duc Tho in Paris in 1973. Several predicted the pope might earn a Nobel Peace Prize as had Henry Kissinger after the Vietnam War.

At two p.m., Kevin, Max, and Toby were still glued to the TV. Because of their success with Roberto the previous evening, the duo, Kevin and Toby, were encouraged about finding the secret's hiding place.

MC sat in the corner of the room, clearly discombobulated. Because she'd ratted out Roberto, identifying him as the priest she'd known in Opus Mundi, she knew about his having been tortured last night. When Kevin and Toby had joined her and Max in the van, Toby and Kevin hadn't said much about it. But she knew about waterboarding. It upset her. And it upset Max. Both were subdued the entire day.

The Vatican press conference was being held inside the Apostolic Palace. Security was exceptionally tight. Because of the assassination of the pope by poisoning, Vatican security was taking extra precautions. In the future, there'd be fewer occasions where the pontiff would be set up as a living target to over a million people.

At two p.m., the Vatican chamberlain stepped onto a podium and addressed the diplomatic corps assigned to the Vatican, news correspondents from around the world, and senior officials of the Italian government.

The chamberlain, dressed in a dark suit with a long silver chain around his neck, introduced His Holiness, Linus II.

The audience rose. The pope was wearing the house dress, a white silk cassock with a matching shoulder cape. The white zucchetto, exclusive to the pope, capped his head. A gold pectoral cross hung from his neck.

Kevin thought Porter looked splendidly papal.

The pope smiled at the audience, turning his head from side to side.

"Good looking guy," Toby commented.

His Holiness took his place at the middle lectern and waved to his right and left. Two men, on cue, walked to the middle of the room. The pope was joined at the lectern on his right by Itzak Reuben, the prime minister of Israel, and on his left by Amir Esfahani, the new president of Iran. The crowd erupted in a spontaneous round of applause.

"Looks like he pulled it off," Toby said.

Kevin nodded. "It answers the question of whose side he's on. Opus Mundi isn't going to like this."

The pontiff began by welcoming his guests. He spoke in Italian, which was both appreciated and approved of by the media. As he stood tall and handsome at the lectern, his white silk vestments shimmered on the wide screen TVs around the room.

"I'm pleased to announce that an agreement has been reached between the leaders of Israel and Iran. You'll hear from the leaders shortly. Iran will renounce all previous statements on Israel's right to exist. The Israeli armed forces will stand down and delegations from both sides will meet with a mutual goal to establish diplomatic communications."

Left unsaid by the pontiff was the fact that the two countries weren't yet ready for the full embrace; there'd be no immediate exchange of ambassadors. But a defrost was a beginning. Inspectors would be allowed to visit any and all nuclear sites in Iran.

"I am grateful to the parties for the good faith exhibited by all sides over the past few days," the pope continued, "and I thank Our Lord for His Divine Intervention. We have many faiths represented here. The God of all was present, and we join together in offering our gratitude."

The pontiff looked to his right and introduced the prime minister of Israel, who was approaching the lectern. As the Israeli leader thanked the pope for his efforts at mediating the crisis, chaos erupted in the crowd. The television cameras remained focused on the three principals behind the lecterns, but they all stopped talking. Instead, they looked out into the audience with surprised and fearful looks.

A priest in the audience, about ten rows back, jumped to his feet and started yelling unintelligibly at the men on the podium. The crowd froze and turned to see who was causing the commotion. At that point, the priest removed a pistol from his cassock and pointed it straight ahead. Screams pieced the air. As the assembled press corps and dignitaries jostled away from the gunman, chairs were knocked over. A shot rang out. The screams resumed at a higher pitch.

Security men leapt onto the podium, throwing their bodies over the leaders.

"My God!" Max said, leaning forward.

"Please, God, no!" shouted Kevin at the TV screen.

"Good God Almighty!" said Toby. "They're trying to assassinate the pope!"

MC stared at the TV with shock all over her face.

The pope remained standing, immobile, and was shoved to the side by his security guard. But he insisted on staying where he was. Standing. The leaders of Iran and Israel lay covered on the ground, shielded by their security guards, while a group of unidentified men, guns drawn, shoved through the crowd.

The camera captured a close-up of the shooter, a young priest with dark hair and a tan, oval face, dressed in a black cassock. He continued to shout in Italian, his pistol waving wildly in the air, when one of the security guards, waiting for a clear target, shot him in the chest. The crowd fled from his area, stampeding the doors.

Max made the Sign of the Cross and cried out, "I hope His Holiness is safe."

The cameras focused on the stage, where the two visiting leaders had already been escorted backstage. At the lectern, His Holiness, Pope Linus II, remained standing, flanked by two Vatican policemen.

The gunman lay immobile and was presumed dead. Now with some degree of calm restored, the TV commentators re-emerged from hiding, trying to make sense of what had just happened. All were thankful that no one besides the shooter had been harmed. The leaders of Israel and Iran were safe and secured in undisclosed locations. The only one standing, still exposed, was the pope.

Commentators marveled at the pope's courage, his *sang froid*, as the anchor for France One Television put it.

"An awesome display of courage," added the BBC.

"The Jews have a word for a guy like that," Toby said to no one in particular. "A *mensch*. This pope rocks."

MC hadn't said a word. She was still staring blankly at the screen, as if she'd seen a ghost.

"Mary Catherine?" Kevin called out, as he suddenly noticed her white face and blank eyes.

She didn't respond.

"MARY CATHERINE!" Kevin shouted.

MC jumped.

"I'm sorry," she said faintly. "I . . . I recognized the priest."

Toby shook his head. "Oh, really? Another one of your buddies?"

"Lay off, Toby," Kevin said. Turning back to MC, he realized she was not just shocked by what had happened. She was in shock.

"They're crazy . . . they're all crazy," she said, shaking her head.

Max said, "You're just figuring that out?"

Kevin lowered the volume on the TV and stepped up. "Listen up, everyone. It looks like Opus Mundi isn't going to stop. They're hell-bent on killing the pope and getting one of their own as the leader of the Church. We've no idea how many more shooters are out there. Unless we put a stop to it, one of them is going to succeed."

He turned to MC, who'd buried her face in her hands. "MC, we need to get a list of everyone in Opus Mundi you know."

She nodded.

"Maybe the missing pages to the secret will help," Toby said.

Kevin nodded. He didn't want to let on that he was under orders from the top man. The missing pages couldn't help because no one would see them. Only the pope could read the missing pages. *Oh hell,* he thought. *Toby won't mind.*

The group continued to watch the news. CNN replayed the shooting and the pope's heroic reaction over and over again.

Finally, Kevin grabbed the remote and turned the TV off.

"We need to plan our mission to get those pages," Kevin said. "Gather 'round, everyone." He moved to the kitchen table.

Kevin started drawing on a yellow legal pad. "Here's where it is," he said, pointing to a spot on his drawing. "With a few tools, and a lightweight folding ladder, tomorrow night we're going in."

∞∞∞∞

CHAPTER FORTY-THREE

Seville, Spain

Early Sunday morning, Toby and Kevin checked in on their prisoners. They were still tied up and weak. They gave them water and gagged them again. "If you've lied to us, Roberto, there'll be dire consequences," Toby said.

"I didn't lie," Roberto said. "Please, let us go."

"We'll be back later," Kevin said.

Checking their ropes were secure, they left their prisoners and locked the door.

Kevin and Toby went back to the suite where Max had stayed with MC. Kevin and Max left for Mass at the Cathedral. Since arriving in Seville, they'd not dressed as priests. Today would be no exception. Wearing slacks and a jacket, they looked like ordinary citizens attending Mass. Of course, Kevin and Max had a major objective: to find the missing pages of the secret of Fatima.

Father Roberto had told them the secret of Fatima was hidden where no one would find it, inside Christopher Columbus's tomb, in the Cathedral of Seville.

"Those bastards are ghoulish," Max commented.

Entering the cathedral through a side door, Kevin and Max settled in a pew in front of the Capilla Mayor, separated from other rows by a black iron grill facade. Behind the grill stood the altar with six large silver candelabras and behind the altar, the well-known gilded carved altarpiece.

Kneeling to pray, Kevin couldn't take his eyes off the gold altarpiece. All he was thinking about was recovering the lost pages of the secret of Fatima.

Deciding to skip the service, Kevin whispered to Max he was leaving. But before exiting, he turned for a look at Columbus's tomb. Then he went to the gift shop and bought an oversized book about the cathedral with full-color photos. Only one page interested him: a large four-color photo of the tomb. He waited to examine and study it before returning later that night.

Returning to the hotel, Kevin paused in a park near the Cathedral to study the photo and read about Christopher Columbus's resting place. The tomb had been in the cathedral since 1899. Before that, it'd been in Havana. Part of a larger sculpture, the tomb was high up, resting atop the shoulders of four larger-than-life figures representing the four kingdoms of Spain: Aragon, Castile, Leon, and Navarre. It was befittingly majestic.

Father Roberto had said the missing pages were inside Christopher Columbus's tomb. But to get to the tomb, Kevin would have to climb above the four towering statues.

Kevin started back to his hotel, the book tucked under his arm. Entering the suite, he found MC by herself on the living room sofa, sobbing inconsolably. *Why was MC always crying? Hard to believe this was the same vixen who'd tried to poison him.*

"What's wrong?" he implored.

"Oh Kevin, I need to talk," she pleaded.

"Go ahead," Kevin said, calmly.

"May I speak to you as my confessor?"

"No. Let's just talk." Kevin sat down by her. Her confessor? He couldn't be bound by its strict confidentiality.

"Kevin, as a young nun I had an indiscretion," she began.

Kevin thought, *So what else is new?*

"There's a young priest at Opus Mundi from Perugia. His name is Francesco. When I first arrived in Rome, he took me under wing. I was lonely and vulnerable. He was the one who introduced me to Opus Mundi. I joined, mostly because he'd swept me off my feet. We had an affair. I thought I loved him, but reflecting on it now, I was just feminine bait for seduction, and for his recruiting efforts. I think he really just wanted me to join up."

"We all make mistakes," said Kevin. "Why bring that up now?"

"Because he just called me. He's scared. He says that Alameda—one of the big OM leaders—accused him of helping me. OM now considers me a traitor; anybody who helps me in turn becomes a traitor."

"What's he scared of, MC?"

"His life! They'll kill him! He wants my help. He says OM is planning something big in the States."

"In the U.S.?"

"That's what he said."

If OM's planning a U.S. operation, it might be retaliation against the Vatican for electing an American pope. On the other hand, Opus Mundi was wildly crazy, erratic, and unpredictably dangerous.

Kevin took MC's hand. "Listen MC, call this Francesco, tell him you'll help him. I want you to fly back to Rome tonight. Toby will find a safe place for you to stay. When we're finished here tomorrow, we'll join you there."

MC nodded. "I'm frightened, Kevin," she whimpered putting her arms around him.

Kevin patted her tenderly on the back. "You'll be okay. Don't worry. I'll make your flight arrangements."

Kevin called Toby, who was souvenir shopping near the cathedral. He filled him in. Toby said he knew a safe house in Rome for MC, and he'd arrange for security for her.

"It's urgent, Toby. When can you have this for her?" asked Kevin.

"Is tonight soon enough?" Toby asked.

"Perfect," Kevin said.

"I'll be back in a few," said Toby, "and you can tell me about it then. I'm almost finished shopping."

"Don't forget the glow-in-the-dark Mary statues," Kevin added.

"You're right—got 'em."

Once back in the suite, it didn't take long for Toby to make the arrangements. Kevin, Max, and Toby drove MC to the Seville airport for her flight to Rome. Kevin gave her final instructions and a warm embrace.

MC wiped her eyes and smiled.

Returning to the hotel for the equipment, they agreed to meet at the cathedral after its ten p.m. closing. Kevin and Toby both dressed all in black, slacks and sweaters. Toby carried the satchel with tools, and Kevin toted the portable ladder, concealed in an oversized nylon artist's folio. Max was assigned to be the lookout, which suited him. He didn't like this burglary idea, even if they were retrieving "secret" pages that'd prevent worldwide catastrophe.

Pointing to the map he'd drawn, Kevin also showed them the picture in the oversized photo book he'd bought. "Here's where we enter, through this side door," he said. "It's a simple lock we can break easily. Max, you stay outside. Good you're dressed as a priest. No one will question your presence." Kevin smiled. "You'll have a walkie-talkie to warn us if anything goes wrong."

Max nodded.

They left the hotel together and walked to the cathedral separately. Not a soul was on the street. At this late hour, most Spaniards were just starting dinner.

Near the cathedral, Toby pointed at the Doorway of Forgiveness, located on the quiet Calle Alemanes. The doorway led to a courtyard and a grove of orange trees, a memento left by the Arabs of a different era.

Max stayed discreetly at a distance, sitting on a bench under the orange trees, clutching his walkie-talkie, just in case.

In a matter of seconds, Toby unlocked the first door and approached a second door leading from the courtyard into the church. He unlocked it quickly.

Kevin looked up at the cathedral's majestic vaults, barely visible in the dark. He motioned to Toby to follow him across one of the middle aisles to the Christopher Columbus monument.

As they crossed, Kevin blessed himself, glancing at the chancel, the cathedral within the cathedral, where he'd prayed earlier.

"It's higher than I'd thought," Toby commented as they came upon the Columbus monument, his voice echoing resoundingly throughout the empty cathedral. He looked up at the four tall bronze statues carrying the coffin. "Let's get started," he whispered, opening his satchel.

Unzipping the leather portfolio, Toby assembled the aluminum ladder, placing it on the pedestal between two of the bronze statues. Kevin held it steady with one hand, a flashlight in the other. Toby climbed to the top of the coffin.

"Hand me the crowbar," he said.

Lifting it out of the bag, Kevin handed it to Toby. Using both hands, Toby applied pressure on the lid to move it. Once open, Toby stood on top of the small ladder and peered down into the tomb. There was a putrid stench; the smell of death, which mysteriously lingers.

"Kevin, there's room for both of us up here."

Kevin steadied the ladder and cautiously climbed the three rungs. Now they both stood precariously on the top, peering down into the tomb. To their dismay, they could see nothing but the bony remains of a body wrapped in a dark, decayed, rotting cloth. There was no sign of paper. Or of anything that might contain papers.

Using a crowbar, Toby calmly and methodically moved the remains. Both Toby and Kevin pointed flashlights on all the corners of the dusty, smelly tomb.

Nothing.

"Damn," Toby said.

"Wait a minute," Kevin muttered, aiming his beam on the crown of the head of the leader of Aragon. "Roberto referred to Columbus as *capo*. In Italian that means 'head'. Maybe he wasn't talking about the body of Columbus, but about the hiding place." Kevin flickered the light around the crown, onto the statue of the leader of Aragon.

"Okay, let's have a look. We'll need to move the ladder." Toby jumped off first.

Kevin's walkie-talkie squawked.

"Somebody coming!" Max whispered. He was panicking. "Maybe it's a security guard."

Kevin and Toby turned off their flashlights. In the distance they could hear the sound of heavy footsteps. The two quickly scrambled down the monument.

"They've got security sensors," Toby whispered, pointing to the ceiling. "Let's hope they don't call for backup."

They darted to the pews in front of the altar. At the end of one of the pews, Kevin knelt quietly. Toby crossed the aisle and positioned himself behind a massive stone pillar. Without moving, they listened carefully to the clickety-clack of the approaching steps. From the direction of the steps, a beam of light was zigzagging up and down.

Kevin, in plain sight, remained calm, kneeling . . . praying.

As the man approached, the beam of light marked Kevin's back. "You!" the man shouted. "What're you doing here?"

Kevin slowly turned around until he was facing the guy. "Praying." His words were deliberately calm.

"May I see your identification, señor?"

"Certainly." Kevin rose slowly, moving to retrieve a wallet from his jacket.

Toby was now moving behind the guard. The fellow was rotund, past his prime. This shouldn't be hard, Toby thought.

Putting his hand over the man's mouth, Toby stuck a gun in his back. "Don't move,"

he said in English.

The guard nodded agreeably.

Kevin felt sorry for the old guard.

"Be gentle with him. I'll finish up," Kevin said. "Please get him out of the way."

With the gun pressed to his back, Toby escorted the guard to the rear of the cathedral. The man's legs trembled. Toby assured him there'd be no trouble.

Out of sight, Kevin climbed the ladder until he was facing the statue of Aragon. With both hands, he grabbed the crown, pulling it upward. At first it resisted, then loosened, giving way. Kevin peered into a small crevice on the top of Aragon's head. Nothing. Scurrying down the ladder, at the bottom he moved it to the next statue, Navarro, and started up again. This time, the crown wouldn't budge at all. Kevin tried again, but still it wouldn't budge. He reached for Toby's crowbar on the second step and tried again. Now the crown moved. Kevin laid it on top of the tomb and pointed his flashlight deep into the opening.

His heart nearly stopped beating. *Oh my God!*

Inside the opening was a leather folder with a wax seal. Kevin exhaled with relief: He knew he'd found what he was looking for. He lifted the folder, replaced the crown, and climbed down.

Kevin quickly put the tools and the ladder away, and called for Toby, who was waiting at the rear of the cathedral. "Got it!" said Kevin. "C'mon, time to get out of here."

Toby directed the guard back to the Christopher Columbus tomb where Kevin was waiting.

"Check the bag," Toby said to Kevin. "You'll find rope and masking tape in there."

When Kevin retrieved the rope and masking tape, Toby tied up the guard and pressed the tape over his mouth. He left him in a pew where he could lie down and sleep. He wouldn't be found until morning.

"You got it?" asked Toby.

"Yes, I think I found it," Kevin whispered.

"C'mon, then, let's get the hell out of here!" said Toby.

The men fled the cathedral the way they'd come in.

On seeing them, Max, who was pacing in anticipation of the worst, breathed a sigh of relief.

They walked quickly back to the hotel, excited and relieved to have uncovered the secret pages. Inside the suite, Kevin's phone buzzed.

It was Katie. She apologized for calling so late. His first thought was Maggio. But Katie assured him that he was under control. He wasn't pleased but he had reluctantly accepted the story that Katie couldn't travel for a while. And, yes, he was still getting billed. Kevin asked about the baby boy.

"He's fine, Kevin. The doctors will examine his clubfoot tomorrow. We hope it's not serious. Anyway, that's not why I'm calling."

There was an awkward silence. Then Katie continued, "I'm sorry to ask this, Kevin, but it's bothering me." She paused again. Kevin waited. "Did you tell me the whole truth about your court martial?"

"What do you mean?"

"I'm not sure . . . I just—"

"Who's putting you up to this, Katie?"

"I just want to know the truth. The whole truth. Did you kill an American soldier in Iraq?"

"I killed a rapist. The rapist's country of origin, his nationality, is of no importance. The truth is that I didn't know he was an American when this happened. And I don't think it would have mattered. Where's this coming from, Katie?" Kevin's jaw was clenched.

"Jimmy told me."

While Jimmy's name sunk in, Kevin paused. "I have nothing else to say about this, Katie, except you might want to ask your boyfriend why he's digging up dirt on me and recommending questionable clients to you."

Silence again.

"I'm sorry," Katie said. "Good-bye."

"What was that about?" asked Toby as Kevin pressed his cell's off button.

"Nothing," said Kevin. "Seems like Katie's fiancé is spinning webs about me."

"What webs?" asked Max.

"Jimmy told her I'd killed an American soldier in Iraq."

"Remember, Kev," said Toby, "I told you that Jimmy Stein guy was snooping around your Army record."

"Yeah, I remember. And he also referred Maggio to Katie."

"We need to figure out what his game is."

"I'll deal with it."

Max was looking at him with big eyes. Kevin was always surprising him.

Kevin couldn't think about this right now.

"Have we heard from MC?" asked Toby.

"No," Kevin said. "Let's wake her up." He put the phone on speaker.

MC answered on the first ring. Right away, she assured Kevin she was safe and comfortable, thanks to the safe house Toby had arranged in the Parioli district.

"Did you see your friend?" Kevin asked.

"Uh, yes, last night."

"Well? What did he say?"

"Kevin, we have to help him. I promised."

"We'll deal with that later."

"He said that Alameda, who he also called Columbo, and some of his people are planning an operation in the United States."

Toby said, "Why, MC? Did he say?"

"I asked," she replied, a tremor in her voice. "He doesn't know. He swears he doesn't."

"Well, we'll see about that," Kevin said. "We're coming back tomorrow."

"You can't torture him, Kevin. I know him, he's telling the truth!"

Kevin wasn't about to debate about whether Sister Mary Catherine's friend was telling her the truth. "I just want to talk to him," he said. "Go back to sleep."

∞∞∞∞

In bed that night, Kevin tossed and turned, barely sleeping. They'd stayed up late making travel arrangements to get to Rome the next morning. Toby had suggested getting out of town early, since the guard at the cathedral probably would be found after sunrise. It'd be nearly impossible for the Seville police to trace the incident to them, but it was pointless taking a chance.

Kevin took inventory. First, he'd successfully recovered the missing pages of the secret—a major accomplishment. The leather envelope lay securely under his mattress, its wax seal intact. Second, he uncovered Opus Mundi's plan to go to the U.S. for an "operation." "Operation" was deadly when it came to Opus Mundi.

Third, Kevin wondered about Katie, if she was in danger. *And who was this Jimmy Stein? Could he be setting up Katie to get at Kevin?* Perhaps. If that was the strategy, it would get his full attention. *And if so, how was Jimmy Stein involved? Who was Jimmy Stein? What was his game?* Too many unanswered questions.

Fourth, Kevin had decided to talk to MC's priest friend, get whatever information out of him he could, regardless of the cost in lives, or in lofty principles.

Fifth, soon he and Toby would have to go release the prisoners at the apartment building. *Or, maybe they should just leave them,* he thought. *But no, not possible, bad idea. He wouldn't want them to die of dehydration.*

∞∞∞∞

The next morning, Kevin and Toby awoke early and went to the apartment. Entering, they could see Roberto and his friend weren't there—they'd escaped!

"Well, that's either good news or bad," Toby said.

"Meaning what?" Kevin asked.

"Well, either they got free by themselves and have split town; or some of their Opus Mundi operatives found them, which means they're now hunting for us," said Toby.

"Another reason to get out of Seville," said Kevin.

The two hustled back to their hotel and started packing. Already packed, Max was patiently waiting for them. He asked if Kevin was going to try to see the pope.

"Yes, as soon as we get back to Rome," Kevin replied. "I've got something he wants." Kevin smiled and held up the pouch. He then put it in his leather briefcase and locked it.

"Aren't you going to read it?" Toby asked as he closed his suitcase and put it on the floor.

"I've got orders from the pope not to read it," Kevin said.

"Look, pal," Toby said. "As far as I'm concerned, there may be something in those pages having to do with national security. You've got some extremely radical Catholic group killing people based on whatever's written in there. I'd vote to go ahead and read it."

Kevin shook his head. "It's sealed, Toby. I gave my word. I do a lot of questionable things, but countering a direct papal order isn't one of them."

"Kevin, think hard about this. Uncle Sam financed this little expedition. I need to account for it."

"Okay, I'll think about it," Kevin said.

"It's a wonder we're all alive," said Max.

"Well, it's not over yet," Toby said. Max looked at him with terror in his eyes. Toby laughed and punched him in the arm. "Just kidding, big guy. We're safe . . . I hope."

The three men grabbed their bags and left quickly for Seville's airport. In the taxi, Kevin's cell buzzed. He didn't recognize the number but answered it anyway.

"Father Thrall, this is Ivan Koncik."

"Who?"

"Ivan. Your friend from Medjugorje. I showed you around when you were here."

"Of course. Sorry, Ivan. Bad connection," Kevin fibbed. He remembered now.

"Kevin, I have a message for you."

"A message?"

"Yes, one of the visionaries came to see me. She said that I must tell you something."

"Who is it?" Kevin asked.

"I'm sorry. I can only tell you the message comes from one of the visionaries to whom Mary appears."

"What's the message, Ivan?"

"I wrote it down. Please hold." There were sounds of paper crumpling. "Here it is," Ivan continued. "You will soon have answers to questions important to you. Follow your destiny."

"Follow my destiny? Ivan, I can get advice like that from a fortune cookie. Was there anything else?"

"That's all, my friend."

"Thank you, Ivan."

"What's that about?" asked Toby.

Kevin shook his head. "A message from heaven," he said. "Allegedly."

∞∞∞∞

CHAPTER FORTY-FOUR

Rome, Italy

Among the CIA's many qualities, one that goes uncelebrated is its keen eye for valuable real estate. If the CIA were to cease to exist, it'd reap a fortune from its exquisite residential real estate holdings acquired over the years in some of the world's most beautiful, coveted spots. These properties were lumped under the misnomer of 'safe houses.' Lodged in one of them, a nineteenth-century townhouse in the Parioli district of Rome, was Sister Mary Catherine.

When Kevin had first studied in Rome, he enjoyed dinners and receptions in Parioli, a residential area of parks, tree-lined streets, and a mix of old villas and modern luxury apartment buildings. It's Fellini rather than Borghese, Ferrari instead of Michelangelo, a modern twist on residential luxury.

When the three arrived from the airport, an official minion opened the door. He looked for the approval of a CIA officer standing behind him. Recognizing Toby Beck, he allowed them entrance.

Dressed in her usual spray-on jeans, Sister Mary Catherine greeted them in the drawing room, activating her brightest, toothy smile.

"It's good to see you guys," she said, smiling and hugging them.

"MC, I need to meet your friend," Kevin said.

"He's upstairs," she replied. "But, Kevin, remember what I asked you . . ."

"Don't worry," said Kevin.

"We'll be on our best behavior," added Toby.

Toby and Kevin made their way upstairs. An attendant pointed to a room on the right of the staircase. Before entering, Toby said, "Your turn as bad cop."

Kevin nodded.

Kevin knocked on the door, but didn't wait before entering. Father Francesco Garibaldi was propped in a wing chair. As they entered, he turned to face them. Garibaldi was youthful, svelte, with long black hair, an aquiline nose, and the look of the fetching playboy models in Gucci ads. *No wonder MC liked him,* Kevin thought.

After introductions, they invited the priest to join them at a nearby card table.

"May I smoke?" Francesco asked with a pseudo-British accent. He didn't wait for a reply before pulling out a Marlboro and a shiny gilded lighter.

"We need to talk and don't have much time," Toby began.

"I am at your disposal," Father Garibaldi replied with a guarded smile. He opened his arms, bowed slightly, and simultaneously exhaled a heavy stream of smoke.

Kevin thought he was quite full of himself.

"I'm going to be blunt, Francesco," said Toby. "You are in a CIA safe house. Don't let the plush surroundings fool you. This serves two purposes: to protect some people and to get information from others."

"You are in the latter category," Kevin said, leaning forward, inches from Francesco's face.

Francesco smiled again. "Of course," he said.

"Tell me what you know about Opus Mundi's mission to the United States," said Kevin.

"Well," he began. "First, let me say, I was recruited under duress. I don't agree with their methods, which have become very, shall we say, harsh and unacceptable."

"Go on," said Kevin.

"I overheard conversations about a mission to Washington, D.C. Carlos Alameda is going, which leads me to believe it's important. This Alameda—we also call him Columbo—indicated they plan to talk to a woman named Kate O'Connell."

"Why?" Kevin demanded.

"I don't know."

"Hey, not acceptable," Kevin said. "Look, we can do this the easy way or the hard way. Are you with me?" Kevin rose and stood behind Francesco. Without warning, he locked his arm around Francesco's neck and began strangling him.

The young priest was shocked. He gasped for air and struggled to loosen Kevin's grip, but Kevin was too strong.

"Answer the question," Kevin said, keeping his grip tight.

"Wait a minute," Toby said. "Give him a chance to talk." *Toby playing Mr. Nice Guy.*

Kevin released the priest and sat down facing him. "Next time I have to get up, we're going downstairs to the basement," Kevin said. "You won't like it down there." Kevin didn't know if the townhouse had a basement or not, but he was assuming Francesco didn't, either.

Toby shot a look at Kevin which both men understood. This guy wasn't going to take a chance on ruining his pretty looks. In no time, he'd be singing like a canary.

"If I talk, will you protect me?" Francesco asked. He seemed afraid, and eager to cooperate.

"We'll get the Italian authorities to protect you," Toby said. "But only if you tell us everything you know. If you don't, we'll let you walk out of here, but we'll make sure the whole town knows you talked to us."

Francesco shuddered.

"Tell me about the mission to Washington," Kevin said, calmly.

Francesco took a deep breath. "It's about the secret, the unrevealed secret of Fatima. I don't know what it says, but Alameda does. Whatever is in the secret is the reason Alameda is going to Washington."

"What about Katie O'Connell? How does she fit in? Is he using her to get at me?" Kevin shouted.

"I do not know, sir. Honestly, this I don't know."

Kevin jumped up from his chair, kicked it over, and reached across the table for Francesco.

"Is he using her to get to me?"

Toby stood up. "Easy, Kevin. This guy doesn't know."

Kevin relaxed his grip, and let the priest slide back into his seat.

Francesco begged to be released. "Please let me go! I know nothing else!"

Toby and Kevin went to the corner of the room to discuss what to do with Francesco. Finally, they came to a decision. "You can go, Francesco," said Toby. "But, don't say a word to anyone about this meeting, or this location."

"I swear, *signori!*"

"Get out of here before we change our minds," said Kevin.

"Please . . . are you going to tell them what I told you? If you do, they'll kill me."

"We won't tell anyone. At least, not unless we hear you talked. *Capice?*"

Nodding, Francesco bolted for the door.

∞∞∞∞

CHAPTER FORTY-FIVE

Rome, Italy

That afternoon, Max Drotti went home, and Toby accompanied Kevin to his quarters in the Vatican. For the time being, MC would stay at the CIA safe house. It was the safest place for her. She had cried when Kevin let Francesco go, and thanked him profusely by wrapping her arms around him. "Kevin, if you need anything—and I mean anything, please ask me. I'll do anything for you."

He knew what she meant as she rubbed her body against his. Once again, she'd conveniently forgotten his priestly calling.

Toby watched them, shaking his head. He couldn't believe this nun was throwing herself at Kevin. Honestly! Kevin—even as a priest—got more action than he did. It didn't seem fair.

Kevin found everything at his apartment the way he'd left it. "I'm really thankful for the security system here," he told Toby.

"It's probably one of the best," Toby said.

Toby dropped his bag in the living room. Kevin made coffee.

"I'm going back to D.C. tomorrow," Toby said while making himself comfortable on the couch. "Time for me to head home. Have you thought any more about the secret?"

Kevin had stored the pouch in his leather briefcase. He hadn't let it out of his sight. "I'll let you know in the morning, Toby."

"My plane's at two p.m."

"Tomorrow?"

"Yes, OK." Kevin nodded. "May I ask another favor?"

"Sure."

"Would you run a deeper check on Jimmy Stein? I need to know why he's digging up dirt on me and if his recommendation of Maggio to Katie was innocent or because he knew something more. Could he be with Opus Mundi?"

"If he is, there's going to be a clue, something pointing to it, either through communications, travel, or money. I'm pretty sure, if he's working with them, we'll find something that tips us off. Might take time."

"Thanks, Toby." Kevin said.

Kevin and Toby turned on CNN to catch up on the latest news.

Since assuming his role as successor to St. Peter and leader of the Roman Catholic Church, Pope Linus II had become a world celebrity. Kevin was proud to call him a friend, but knew his rising star would make access and communication hard. And he had to see him.

It wasn't enough that Porter had become the first American pope—remarkable in itself—but in his brief reign, he'd negotiated a peace between Israel and Iran, thus distinguishing himself as the first in history to do so. He'd become a world-class diplomat. However, the media was now referring to it not as "peace" but as a "Mexican standoff." It didn't matter. Either way, Porter had accomplished a major feat, which others before him hadn't been able to do for several decades.

And the accolades were newsworthy. For his exemplary conduct during an assassination attempt on his life, the United States Army made His Holiness an honorary Green Beret Ranger. The commandant of West Point was making plans to travel to Rome with a sizeable delegation to present the award. The Italian press speculated whether the pope would actually don the Green Beret during the ceremony. Officials at the Vatican made plans to ensure that he did not.

∞∞∞∞

While Toby watched the news, Kevin made phone calls. He was as surprised as anyone when his request for an audience with the pope was granted immediately. His Holiness would see Kevin at six p.m.

Kevin showered, shaved, and donned his finest black suit and white collar. Looking at himself in the mirror, he thought he detected more gray in his hair. Given the stress of the last few weeks, he was neither surprised nor bothered. Vanity wasn't one of his vices. Still, he liked his face. It had the ruddy charm of an almost middle-aged American man.

Where the pope resided, the Apostolic Palace, the security was as tight as in the White House. A uniformed security man requested the leather portfolio in Kevin's possession. Kevin wouldn't let it out of his possession for anyone, and told that to the guard. Sensing a confrontation brewing, a papal aide motioned to the guard to stand fast. Clutching the leather folio under his arm, Kevin followed the aide up the stairs to the pope's quarters.

Porter, being American, had minimized some of the traditional ceremonial pomp and circumstance, the daily rituals accompanying the pope's presentation. For example, there was no chamberlain with a commanding stick banging the floor to announce His Holiness. No lines of visiting clerics kneeling to kiss the pontiff's ring. There were now mostly informal meetings in house dress with the Vatican higher officials.

Instead, Kevin was escorted directly into the room and invited to sit on an embroidered armchair in the papal library. Once again, Kevin found himself admiring the bound volumes nestled in floor-to-ceiling bookcases around the room. The expansive windows offered a spectacular view of St. Peter's Square below and of the basilica to the right. As always, a crowd was waiting to enter the church.

Kevin had been seated for only a minute when the pontiff entered the room by himself, dressed in papal white. As usual, he wore the white zucchetto on his head.

"Hello, Kevin." The pontiff smiled, holding out his hand.

Kevin jumped to his feet, took the pope's hand and kissed his ring.

"Thank you for seeing me, Holiness," Kevin said. He knew the man well enough to know he couldn't be fully adjusted to the papacy yet, his papacy.

"Always good to see an old friend, Kevin. Let's sit over here." They sat facing each other in two plumped, down-filled armchairs. "It's amazing the new friends I've made since becoming pope," Porter added. "Have you found what you were looking for?"

"I did, Holiness, with the help of a few friends." Kevin unzipped his leather case and retrieved the velvet pouch. He handed it to Porter, making sure he could see the unbroken wax seal.

His Holiness took the pouch from Kevin and heaved a weary sigh. "I can feel the weight of this already," he said, "and I suspect you do too, Kevin."

Kevin nodded.

"Shall we see what's inside?"

Kevin was surprised, but pleased. He couldn't help but notice that his friend had aged in the few weeks since taking office. His role as the spiritual leader for more than a billion people was not for the faint-hearted.

"Considering what happened to some of your predecessors who read it, aren't you a bit unsettled?" Kevin asked.

The pope laughed. "Given that somebody was trying to shoot me the other day, I doubt the musings of some young lady about the goings on in 1917 will do me in." He pressed a buzzer on the table beside him and a young man appeared and bowed. After addressing the man in Italian, the pope broke the seal on the velvet pouch. He withdrew two faded pieces of paper. Kevin glanced at the handwriting on the pages. He recognized it as Lucia's, the same as the other four pages.

The pope began to read. After a few seconds, he stopped and handed the pages to the young man, who bowed again and took a seat at a small desk in a corner of the room. He opened a small laptop and went to work.

"He's a translator, Kevin," the pope said. "My Portuguese isn't good enough to make it out. He is reliable and discreet. This should only take a few minutes."

Kevin noted to himself that as reliable as the translator might be, His Holiness had insisted he perform his work in his presence.

The two sat quietly while they waited. An attendant in a white coat brought coffee and pastries. In the silence of the moment, as old friends, they were at ease, sipping coffee and sampling the croissants.

Closing his eyes, Kevin wondered if he should share with His Holiness that Opus Mundi was targeting his friend, Katie O'Connell. He could decide after the pope had read the secret. He prayed the pontiff would share it with him.

A few minutes later, the young man rose from the desk, bowed, and handed the pontiff a handwritten piece of paper and the two original, yellowing pages from which he'd translated.

Taking the handwritten page from the man, the pope dismissed him. Then he looked at Kevin, his eyes wide. "Here goes," he said.

Kevin watched Porter's eyes. While he read, the pope clearly was making an effort to remain composed, but his eyes betrayed him before he spoke. "Good Lord," he muttered.

As the pontiff finished with the page, he held it in his hand and looked up at the ceiling. He didn't speak. Then, composing himself, he turned to Kevin.

"Takes your breath away," he said soberly.

Kevin debated whether or not to ask the pope. Instead, he remained silent, hoping the pontiff would confide in him. Something—anything.

The pope handed Kevin the single sheet of paper. "Read this. Keep it to yourself," he said. "You deserve to know."

Kevin began reading. When he'd finished, he read it again, making sure he'd fully grasped what it'd said. He broke out in a cold sweat. Could this be? He thought about the message Ivan had given him in Medjugorje, from one of the visionaries to whom the Virgin had appeared. Follow the path of your destiny. At the time, it seemed silly, but now much less so.

He handed the page back to the pontiff.

"Holiness, this is startling. Mary talks of a dramatic event that'll occur in one hundred years. From then. That time is now."

The pope nodded. "Fatima was in 1917. That's just about one hundred years ago."

"Yes, Holiness, and there seems to be a pattern here. The visionaries in Medjugorje said Our Lady spoke of Fatima in her appearances to them, which wasn't so long ago."

"There is likely a connection here. I wish I knew what it was." The pope was folding and unfolding his hands.

"I have some ideas, Holiness, but I won't speculate until I'm more certain," Kevin said.

"I understand, Kev. My concern is Opus Mundi. What do they plan to do with the information revealed in the secret?"

"Opus Mundi will certainly play a role. Do you know their leader?"

"Based on new evidence, I have suspicions," he said.

"May I remind you, Holiness, that you brought me here to take care of Opus Mundi. I can't be effective with one hand tied behind my back."

"I understand, Kevin. Truly, I do. But I won't mention names just yet."

And then Kevin got it. He smiled. "That's not necessary, Holiness. I am reading your mind."

∞∞∞∞

CHAPTER FORTY-SIX

Rome, Italy

Later, when Kevin went back to the apartment, Toby presented him with a care package. "After you leave, open it," he said. "And Kev, whatever you do, be careful tonight. These Opus Mundi guys are ruthless."

"Thanks," said Kevin. "I appreciate your help."

"You don't want me to come along?" asked Toby.

"No, it's best I brave this one alone," said Kevin.

"OK. Good luck. I'll be here, just call."

Leaving on his mission, Kevin opened the small package Toby gave him in a plain cloth zippered case. The tools included a set of master keys, a notepad with codes and passwords for a computer, a miniature crowbar, an LED flashlight, a miniature camera, and plastic gloves. Brilliant! Also, there was a card in an envelope:

Dear Kevin,

I don't need to tell you to be careful. These tools should help. Consider them a birthday present. May you live well this year. Onward! Happy Birthday.

Toby

Kevin was touched. It was just like Toby to remember his birthday. Kevin himself had nearly forgotten it. *Ugh, forty-three.*

The tools were only part of the gift. While Kevin was visiting the pope that day, Toby had learned, from his intelligence connections, the secure address of Cardinal Marini's private residence. Cardinal Marini had long kept it secret. Kevin knew that if the leader of Opus Mundi was a cardinal of the church, it left few places to look. It'd have to be someone high up inside the Vatican with access to confidential information. As head of Vatican security, Marini was suspect. He'd brilliantly derailed the investigation of his unlisted personal address, shifting all the attention to the attempted assassination of Pope Quintus II. This was a major clue.

The difficulty: proving it. There was nothing tangible to connect Marini with Opus Mundi. Only a handful of individuals knew the true identity of Visitor, the leader of Opus Mundi, and all of them would give their own lives not to reveal it.

The big break came when Toby secured the address of Marini's secret residence. Tonight, Kevin was heading out, undercover, to let himself into Marini's townhouse in Trastevere. The cardinal was scheduled to be at an ecclesiastic affair involving a religious delegation from Poland. Kevin had checked the schedule; the event started at seven p.m. and ended at eleven p.m., leaving ample time to get in and snoop around his digs.

At nine p.m. Kevin left his apartment, dressed in black slacks and a sweater, dark sneakers, and Toby's magic bag of tools. Kevin wore a black knit cap.

Kevin took two buses to get to the address. He got off the second bus at Viale di Trastevere, a residential neighborhood in the oldest section of Rome.

The building was on a tree-lined side street off the main bus line. Kevin double-checked the stone building's address, noting a massive double door at the entrance. Not a problem; it creaked open. Inside, as the centerpiece for the residential complex, was an elegant courtyard featuring an angelic three-tier marble fountain surrounded by lush foliage. There were four building entrances, for what Kevin estimated amounted to twenty individual units, two per landing on each of the five floors.

Toby's intelligence had pinpointed the cardinal's residence as unit C-4.

Kevin crossed the courtyard, tiptoeing gingerly on cobblestones. When he got to unit C-4, the door was locked. Kevin fiddled with the master keys, trying one, then another, without success. The third did the trick. With two apartments on the ground floor, it meant unit C-4 would be one flight up. Kevin climbed the stairs encircling a small elevator.

On the second floor, Kevin located a brass plaque with the number four. The wooden door was ornate, about ten feet high. There were two locks, a fairly modern upper bolt and an old-fashioned lock below, with a large keyhole. A cinch. Starting with the upper lock, he opened it on the first try. The second lock was even easier. Piece of cake.

Kevin surveyed the landscape outside one last time before turning the knob to enter. It was dark inside, but he waited until he was inside and had closed the door before activating his flashlight. Suddenly, the room lit up. An overhead chandelier, lamps on tables, picture lights over oil paintings—all at once, in a flash, everything illuminated. *Trouble.* Kevin withdrew his pistol and crouched low on the floor, waiting . . .

Nothing.

He took measure of the room, now that it didn't seem as though anyone was there. Slowly, he rose, his eyes peeled for possible hiding places for someone to pop out. He was in the foyer of a luxurious home with fifteen-foot ceilings, eighteenth-century oils lit by gold plated lamps, eighteenth-century period furniture, Persian carpets, and a Venetian crystal chandelier.

In the corner of the room high on the wall, Kevin sighted a small black box. Definitely not a period piece: it had a blinking red light. He breathed a sigh of relief. The box was a sensor that turned on the lights when someone entered the room. Maybe Cardinal Marini had been to Las Vegas. But could the box have a security alarm signaling to the owner that someone had entered? Kevin had to act fast.

The pistol firmly in his grip, Kevin entered the living room, which was equally as majestic as the foyer, only twice as large. An oil painting of a cardinal hung over the marble fireplace. The air was musty; the windows probably hadn't been opened in days, but if musty air could smell rich, this air was luscious.

Kevin walked into the master bedroom and noted a massive California-style poster bed with carved bedposts. Gold sconces with faux candles decorated the walls. Past the bedroom, Kevin found a small door and opened it into a dark room. Fumbling about, he located a light switch and found himself in a modern space—an office with contemporary furniture, an iMac desktop, a laptop, two viewing screen monitors, and on a parallel opposite wall, a huge flat screen TV. A dramatic, high-tech contrast to the centuries-old elegance of the apartment proper.

Kevin put the pistol and flashlight in his bag and hurried to the desk. He sat down and turned on the iMac. The screen came on, asking for a password. Kevin got his notebook out of his bag. Fortunately, the CIA had been able to locate the computer's IP address and the folks in Langley, Virginia had monitored it for several days. They believed they'd captured the password from keystroke mimicking software, which tracked keystrokes using the computer's IP address. All highly illegal, of course, unless it was part of the agency's work to safeguard the United States from terrorist activities. In moments like these, it paid to have friends like Toby.

Typing in the password, folders popped up. Kevin opened some with self-explanatory names. Nothing worth getting excited about. Some folders involved humdrum church business, appointments with visiting dignitaries, budgets for various Vatican departments, and notes from meetings with the Curia. Then Kevin opened a subfolder. The text was garbled, in code. No way of deciphering it. He couldn't chance emailing the info; it'd leave an electronic fingerprint. He didn't want to use the printer, either; too easy to trace. Instead, he took his iPhone and snapped pictures of five pages of gibberish. Now he could safely enlist the CIA to decipher the code. Kevin was guessing these docs had info related to the security of the United States. After all, these were the same guys who'd started the Israel-Iran war.

Totally psyched about what he'd found, Kevin turned the computer off to check out the rest of the apartment. *Why would a high-ranking Vatican cardinal opt for such a secret, high-rent apartment?* Something was smelly—raunchy. For a moment, Kevin wondered if he'd find a pair of lacy fishnet thongs in the closet.

Something told him he would.

Exiting the office hideaway, Kevin went back into the bedroom. He opened the closet door and found an array of tailored, high-end men's clothes. Rifling through them, he marveled at the Italian designer tags: Zegna, Gucci, Brioni, Ferragamo. Even the shoes had Italian labels. Not a thread of clerical garb.

Kevin reached for the back of the closet and felt something like a drawer. Pushing some suits aside, behold, an almost imperceptible built-in safe, blended in with the wall. He felt around and found a tiny keyhole. Fumbling through his set of master keys, Kevin inserted one. Three tries later, the lock turned. Inside the safe were two items, a stack of 500-euro notes and a leather album.

Kevin took the large, bulky album to the desk and sat down. The album contained photos. They were medium close-up shots and head shots of young seminarians, dressed in robes, adolescents in training for the priesthood. Kevin smiled as he remembered those moments—but as he kept turning the pages, the pictures became disturbing. Now there were full disclosure shots of the young men without clothing, performing sex acts on an older man. In some of the photos, the older man's face was shielded by a mask. In others, the perpetrator's face became recognizable. Cardinal Marini.

"Good God!" Kevin said quietly to himself. "Good God!" For a long time he looked in horror at the pictures. He thought he'd be sick. Whatever else Marini was, he was a pervert. Kevin gagged and ran to the bathroom. He threw up in the toilet, and then waited while his stomach settled. He still had pain from the knife wound Alameda had inflicted on him. The retching made it worse.

Coming from the foyer, Kevin heard a creaking noise from behind him in the foyer. Someone had opened the large door. He could hear two men jabbering in Italian. *Shit!* He rushed to the den and with a flick of his wrist, grabbed the album and his bag. He wouldn't have time to put it back in the safe. He tore out two pages from the album, stuffed them in his pocket, and set it on the desk. He located his pistol and hid by the wide screen TV in the corner of the den. From there he'd have a clear shot at the door.

Of the two men chatting in Italian, one voice was Marini's.

"Yes, the lights are on. Someone's been in here," Marini said.

"I called you right away, Eminence," the other man said. "I heard the footsteps on the steps as I was leaving to inspect the building before retiring. I knew it wasn't you. That is why I phoned you."

"Thank you, Renaldo. You will be rewarded. You may leave now."

"Sir, the intruder may still be in the apartment. It isn't safe. I'll stay with you while the police are called."

"No need, Renaldo. I have an idea who it might be; there'll be no danger."

A few moments later, Kevin heard the door click shut.

Then a deep voice called out, "Father Thrall! If you're here, I suggest you come out!"

Kevin walked calmly through the bedroom and into the lounge area. His Eminence stood wearing a simple black clerical suit with the line of scarlet buttons. Kevin entered the room and stood at a distance facing the cardinal, keeping the gun visible in his hand.

"You've become something of a nuisance, Father," Marini said calmly.

"And what shall I say of you, Eminence?" Kevin spit out the word with an intonation of contempt.

"If you'd like to shoot me, be my guest. I should like to point out that the black box over there does more than turn on the lights. It's a hidden camera."

"Good to know. Then we'll just move to another room," Kevin said.

Marini shrugged. "Same thing, I'm afraid."

"I believe you, Marini, if only because I cringe to consider in what creative ways you've used those cameras."

"Let's not get sidetracked. What you and I need to discuss is how we might come to a mutually agreeable arrangement between us. Shall we sit down?"

Kevin stared at him with anger and contempt. "I'm quite comfortable standing on my feet." He raised his gun.

"As you wish," Marini responded. "No doubt by now you and your clever friends have deduced what I stand for. I am the leader of Opus Mundi."

"And a pervert," Kevin said.

Marini raised his hands in a gesture of surrender. "Please, Kevin, let us not digress into sins of the flesh. Suffice it to say they afflict us all at some point. As I believe you know all too well, we mortals all wrestle with these burning, salacious inclinations."

"Okay, tell me, how does someone like you get to be a cardinal in the Catholic Church?"

"Besides my *human* shortcomings, I have numerous qualities to recommend me. Many clergymen look to me to be the salvation of the Church. The Catholic Church has been losing members for decades. Many devoted to the Church pay little attention to our important teachings."

Marini pointed a finger at Kevin. "By the way, the American church is among the worst. And we intend to reform it before the true mission of our Church becomes archaic."

Kevin held his gun in one hand. With his other, he plucked his phone from his pocket.

"What are you doing?" Marini asked.

"Calling the Vatican police."

"May I suggest you wait?" He held up a hand. "A little patience, Kevin. I haven't conveyed my offer."

"There's nothing to offer."

"Well Kevin, I'm offering a way to save your friend, Miss O'Connell. Surely that might be of interest."

Fear overcame Kevin. He knew Opus Mundi was targeting Katie. MC's friend, Francesco, had told him so. Francesco also had told him Alameda was on his way to Washington to "talk to her." Kevin got it. And he had to make sure it didn't happen.

"You son of a bitch. She has nothing to do with this," he said. He clenched his jaw.

"Of course not," Marini said with a patronizing smile. "But if you care for her, listen to me. Leave quietly. Forget about this encounter with me, and anything you may have seen tonight. Do this and I will give you my word no harm will come to your friend."

"And if I don't?"

Marini shrugged his shoulders.

Kevin considered his options. The threat against Katie was real. Carlos Alameda, aka Columbo, was planning an operation in the

United States. But there was more to it. *Would Alameda actually go after Katie? If he agreed to his terms, could he trust Marini to honor his word, his side of the bargain?*

Then again, could he in good conscience allow someone as repugnant and perverse as Marini to get away? One thing was certain: If Marini were allowed to live, Opus Mundi would make Kevin disappear, probably kill him.

Kevin made his decision. "No deal," he said. He raised the pistol, pointing it at Marini.

For the first time, Marini grimaced, looking genuinely worried. "Remember the cameras, Father!" he said.

Kevin pulled out his cell phone from his pocket and punched in the Vatican emergency number.

"The only way I'll get the satisfaction of shooting you, Marini, is if you run. And let me warn you, if you do, don't expect a clean shot. You will suffer."

"Don't be an idiot. You're throwing your life away."

"Not after the Vatican police sees that trophy album."

Ten minutes later, a knock on the door signaled the Vatican police's arrival. Kevin opened the door and identified himself to the commandante, a short, stubby policeman wearing a plain wrinkled suit. Accompanied by two uniformed armed Vatican detectives, the commandante was stony-faced.

"This is Cardinal Marini," Kevin said to the group, although his identification was hardly necessary to members of the Vatican constabulary. "Place him under arrest."

Marini looked at the policemen and smiled. "My good men, please forgive this poor misguided American priest. He doesn't know of whom he speaks. And, please, for his own safety, see him out. As you can see, he is under duress and suffering." With his index finger Marini made an elaborate twirling gesture, pointing at his forehead. "*Pazzo*," he whispered. *Crazy*.

Saluting Marini, the commandante turned to his men.

"Secure him," he said calmly, pointing at Kevin.

"No!" Kevin shouted. "You've got this all wrong! Wait 'til you see what I have to show you. In the bedroom."

Marini smiled at the commandante. "It's always something!" he chuckled to the policemen. The officers nodded in agreement, dutifully.

Marini opened the door. "Now, please go," he said. "I am truly exhausted. I would like to retire for the evening."

As he exited with his men and their hapless prisoner, the commandante saluted the cardinal. Kevin remained silent. *What had he been thinking?* It was futile to protest. He felt beyond stupid. Naturally, the Vatican police would take the word of a cardinal over that of an American priest.

In the police car, Kevin was grateful he was spared the handcuffs. Suddenly, he remembered the pages in his pocket. He reached into his pocket and retrieved one of the pages he'd torn from the album—two vulgar shots of young men performing sex on Cardinal Marini. He held up the pictures before the commandante's eyes. "Look at this!" Kevin said.

The commandante seized the two pictures, put on his glasses, examined them, and turned back to Kevin, alarm on his face.

"Good Lord!" the commandante said. "I am appalled. What to do?" He frowned as the wheels in his brain were spinning. The commandante nodded once, and reached for his phone to dial headquarters. He wasn't going to make this decision by himself. In rapid Italian, an agitated discussion ensued. Kevin couldn't keep up. But in the end, the energetic nodding made it clear an agreement had been reached.

The commandante turned to his men. "We've made a big mistake. We're going back upstairs."

"Why?" asked one of the policemen.

The commandante shoved the photos in front of his face. "Here's why."

"*Jesus, Mary and Joseph!*" said the policeman.

When they arrived at the landing, Marini, a small leather suitcase in hand, was already opening the door to exit.

"Cardinal, I'm afraid we need to detain you," the commandante said.

"You can't arrest me!" shouted the cardinal. "I've done nothing wrong!"

The commandante held up the two pictures. "You're a sick bastard," he said calmly.

"I'm sorry, Father, for any inconvenience. You may go," the commandante said to Kevin. "But you'll need to give evidence, starting with how you came upon these photos and who authorized you to search in the cardinal's flat."

Kevin nodded. He knew a highly-placed Vatican source who'd ensure he wouldn't have to explain much of anything.

∞∞∞∞

CHAPTER FORTY-SEVEN

Rome, Italy

When Kevin arrived back at his flat, the smell of Italian grilled cheese sandwiches permeated the air.

"That smells fantastic," Kevin said. "Any leftovers?"

"Sure," said Toby. "And they're still hot."

Kevin dropped the bag of tools in the middle of the floor and went to the counter by the stove. Sandwiches were stacked on a plate. Toby was famous for his grilled cheeses, just what Kevin needed after his ordeal.

"OK," said Toby, "spill it. What happened?"

"Well, first off . . . I'll be with you on the plane tomorrow to Washington," Kevin said as he bit into his sandwich while simultaneously opening the refrigerator and grabbing a Peroni. Toby joined him, taking another beer for himself.

"You're going home tomorrow, too?" asked Toby.

"Yes."

Toby laughed, pointing at Kevin's black garb. "It must have been quite an evening. I haven't seen an outfit like that since the last time I watched *CSI Las Vegas*."

Kevin shrugged. "Gave me lots of street cred. And, by the way, thanks for the tools and the intel. Nice birthday gift."

"Well, did it help?"

"Yes. Cardinal Marini's finished."

"Finished?"

"Not only is he the head of Opus Mundi, he's an active pedophile. I found photos to prove it. He's now in custody."

"A pedophile?" Toby said. "No way! And he's a cardinal? Good Lord! It's been quite a day for you, hasn't it?"

"Yeah, the cardinal is a truly sick bastard. The whole mess makes me sick."

"How did the meeting with the pope go?"

"I can't say much, but I still need your help. I can tell you there wasn't any threat to national security regarding the secret. But Marini threatened Katie, and offered me a deal to let her go free."

"But you didn't?"

"No, I didn't. I declined."

"Shit! That means you need me to protect her from Opus Mundi."

Kevin shook his head. "It's not Katie they're after."

∞∞∞∞

CHAPTER FORTY-EIGHT

Washington, D.C.

After a nine-hour flight from Rome, the Boeing 777 skidded onto the runway at Washington's Dulles Airport. Toby and Kevin retrieved their bags, went through customs, and got in separate taxi lines. "Talk soon," Kevin said.

"Be safe," Toby told him. Toby would head to his home in McLean, Virginia, and Kevin to Anacostia and his small flat near the school where he'd taught.

Before leaving Rome, Kevin alerted the school's headmaster of his return, explaining he couldn't resume teaching for a while. He'd also checked in on Sister Mary Catherine, who'd continue staying in the safe house in Parioli. Given the alternatives, she didn't mind a bit. Also, he called Max Drotti. "I'm sorry to hear you're going back to the States," Max had said. "I'll hope to see you again before long."

The most difficult call he'd make was to Katie, which is why he saved it for last. In his mind, Kevin had rehearsed several different conversations. None of them seemed to work. His challenge was to get her to agree to what he wanted from her—purely on her faith in him, no questions asked, no explanations. It'd probably be an uphill battle. Given the urgency, he decided not to wait. He'd call her from the cab.

The line of people waiting for taxis was long, but the bright sun and cool weather made the wait tolerable. It was good to be home. In faded jeans and a pale blue sweater, rolling his beat-up two-wheeler behind him, Kevin looked like a run-of-the-mill tourist returning from abroad.

While waiting, Kevin's mind drifted back to his conversation on the plane with Toby. Kevin needed him for his mission, but didn't have much to go on yet. He knew this was frustrating Toby. In turn, Toby was limited in what he could do. For one thing, the CIA had no jurisdiction within the United States. If Toby needed to tap friends at the FBI, he'd need some real leads to be very convincing.

"But the help you want has to do with the secret, right?" Toby had said on the plane as they sipped Scotch before lunch. "And you can't tell me what the secret says?"

"Toby, I know it's asking a lot. I can't tell you what it says, but I can tell you this: I know more about its meaning than anyone, including the pope."

Toby looked at him quizzically, putting his glass down. *A riddle?* "Kevin, do you realize what you just said?"

"Yes," Kevin said. "I know I sound pompous, but it's true. The secret itself is startling, and the pope has to figure out how to deal with it. But I know much, much more. For now, I can't share it, not even with him, nor with you."

"You're skating on thin ice, Kevin. I've been there before. I know what I'm talking about."

"Yeah, well you'll have to deal with your superiors, I'll have to deal with mine. Mine just happens to be the pope."

Finally, Kevin moved to the head of the taxi line. The agent in charge waved Kevin over to a beat-up Ford van. The taxi driver got out, taking Kevin's suitcase and putting it in the trunk. Kevin climbed in the back and gave the driver the address of his destination. Now it was time to call Katie, the dreaded call. It was Friday. She'd be at work.

"Kevin? Everything OK?" Katie's surprise was heightened by his calling her at work.

"I'm back in Washington," he said.

"Really? That's wonderful! When will I see you?"

"Katie, I need you to listen to me, and if you've ever trusted me, I need it from you more than ever. Without asking questions."

"Sure . . ." she said slowly.

Kevin swallowed hard and continued, "I want you and your son, William, to get out of town for a while. A vacation from work. Tell no one where you're going—not even Jimmy."

Silence.

"Kevin, I have a case next week. I can't just walk away!"

"You have to, Katie. Work remotely. Everyone does it these days. Just don't tell anyone where you are."

"Look, I know you're serious. You're concerned about me. Just tell me why this disappearing act is necessary."

"I can't. You'll have to trust me."

More silence.

"Why can't I tell Jimmy?"

"Trust me. Please."

"Are you coming with me?"

"No. I'll stay in your apartment."

"What?"

Silence.

"You're really serious, aren't you?"

"I couldn't be more serious."

"Well, you've got me scared as hell, Kevin. If that's what you intended, it's working."

Kevin could hear resentment and protest simmering in the timbre of her voice. But he also knew she was sensible and trusted him.

"All right, Kevin."

"Thank you, Katie. I have a place for you to go. I'll come over later to give you the details."

The last part of the conversation, the part about having a place for her to stay, wasn't exactly true. But he hoped he'd have it after talking to Toby.

∞∞∞∞

Kevin found his apartment the way he'd left it. His living room with its simple Crate & Barrel furniture seemed austere next to the opulence of his Vatican apartment, but he was glad to be home. He unpacked, putting his laundry in a bag, then rummaged for clean clothes in the closet, a welcome change from the outfits he'd been wearing.

Kevin took his favorite rosary beads out of a chest of drawers. Unwittingly, he'd forgotten them in his rush to pack for Rome. He held the rosary in his hand and said a silent prayer. The next few days would be crucial. He needed all of the spiritual help he could get. *Please, Lord, let me be strong.*

After his prayers, Kevin unpacked his suitcase, which he had checked in rather than carried on, due to the two pistols he'd brought from Rome. He would need more ammunition for the pistols. He decided that he'd also need a shotgun.

Before going to the garage to start his car, Kevin phoned Toby and told him what he needed.

"Listen, buddy," Toby said, "my name's not Marriott. I can't keep coming up with safe houses with no explanation. I've got bosses, too."

"I need to get Katie and her kid to a safe place, Toby. I'm counting on you."

Toby grumbled, "OK, pal. I'll work it out. I guess you're expecting Opus Mundi to come calling. Will you get the D.C. police involved?"

"I can't. I have nothing to go on. I'll have to do it myself. After we get her out of town, I'm going to hole up at Katie's."

"I'll take some leave. Keep you company."

"Thanks, friend. I won't forget this."

"Don't worry. I won't let you," said Toby.

∞∞∞∞

CHAPTER FORTY-NINE

Washington, D.C.

Kevin arrived at Katie's apartment in Dupont Circle and found a parking place easily on a side street off Connecticut Avenue. After he parked, he dragged his suitcase up the three flights of stairs.

Katie greeted him with a nervous hug. She looked radiantly fresh, in spite of the stress Kevin must have caused.

"They were truly understanding at work," she said after they settled in the living room. "But they must be wondering what I'm up to."

Kevin noticed Katie had packed. Three suitcases were waiting in the front foyer of the apartment, along with a stroller, a diaper bag, and a few stuffed animals.

"Where's William?" Kevin asked, looking around the room.

"He's in his crib, in the baby's room." Katie smiled. "It sounds strange—so surreal—to say that."

"Again, Katie, I'm so happy for you."

"Thanks," she said. "Now, tell me, where are you sending me?"

"Fredericksburg, Virginia. You'll be in a small house with security, but since no one will know you're there, you needn't worry. My friend Toby has arranged everything."

"Good so far," said Katie.

"It is." Kevin remembered Toby telling him that Fredericksburg was the kind of small town that defined America. Its historic district was part of American nineteenth-century history. George Washington's family had roots in Stafford County and the first president's mother lived in Fredericksburg until her final days.

"You'll be in an attractive, single-family, brick, ranch-style house with green shutters and a grass lawn on a tree-lined street in a residential neighborhood near the center of town. A Norman Rockwell painting." Kevin smiled. "You and little William will fit right in."

"A dull, picturesque town where nothing much happens," Katie said, smiling. "Since you're staying in my apartment, you must be expecting somebody to be coming after me, right?"

"Something like that," Kevin replied.

"And I assume they want to get at me in order to get to you, right?"

"Hey, counselor, I'll plead the Fifth." Kevin managed a smile.

Katie raised her hands. She wore a red cotton sweater and tight jeans. Kevin felt a moment of weakness, remembering how she'd lingered with the hug when he arrived at her apartment.

"Okay," she said. "I won't ask any more questions."

"That's great. I appreciate it," Kevin said.

"Let me show you where everything is, and how to work the techie stuff," Katie said as she took Kevin through the apartment. She explained how the appliances worked, her timers for the lights, and home security. She pointed to the garbage chute down the hall, which he remembered from the dinners they'd enjoyed there together. *Sweet memories. Hot, passionate memories. Shut up,* he told himself. *Good God! Think about something else!* She had a small washer/dryer and Comcast internet service, which Kevin had in his own apartment.

"No dirty movies, OK?" Katie grinned as she tossed the remote to him.

"I'll try," he said as he caught it with one hand.

"I've got wine and beer and a little food in the refrigerator," she said. "You're welcome to whatever I have."

"Thanks, Katie. Your hospitality hasn't changed a bit."

"I remember that once upon a time my reward for hospitality was some physical affection," Katie said.

Smiling, Kevin looked away.

"One last question," she said. "How long will I be gone?"

"Can't say for sure, but not more than a week."

"Good. That's what I told them at work."

"You ready to go?" asked Kevin.

"Yes, let me get the baby," she said.

Katie went into the baby's room, picked up William, and placed him in a portable baby pouch affixed over her shoulders. He smiled and gurgled and nodded back off to sleep. Grabbing the suitcases, Kevin and Katie went down the stairs and out to the sidewalk.

"Your building doesn't have an elevator?" he asked.

"Well, even though it's a modern apartment, the building itself is old," Katie mentioned.

"Isn't it difficult getting the stroller in and out on the three floors?"
"Yes," she said. "My fiancé helps out."

Ouch! That hit a nerve.

Katie's BMW was nearby in a parking garage. Katie fastened William into his car seat, then settled into the driver's seat. Kevin put the suitcases in the trunk, then joined her in the front seat to give her instructions while Katie punched the Virginia address into her GPS.

"Take this cell phone." Kevin offered her a black nondescript phone. "It's a burner phone, can't be traced. I'll take yours; they can trace your whereabouts with it."

"Kevin, are you putting yourself in danger by staying here?" She reached over and took his hand.

"Not that much," he lied. "No one expects me to be here. And Toby's my backup."

"You sure?"

"Sure. Thanks for caring," he said, pressing her hand in his.

"That's never been the issue, has it?" Katie said, as she slowly withdrew her hand.

Kevin repeated the instructions he'd given Katie earlier. First, she should drive to Baltimore, the opposite direction of her destination in Virginia. Be on the lookout for a vehicle following her, and if she sees one, turn around and head back to D.C. If she sees someone tailing her, she should return home, not go to the safe house. Otherwise, go directly to the safe house in Fredericksburg. Any problems, call Kevin.

Katie noted the instructions with a nod, turned back, and smiled at William, who was gurgling with slobber dribbling down his mouth. Then she turned back around and kissed Kevin on the cheek. He got out of the car, stood there for a few moments, and watched her drive away.

Once Kevin was back and alone in Katie's apartment, he unpacked his things. He placed one of the pistols in the top desk drawer, ready to grab at a moment's notice. He assembled the shotgun he'd purchased, putting it under the bed. He'd keep the Glock on him at all times—this reminded him he was glad he had a carry permit for the District of Columbia.

Toby arrived in the early afternoon with a bag of hamburgers.

"How'd you know I was hungry?" asked Kevin.

"You're always hungry," Toby said. He dropped his duffle bag on the floor. "Nationals on at one o'clock," he said.

Kevin had been watching CNN. "It's amazing," he said. "Not a word about Marini. The Vatican is keeping it on ice." He retrieved a few beers from Katie's refrigerator.

"Isn't that standard protocol for the Church?" asked Toby.

"Well yes . . . and no," said Kevin.

"Do you blame them?" Toby and Kevin both sat down on the sofa, and Toby took out the burgers, placing them on the coffee table.

As the men settled in with their burgers and beer for what they'd hoped would be a quiet Sunday afternoon, Kevin was thinking about Katie. He hoped he'd done enough to ensure Katie and her son's safety. No one knew where she was going. *Check.* She had a cell that couldn't be traced. *Check.* She was drilled in some basic precautions against being tailed. *Check.*

His mental checklist reassured him. He'd now wait until word came that Katie and William had arrived safely.

∞∞∞∞

CHAPTER FIFTY

Washington, D.C.

Nothing out of the ordinary happened on Sunday or Monday. Kevin and Toby occupied themselves with reading, watching TV, cleaning their weapons, and taking short walks in Dupont Circle, where the bustle kept their minds off their mission.

On Monday night, it all changed. Around ten p.m., Kevin heard something unusual while watching TV. He motioned for Toby to be quiet and lowered the volume on the TV. Then the lock on the front door started jiggling.

Kevin signaled for Toby to turn off the lights. Each of them retrieved their pistols. Kevin motioned to Toby to get on the far side of the front door, while Kevin positioned himself on the other side. They waited until the lock clicked open.

From his vantage point, Kevin could see the hand on the doorknob as it opened into the room. The light in the hall framed the silhouette of a man. Kevin didn't wait. He grabbed the intruder by his arm and yanked him into the room. The man stumbled to the floor and Kevin whacked him with his gun on the side of the head.

Toby looked out into the hallway to see if the intruder had friends.

No one. He slammed the door shut and joined Kevin, pointing his gun at the man on the floor.

"Get up!" Kevin ordered, kicking the man in the legs.

The man rolled over, his eyes full of fear. "Who . . . who . . . are you?" he asked.

"Funny guy," Kevin said.

"Kevin?" Jimmy stammered. He stared at two gun barrels poking in his face. "I'm . . . I'm Jimmy Stein, Katie's boyfriend."

Kevin and Toby looked at each other, shook their heads in disbelief, and put their guns away.

"Get up, Jimmy," Kevin said, exasperated. "Now tell me what brings you 'unannounced' to Katie's apartment?"

"What kind of priest are you?" Jimmy asked, rubbing his head where Kevin had struck him. *It hurt like hell.*

"The kind that hits people who break into apartments," Kevin said. He pointed at Toby. "And this is Toby Beck. He doesn't like intruders, either."

Toby exaggerated a fake smile.

Jimmy got up and brushed himself off with his hands. He looked nerdy, wearing a dark gray suit and yellow bowtie. "I came to check on Katie," he said. "I haven't been able to reach her. I was concerned."

"She's fine," Kevin said. "She's gone out of town."

"Why?"

"None of your business."

"I'm engaged to her, for Chrissake!"

"We know that, dufus," said Toby.

"Sit down, Jimmy," Kevin said. "It's my turn to ask some questions."

Toby pushed Jimmy down on the couch, then sat in a chair across from him. Kevin sat down in the other chair and said, "Who do you work for, Jimmy?"

"I'm an account executive as Wellesley Ferrer, an investment firm. I told you that in Sarajevo."

"Not what I meant, Jimmy. Tell me what you know about Greg Maggio and Opus Mundi."

"Opus Mundi? What's that? Maggio is a client of mine. He was a walk-in at my firm."

"Don't play games with me," said Kevin. "I'm in no mood for fibbing. Think again. What do you know about Opus Mundi?"

"Something about it being the right-wing Catholic group that wants to take over the Church . . . If I'm not mistaken, I read about them in the *New York Times Magazine* and—"

"Cut the crap!" Toby said loudly.

Startled, Jimmy jumped in his seat. "I don't know why you're asking me about Opus Mundi. I have nothing to do with them. I only know what I've read!"

"Let me try something else, then," Kevin continued. "Have you been spying on me and digging up dirt on my background?"

Jimmy Stein's jaw dropped. He stammered before realizing that lying would do no good. "Yes," he whispered.

"Now, why would you?"

"I love Katie," Jimmy said softly. "And I . . . I . . . guess I was jealous. She loved you, Kevin. Now she loves me, but there were times . . . I don't know. I'm sorry."

"What did you find out about me?"

"That the U.S. Army whitewashed your record, covering up your killing of an American soldier who'd assaulted an Iraqi girl, not an al Qaeda terrorist who you said you'd killed. I just wanted Katie to know you're not as wonderful as she thinks." Jimmy looked pathetic, really.

Kevin glanced at Toby. At this point he didn't know what to do.

"Let him go, Kevin," Toby said. "He can't help."

Kevin motioned for Jimmy to get up.

Leaning over, Toby whispered in Kevin's ear. "I meant to tell you I finally got word from my investigative contacts. They looked into this guy. He's clean. There's almost no chance he's working with a foreign group. And it's true that Maggio just walked into his firm and asked for him. Maggio used him to get to Katie. And we'd know if he had any overseas contacts. He didn't."

Kevin nodded and followed Jimmy to the door. "I'm sorry, Jimmy," Kevin said. "I know Katie loves you, not me anymore. But don't try to contact her for a few days, okay? This is a safety thing. She'll explain more in due course."

Jimmy nodded and opened the door. As he left, Kevin called out to him. "And Jimmy, you were right. I'm not so wonderful."

∞∞∞∞

CHAPTER FIFTY-ONE

Washington, D.C.

Another uneventful day passed for Toby and Kevin. They woke up, had breakfast, and hung out in the apartment.

In midafternoon, Toby's phone buzzed. He checked the caller ID and took the call. He nodded a few times, asked a couple of questions, and hung up.

"We have visitors, buddy," Toby said.

Kevin put down the *Washington Post* he was reading. "Who?"

"According to U.S. Customs, one Carlos Alameda and two male travelling companions arrived at Dulles last night. We have no trace of where they're staying. They lied about where they're headed."

"That means we have to cancel our dinner reservations," Kevin said. "We wouldn't want to miss anything."

Toby plopped down on the couch with the TV remote in his hand. "No problem, I'm getting kind of attached to this soap opera," he said. "Let's order in pizza."

"Okay, but none of that squiggly stuff you like on it, okay?"

"They're called 'anchovies' and every pizza connoisseur savors them."

Kevin grimaced. "How'll we track Alameda and his gang?"

"You've got to assume they have fake U.S. identities, like South Dakota drivers' licenses or something," Toby said.

"Probably."

"Kevin, let's go through the instructions you gave Katie."

"Sure." Kevin explained that he'd given Katie a quick lesson in anti-tailing strategies; he replaced her cell phone and gave her a secure one; gave her instructions not to contact anyone, and Kevin was certain she'd comply.

"Shit!" Toby stood up.

"What?"

"Those guys have cohorts here. Did you sweep her car for a GPS tracker?"

Kevin's face turned white. "My God."

"Likely Maggio took care of that. We've got to get to Fredericksburg," Toby said.

"Anyone with her at the house?"

"She's got security—but it's all electronic; they can get there in minutes if needed."

"Looks like we need it now," Kevin said.

Toby grabbed his jacket. "Get the weapons," he said. "We need to get on the road."

∞∞∞∞

CHAPTER FIFTY-TWO

Fredericksburg, Virginia

Kevin had never been to Fredericksburg, Virginia. This sleepy, bucolic town had seen little of the kind of feverish activity it was about to witness. Kevin had often thought of taking a Sunday afternoon drive there to stroll the cobblestone streets and visit the historic houses. Not on this visit.

While on the road, Kevin called Katie. "Katie, this is Kev. I want you to go right now and make sure all your doors are double-locked securely."

"Yes, of course they're locked. But I'll double-check. What's going on? You're frightening me, Kev." She was in the upstairs bedroom, reading, with a glass of Merlot. The day had been uneventful. William was sleeping soundly in an adjacent bedroom.

"We're on our way there. I don't want to alarm you, but be on the lookout for anything unusual."

"Why, Kevin? What's going on?"

"Nothing for sure. We're just being cautious, OK? I'm on my way with Toby. We'll be there in less than half an hour. Is your phone charged?"

"Yes."

"Stay on the line with me."

"What about the baby?" asked Katie.

"Go get the baby, and hide him in a closet," said Kevin. "Do it right away."

While keeping the phone line open, Katie ran into the bedroom and grabbed William. He barely moved. Thank goodness he was a sound sleeper. She took him into her bedroom and opened the closet door. Inside were several cardboard boxes. She placed him in one of the boxes, covering him with one of his blankets. Then she closed the door. William gurgled and cooed, and went back to sleep.

"OK, he's hidden," Katie said. "He's asleep, he should be alright."

"Good," said Kevin.

In a couple of moments, she screamed, "Kevin!"

"What? Katie. I'm here."

"Someone's ringing the doorbell!"

Shit.

"Can you see the front door?" Kevin asked.

"Yes, out the bedroom window."

"Okay, look out. But make sure your lights are out."

Kevin looked helplessly over at Toby, who was already calling CIA security and the local police.

"There's a man in dark clothes out there."

"Stall, Katie," he said as calmly as he could. "Toby's calling the authorities. We'll be there in a few minutes."

"How do I stall?" she asked nervously.

"Stay in your bedroom. Lock the doors."

While Kevin was speaking, Katie heard a thunderous crash downstairs. The back door had been kicked in. She heard footsteps at the front door. Someone was opening it, letting someone else in.

"Oh my God! They're in the house! Hurry!" Katie said.

Kevin heard someone pounding on the door to her bedroom.

"Miss O'Connell!" The voice was deep, throaty, and accented.

Katie shook and her teeth chattered. Her heart thumped in her chest. *Could they hear her heartbeat?* Now in the distance she heard police sirens. *Where was Kevin?* The sirens grew closer and louder.

"I'm crawling under the bed," Katie whispered into the cell, hoping Kevin could hear.

The next sound Kevin heard on the phone was the bedroom door smashing open. It didn't take the intruders long to figure out where she was hiding. One of them kicked the bed aside.

"Get up," the deep voice ordered. He grabbed Katie's arm.

Kevin could hear as she struggled to her feet.

"What do you want with me?" Katie asked. Now William began to cry from the closet.

"Well, well . . . what have we here?" One of them had opened the closet door, and saw little William squirming in the box.

"Please don't touch him!" Katie yelled.

"Shut up."

There was the sound of someone slapping Katie's face.

The phone went dead.

Toby and Kevin's car screeched to a halt in front of the house. Two police cars arrived seconds later, sirens blaring. Red, blue, and green lights were flashing throughout the neighborhood. The neighbors were fully awake and clusters of people were gathering in their pajamas in their yards and on their wraparound porches.

Kevin rushed into the house. "Katie! Where are you?"

He spotted the open back door and ran back out.

Toby told the police chief, "They're gone. They kidnapped a woman and her baby. You need to form a perimeter around here immediately."

The police chief wasted no time. Rushing to his car, he spoke into a microphone, giving orders. He went back to Toby and Kevin. "I've got a helicopter taking off and we've got a security perimeter of a half a mile. They don't have a chance."

"We're going out after them, too," Kevin said. "Give me a radio and make sure we get clearance." Kevin gave him the description and license number of his car. A young officer came over with a portable radio tuned to the police frequency.

Toby and Kevin ran to his car. "I'll drive," Kevin said.

Tires screeched as Kevin maneuvered around a blockade of police cars with spinning multicolored lights. Police barricades were being set up everywhere. The sound of a police helicopter thumped overhead, its two spotlights circling the surrounding streets. Kevin drove at high speed back toward the main road into town, the one leading to Interstate 95, the only viable escape route out of Fredericksburg.

While Kevin drove towards I-95, Toby listened to the portable radio. It squawked endlessly with chatter about every car they were seeing and what the helicopter was observing. Finally, there was something significant. The helicopter tracked a vehicle traveling at high speed out of the neighborhood. It was a blue Ford Taurus. The order boomed from the helicopter bullhorn to stop for questioning.

Kevin listened and noted the route the Taurus was taking. He checked his GPS screen and immediately changed course to pursue it.

Kevin screeched and twisted through the side roads, and quickly spotted the suspect Taurus. It was about to take the ramp to I-95 when the driver suddenly veered away, heading toward the river. Kevin was following at a safe distance. Near the Rappahannock River, the road running parallel to the highway had a series of small parks shaded by tall trees. *The bastard did his homework*, Kevin thought. The only way to escape the helicopter was to get undercover where the chopper couldn't see them.

But the helicopter hung close. As the Taurus veered along the dark streets around the corner, the chopper stayed with them and the spotlights circled closer.

Kevin and Toby still could hear sirens in the distance.

The Taurus tore into a parking lot next to a bank with a railroad-crossing style gated entrance. At this time of night, the entrance wasn't manned, and the gate was down.

Kevin continued to follow, wondering why the Taurus had picked this spot. He saw an old-fashioned wooden riser at the gate house that wouldn't stop a runaway baby carriage. The Taurus driver approached the barrier slowly and ran the car right through it, sprinkling shattered wood fragments in its path. Then the Taurus pulled into the vacant lot and moved under the parapet covering the drive-in teller machines.

Kevin slowed, following them, staying far enough behind not to be noticed. When the Taurus stopped, the driver got out and opened the trunk. Kevin stopped a hundred yards behind and turned the car lights off, out of their line of vision. The driver unzipped the duffel bag and removed a submachine gun. He pulled back the lever and chambered the first round.

Lights way above were circling around the bank. The helicopter had found them.

In the empty parking lot, the gunman walked out into the open, waiting for the lights to find him. The spotlights continued to circle, zeroing in on their target. He was ready. Now the lights were on the bank and the teller machines. The front of the car was visible in the bright spotlight. The other light came around and shone on the gunman. He waved and kept the gun hidden behind his back.

A blaring voice came from the helicopter. "Drop to the pavement, spread eagle!" The helicopter was slowly descending.

In one swift motion, the gunman jerked the machine gun around, pointed at the helicopter and started firing away, spraying bullets right and left.

"He's going to down the chopper!" Toby said.

"We can't go in now, Toby," Kevin said. "I can't risk Katie and the baby getting hit by the guys in the car."

The spray of gunfire hit the helicopter, glass shattered, the engines sputtered and smoked, and the helicopter gyrated wildly. The pilot swerved the control stick right and left, trying to regain control, but to no avail.

The man on the ground kept firing. Now the rotors stopped and the helicopter started its descent, very slowly at first, then accelerating. It finally hit hard on top of the bank. Moments later, the deafening crash gave way to a series of explosions. Flames spewed out from the roof and down the sides of the building. The copter's rotors came loose, rolling and tumbling to the ground. Seconds later, all that was left was a torrent of fire.

"Call it in!" Kevin shouted.

The gunman jumped back in the car. The Taurus took off. Kevin started up his engine and pursued.

Dear God, if I ever needed you, it's now.

Doing eighty miles per hour on the empty road, the Taurus screamed past them. Kevin braked and spun his car around in heavy pursuit. Toby held his pistol, aiming at the car. "Stay with them, Kevin."

They followed the Taurus at breakneck speed, until reaching the entrance to a recreation park marked by a row of tall trees clustered together. The park entrance welcomed visitors with a wooden sign: CLOSED AT DUSK.

The Taurus sped faster and Kevin's Toyota followed in hot pursuit.

Toby radioed the police chief. "We're going in."

"I don't want you guys to get in the way, ya' hear? Stay in your car and let the police handle this. We'll be there in a few minutes."

Kevin and Toby looked at each other, knowingly. *No way would they just let the police handle this!*

The Taurus continued barreling along the road, which was turning into a gravel path. It was dark and hard to see. The height of the trees blocked the light of the crescent moon from filtering through. Kevin followed at a moderate distance, knowing that the showdown was near.

Sure enough, the gravel road ended and the Taurus stopped. The occupants surely knew that the Toyota was about to catch up with them. Seconds later, the Taurus driver got out of the car with his machine gun.

Toby turned to Kevin. "I can take a shot before we stop," he said.

"Don't. Katie and William are in the car. We can't risk it."

Kevin pulled up to within fifty feet of the Taurus, his headlights shining on the car and the tall, dark, armed man standing in front of it. Kevin instantly recognized Carlos Alameda, aka Columbo. He stood and held the machine gun prominently in front of him, his finger on the trigger. The sight of him reminded Kevin of the many combatants he'd encountered over the years, all eager and ready for a fight. Kevin knew the feeling. He was one of them.

Through the car's rear window, he could see the back of Katie's head. Kevin kept his eye on the machine gun Alameda was clutching with both hands.

"Now what?" Toby asked.

"I'm getting out of the car."

"That'd be suicide, Kevin. We don't know how crazy this guy is."

"I know him. I'm betting he's rational crazy, not *crazy-crazy.*"

"Well, if he does something stupid, I'm taking him down, not that at this point it'd help you much," Toby said.

Kevin opened the car door and got out slowly. He kept his hands by his side where Alameda could see them.

"Turn the lights down," Alameda ordered.

Kevin nodded. Toby turned the brights off, leaving only the parking lights on. They were in a gravelly patch at the end of the road surrounded by tall trees.

"Don't do anything stupid, Father," Alameda said. "Your friend is in the car with two unpleasant colleagues of mine."

"What do you want?" Kevin asked.

Alameda smiled. "I want to leave with the child. You can have your friend back."

Kevin shook his head, as if to say, *I don't think so.*

"Then let's see who'll die first," Alameda said.

Standing by the car, Kevin heard the sound of the front seat window being lowered. He knew Toby had to make some decisions. He prayed they were the right ones.

Toby pointed his pistol at Alameda. "My bet is you go first," Toby said, drawing Alameda's attention. Before Alameda could react, Toby fired a shot, hitting him in the arm. Alameda cried out, dropping his weapon.

One of the men in the Taurus got out with a pistol in his hand. When he hesitated for a few seconds, deciding who to shoot first, Toby shot him in the chest. He went down.

The third man remained in the car with Katie and the baby.

Kevin approached Alameda, who got up slowly, clutching his wounded arm, trying to stop the blood flow. Police sirens shrilled in the background. They'd be there soon.

As he pointed his pistol at Alameda, Kevin's heart was racing. *Should he or shouldn't he?* One shot would finish him off. *Then what?* The decision had to be fast. Katie and the child were still in the car with one of Alameda's thugs.

"Here's your deal," Kevin said. "You let Katie and the child come with us, and I'll let you live. The police will deal with you."

Alameda hesitated, which worried Kevin. *What was he planning?* The answer came quickly. Alameda was a strategist; he'd recognize when retreat was his best option. Alarmed, he glanced at his wounded arm, nodded to Kevin, and called to his man in the car to get out.

The man obeyed and got out, looking puzzled. Alameda repeated his order. The man stood by the car, next to his fallen comrade, his hands by his sides.

"Katie!" Kevin called out. "Get out of the car!"

Slowly, from the other side, with William in her arms, Katie exited the Taurus. Kevin could see her trembling.

"My car, NOW!" shouted Kevin, waving to her. In a flash, she fled to the Toyota. Toby helped her and the baby into the backseat.

Kevin looked at Alameda, holding the gun steady. "You were going to kill them, weren't you?" Kevin hissed.

"Calm down, Kevin," said Toby. "Don't do anything stupid."

"And you've already murdered a pope," Kevin continued.

Alameda walked toward his car, still clutching his bleeding arm. "Listen to me, you poor excuse for a priest," Alameda hissed. "What other vows have you broken? So, now you're reneging on the bargain we made? You're going to kill me? God will personally escort you to hell."

"Maybe I just changed my mind," Kevin said.

"Kevin, let him go," said Toby. "It's not worth it." The sirens were louder—getting closer.

"You don't know what I know, Toby. We can't let this guy go."

"Let the police deal with him."

"He'll get off and do it again," Kevin said.

Recognizing the freedom deal was turning sour, the second man by the Taurus reached into his pocket. Just as his pistol came out, Toby aimed and fired, hitting him in the chest. He slumped forward, hitting the ground.

Suddenly aware of the rage mounting in Kevin, Alameda's expression turned to fear.

Kevin's moral compass, his internal voices, were struggling with the dilemma facing him. The right and wrong of eliminating this monster, justice and retribution, the future of Christianity. He wanted to quell the danger, *but how would he justify murder?* And he knew the consequence of letting Alameda run free, of letting him live. The stakes were very, very high.

"You were the one who tried to kill Sister Mary Catherine," Kevin said, his voice now strained. "And you also killed the pope. You don't deserve to live."

"Whatever I deserve, Father Thrall, matters not. You're an ordained priest. You cannot, you will not, assassinate me in cold blood. If you must, turn me over to the police."

"Sure, and thanks to your friends in high places, you'll walk, and we'll be starting up with you where we left off."

The police vehicles were in sight now, entering the park. Their sirens blared, their lights flashed red and blue on the trees and on the ground. Paramedics trailed behind them in an ambulance.

"Calm down, buddy," Toby said.

Kevin turned to face Toby. Just as he did, Alameda reached into his pocket and pulled out a throwing knife, hurling it at Kevin.

"Kevin, MOVE!" Toby yelled.

Just as the knife ripped into his jacket, slicing him in the side, Kevin jerked to the right. Kevin winced, then glowed. *Thank you, Lord, for easing the burden of my decision.* Ignoring the pain in his gut, he raised his gun.

"Remember, who you are, Father Thrall! You're a priest!" Alameda cried out, raising his arm to shield his face.

"I'm taking a short leave of absence," Kevin said calmly. He fired two shots. One entered Alameda's head just above his right eye. The other pierced his heart. Alameda collapsed into a heap on the ground. *Good riddance, you holier-than-thou piece of shit,* was all Kevin could think.

The first police car stopped a few feet away. The police chief got out and went to Kevin.

"Give me the gun, padre. The medic will see to your wound." He looked at the three lifeless men on the ground. "Hmph . . . nice job."

Kevin handed over the pistol. "I've got a permit," he said, reaching into his wallet and pulling out a card.

"That's for the District of Columbia," the chief said. "This is the Commonwealth of Virginia. We don't issue carry permits easily."

"It was self-defense, chief," Toby piped in.

The chief shook his head, handing Kevin's gun back to him. "These bastards killed two of my helicopter pilots," he said.

The chief walked around and saw the two other casualties, Alameda's thugs, lying on the ground. Then he looked at Toby and Kevin and said, "I need your IDs!"

The chief checked Kevin's Vatican ID, hesitated a moment, looked at Kevin again, then back to the ID. He shook his head, scribbled a few notes in his pad, and returned the documents to the two men.

"Let the paramedics take a look at you," the Chief said, "then you two get out of here."

Kevin looked at the bodies splayed grotesquely on the grass. He ignored the flashing lights and wailing sirens. He felt nothing but a deep satisfaction for what had just happened. *Who am I?* he thought. Then he looked over at the Toyota with Katie and William in the backseat. Mother and child.

I have the answer. I know who I am.

∞∞∞∞

CHAPTER FIFTY-THREE

Washington, D.C.

As Toby drove the car, Kevin was sitting next to him in the front seat. Kevin wasn't in any shape to operate anything. The paramedics had wrapped him in bandages. The knife had penetrated deep into his abdomen. Fortunately, it'd missed vital arteries. The bleeding had slowed to a trickle and Kevin had been given painkillers, which were making him woozy. Katie was sobbing in the backseat.

"It's okay. Katie . . ." Kevin tried to console her.

"Why would they come after me, Kevin? What's this all about?"

"I'm going to Rome tomorrow for a couple of days. When I come back, I'll have some answers."

"Include me in that little lecture, pal," Toby added. "I think I've earned it."

∞∞∞∞

Though sore and needing pain meds, Kevin left for Rome the following evening. He sent word ahead arranging for an immediate audience with Pope Linus II. Meanwhile, Max Drotti had arranged for him to stay in his old apartment at Villa Dominica in the Vatican.

∞∞∞∞

On the night flight to Rome, Kevin's self-recriminations about what he'd done were haunting him. When the cabin lights dimmed, he ordered a second Scotch, and prayed. He spoke to God and the Blessed Mother, asking forgiveness. On reflection, he wasn't certain he'd made the right decisions, but he was prepared to live with the consequences, whatever they were. He was dreading this visit to Italy. During his flight, he napped fitfully, but it wasn't restful.

On arrival, Kevin took a taxi to the Vatican, then stopped by the administration building and picked up his keys. Strolling along the stone path up the hill to his apartment, pulling his suitcase behind him, it felt good, comforting, to be back at the Vatican. The early morning sun was warm and beautiful to behold. Was the light and warmth of the early morning sun an auspicious sign?

Entering his apartment, he wasn't surprised to see Max sitting in his living room. He sat there listlessly, slumped in the armchair. His eyes were vacant, his face pale and drawn. Kevin knew this meeting had to happen. It was inevitable.

"Hello, Max," Kevin said.

"I've been dreading this, Kevin," Max said without getting up. "I assume you've figured some things out."

"A lot of things, Max," Kevin replied. "But only one that concerns you."

"I had to do it, Kevin. You weren't supposed to find out. I prayed you wouldn't."

"When I knew Jimmy Stein wasn't working for OM, there was only one other person who knew enough about Katie to tip them off."

Max nodded. His face looked old and sad. "I don't work for them, Kevin. I hate them, in fact. But when they threatened me, I was left without a choice."

"What could they possibly have done to you, Max, to make you betray everything you stand for?"

"I come from a humble Italian family, Kevin. And they're proud of my priesthood, especially when I rose to a monsignor in meteoric time." There was great sadness in Max's eyes which Kevin hadn't seen before. Here was a pathetic, broken man.

"Kevin, have you ever stopped to consider how one with as few intellectual gifts as I might have become a monsignor so quickly?" Max looked down at his hands.

Kevin remained silent. His heart was sinking as he watched his poor friend dissolve and dissemble before him.

"You surprise me, Kevin," Max continued. "Father Kevin Thrall, the gifted, brilliant man who so fearlessly does everything and anything!"

"Max, I trusted you. I didn't know much about your past. I trusted you intuitively." Kevin reached into his pocket and withdrew one of the photos he'd taken from Cardinal Marini's album. He handed it to Max, who glanced at it quickly and then tossed it to the ground, like a puritan shaking off the devil.

"Yes, that's me . . . He ruined me, among dozens of others. But you don't know the worst part! Marini made me recruit for him. I rounded up teenage seminarian candidates, brought them to his flat, and initiated them in Marini's ways to advance in the Church. I hated what I was becoming. I hated everything Opus Mundi stood for. But once it was underway, there was no way out. I was trapped."

"I'm sorry for you, Max. I really am. I won't judge you, but I'm having trouble getting past what happened to Katie and William."

"I don't want or expect your forgiveness."

"We were friends, Max. There had to be another way to handle this."

"I wish I knew what it was. I made bad decisions. Katie is safe now, and that's some consolation. All's well that ends well, right?"

"It might have gone the other way."

"I'm so sorry." Max smothered his face in his hands.

"Marini is in custody, and sooner or later, the whole sordid mess will come out," Kevin said. "I think you'd better go."

Max stayed in the armchair. He looked up. All of a sudden, something changed. The tone in his voice became harsh. "You forget. I still have the pistol you gave me, Kevin." Max took it from the inside of his jacket and pointed it in Kevin's direction.

What the hell? Kevin stepped back. "You think that'll solve the problem?"

"I've run out of options, I'm afraid. With you out of the way, I can disappear somewhere before they find out."

"So this is what you want, Max? To kill me?" Kevin was stalling for time, trying to get a handle on how he'd escape. It didn't look promising. No matter how fast he moved, he'd take one bullet, maybe two.

"Kevin, if you were in my place, what would you do? Oh, but you've killed before, so it'd probably be much easier for you, wouldn't it?"

"Don't do this, Max. This isn't who you are. Don't let it end this way."

"Not quite that way, Kevin." Max Drotti pointed the gun and stared blankly at him. His eyes were moist, a sure sign of despair. Kevin could see his lips were quivering. Kevin knew he was at the mercy of a man who was distraught and deranged, a man no longer in control of his faculties.

Max raised the pistol, his hand shaking. Then, in a jerky motion, he shifted the direction of the barrel of the pistol toward his temple.

"Max, NO!"

Before Kevin could react, with an eerie grimace, Max smiled, pulling the pistol's trigger. The shot reverberated around the room. It was a shot that'd haunt Kevin for years to come.

Max slumped over in the chair, a fountain of deep scarlet blood gushing from the hole in his head.

Oh, God, no!

Kevin called security, requesting an ambulance. But he knew it was too late.

For the first time in a long while, Kevin wept inconsolably.

∞∞∞∞

CHAPTER FIFTY-FOUR

Rome, Italy

The audience with His Holiness, Pope Linus II, was granted immediately. Before presenting himself at the Apostolic Palace for the meeting, Kevin took his time dressing appropriately in his priest's clothing. He was admitted at once and soon found himself in the pope's library awaiting the presence of the leader of the Catholic Church.

Pope Linus II, wearing full papal white, entered the library unceremoniously, a leather folio case under his arm. He greeted Kevin with a handshake and a warm embrace.

"I heard about Monsignor Drotti," His Holiness began. "I'm very sorry. I know you'd become friends. God bless him. I pray for him."

"Thank you, Holiness," Kevin said. "This has been difficult for me."

"I understand, son." The pontiff invited Kevin to sit in his library, at the round table. The windows overlooking St. Peter's Square were open, a soft breeze blowing in. The hum of the crowd below was echoing upward.

"I have important news to discuss with you, Holiness. It's about the secret of Fatima."

"I have it here with me, Kevin," the pope said. "It's a copy, but here it is." He lifted a single sheet of paper from his folio, placing it on the table. "And for both our benefits, this copy is in English."

"Thanks, that does make it easier."

Kevin looked at the page and began reading the words that the young Lucia had inscribed so many years ago, the missing two pages that had been kept secret for decades:

Our Lady told me the most important revelation during the final vision. She said that Our Lord will grant the world a period of one hundred years to return to prayer and reverence to God. She said that angels would remain among us to monitor the progress of the people for whom He sent his only son to die for their sins. After the period of one hundred years, Our Lord will again send an emissary to live among us and once again, show the way toward a life of prayer and penance for our sins. He will come to a new part of the world and live among us until the designated time arrives for Him to be revealed to the world. I say to you, Pray! Pray! Pray! until the time has come. It shall not be a time of peace and universal love. There shall be dangers and tragedies which can only be solved by devotion to Him. This applies to all religions and all faiths who genuinely worship God in different ways. There is salvation for all. The Lord's emissary will live among us as one of us. He shall share in human pain, for he shall be deformed in one leg as a sign of the imperfections he comes to succor. He will be in mortal danger from enemies of the Church and his mission will depend on the courage and resolve of the true believers in the Lord. I say again, Pray! Pray! Pray! Through prayer and devotion to Our Lord peace will come to those who truly believe.

Kevin placed the page gently down on the table. He felt breathless and composed himself as the message sank in again. He looked at the pope, who also was absorbed in his own thoughts.

"Holiness, is this predicting the *Second Coming of our Lord*?"

The pontiff nodded. "Perhaps, Kevin, perhaps not. We don't know what is meant by *emissary.* I have had two trusted academics looking at this with me, in my presence. One believes it refers to the Bible's prediction of the Second Coming of Jesus, and another believes that it foretells the arrival of a messenger, perhaps an angel. Remember, the message refers to a period spanning one hundred years. That was in 1917. So we're just about at the one hundred year mark."

"How will we know which it is?"

Pope Linus II shrugged. "Time."

The time had now come for Kevin's major revelation. "I have some important news for you, Holiness," Kevin said, his heart beating faster. "I know the identity of the Lord's emissary."

The pope's startled look was dramatic, surprising Kevin. The pontiff sat back in his chair and stared at his junior colleague. "How could that possibly be?" he asked.

"Holiness, allow me to explain."

Kevin went through the entire story from the beginning—his calling, his relationship with Katie, his decision not to marry but to follow his calling, Katie's decision to adopt, his visit to Medjugorje, the strange feelings he'd had upon meeting the child's birth mother, and finally, the message from the visionaries. Then he took a deep breath and recounted briefly what'd transpired at the baptism in Sarajevo.

"Holiness, when I went to Sarajevo to baptize Katie's adopted son, the doctor at the orphanage gave the child a clean bill of health." Kevin took a deep breath, then continued. "Expect for one impairment. The baby had been born with a clubfoot, a malformed leg. That is precisely what the secret foretold."

The pope gasped. "Extraordinary."

Kevin continued, "When I read the secret for the first time here—in your presence—I knew . . ." Kevin's voice trailed off as he lowered his voice as if speaking only to himself. "I knew," he whispered, casting down his gaze.

The pope didn't speak. A thick silence hung over the room, broken only by the ticking of a grandfather clock, and the hum of the crowd outside.

Several moments later, the pope reached over and touched Kevin on the forehead. "It seems you've had much weight on your shoulders, son. You've been given an enormous and grave responsibility," he said.

"I know, Holiness. And it weighs heavily."

"But how did Opus Mundi know about the child?" the pontiff asked.

"There was a local priest at the baptism in Sarajevo, where we first heard about the baby's infirmity. I suspect the priest tipped them off. Until we found the missing pages of the secret in Seville, Opus Mundi's leadership had sole possession and knowledge of it. They also knew of my mission against them—they must have put it all together and figured out about the child, just as I had. Since they discredited the message, Opus Mundi saw the child as a threat. They were out to kill him. That's what I prevented." Kevin took a deep breath before speaking again.

"Holiness, remember when Drotti and I were in your office and you read from Matthew: 24? The passage speaks of war as a prelude to the final days. But it also speaks of the Second Coming and false prophets. I remember one passage you read to us: '*For many shall come in my name, saying, I am Christ; and shall deceive many*.' I'm convinced Opus Mundi thought the emissary from God would be one of them, and that Katie's baby, although clearly the child predicted in the secret of Fatima, must therefore be a false prophet. They had to kill him."

The pope closed his eyes and made the Sign of the Cross. "This is a major event for the world, Kevin. My challenge as pontiff is what to do about it."

"Well, we know who the leader of Opus Mundi is, or I should say, *was*. He's now in Vatican custody," Kevin said.

"He disgusts me. We'll deal with him," Porter replied. "And we will dismantle Opus Mundi."

His Holiness rose from the chair and walked over to the bookshelf in his library. He removed a leather-bound book. "This volume speaks of the Second Coming," he said. "When I was a young priest, I loved reading this book."

"Holiness, there are decisions needing to be made before I leave Rome, and I'm here now for your guidance and instructions."

"I am still absorbing this turn of events myself, my son."

"The first question is this: Do we tell Katie what we know? After all, she's the mother of the child."

The pope remained standing by the bookshelf. "My own feeling is it'd be too much of a burden for her. I will pray on it; my instinct tells me she should not know. At least not now."

Kevin nodded.

"Only a handful of top clerics will be told, Kevin," the pope continued. "It must remain a secret until such time as the Lord makes the revelation in whatever manner He chooses." The pope returned to the table and sat down. "Now I have a request of you."

Now what? Kevin thought. *How much more of this can I take?*

"Kevin, I want you to stay here in Rome working at my side. I will appoint you a bishop and provide you with comfortable quarters here in the palace next to me."

"Holiness," Kevin began, and now he couldn't look him in the eye. "I am at your command at all times, but I must respectfully ask that you allow me to return to my job at the school in Washington. I'd be honored to work with you, Holiness, but I believe I was called to this duty by the highest authority and that my task is not finished."

"What do you mean?"

"Perhaps my duty in life, and the reason I was called to the priesthood, was to protect the new emissary from God, be he Jesus or whoever he turns out to be. I want to stay close to Katie and the boy, and be there for them."

The pope looked at Kevin, hoping for an explanation for what Kevin had just said.

Kevin added, "She's engaged to be married, Holiness, and I will officiate at the wedding. I should add that she is marrying a Jew. Perhaps Our Lord is sending us another message having to do with interfaith harmony."

The pontiff looked away for a moment, composing his thoughts, and looked back across the table at Kevin. "All right, Kevin. Go back to Washington. I'll authorize an assistant or two to help you with your assignment. But I warn you, I may change my mind at any time and call for you to join me here."

"Yes, Holiness." Kevin inhaled a big breath and let it out with a sigh of relief. "Thank you."

CHAPTER FIFTY-FIVE

Rome, Italy

Toby's flight from Washington arrived at the Leonardo da Vinci Airport on time. As instructed, he took a taxi to the Basilica of St. John Lateran on the outskirts of Rome. At the basilica, he asked an attendant for directions to the Scala Santa. The man pointed across the street, adding, "But it's closed now, *signore*."

"I'm meeting a friend here," Toby said. "Father Kevin Thrall."

The man's eyes opened wide. "Father Thrall is waiting for you in the chapel. Follow me, *signore*." He led Toby across the street and unlocked a massive wooden door. Inside, Toby's eyes needed adjusting to the darkness.

"I'm up here," Kevin said from a distance. Toby looked up and as his eyes adjusted, correcting his vision, he saw a staircase and the shadowy outline of his friend all the way at the top.

"Don't use the stairs unless you want to come up on your knees," Kevin said.

"Huh?"

"This is the most important stairway in Christendom, my friend. Those twenty-eight marble steps," Kevin added, pointing down, "are known as the Scala Santa. They once stood in the office of Pontius

Pilate when he was Governor of Jerusalem. Some say these were the steps Jesus climbed when Pontius Pilate condemned him to death."

Toby looked down at the steps. They weren't marble, but marble covered in wood. He stooped for a closer view and noticed cutouts in the wood where blood stains were visible on the marble below.

"Those are said to be Jesus's bloodstains."

"How do I get up there?" Toby asked.

"If you're not going to kneel, there's a stairway over to the side."

Toby took the stairs and joined Kevin in a pew. Placing his small travel bag on the floor, he sat beside him.

"Geez, you look like hell," Toby said.

"Thanks. How was the flight?"

"Expensive. I had to pay for it myself. Listen, pal, if I didn't love you like a brother, I wouldn't have dropped everything to come here for a little private chat."

"I appreciate your coming."

"Well, like I told you, I'm booked on a flight back to D.C. this afternoon. I'm all out of vacation time."

Kevin faced the altar, crossed himself, and turned. "Let's take a walk," he said.

They left the chapel and walked down the steps. Outside, they strolled through the nearby gardens of the basilica until they came upon a bench.

"You're my best friend, Toby, and you're someone I'd trust with my life. I'm going to tell you the whole story, so you'll know how you've been helping. I need your word this will stay with you."

"Does it involve national security?" Toby asked.

"No. Only Church security."

"Okay. You have my word," Toby said.

Kevin took a deep breath. "I know you're not religious, so I need you to keep an open mind about what I'm going to tell you. If you must, judge it on the evidence alone."

Toby nodded.

"First, and you may have heard this through your own channels, we've taken down the leadership of Opus Mundi."

"I heard that."

"Second, in the presence of His Holiness, I read the missing pages of the secret of Fatima," Kevin continued, "and I'm going to tell you what it says and what it means."

Toby's attention was fully engaged.

"You know me well enough to appreciate how I've struggled with my spiritual calling to the priesthood," Kevin said. "It's been a tortured conflict. How could I have renounced the only woman I've ever loved, for the solitary life of a priest? But that's exactly what I did."

"So you found the answer?" Toby said.

"Yes," Kevin replied, with a smile. "And I know you're thinking: 'Did I really cross the Atlantic Ocean just to hear my buddy Kevin talk about his calling in life?'"

Toby smiled back. "Yeah, but go on."

"The missing secret revealed the coming of a child. This child might be an emissary from God, or the Second Coming of Jesus."

"You just lost me. You can't be serious, Kev."

"I'm very serious. Better still. I know this child. It's Katie's adopted son."

"C'mon, Kevin. How could you know that?"

Kevin told the whole story methodically. He spokc of the clues that'd come to him, of the birth mother of Katie's adopted child in Sarajevo who'd said *shukran* to him, going all the way back to the young girl's life he'd saved in Iraq. But the most telling clue for him was the boy's clubfoot.

"When I read the secret, my heart almost stopped," Kevin continued. "Our Lady revealed that the emissary from God would live in a new part of the world—I'm assuming that's the U.S.—and would be born with a deformed foot. When I read that, I knew immediately why I was called to the priesthood. My mission was to protect this child who'd be adopted by Katie."

Toby shook his head. "This is wild. Can you believe we're sitting here talking about the Second Coming of Christ?"

"I don't know. The message just speaks of an emissary. His Holiness asked two trusted experts to review the secret. One thought it's just an emissary, the other said it's the Second Coming. Take your pick."

Toby was quiet for a moment, staring at the gravel. "Does Katie know?" he whispered.

"No. And it's been decided, she won't for a while."

"What will you do?"

"Protect the child, Toby. Opus Mundi believes the message alluded to a false prophet who'd interfere with their scheming to overthrow the church. So they want the child killed. After we've dismantled the leadership of OM, who knows how many wacky followers will remain? We can't get rid of all of them, I don't think."

Another pause, then Toby looked at his friend. "I changed my mind," he said.

"About what?" asked Kevin.

"My trip. I originally thought it was a waste of time. I don't think so anymore."

Kevin smiled. "Now comes the part where I ask you for one big favor," he said. "If any followers of Opus Mundi find out about Katie's child, my life may be in danger. I'm asking you, if something happens to me, to be my backup and look after Katie."

"Look, Kevin. I have my own life and career. And you know, I'm not totally sold on this spiritual stuff."

"I'm praying you'll get a sign of your own. I need you with me on this."

"All I can promise is, I'll think about it."

Kevin stood up. "That's all I'm asking," he said.

They walked down the path to the street. Kevin hailed a taxi. "I'll buy lunch," he said. "Oh, and Toby? You've been designated as the baby's godfather. Hope that's not a problem."

∞∞∞∞

CHAPTER FIFTY-SIX

Rome, Italy

That evening, Kevin stayed home. There was beer in the refrigerator, and he helped himself to one. Watching the news for a few minutes, he enjoyed the headline news of His Holiness Linus II. He was a top contender for the Nobel Peace Prize for his work in the Middle East. Then Kevin switched off the television to take a moment to meditate and think.

The questions driving his life were finally coming into focus. How a man with his faults and temptations had such a powerful calling to the priesthood had always been a mysterious unknown. It was now clarifying itself. Prayer was coming more easily. When he held little William in his arms, his heart would pound with love and his sense of purpose would be forever engaged. He knew why he was here. He looked forward to fulfilling it and to serving the highest authority.

He checked his phone, looking for a message from Toby. None came. Before going out again, he made a phone call.

"MC, it's Kevin."

"Oh Kevin, I'm so happy to hear from you! I've been miserable here. I mean, the place is fine, but I can't go out and TV is boring and . . . "

"MC, be quiet and listen to me. You're coming to Washington with me tomorrow, understand?"

"No, Kevin, I don't understand. I've never been to Washington, I—"

"Just listen to me. If you stay here, you're going to get implicated, caught in the takedown of Opus Mundi. I'll get you out and give you a meaningful job."

"What kind of job?" she asked suspiciously.

"You'll be my special assistant, do whatever I tell you to do."

"I think I'd like that, Kevin," she said. "How will you pay me? You know, I'm thinking about leaving the Order."

"Leave if you want to, and don't worry about how I'll pay you."

"It's a deal, Kevin. But I need more details. Can we have dinner tonight to talk about it?"

"No. I'm meeting an old friend. Maybe tomorrow after we land."

Kevin turned off his phone and put on his coat. He checked himself in the mirror. He was a priest in a black suit and turned collar. This is who he was. And who he was meant to be. He knew it now. An enormous weight had been lifted from him. He felt he could float in the air. *Thank you, Lord. Thank you, Mary. I wish it hadn't taken so long, I admit, but now I know the purpose of my life. I'll do everything I can to fulfill it.*

He walked out of his quarters into a moonlit night. His euphoria was now giving way to a new concern, a new weight on his shoulders, the responsibility for a new life. A life? Perhaps the most important life in two thousand years. As he strolled, a gentle breeze accompanied him, propelling him along the path to St. Peter's. A guard at the back entrance nodded, allowing him to enter the now empty, cavernous basilica. As he crossed the apse to a side altar, his footsteps echoed loudly. He knew where he was going.

When he crossed the main aisle, Kevin genuflected and continued to a small cove behind the main altar. Inside the cove, a gold tabernacle sat atop a cloth-covered marble altar. To the right stood a life-size statue of Mary on a concrete pedestal. At its base, an array of votive candles in red glass cases cast a flickering light on the figure above. Kevin dropped a few coins in the black metal box and lit a candle.

He watched it for a moment, looking up again at the statue. The light on Mary's face shimmered from the candles' reflected light, creating a sense of movement. He continued looking into her eyes. His mind was playing tricks on him as a kaleidoscope of familiar faces appeared on the statue. He recognized them: his mother, Katie, the Bosnian mother of Katie's child, and the young girl he saved in Iraq. *Shukran.*

It had been a long day.

Kevin bowed his head and knelt in front of the statue.

"Hail Mary, full of grace, our Lord is with thee . . ."

Kevin finished his prayer. His eyes drifted up to the statue.

Mary smiled.

CPSIA information can be obtained at www.ICGtesting.com
Printed in the USA
BVOW08s0054300616

454036BV00001B/2/P

9 781504 035118